"PETITE ANGE,
HOW DARING YOU'VE BECOME."

She gasped when she saw him and instinctively crossed her arms over her breasts.

"A gentleman would not look!" she accused. The heated pink on her cheeks made her look all the more innocent, but the wet chemise clinging to her skin called an ancient allure.

"Am I a gentleman, *chère*?"

"You are wicked!"

He stole softly, calculatingly, into her thoughts.

"There is no one here to chastise you. No one will blame you." He pulled his own shirt off over his head and flung it away, then started toward her, slowly, careful not to cause her to flee. "No one will even know."

Hunter moved toward her with fluid grace, a smile on his face, but his pulse darkly hammering out a warning to leave her alone. But the desire to have her had overrun him days ago, and he was weary of trying to outdistance it. . . .

LIBBY SYDES

STOLEN DREAMS

A DELL BOOK

Published by
Dell Publishing
a division of
Bantam Doubleday Dell Publishing Group, Inc.
1540 Broadway
New York, New York 10036

The trademark Dell® is registered in the U.S. Patent and
Trademark Office.

ISBN: 0-440-21544-7

Printed in the United States of America

Published simultaneously in Canada

May 1995

10 9 8 7 6 5 4 3 2 1
OPM

For Fred and Betty Sydes, with love

AUTHOR'S NOTE

When the Napoleonic wars began lashing Europe, America was caught in the international controversy. Its shipping and neutral rights were violated repeatedly by both England and France. England's navy, being superior, was the more flagrant offender. Its warships frequently lurked close to American harbors, awaiting the chance to capture able men to fortify the English cause.

American ships were stopped and boarded, their cargo falsely confiscated as contraband bound for the enemy, their seamen seized and impressed into British service. Protests by the United States went ignored. In an effort to retaliate, Congress enacted an embargo prohibiting American vessels from departing for any foreign port and all foreign trade was stopped. The results were drastic.

American harbors were filled with idle ships, and thousands of men were thrown out of work. The New England states' exports fell, and the South was thrown into a severe economic depression. America's foreign commerce was at a virtual standstill, and sailors were encouraged to violate the law and carry goods at their own risk. Many did, with England and France poised to seize them upon entering European waters.

Chapter One

*When I surveyed all that my hands had done and what
I had toiled to achieve, everything was meaningless, a
chasing after the wind . . .*

—*Ecclesiastes 2:11*

Ravenwood Castle, England
1821

Blackmail. It was such an ugly little word to someone
who always presented herself with the utmost propriety.

Lara Winthrop Chalmers smoothed back an imagi-
nary curl from her perfect coiffeur and gazed at the
handwrought silver chalice dating back to the elev-
enth century. Her palms were clammy beneath her
gloves, her pulse rate unstable, but she composed her
expression with iron fortitude and kept her smile
vague and serene. She mingled with the Society for
the Preservation of Antiquities, going from room to

1

room and making the proper reverential responses over each relic as if truly interested. Making cool, mechanical observations kept the ever-present terror thudding in Lara's heart from showing in her voice.

"Oh, Lara dear, look at the Greek sculptures!" Lady Marion Fitzworth cooed, pointing to a carved fragment from a set of Elgin Marbles on loan from the British Museum. Her voice lowered deliciously. "Shocking, aren't they, all that exposure? However do you think the duke obtained permission to bring them here?"

Lara gave an appropriate moment's pause for thought. "I imagine he is a substantial contributor."

"Yes, of course. I must be daft," Lady Fitzworth tittered. "Don't you think it quite smart of Lord Elgin to collect the sculptures while serving as ambassador to Turkey?"

Lara nodded politely while urgency sang through her blood. She generally adored Marion Fitzworth with the convoluted sort of affection one reserved for pesty but dear maiden aunts, but today there was little generosity in Lara for the elderly lady. Her mind raced ahead to the next corridor where she had sent her solicitor, Smythe. She slid a surreptitious glance in that direction, but the hall ahead remained empty. Almost as if from a distance, she heard Lady Fitzworth ramble on about how Elgin had funded the project himself when the British government wouldn't, but there was little she could contribute to keep the conversation going when her attention lay elsewhere.

". . . so, what do you think of that?" Lady Fitzworth added in a sly, scandalized voice.

Having missed part of the conversation, Lara tried to attend the lady's tone. "I understand Lord Byron denounced Lord Elgin as a vandal for removing the art objects."

Lady Marion's offended nose rose a notch and her expression flattened with disdain. "Fie on Lord Byron! He was removed from Oxford for passing about atheistic literature and has been linked with more lascivious infamies than I can recall." Her hand went to her heart in a show of great melodrama. "What Lord Byron thinks is certainly of no consequence to me." She blinked myopic eyes and smiled sweetly. "Now, dear, aren't you glad I convinced you to come along today?"

Lara smiled back at the seasoned collector from whom she had carefully manipulated her invitation. Smythe had slipped away a quarter hour ago, and she only awaited his signal before attempting the same.

She studied another part of the frieze from the temple of Athena Nikē and waited for Smythe through interminable seconds that ticked away slowly, as annoying as the constant drip, drip, drip of a leaky pump, as annoying as Lady Fitzworth's immutable conversation. But Lara had become adroit at waiting, and not even a flush of impatience showed on her placid face.

The signal finally came, a nod of Smythe's head from just around the next corridor. She caught the movement out of the corner of her eye and hung back as the group began moving forward again, filing past her one by one, monocles and viewing glasses perched just so to best absorb each display.

"Coming, dear?" Lady Fitzworth called.

"In a moment," Lara answered absently, and continued to study the frieze.

As the group would not be hastened beyond their studious pace, Lara took her breaths by their steps, slow but constant, at least thirty in number, their muffled exclamations filled with either veneration or affront, depending upon their sensibilities. She waited until she stood last in line, then followed at a snail's pace, a lag-behind in utter enthrallment of the various artifacts should anyone care to notice.

Turning down the next corridor, the group paused at the entrance to the elegant library of Ravenwood Castle, and the first show of impatience exerted itself on Lara's countenance. It was the very room she wished to enter.

Other than the duke's private quarters abovestairs, this was the only area restricted to the Society. It made for wondrous speculation about just which leather-bound tomes and signed first editions made their homes beyond the stately doors. Speculation ran through the crowd in whispers and titters and sage conjectures. But for all their educated presumptions, not one of them had been beyond the carved wooden entrance. Except Lara.

Lady Fitzworth, feeling bold and entitled at eighty years of age, even went so far as to walk right up and grasp the handle to rattle it. The action brought gasps and snickers from various members, which satisfied

Marion immensely. But other than a few dramatic sighs and longing glances, the members did nothing more and proceeded on. They knew their manners and would never risk forfeiting future invitations.

Lara had no such reservations. She waited until the group was out of sight, then slipped into the arched entrance and remained there, slowing her breathing so she wouldn't be found flushed should someone come back to look for her.

The sound of hushed voices faded further as the ladies and gentlemen moved on down the hall to complete their tour. Lara paused a second longer, then turned. Cut from stone and coldly majestic, the entry towered at least fifteen feet above her head. She felt small and insignificant beneath it, but retreat was not a consideration so she voiced a silent prayer and entered the double doors.

She was consumed at once as she stepped inside, almost overcome by the scent of age. A hint of beeswax and leather mingled as well, but it was the more dominant ascendancy of the ages that arrested her.

Glancing around intently, she quietly pulled the doors shut behind her and continued forward, deeper into the heart of a place that seemed to pulse with a life of its own. The whisper of her slippers upon the carpet sounded unnaturally loud, intrusive. She was an outsider here, vulgar and colloquial to dare trespass upon unwelcome ground. She could feel it in every step she took.

A lowered voice seemed requisite beneath the high ceilings, ornately painted by whichever master happened to be *en vogue* at the time of the library's last

5

restoration. The architecture was superb, as was the artwork gracing the ceilings and walls. As with all of Ravenwood, this room was richly but simply appointed with furnishings that would appeal to nobleman and commoner alike. There was an allusion of warmth in the damask draperies, velvet upholstery, and silk carpets.

Yet the air of austerity remained.

Great young minds had been tutored here, destinies shaped, fates altered by the sheer force of will of the Ravenwood sons. Cozy warmth was not something the castle boasted easily when indomitable power had bulwarked the very foundation upon which it stood. Terribly old, meticulously updated, the castle resonated with the generations of wealth and authority that had resided here.

Lara, standing in the midst of it all, felt the weight of her mission settle like a stone around her neck. Her purpose was set, her path unalterable, yet her heart beat with the slow rhythm of dread as she approached a dapper young man in professionally sober attire. Their meeting in this room had been prearranged, but the outcome was far more uncertain. Percival Smythe nodded when she reached him.

"Well?" she asked, her entire being arrested.

He reached behind him and brought out a packet of plain brown paper and folded back the edges.

"You found it," she breathed with equal portions of relief and trepidation.

She stared at the sheets of parchment for a long moment, then took them and began sifting through the old papers as carefully as one touched a newborn

—with reverence, awe, and the subtle fear of endangerment. The ancient pages dated back as many centuries as the wood and stone that formed the castle's outer walls and were so exquisitely illustrated she was forced to ignore the intricate beauty of each drawing in order to continue the search.

Not a hint of her shock or despair showed on her lovely face, but her fingers trembled slightly when she finally found the sheet she had come seeking. Moldy at the edges and yellowed with age, it gave off the musty scent of the passage of time despite being well preserved.

Carefully she removed the fragile page from the others, though it almost seemed a sacrilege to do so. The sound of crackling parchment echoed throughout the cavernous room in slithering rustles, like a serpent disturbed from its nest. She held the sheet up to catch the light streaming in through leaded glass windows that had once been covered only by thin scraped hides.

With painstaking exactness, she studied the drawing, going over every minor detail with almost ritualistic accuracy, as if it were of upmost importance that she define each singularity.

She need not have bothered. She'd committed this particular sheet to memory a decade ago, then kept the secret it contained close to her heart out of revenge, retribution, and, she realized now, some misguided sense of justification. She had fully intended to use the knowledge one day, primarily in the early months when the memories were still fresh and painful, but those hours spent in vengeful plotting and planning had yielded nothing but an empty sense of fruitlessness.

The paper wavered and Lara realized she was trembling, but there was no help for it, so she ignored the fact that her shattered nerves were revealing themselves when composure had always been vital to her—at least for the past ten years. She held the sheet out to test her control and watched it flutter once then go perfectly still. She wouldn't allow the force of her anxiety to overcome her determination. There was too much at stake for nervous interference.

It was too late for revenge, as well, and it was much too late to continue ignoring what lay before her, for it held her only hope.

Upon the sheet in exquisite detail was the drawing of a jeweled brooch dating back to the eighth or ninth century. She'd been fascinated by it as a young girl on her infrequent visits here, visits made because her father was a great lover of medieval antiquities, a prominent member of the Society, and could claim a very distant kinship to the first Duke of Ravenwood, Borgia de St. Brieuc.

Before the library became restricted, her father had spent much of his free time engrossed in the old manuscripts and artifacts. At his side, Lara had learned to appreciate the detailed sketches, paintings, and writings of the early ancestors who had kept daily accounts of castle life down through the ages.

But the records were not complete. No one knew exactly what had happened to the jewel after Philip, a younger son, had taken it when he journeyed to

France in the early eighteenth century to make his own way in the world.

It had caused quite a scandal when Philip stole the brooch from his older brother and kept it for himself. The reason for the antagonism between the brothers had been lost—proud English lords being adverse to spreading their dirty linen before the populous—but with the disappearance of Philip had come the loss of the family's most treasured heirloom.

Even upon his older brother's death and his own ascent to the dukedom, Philip had not returned to England, a fact still remarked upon in drawing rooms and gentlemen's clubs when conversation lagged. One's choosing to live abroad without specific political ambitions was too tedious to consider, so of course it was assumed that there must have been a woman involved.

Proud English lords also being given to many such anomalies, the matter was usually dropped in favor of more tantalizing and current gossip. Philip had carried out his duties as duke from afar, using solicitors and managers, and setting a precedent for the generations to follow.

Lara lowered the parchment and took a deep breath to still the uneasiness in her stomach. The many barristers and counsel employed by the estate might not know what had become of the priceless antique, but she did.

She knew exactly where it was, for she had seen the stolen artifact firsthand—no longer a brooch now but reset into a locket—aboard a pirate ship when she was seventeen years old.

9

A dreadful feeling of inevitability washed through her, as it had so often over the past few days. She suppressed the accompanying shudder and slipped the sheet back into its rightful place, then turned to her solicitor. Her face was cool and tense in the waning light.

"We may go now, Mr. Smythe."

The solicitor was not fooled in the least by her calm demeanor. Grief and fear were etched along the exquisite planes of her face, hidden from most who thought they knew her beneath the regal tilt of her chin and the proud and graceful way she carried herself. Her dark sable hair was pulled back away from her face, revealing clear hazel eyes that stared sightlessly ahead.

She was the most beautiful woman he had ever known. She had the slender figure of a dancer, deceptively strong. The horror of the past few days had not managed to strip her of her loveliness, but it had given a hollow depth to her eyes and a stony dignity that was unbecoming to the woman she had once been.

Smythe drew himself up stiffly as befitted a man of his background and education and tried to cloak his compassion. She would not appreciate knowing how his heart broke a little every time he bore witness to her pain and distress.

"You are certain then, Lady Chalmers? It is the same?"

She nodded once. She would never have taken precious time to journey here in these perilous days had it been otherwise.

"Locate him immediately." Her face paled slightly, but she continued with quiet resolution. "But be very careful, Percy. He can be quite . . . dangerous." She took a deep breath and handed the papers back, her eyes calm but fiercely direct. "And above all, be discreet."

"Of course." He nodded, uneasy at the sudden hard grief in her eyes—eyes that had once, in their youth, been full of childish vitality and bright pleasure. He glanced down, not quite able to meet those eyes now. "Will he come, do you think?"

"He'll come," she replied with toneless confidence. "He owes me that much at least."

Chapter Two

New Orleans 1821

The seedy riverfront tavern boasted nothing in the
way of gentility. Its patrons had neither noble intentions nor ambitions to recommend them, save for the
occasional Creole aristocrat out for a night of slum-
ming. Even the sale of contraband was done in nicer
places.

The tavern's usual clientele consisted of sailors
down on their luck, vagrants trying to empty a pocket
or escape the damp night air, and scurvy pirates who
didn't have the know-how or desire to lead a law-
abiding life, even though they'd been granted am-
nesty years ago for their participation in the Battle of
New Orleans. And, of course, scattered among the
scum were the diseased slatterns whose better days
were long past, their bodies and souls too wretched
to make a living in the cleaner brothels.

It was not a place Matthew Huntington Hamilton

13

frequented—not anymore—but he'd been summoned earlier in the day by a cryptic message he did not choose to ignore.

The Laranne
Imperative! Come at once to the Blue Gull.
My solicitor will meet you there.

There was no signature, but Hunter knew without the faintest trace of hesitancy who had sent the note and that she would never have contacted him had the matter not been one of life-and-death importance. Whose life mattered little; *his* death, or the advocation thereof, he didn't doubt. Admittedly, Lara deserved a chance at revenge; he just wondered why it had taken her or her influential family so long to go about it openly. And why, for God's sake, had his transgressions decided to rear their ugly heads at this point in his life?

He slid onto a crude wooden bench, his back to the wall as was prudent in a place like this, and waited for the game to be played out. At thirty-three years of age he could still be intrigued by a challenge, keeping his neck being the greatest challenge of all, but he had little tolerance for petty vengeance these days and none at all for the cloak-and-dagger affectations of such a clandestine arrangement.

To a degree, his life was staid and settled. He had reached a place of suitable conformity that allowed social acceptance without too much compromise on his part and carried none of the guilt of his past. If his peers were an unusual tangle of New Orleans aristocracy and salvaged street toughs, he never mixed the two or mistook them, leaving the unblemished social strata safe from the contamination and folly of his younger days. His life had become well ordered, if a bit boring, and comfortably predictable.

Which was why the note had caught him off guard. It was unexpected and unwise . . . and thrilling in a ghastly sort of way. It also unfortunately made his blood run hot for the first time in years in the manner he had never been able to ignore.

He peered through the dull haze of the lantern-lit room, knowing why Lara had chosen this despicable place. It wasn't a deliberate slight against his character—though there was that, of course—but rather that she wouldn't have known to simply send a message to his plantation on the outskirts of New Orleans or the town house he kept in Mobile. He'd received the note through a chain of spies from the New Orleans underworld with which he'd once had dealings.

How histrionically appropriate.

A drunkard staggered near, reeking of stale sweat and river mud. Hunter lifted a forearm as if to deflect the man's progress, then negligently twisted the thief's arm up behind his back and snatched back the watch the swindler had so neatly lifted.

Carl Partridge screeched in agony and leaned back into Hunter to lessen the pain. "Gawd! It were just fer fun, I swear it. I've a message from Connie."

Hunter shoved the pox-scarred man at arm's length and waited.

"Her ship docked last night. Connie ain't seen tit

nor toe of her though. It took her messenger till this mornin' to find you and deliver the note.''

Hunter flipped the man a coin, then turned his attention back to the front entrance. There was nothing at all in his expression beyond bored curiosity, but a hint of cold calculation lay in the eyes that glittered strangely at the front portal as if he could see right through the slatted door.

Come yourself this time, Lara. If you're determined to stir this up, don't bore me with some inept henchman who'll bungle the whole thing as did those in the past.

She wouldn't, of course. It was unthinkable. She needed the bald exposure of the two of them coming face to face even less than he did. And he needed it none at all. Past sins creeping back to haunt him were not his brand of entertainment these days.

A sardonic smile tipped one corner of his mouth as he tried to picture her as she would look now, a decade older and apparently not wiser, walking through the tavern entrance. But he could see only a vivacious seventeen-year-old with too much innocence in her eyes to realize the danger she was in. And too much pampered arrogance to care.

He had never encountered anything like her eyes, neither before his skirmish with her father's ship, the *Laranne*, nor in all the years since. The memory had traveled with him, a vexing tag-along undiminished by time, a reminder of things left unfinished. They were a changeling's eyes—deceptive hazel at first glance that could bend toward an unsullied blue one moment, lending credibility to her innocence, or an enchanting green the next that empowered her with the weapons of a Siren. And at times, depending upon her disposition, they ranged every shade in between.

They had been a mixture that last day, moody as the sea, the eyes of a frightened and subdued young woman whose innocence had been shattered—as his had been at a much younger age—by men's lust, greed, and the general and inescapable injustices of life.

He ignored the slight twist in his gut, evidence of a predilection toward blame that never seemed quite capable of surfacing into full guilt. It wasn't that he had been given to ruining virgins—he'd never been quite *that* jaded. He simply hadn't been able to abide the guilelessness in Lara's eyes. It had called to him, mocked him, made him want to lose himself in the fleeting sweetness of her youth and be washed clean.

Which, of course, was impossible. Thus, he had destroyed it.

Simple. Easy. What an uncomplicated piece of work she had been. The wrench in his belly tightened. The complications had come later, damn her. So, why now, after all these years, did she want to resurrect what had finally died by the natural sequence of time, distance, and maturity?

He neither needed nor wanted this complication in his life. He had just recovered his equilibrium from an unexpected breakup with a mistress of whom he had imagined he was truly fond. He should have seen it coming—his inattention was one of her complaints—but, just as with the note, he felt maligned and mis-

17

treated, pole-axed from behind by a bolt of bad luck hurled from a cloudless sky. The fact that he hadn't seen it coming and probably should have—one always reaps what one sows, after all—made him downright surly with himself and consequentially with whomever Lara chose to send through the tavern door.

The hum of voices rose and fell as the tavern's motley patrons continued downing libations. An occasional burst of laughter broke through the din but was usually short-lived. There was little to be joyous about in this part of town.

Hunter checked to see that his people were in place, an old habit that had proved reliable for longevity. Gal, so called because she didn't know her real name, stood near the scarred wooden bar and smiled a coy invitation. She was dressed in boy's britches and vest with her pale blond hair twisted up beneath a ragged cap, but her flawless skin, huge topaz eyes, and lean graceful figure would always give her away as female.

Hunter shook his head once at her affected invitation and ignored her equally unnatural pout. Gal was bored with waiting and trying her hand at mimicking the whores, but he was in no mood to humor her theatrics.

Shaken by his inattention, she tried once more and his eyes turned cold as ice. Fearful hesitancy shivered through her at the realization that Hunter was in no mood for teasing and she had pushed the game too far. He would withhold his devil's charm and the polite favor he bestowed for good behavior. Days or weeks of nothing but his icy regard stretched before her, a living Hades of vacant, silent disapproval. Furious at the prospect, she turned to look for the little man they called Weasel.

Weasel noted Gal's frenetic flush and glided toward her quickly. He was small and spry, having the appearance of a wizened old man of ancient lore, a fabled leprechaun or elf. He had the uncanny ability to be everywhere or nowhere, and more than a few of the superstitious New Orleans fortune-tellers had called him charmed. Though he knew better than to touch Gal, he leaned close and crooned, "Now, sweeting, no need to tie yerself in a knot. He's in a mood for certain, but it ain't gonna last. You'll see."

"Oh, but . . ." She glanced back at Hunter, angry yet wanting to make amends.

Her breathing grew a bit fast and shallow by Weasel's way of thinking. He drummed his fingers rhythmically on the bar, trying to divert Gal's attention before she flew off on a tangent and ruined everything.

"You know he'll not be pleased if you get to feelin' bad," he said placidly. "He knows it were all in fun, but he's got other things on his mind right now."

Wrath flashed in her eyes, but the effect was ruined by the petulant pout of her bottom lip. Weasel relaxed when Gal dropped her chin and wilted morosely against the bar.

" 'At a girl," he encouraged. "Now, look sharp. We've a visitor."

Gal shot back upright, alert, when the tavern door

swung open to admit a small, jaunty man. "That the one?"

Weasel studied the newcomer with a practiced eye. The man's clothing was well tailored and immaculate, the golden chain of his watch fob stupidly displayed upon his silk vest. His presence was spectacular in light of his obvious misplacement in this hovel.

"Aye, signal him."

Having already noted the man's entrance, Hunter stood abruptly. Dressed in severe black from his tall boots to his cape, he rose like an ominous dark-winged beast, his intent to discourage the tavern's clientele from stripping the man clean of valuables and livelihood before he had a chance to question him. Although as finely turned out himself as the sober little man he approached, no one would have dared accost Hunter. They knew him by face or reputation and either feared or respected him. Those who didn't were soon disabused of erroneous notions by their colleagues, who never in their deepest nightmares wanted Hunter or his minions as enemy.

Percival Smythe almost choked as much from fright as revulsion when he stepped into the Blue Gull. He'd never seen such a sordid horde of humanity grouped into one small space. England could, of course, boast its own collection of squalid grog shops and alehouses, but Thaddus Percival Smythe was acquainted with them only by hearsay. He'd certainly never been inside one.

He took a monogrammed kerchief from his pocket and dabbed the thin film of sweat on his upper lip as his eyes scanned the crowd. Smoke from cheap tobacco hung like fog over the room and mingled with the stench of years of spilled ale and the even ranker smell of unwashed bodies. He swallowed back his offended sensibilities and apprehension, praying the man who approached him with unhurried but somehow intimidating grace was the one he had come seeking.

Their path was bisected by a hag reeking of a musky scent so vulgar Percy ignored its probable origin. She sidled near him with a partially toothless grin and cooed a greeting as her dirty nails fingered his chin while her other hand neatly tried to palm his valuables. Sent screeching back by a hard grip on her shoulder, she turned angrily to rebuke her nemesis, then cringed away like a stray dog when she encountered the tall dark man known only by his alias.

Percy strained his head back to look well above his own meager height to meet the man's eyes. He would know him by his eyes, Lara had said. She was right. Even in the dim room there was no mistaking the strange amethyst-indigo coloring, icy outside, burning beneath.

"Mr. Hunter?"

Christ! How like Lara to send this milk-faced puppy into the bowels of Hades and expect him to return unscathed. Hunter took the man's arm in an uncompromising grip, swung him around, and ushered him back outside. A small band of outcasts collected immediately and followed. After slipping out the front door, they dispersed again like nervous rats into the dark alleys, doorways, and other hidey-holes lining the waterfront.

Libby Sydes

Willing or unwilling, Smythe allowed himself to be dragged along; he had no choice really. But once away from the foul odor of the tavern, he found himself relieved enough to be in the clean air to draw a deep breath.

"Where is she?"

If the man's eyes were the cold, deathless fire of Hades, his voice was even more so. Smythe lost the breath he'd taken and suddenly feared he was only two steps away from disgracing himself by whining. With nothing more than a few words Percy was convinced that Lara's warnings (which he had assumed were merely the concerns of a distraught woman) had not been spoken lightly after all but were based purely on fact. And, more sadly for the young woman, from experience.

"She is still in England," he offered.

"State your business."

He swallowed hard, grateful for Lara's foresight, and fumbled for the letter in his pocket, realizing he wouldn't be able to find proper command of his voice to explain what was already plainly written. Ashamed of his cowardice when this errand was so important to his client and friend, he shoved the letter forward with forced bravado.

Hunter smiled—which didn't alleviate Smythe's terror a whit, for it was the cruelest twist of the lips he'd ever seen—then took the paper and broke the seal. He was still for tense, endless seconds as he read and reread the message, then crumbled it in his fist as if it were nothing but an insignificant bit of rubbish. Tossing it to the ground at Smythe's feet, he gave the solicitor a belittling glance, then turned and walked away, his cloak billowing out behind him like an avenging raven.

"Come along," he said into the night.

At once three bodies crept from nook and crevice, their movements both wary and cocksure. Smythe noted a thin man of indeterminate age who moved with the quick darting scurry of a ferret. A girl in tattered boy's clothing followed, a hat in one hand, the other swinging a gnarled stick like a cane. Her hair was as light and soft as the moonlight falling just below her shoulders. She turned to say something to a robust man behind her, and Smythe was struck speechless momentarily by the pure lines of her face and alabaster reflection of her skin in starlight.

"Wait!" he called, frantic for Lara at the possibility that his mission had served no purpose whatsoever. He snatched up the crumpled paper and hurried after the group. "Sir, please, what do I tell her—"

Hunter swung back, stopping the young solicitor dead in his path with a lethal stare from hard, amethyst eyes. "You need tell her nothing. I will arrive there before you will."

Percy watched, astounded, as the man strolled away without a backward glance and dissolved into the eerie night as if he were one with it, an otherworldly part of the darkness followed by a fallen army. Only the girl paused to look back at him, and the strange void in her eyes chilled him to the bone.

Percy shook off the uneasy sense of foreboding and pulled himself up stiffly, reckoning everything he had heard was true. These Americans were indeed impertinent, crude, and too arrogant by half. He had been left rudely standing alone in a place not fit for decent persons, and he wasn't even certain he had fulfilled his mission. There was nothing for it but to return to Lara and hope the man's word could be trusted. His brow creased as he stared into the fog-laden blackness and searched for one last glimpse of the girl.

She was gone, of course, but the nothingness in her eyes stayed with Percy even as he opened the note and smoothed the rumpled edges out against his thigh. Holding the paper up to catch the glow from a street lamp, he read the short message, astonished that the man had asked no questions after reading such a simple communication.

I have information that will interest you. I am willing to bargain for it in return for a favor, but be warned there is grave danger involved, and you must be willing to come immediately. All is lost otherwise.

Chapter Three

The night was black as a witch's kiss when Hunter sailed into the isolated cove off Hythe. He had brought only the sparest number of trustworthy souls necessary to sail his sleek barque, a far cry from the numerous crew members he had employed as the pirate Hunter. The dinghy dispatched from the ship scraped the moonlit beach and he disembarked, then stealthily made his way into the cliff overhangs for cover.

He would not risk ambush or abduction until he discovered Lara's scheme, and he would meet her on his terms only. Behind him, water lapped against the sides of the small boat as it was rowed back into the night mist toward the *Huntress*.

Ian O'Connor, dressed in sandy-colored buckskin, appeared like an apparition out of the fog, leading two saddled horses. "You're a day early."

Hunter nodded as he mounted. "Good winds. Lead

the way, Connie. Let's see what sweet little Miss Winthrop has in mind."

"Lady Chalmers," Connie corrected, and took satisfaction from Hunter's sharp glance. "Or don't you remember they married her off?"

Hunter kicked his horse forward. They both remembered.

They took the easiest route, the land having been scouted by Connie ahead of time, and slowed only when they reached the outskirts of Dover proper.

"It's there." Connie pointed. "That monolith they call a castle. They keep it locked up tighter than a nun's knees."

Hunter eyed the massive stone structure. "Her husband?"

"Died a few months ago," Connie replied, his gravelly voice so like his weatherbeaten face. "By my reckoning, she must have sent for you within days of the burial."

Hunter ignored the underlying insinuation. "What else?"

"I couldn't find out anything more; they guard their secrets as carefully as their doors, but there is something not quite right. I could feel it in my bones. Her servants are either loyal or scared, and I didn't want to dig too deeply and arouse suspicion."

Hunter slid from his horse, then handed the reins over. "Which room?"

"She sleeps in the west wing, the corner suite there. Any number of windows will grant you entrance, if you make it across the grounds undetected. Hunter . . ." Connie paused and gave his companion a direct look. They had been together a long time, from victims of England's pressment gangs to Jean Lafitte's army of corsairs, to the discreet lives they had led since the Battle of New Orleans. They knew the rights of friendship and its inherent boundaries well.

Connie chanced overstepping those confines. "The past is dead; let it rest. She's not her father, never was. It was Henry who took your ship and cargo and pressed you into service all those years ago, but it was Lara who got caught in the middle and paid the price for revenge."

"So now it's her turn." Hunter shrugged. "Her other tries have failed. She has simply grown more aggressive." He glanced over at Connie and smiled. "I should applaud her tenacity."

Connie shook his head. "I don't think she's after retaliation. Just a feeling, mind you, but—"

"Enough," Hunter said. Speculation was as bankrupt as an empty pocket, and he'd never cared for either—too unreliable. "I'll find out soon enough her reasons."

Dressed in black, he melded with the night as he made his way across the elaborate grounds, attuned to the slightest sound, the faintest disturbance in the expanse surrounding him. The grass was a closely cropped cushion beneath his feet, aiding his stealth, the shrubs precisely manicured silhouettes in the moonlight that provided intermittent cover. There were no dogs out, and upon closer inspection, the watchmen in decorative livery seemed more for show than anything else. They seemed to patrol the grounds by rote rather than any obvious desire to catch an intruder.

It was that very nonchalance that alerted Hunter.

Lara awoke to a smothering sensation and realized her mouth and nose were covered. She reared up against the gloved hand, then forced herself to release the frantic urge to lash out with her arms and legs. If an assassin wanted her dead, she would already be so. She jerked her head to the side and fought for a breath, just one, just enough to scream for her manservant Barrows. The hand only pressed her head ruthlessly back into the bedding until dizziness assailed her and she thought perhaps her earlier assessment had been hasty.

It had been foolish not to resist when she still had the strength to be effective. She tossed her head to the other side and tried to pull her arms from beneath the covers, but she was trapped in the bedcovers. Just when she was certain she would suffocate, the hand moved down slightly from her nose so she could draw air. Her nostrils flared and pinched as she sucked in deep breaths, and her eyes flew open to face her assailant.

"Ah, Lara," a voice crooned sweetly from the darkness. "Still fighting me in bed, I see."

Hunter! Dear God, he was here. Her body went limp, and she shut her eyes in relief and waited for him to release her. His hand drew away only a cautious fraction and hovered, ready to pounce again. Lara wouldn't give him the satisfaction just yet of assuring him she wouldn't scream. A small struggle for power on her part and probably useless, but she needed to retain whatever bits of herself she could before casting her soul to the devil.

His fingers touched her cheek and lingered there for immeasurable seconds that ticked away as slowly as her impeded heartbeats, then lightly slid down her neck with an excruciating deftness that held her suspended in mingled portions of fear and anticipation and relief that he had arrived. But when he reached the top edge of her gown and flicked one button loose, she reared up and pushed him away, disgusted.

"Light the lamp, Hunter," she said tiredly. "I'm in no mood for your midnight drama."

But she was vastly grateful he had come so soon—that he had come at all. There had been, of course, the terrible fear that he would not, but she hadn't let Percy know that. It had been too necessary for her own peace of mind to keep the hope alive.

She eased up against the bed's stately headboard and gripped the counterpane to her chest. "The lamp, please," she repeated.

As silently as he had come, he drew back and closed the heavy draperies so the glow would not summon the guards, then lighted a bedside candle that could be easily snuffed.

"You're in no danger here . . ." she began, until he turned with the lighted candle in his hand. Her throat closed, cutting off the words and whatever hope she had held, at her first glimpse of the man she had not seen in a decade.

He was nothing like she remembered . . . yet everything.

Well over six feet, he stood tall and commanding, a dark force tightly leashed in clothing tailored to perfection to fit his lean, well-built frame. His shoulders were broader, his face more mature, but she had expected those changes. It was the others she could not acknowledge.

His ebony hair no longer hung wildly down his back past his shoulder blades in pure jet rebellion, but had been cropped just below his collar, sedate and proper, fashionably unkempt. The jeweled earring no longer dangled defiantly from his lobe but had been replaced by a single tiny diamond, not as an ornament, it seemed, but more like a reminder or proof of bygone days.

Her heartbeat paused at the transformation, then rushed painfully on. Angry tears rose to the surface of her eyes, revealing her sudden hopelessness. Through a mist of seething distress, she stared harder at him, frantic to find some remnant of the man she remembered in his gracefully polished features. But she couldn't feel the sting of sea spray as it crashed against the hull of the ship, couldn't taste the salt on the wind, couldn't feel the rolling motion of the barque beneath her feet.

Her pulse struggled to find what her eyes could not, but she could make no sense of the refined man who could have walked straight into Almacks or Whites and not have his presence questioned.

Despair threatened to overwhelm her. *Dear God,*

he was so changed! In his dress, in his bearing, he was so changed. He might not serve her purpose at all.

The realization was staggering and sickening for Lara, who had placed all her foolish hopes on one disreputable, disloyal pirate from her childhood. The man she had known then would have done anything for the money she was prepared to offer, would have committed any unholy deed for the challenge she would have presented.

But this man . . . this seemingly well-bred and worldly person who stood with the ease and command of a titled aristocrat was not at all whom she had summoned, whom she had counted on as capable of being bought or blackmailed into doing her bidding.

Her optimism languished and everything in her went mortally cold. All the carefully built defenses she had erected over the past ten years had been penetrated so effortlessly. Not by what he was, but by what he had become. Damn him for growing up, for maturing into a man of obvious means who would not need her piddling bribe money.

Overcome by a surge of emotions, she turned her face aside to hide the bitterness and betrayal and helplessness. Tears threatened but she refused to let them fall, to show any hint of weakness. She could not bear to be near him now, to witness his heinous evolution. Taking a deep breath, she gathered her failing composure to demand that he leave her home, her life.

She looked back and met his eyes.

It was there that she finally found everything she

had hoped and expected to see. Deepest amethyst, almost indigo in the glow of a single candle, stared back at her with lazily tempered vitality, dangerous and compelling. She was shocked by the nimbus of dark power, the undiluted energy contained and controlled within him. She hadn't realized how much the years had managed to temper it in her memory, but not in the man. He moved closer to the bed, lithe and silent, an elegant phantom mingling with the shadows.

Ten years might have changed the outer man, but within, coiled and barely restrained, he was still completely uncivilized.

Lara felt something in her give. A shudder rippled along her arms and she gripped the covers tighter. There was energy and dark ambition in his gaze and a cruel promise that no longer had the power to frighten her outright. No, his eyes had not changed at all, and for all his impeccable dress, there was no doubt that the man inside the clothing had not changed either.

His teeth suddenly flashed white in a sensuously cynical smile that she knew was meant to intimidate her.

But Lara had changed as well from that seventeen-year-old girl he had held captive aboard his ship. There was nothing Hunter could do to terrify her now—except refuse to help her. Relief filtered through her in slow waves, quieting the anxious beat of her heart. Her pulse steadied as her eyes settled calmly on his.

"Hand me my wrapper," she requested, "then take a seat. Your towering over me is tiresome."

"Sweet Lara, you've grown claws," he said with approval as he collected her velvet robe and tossed it onto her lap.

"Not sharp enough, I imagine." She shrugged into the wrapper, then folded the counterpane back and swung her legs over the side of the bed and stood, her toes sinking into the deep Aubusson rug. "Do sit down," she repeated, but did not follow her own command.

Instead, she walked to the window and folded back the drape to peer out over the cliffs. Folkstone Castle was a haunting, moody place situated in a land of unpredictable weather and the constant motion of sea. Waves crashed against the dangerous rocks below, never at rest, sending up a glittering spray in crystal rainbow colors as the night slowly gave way to dawn.

For all its hostile appearance, being here suited her better than the finest spring day in the less harsher climes of the English countryside. Folkstone was like life, capricious and uncertain, stunningly beautiful but always potentially lethal. In its own fickle way, there were no surprises here.

She turned back to see Hunter still standing, negligently now against the bedpost, one finger running idly over the soft coverlet while his eyes ran indolently over her. He didn't reveal by so much as a whisper what he was thinking, but the unholy quest in his eyes was unmistakable. She glared back at him, ignoring the tightened muscles in her shoulders and spine, braced against the emotions such bold casualness called forth. After strolling to the nearest chair, she sat down and smoothed the folds of her robe around her with utmost and necessary composure.

Through it all he watched her, one eyebrow arched ever so slightly, the faintest hint of a cynical smile at his lips.

Lara looked away from that smile and laced her fingers together in her lap. "I suppose you are wondering why I sent for you." It wasn't a question, just an obvious effort to control the silence that had grown oppressive in the room.

"Not at all."

She ignored his silken sarcasm and tried to formulate her words to best advantage, but his image of a decade ago kept intruding. The fierce intolerance in his expression when he realized her father was not aboard the ship he had seized, the wicked delight when he realized the man's seventeen-year-old daughter was. Ignominiously hauled aboard his ship by two burly sailors, Lara had been treated with less respect than the case of brandy in her father's cabin that followed her.

Hunter studied the sculpted angles of her face, the subtle changes wrought by the passage of time. She no longer bore the first blush of womanhood. Her cheeks were more carved and slender, as was her body. Her fingers were long and elegant, white against her emerald-green wrapper, not baked golden by the sun as he had last seen them. The brilliant eyes that had shone with such fire and innocence, then later with confusion and fear, now held deep shadows and secrets. She was neither lush nor exotic, but sleek and cool and patently adult. At seventeen she had been charmingly pretty. At twenty-seven she was beautiful.

He ran one finger lightly over the counterpane again, then curled his hand into a fist. "I assume you brought me here to enact vengeance," he said. "I don't deny that you deserve the chance, but understand, Lara, I can't let you succeed. I've grown rather attached to my blood pumping regularly through my veins."

She looked startled for a second, then perplexed. "No, I haven't brought you here for revenge." She stood suddenly, too confined by her own leisure to tolerate it, and glided back to the window, smooth and graceful in her maturity. "Actually, I've brought you here in order to bribe or blackmail you, whatever it takes, to do something for me."

"I'm intrigued."

His tone was clearly bored, but for Lara there was no turning back. She plunged ahead without caution or self-preservation, mindful of the danger she put herself in but not caring. "There exists a piece of jewelry, an antique locket. I saw it aboard your ship ten years ago. I don't know if you are aware that it was once a brooch and part of a larger collection. As I know its origin, I must conclude you either stole the locket or bought it from a disreputable source." She spun around to face him. "Do you remember the piece?"

"Perhaps." He shrugged casually. "Trinkets come and go."

"Do not toy with me!" she demanded quietly. "Which is it, Hunter? Did you buy it or steal it?"

His nonchalance was contemptible. "I've not seen you in ten years, Lara, and you send for me to ask about a locket? What absurdity is this?"

"I am certain the estate to which it belongs would pay a sizable sum to get it back, a reward if you will." At his continued silence, her voice grew threatening. "They might also use other means to ensure that the jewelry is returned to its proper owner. You could be charged with thievery and imprisoned, Hunter, perhaps even hanged when your crimes of kidnapping and piracy against the Crown are known."

He smiled. "And I could slit your throat before you run off to tattle, Lara."

"Yes." A shiver crept along her limbs, though she could not afford to be afraid. She didn't doubt for a second that he was capable of such, but she had known the risks before sending for him. "Hear me out before you dispose of me, please."

"Sarcasm doesn't become you." He pushed away from the bedpost and strolled across the room to pick up a figurine on the mantel. He placed the delicate piece back and moved to another, idle and unconcerned.

Lara watched him study the porcelain, a sleek panther on the prowl, silent but restless. He balanced each valuable piece on his palm, and she remembered with vivid clarity how those hands could easily crush something he considered inconsequential—

36

how gentle they could be when he chose. Both memories made her highly uncomfortable, and she turned away to stare back at the cliffs.

"If you were innocent of the locket's origin when you bought it," she continued in a voice that hinted the idea was ludicrous, "you stand to gain an enormous reward for its return. It needs only me to inform the estate of its existence and yours." She looked back over her shoulder. "It's been missing for centuries, you see."

"Oh, I see," he remarked. His smile flashed again, clearly mocking in the awakening dawn.

Furious at his blithe reaction and everything else that had led up to this moment, Lara whirled back around to face him. "This is no game! I need your assistance desperately, and I mean to have it no matter what I have to do. Blackmail or bribery, Hunter, you decide."

"My dear, *dear* Lady Chalmers," he said with such grating indifference it set her teeth on edge. "You're growing quite distressed."

There was no longer French or any other discernible accent to his speech, not even the patois Cajun that had been so evident ten years ago. Instead, he sounded like any cultured and well-traveled gentleman. Lara greatly feared that he had purchased the jewelry after all and not stolen it. Either could work in her favor, but blackmail had been much easier for her to stomach than merely handing over a potentially exorbitant reward to a man who did not deserve it.

"Distressed?" she said faintly. "Yes, I am quite distressed. Name your price, Hunter. I need your services too badly to quibble about whatever it takes to buy you."

His eyes swept her slowly from head to toe, direct and implicit and without apology. At one time she wouldn't even have recognized the look; later it would have shocked her to the core. Now she expected it of him and didn't cringe even a small bit from the irreverent perusal. That, too, she would pay if he demanded it.

He saw the added bargain clearly in her eyes. "I see. You truly *are* in trouble." He couldn't fathom the depths to which she had sunk to send for him. Gambling debts were his first guess, but he still couldn't make the connection. "What makes you think you can buy me at all?"

"Have you changed that much?"

His eyes swept her again, and he smiled. "I haven't changed at all."

"Then you can be bought." For all that her tone was cutting, she preferred not to match words with him. She could not afford to lose.

Hunter grew genuinely intrigued by the hint of recklessness in her tone, by whatever problem was so profound it had moved her to such desperate measures. "What is it, Lara?" he asked smoothly. "What is so bad that your dear papa's money can't bail you out?"

"He has nothing to do with this," she said, a brittle edge to her voice. She'd broken with her powerful family ages ago, too long now to dredge up any guilt or remorse to heap on top of the devastation she was already feeling. It was her late husband's family she had to deal with now, and Hunter's help she needed to do so.

She clasped her hands in front of her and stared straight into his strange, compelling eyes. Diffuse light spilled into the room through the slit in the drapes, but it in no way negated the shadows inherent in the man.

That it had come to this was so unfathomable, so surreal, it wasn't even hard for Lara to speak. "I need for you to kidnap someone."

She spoke the words as if it were the most normal thing in the world, as if she requested nothing more than cream from the buttery and buns from the kitchen. When Hunter gave her a droll look, she realized her gaffe and added forcefully, "Rescue, actually. John Byron, fifth Earl of Folkstone, has already been kidnapped by my late husband's family. I need for you to find and return him to me."

His smile vanished. One black eyebrow rose over his implacable eyes. "I've never before found myself so impaired by stupidity," he said, his voice as sweet and deceptive as poisoned honey. "You must forgive my lapse and the fact that I find this a tad hard to follow."

"Yes," she said softly, then sank down upon the settee and lifted a hand to her throbbing temple. "I'm not thinking too clearly these days; you must find my conversation as addled as the ravings of a lunatic." She lifted her eyes to implore him to bear with her and continued with agonizing control. "John Byron is my son. Upon my late husband's death, George's brothers took the child away and left a note detailing their demands. They want control of Folkstone, but they can only have it through John Byron."

Hunter's eyes narrowed and his expression changed abruptly from grudging interest to sneering cynicism. "What can this possibly have to do with me, Lara? Whatever possessed you to think that I would care about your domestic problems? I don't need your bribe money or the reward you dangle before me, and I certainly can't be blackmailed by your threats." He turned to leave and delivered the parting shot with cruel indifference. "Go to the authorities if some crime had been committed, *Lady* Chalmers, or hire some local henchman as you're so fond of—"

"No!" She leapt to her feet to stop him along with his ruthless, condemning flow of words. "I can't go to the authorities or anyone else!" She paused, her eyes stark and angry, her breaths coming in staggered gasps. "John Byron is my only child; he's all I have. They've taken him away, and he must be frightened out of his mind. He's just a boy, only . . . eight years old. He—"

Hunter rounded on her with a look so brutal it stopped her cold. "He isn't eight," he said with icy softness, "he's nine. And he isn't the legal heir to your husband's estate. He's the bastard heir to mine."

Chapter Four

Lara's hand went to her throat. She felt strangled, choked on her own air. Eyes desolate and unblinking, she stared back at Hunter with a face that had gone parchment white.

"Did you really think I didn't know?" His voice ripped through her with force, a carefully civilized rage far worse than mere anger. "You kept him from me all this time, Lara. I don't know him, can't feel him. He doesn't exist for me. Whatever possessed you to think I would care what happens to your misbegotten child?"

The cruelty of his words seeped through her, an icy black despair that chilled her to the bone. Crueler still was the sight of his back as he turned again to leave.

"Wait!" she demanded, but he continued to desert her, his long strides taking away all hope. She had insufferably few choices left. She crossed the room and grabbed his sleeve in a frantic grip.

He stopped immediately, but she could feel the suppressed violence beneath his linen shirt, quivering and ready to strike.

"I don't care what you feel or don't feel," she bit out, each word carefully modulated. "You will do this for me, Hunter. You owe me!" Her voice broke, and she took a deep breath to reclaim it, knowing how well he could use her vulnerability against her. "John Byron is everything to me. I had no desire for him to know his true sire, and you certainly didn't deserve—"

"Then why am I here?" he interrupted with disturbing patience.

Lara stepped back and dropped her fists to her sides, feeling foolish for trying to restrain him. She had seen him backhand grown men and send them to their knees. She knew his strength firsthand and the utter menace behind his composure. He could dominate and defile by nothing more than a look; with a touch he could annihilate.

She gathered her own poise around her like a shield and walked to the window to stare out at the cliffs. Betraying George tasted like bile but there was no help for it, so she forged ahead and spoke in the dull frank tones of one who needed to be done with what she had to say.

"My late husband could not sire a child. His brothers either knew or suspected it. They stole John Byron after the funeral and are holding him in order to obtain official control of George's estates. They don't need it, of course. Their own holdings are diverse enough, but they cannot abide the thought of John

Byron possessing one share of George's bequeathal. They have commanded me to have my solicitor draw up papers claiming that I am too distraught since my husband's death to handle his affairs and are turning them over to his family to be held in trust until John Byron reaches his majority."

Her fingers curled over the ledge of the window. "But they will . . . John Byron will never come of age no matter what I sign over. They will make certain of it."

Her back was rigid, her entire body braced to keep the panic and despair at bay, but when Hunter touched her shoulder, she crumpled beneath the weight of her helplessness. She spun around and grabbed a fistful of his crisp shirt, her eyes flashing fury and determination and a terrible fear.

"You will help me," she said distinctly. "I can't go to anyone else. John Byron would be publicly disgraced, and he is the only one innocent in all this." Her eyes grew cold, her voice frighteningly calm. "If he isn't rescued, George's brothers will murder him. They'll let nothing stand in the way of their ruthless ambitions, least of all an illegitimate child."

Hunter glanced briefly at the slender hands making a mess of his shirt and said evenly, "Why choose me?"

She searched his face, the beauty and masculine refinement of his perfectly hewn features, then looked into his eyes. "You are the only man I know," she whispered with assurance, "who is as ruthless as they are."

An indrawn breath hissed between his teeth. He

43

took her wrists and pulled her hands from his shirt with a sharp jerk. "I suppose I deserve that. Good-bye, Lara."

He had taken no more than a step when she played her trump. "Barrows!"

A man stepped from the shadows, an elderly servant with stern loyalty and affinity written all over his strict features. He held a derringer pointed straight at Hunter's chest.

"Well," Hunter said smoothly, "I see I must reassess." For all that he smiled, his eyes remained bitterly cold. "When do we begin?"

Air expanded Lara's lungs. "Tonight."

Hunter glanced over at the elderly servant. "Be a good fellow and put that away before one of us regrets it."

Lara held up a hand to stay any movement. "I want your word first."

"But of course." His elegant hand went to his heart. "I pledge you the full measure of loyalty attainable by a man at gunpoint."

For all that he mocked her, it was enough just now to have his promise no matter how weightless. She would pay for forcing his hand, of that she had no doubt, but as long as he rescued John Byron she didn't care. She nodded at Barrows and the servant slid the small pistol into his pocket and asked quietly, "Will there be anything else, Lady Chalmers?"

"No, thank you." She closed her eyes briefly. "We'll get him back now, Barrows, you'll see."

He nodded and exited the room as silently as he had come.

"Efficient fellow," Hunter said. "I applaud your good judgment. It was a full quarter hour before I realized he was lurking about in the shadows."

Heat rushed to Lara's face. "No, we are not so accustomed to sneaking about here. Why didn't you let on?"

"It was too intriguing to wait and see how far you would go for the child."

"Is this a game to you?" she accused furiously. "I assure you, to me it is not."

John Byron was the light in her life, the only thing she truly held dear. He filled the void in her heart, slayed the dragons of empty dreams. George was gone; she'd long been estranged from her parents. Her friends were little more than acquaintances, George's choices from academic circles, and a few from her girlhood she kept at a safe and comfortable distance. In isolating herself, she had alienated them. Now there was no one to turn to, no one with whom to share her grief or fear.

She glanced up to find Hunter's piercing amethyst eyes staring at her without compassion or kindness, and said bitingly, *The child*, as you call him, is *your* son."

A spark of something indefinable flickered in his eyes then was gone. "Yes, well, that has never really been the case, has it?" He reached out and touched the pulse point in the hollow of her throat, and Lara wondered whether he would caress or strangle her. "If I do help return your son, what makes you think they won't come after him again?"

She stood before him for all of two seconds longer,

then stepped back and gripped the arm of the settee. "Nothing." She lifted a palm as if to explain, then collapsed like a wilted flower into the seat and dropped her face to her hands, her hair falling forward to hide her distraught features. "Nothing at all."

Hunter watched her crumble and remembered another time, another place, when the fire had suddenly gone out of a young woman, leaving her vulnerable and unprotected. He took a step back and added crisply, "They will come after him again, won't they?"

"Yes," she whispered. "As long as he's alive, they will try again and again." Her eyes lifted, and her expression was as grave and despondent as her voice. "But I will think of something to satisfy them, or I'll take him away where they can't touch him. Or I . . . I will hide him—"

"For the rest of his life, Lara?"

The words were softly and intelligently said, but their meaning ravaged her heart with the brutal truth. "I can't leave him to those vultures. Surely you understand this."

"Black-hearted demon that I am?" he asked cryptically.

She winced, remembering the name she had once called him. "That was a decade ago."

"Nothing has changed, Lara."

"Everything has," she countered. She pulled the heavy veil of her hair over one shoulder and began braiding it, mechanically, methodically, her nimble fingers pale against the dark tresses. When she reached the end, she looked around her, confused suddenly by what she was doing. She had no ribbon to secure it; the entire process had been in vain. Tears sprung to her eyes, undoing her completely. She rose to her feet. "Just say that you will do it!" Despite the glassy surface of her eyes, there was no tremor in her voice. There was no shame either, and her eyes promised all.

Hunter reached out and lifted her loose braid then twisted the sable mass in his fist. It came unraveled, filaments of silk that flowed like water over his hand and wrist and rushed to life old memories that had lain dormant and waiting on the fringes of his consciousness. The snare was lush and strong, a gossamer web with the scent of springtime and the strength of steel. His hand slid down her neck slowly, testing and tormenting, a controlled insanity beneath his purpose.

He reached the low neck of her robe and still she did not move, just stared back at him with everything she possessed offered in her eyes. The luxurious velvet brushed his fingers as he parted the edges. She flinched slightly but her eyes never wavered. His hand slipped inside and cradled her breast, weighing its fullness and her commitment. Her lashes fluttered once but she remained stoic, her back rigid, her gaze direct.

She never moved, never retreated, but when his thumb brushed over her, once, twice, her eyes flared with loathing. Hunter uncurled his fingers and laid the flat of his palm over her heart. "I begin to understand."

With a smile that cut like a blade, he withdrew his hand and stepped back. Cool air hit her bared flesh, and she dug her nails into her palms to keep from pulling the neck of her robe together. Most of her was concealed beneath the edges of emerald velvet, but his gaze found all the exposed and vulnerable parts: the fair flesh of her throat, the gentle hills of her breasts, the flushed tint of her discomfiture.

He eyed her clenched fists and said smoothly, "No need to sell your soul, Lara."

He moved toward the window and opened it, then paused to send her a telling glance. "I will name my reward later, but if you have betrayed me in this, if you've laid some trap or scheme, be warned you won't like the method of payment."

She watched him disappear into the night, in the same manner he had first come into her life—a dangerous intruder from a lawless world. No rules, no truces, no assurances. Nothing bound him but his word, and she didn't really know how much of that she could trust. She dropped back to the settee and lowered her head to her knees, no longer capable of fighting the tears.

She had never imagined that the man who had once been her damnation might also prove to be her salvation.

The sails unfurled to catch the wind, and the barque lurched forward, slicing through the English Channel with razor-sharp precision. Lara reeled from the impact and gripped the ledge of the portal to steady herself. She'd been in this cabin since before dawn, spirited aboard under the cloak of darkness to conceal her identity from anyone who might be spying.

As theatrical as it seemed, she didn't doubt for a second that there were spies about. The naïveté of youth had been stripped away a decade ago, and now even her trust in basic human nature had been slaughtered. She believed no one—not her son's kidnappers or his potential rescuer.

She gazed out at the channel, knowing Hunter hadn't wanted her to accompany him, but she had refused to be left behind, miserable and waiting at Folkstone. She knew from their note where George's brothers held her son, and that knowledge was vital for the mission to succeed. Still, a carefully drawn map would have been enough to guide Hunter.

The obvious reason he had allowed her aboard ship was too vile to contemplate. She pressed her face to the window and let the cool glass draw the shame from her cheeks. If it came to that, if she were forced to play the harlot in exchange for her son's life, she would do so.

She gripped the ledge of the portal tighter and concentrated on the world outside the cabin. Inside there were memories, too many of them rushing at her from every corner. She had endured for months after her son was taken, had been able to keep her emotions at a manageable level of despair while waiting to see if Hunter would help her. Yet within moments of stepping aboard this ship she felt that just one word, one touch, would snap her fragile composure in two. She held onto the raveling threads of control with a tight fist. If she collapsed she would be no good to anyone, least of all John Byron.

She watched the ocean slide by with amazing speed where the barque cut through the water. Their journey would take them around Land's End to St. George's Channel, then through the Irish Sea into the North Channel and finally past the Barra Isles off the cold, inhospitable coast of western Scotland. Sorrow washed over her. It was no place for a boy who loved warm sunshine and vigorous outdoor play.

Lara closed her eyes and tried to think of John Byron elsewhere, anywhere, than with George's despicable brothers, tried not to think how scared and confused a nine-year-old would be who had been stolen from his home. She hoped Robert and Claude would be fair with the child but had little hope that they would treat him any better than the pawn he represented.

She glanced over her shoulder as the door clicked shut behind her, but it was only a sailor bearing a breakfast tray.

"Lady Chalmers," he greeted.

Something about his accent caused her to turn and stare fully into his face. "Connie?" she whispered. At his nod, she smiled thinly, embarrassed. "I'm sorry, I didn't recognize you."

"Aye, it's been awhile." He set the tray down. "Would you pour?"

Tears rushed to her eyes. It was something they had done before. When she was frightened and so far from home, when nothing else in the world made sense, Ian O'Connor had brought her tea, and she had clung to the English ritual as if it were life-sustaining manna. She lifted a hand, then dropped it back to her side. "No, I . . . would you please?"

"Here now, I've made you cry." He rushed over and handed her a napkin. "I never meant that."

"I know." She turned her face away and pressed the linen to her eyes. "It's just so difficult."

"Well, isn't that a fine welcome? I'm delighted to see you too."

She muffled a watery laugh. His humor helped bring her back to rights, and with a few deep breaths she felt her equanimity return. "Oh, Connie." She sighed. "I *am* glad to see you, but these are not the best of circumstances."

"So I hear." He poured, then handed her a cup.

She took it by rote, her appetite so diminished since her son's disappearance, she couldn't remember the last time she actually tasted anything she consumed.

"Our regular galley hands aren't with us this voyage," he warned. "We'll mostly be fending for ourselves."

Lara nodded. Food held no importance these days except to keep her alive.

Connie gave her a puzzled look, then smiled. "He's right. You've changed."

She almost managed a blush, remembering the pampered girl she had been, fussing for a plate of scones like some royal princess to be waited upon. "I can cook, if you like, nothing fancy but . . ."

Connie frowned. "Can't say as he'd like that much, but I can ask."

Lara didn't really care what "he" liked, but she would be certain not to do anything to antagonize Hunter.

"Saints." Connie shivered. "Ain't you cold, Lady Chalmers? It's frigid as a witch's tit—" A flush reddened his face before he went on sheepishly. "Beg pardon, but it's a mite chilly in here, and you without so much as a cloak."

Lara winced slightly. She didn't seem to feel the cold anymore or the heat. She'd been too outwardly numb with grief for the past few months to notice anything beyond the devastation within her. Her nerves had been centered on that internal pain so long, everything outside was a mere nuisance she hardly recognized anymore.

Connie stoked the small fire in the brazier until the coals glowed. "Can I get you anything else?"

"No, but thank you." Her eyes pleaded with him to understand. "You needn't sit with me. I know you have work to do."

She looked away and busied herself with nonsense, hoping he would leave, perversely wishing he would stay in spite of her wants. Seeing him again was difficult, a reminder of how many lives had been touched so long ago. She needed to be alone, to sort through everything rambling around in her mind and put it in perspective, but she was so desperately lonely since George's death and John Byron's disappearance.

Connie picked up the tray. "I'm no more than a shout away. If you need anything . . ."

"Thank you for coming with him."

"The least I could do." He winked. "For old times."

She tried to smile, failed, and gave him as honest a look as she would allow herself. "Will it turn out all right, do you think?"

"You would not have contacted him otherwise."

She nodded and dropped her gaze. She heard the tray rattle when he left but did not look up again until she was certain he was gone. It was difficult to realize after all the planning and secrecy years ago that Hunter knew about John Byron. Her family had been so careful after her return, quickly marrying her off to George, then sending her far from home to bear the child.

Thoughts of her husband sent a forlorn ache to her chest. Patient, generous, temperamental George. How she had loathed being forced to marry a man thirty years her senior; how she had come to respect him later. He had been a handsome and distinguished man, intellectual and self-assured, but to a girl of seventeen he had seemed quite old.

She smiled sadly, remembering how he had rebuffed the often snidely congratulatory whispers of his peers, then brooded over them later when alone with her. He had been careful to help her through the aversion and insecurity of their hasty marriage, patient when another man would have grown vexed and demanded his conjugal rights.

More companion than husband that first year, he would sit with her in front of a warm fire and talk late into the night. They discussed everything from the strange evolutionary theories being introduced by

the naturalist Erasmus Darwin to the distinctions between opinion and knowledge by the Greek philoso-
phers to, finally, their plans for the child she carried.
The last had been hard for Lara. She'd been wary of
George's calm acceptance after the way her own father had shamed her, but she soon learned that her
new husband was genuinely eager for an heir.

It was only much later when their marriage had
crossed the more normal boundaries of intimacy that
she found out George could have no children of his
own. He hadn't wanted her to know, had wanted so
badly for her to think that he cared more for her than
the son she would give him.

It wasn't true. Her pregnancy was the only reason
George had wed her, but the deception was insignificant. She had returned home ruined, her future
bleaker than anything she had theretofore imagined
possible, to find herself *enceinte*. George had been
her salvation. He had also been everything she
needed in a husband and companion. If it had not
been for George, her father would have banished her
to a convent, and it was debatable whether she would
have found her way back among decent folk. Even
after she was wed, if her father had had his way, she
would have been sent into exile like a disagreeable
wife to be isolated at the country home. Henry Winthrop had never looked at his child in the same doting way after her return, but, blessedly for Lara, he
had greatly underestimated the strength of George
Chalmers's character.

By a man old enough to be her father, Lara had
been given her head and allowed the freedom to be

her own person or at least have her own thoughts. George argued politics and religion and scientific theory with her, and she was never quite certain if he saw her as companion or rival when his voice rose and his face grew mottled in the heat of the debate. But for all their differing opinions, he never berated or belittled her for having her own view. Much later, she realized the talks stimulated him, physically as well as intellectually.

Lara watched dawn turn the channel into a blend of deep violet shadows and warm rosy golds. George hadn't been a saint. He'd had his quirks and foibles and jealousies as any other man, and Lara was careful not to paint him with attributes in death that he had never possessed in life. But he had been a solid, dependable man.

The memory of him made her yearn, made her lie awake nights and long for the sweet warmth of his company, the comfort of a life that had been secure. That ache was the only real indication she had at times that she was still alive, when every other feeling but fear had been severed from her. She crossed her arms over her breasts and held tight, missing him . . . missing their old life.

She was startled by the click of the door latch and turned to see Hunter standing there staring at her with an inscrutable look on a face still fiendishly beautiful. He was as ominous in awakening daylight as he had been in the dark, more so perhaps because the coldness and absolute lack of compassion on his face was more clearly defined.

A decade had brought changes, sun-creases around

his eyes, broader shoulders and thighs. But some things were not altered at all. There had been no softness in his eyes then; there was even less now. They were jaded eyes, full of sardonic coolness and tempered cynicism. He had seen so much, done so much, there was no virtue left in him. Lara's arms fell limp to her sides beneath his stare, but her breasts felt as heavy as her heartbeat from the lingering memories of George that would always be just that, something from the past that she would never recapture—and the much darker memories as well of the man who stood before her.

There was no connection between the two. They were as far apart as night to day. She remembered Hunter's strong fingers manacled around her wrist as he hauled her to his cabin, George's solicitations as he offered his arm for escort. Hunter's slyly cultivated seduction, George's honest request. Her marital obligations to George had been more comfortably endearing than exciting. If there had been none of the wildly euphoric ecstasy that marked the beginning of her short encounter with Hunter, there had also been none of the burdensome guilt and pain that had followed. The act with George had yielded little more than mild disappointment in a physical sense, but it had been more than fulfilling in a spiritual one. Friends, she had learned, were infinitely more trustworthy than lovers.

"Can you really cook?" Hunter asked.

She disregarded the faint mockery in his voice and nodded. She had been too restless to enjoy the tedious art of stitchery but had needed something to occupy her mind and hands during those months of isolation while her body grew round and heavy with child—a child not conceived in any emotion so pure as love or even hate but a terrible mixture of two passionate wills trying to prove dominance.

As much as she had tried to put it behind her, as hard as she had tried to forget, that night still haunted her, the memory of his hands and lips and softly spoken words slipping past her defenses to find an innocence so unready for his experience. And the painful consequence of letting her guard down.

Flushed by the direction of her thoughts, she looked away. "I can prepare simple meals, nothing exotic or elaborate."

"However did you sneak past all the nursemaids, butlers, and cooks to find your way into a pantry?"

There had been few servants in the country estate where she'd been sent to "suffer her iniquities and bear a child in shame," as her father had put it. George had vehemently contradicted Henry Winthrop's statement, but Lara remembered he had kept her there until John Byron was a year old before bringing them to Folkstone.

She tamped down the small dredges of resentment and smiled tightly at Hunter. "The same way I sneaked past you that last night aboard ship. Very successfully."

His answering smile was swift and blinding in his sun-bronzed face. Amusement and admiration underscored his tone. "Very good, Lara. You've grown quick and sharp in your maturity."

Her expression grew pensive. "I don't wish to

trade barbs with you, Hunter. It's too taxing. Can we not put the past aside and be civil?"

"How do you propose to do that when our past is the very reason we are here?"

"A truce then," she demanded.

He only stared at her a moment longer, then walked farther into the room, tossed his cloak over a large stuffed chair, and went to warm his hands over the brazier. His shoulders were wide beneath the loose white shirt, his buttocks and legs athletically firm beneath his fitted pants.

Lara imagined his physical perfection had been admired by many more appreciative than she could be at this moment, but even with the years of antagonism to bolster her, she could not deny the virility that encompassed every inch of him.

"Cook for the men if you like," he said over his shoulder, "but keep hemlock and nightshade from among the seasonings you use."

She blinked in disbelief. "What are you implying?"

"The obvious. That John Byron might be safely playing with toy soldiers at your father's estate while you lead me a merry chase to hell."

"You're mad." She gasped. "How dare you suggest such?"

"How dare you deny the possibility?" he returned. "I've dodged your murderous little henchmen for a decade now, Lara. Do you think I've grown stupid with age, or have you?"

"I don't know what you're talking about."

Hunter eyed her keenly. "Someone has been sending one inept lackey after another since a few months after you returned to England. They are bloodthirsty little creatures, but so far they haven't succeeded in letting mine.''

"I didn't know . . .'' Her voice faded then came back dripping sarcasm. "Really, Hunter, do you think I am your only enemy, the only person who has a grievance against you?''

"No." He smiled. "But you do seem to be the most tenacious. 'A woman scorned' and all that.''

"Not scorned," she bit out. "Raped. And *I* left *you*, remember?''

Stunned amusement flashed in his eyes. "Yes, I remember your midnight flight well, but rape?'' He laughed outright then, cold and mocking laughter that sent a chill down her spine. "My God, Lara, you were with me two months before I even touched you. If that night was rape every man on earth who ever seduced a maid would be in danger of incarceration.''

"I was innocent," she accused, shutting her eyes to block out his handsome face, his contemptuous laughter, and the terrible potent memories.

"You never once fought me," he returned, "not with any energy or intent.''

She shook her head, angry and embarrassed and needing to exonerate herself. "Deny it if it pleases you, if it makes you feel less the knave. It changes nothing.'' She spun away, needing distance, but his fingers curled around her arm and turned her back.

"Why didn't you fight me, Lara?'' he asked softly.

She shrugged off his hold in disdainful defiance. "When you attacked the ship, my maid knew . . .

59

suspected. She said things would go easier—" She looked away, angry at herself for needing to explain.

"Two months, Lara," he interrupted softly, knowingly. "And that day on the beach . . . have you forgotten it so easily?"

She had forgotten nothing, not the wonder of the moment, the thrill of being in his arms, the flushed excitement of her first kiss. The shock and pain and humiliation had come much later. Color stained her cheeks. "I was young and impressionable," she said in a low voice. "You used every ounce of it against me."

"You were spoiled and hungry for adventure," he countered. "You thought it a merry game to be attacked by the pirates you had only heard tales about. You had fantasized about the danger and daring so long you never once considered the real jeopardy you were in or consequences of your actions."

He stepped closer and cupped her face, his thumb tracing the delicate line of her jaw. He smelled of the sea—salt and wind and adventure. His hands were beautiful to look upon, warm against her skin.

His voice, when it whispered across her cheek, was seductively soft and aware. "So young, so pretty, so hungry. How often had you thought the unthinkable, Lara?"

The color left her face. She shrugged his hand off and stepped back, crossing her arms protectively over her middle. "You took advantage of my ignorance in the lowest way."

He shrugged carelessly. "I took advantage of the moment. And you allowed it."

It was, perhaps, what she hated most. The fact that she hadn't fought him until it was too late, that she had been so swept away she had thrown all natural caution and learned morality to the wind. By the time she realized exactly what was happening, her innocence was gone.

"And if I had struggled?" she accused. "You and your men had me convinced you would slit my throat if I disobeyed any command."

"Perhaps I would have." He gave her a careless smile. "I guess we'll never know." He touched a curl by her temple, then laid the back of his fingers against her cheek. "Should we find out?"

She grabbed his wrist hard. "No."

His knuckles were cool against her face, the corded muscle beneath her fingers strong. A part of her yearned to turn her face into his palm, to inhale the salt air on his skin and remember for only an instant what it was like to be young again, blameless and fanciful. To feel the wonder of that first kiss, the startling trickle of desire at the first soft brush of a man's lips against her own. But she wasn't a girl anymore to be both intimidated by his strength and intrigued by his brash behavior as she had a decade ago.

The memories rushed at her with shaming force—the heat and compelling touch of his hands, the way he had known her body better than she ever would. She had been so frightened of him that first month, then so taken with him later—just as he had planned. His pulse beat a warm, steady rhythm against her fingers, reminding her of too much that she could not set aside. When she looked up, she realized his eyes were burning with the memories as well.

She wanted to smile, to gloat, but pulled away quickly. Rebellious pride and misplaced self-confidence had been her downfall once; they would not be again. She knew what he was—powerful and manipulative and cunning. The strength of his intelligence had always been much more dangerous than his sword.

She couldn't tolerate remembering her own ignorance and recklessness, or the way things had been between them—not now when George was only three months in his grave and her son's life in great peril.

She turned her back on him and struggled with the words. "Please go," she whispered, pulling her arms even tighter about herself. "Please . . . just go."

"Where would I go, Lara?" he asked quietly. "This is my cabin."

Her eyes scanned the room, noting things she had ignored earlier in her distress. She whirled back around and stared at him in mild panic. "No," she whispered, and shook her head slowly. "You will find me another. You can't . . ." Her hand went to her throat and she could hardly speak past the sudden dryness there. "Please, I've only been a widow a short time."

His lids lowered over his hard, brilliant eyes, and his manner was questing as he gazed at her cheek, then trailed lower to her chin and continued down her neck, before finally stopping just at the hills of her breasts. "Is the price too high?"

Her shoulders stiffened at the damning warmth of

nothing but a searching look. Anger turned her voice cold. "No. No price is too high for the return of my son."

"Good." He withdrew immediately, retrieved his cloak, and flung it over his shoulders, but paused when he reached the cabin door. "This ship is fast and sturdy, Lara, well suited for our purpose. But it's also small, with few private compartments. I have one, Connie has another, and there are several that now hold storage. Any number of them could be cleared out but, other than Connie and Weasel, there's not a man aboard I can fully trust to leave you alone if you sleep there. Men get . . . rambunctious at sea, as you should be well able to remember."

Her eyes blazed briefly. "What of the girl who accompanied you aboard? Where does she sleep?"

"Gal stays where she will. She is quite capable of taking care of herself, Lara. She'd happily gut anyone who tried to touch her and feed their entrails to the sharks."

Lara's stomach lurched. "What . . . what will you expect of me here?"

"Are you thinking of taking your chances with the men? I would not advise it."

"No," she said between her teeth, "I just want to know exactly what is expected of me."

His eyes raked over her again, but they were depthless, completely unreadable. "Nothing is expected of you in my cabin, Lara. Nothing ever was."

The click of the latch was obscenely loud in the silence, the only sound to follow his departure. Lara leaned against the wall and tried to ignore the awful churning in her stomach. This had been a terrible mistake. She had known all along that it would be, but she needed him so badly, she had been willing to miscalculate or disregard the danger to herself. A laugh grated in her throat, raw as the tears stinging behind her eyelids. Had she truly thought she could handle him after so many years?

She stood upright and dashed the back of her hand over her eyes. No, she would never be that short-sighted or foolish. It was merely that nothing else mattered beyond getting her son back safe—not her morals or her integrity.

Chapter Five

Dawn gave way to a dark and dreary midday. The ship rolled in turbulent swells and drops in the midst of the squall, and the wind howled like a deranged spirit. Lara gripped the foot of the bed to steady herself as rain slashed against the portal.

Time had ceased to be anything but an extension of blended grays. She peered hard out the window to find some break in the storm, some promise of quiet, but outside the world was the color of dull lead, inside a murky black. Without looking at a timepiece, it was impossible to determine whether it was afternoon or early evening or night.

A lantern swung overhead with each dip and sway of the ship, but she dared not attempt to light it. Clinging to the bedpost, she rode the storm as she had all else in her adult life: if not with joy, then with the determination to make it through with some semblance of dignity intact.

There had been a time, very long ago, when a

storm would have frightened her. *Had* frightened
her. It held no sway over her now. She viewed it as a
villainous delaying tactic, the elements conspiring to
keep her from her son. She stared out the portal
again as if she could cut through the descending
darkness by sheer dint of will and penetrate the
gloom to see what lay beyond.

The ship heaved sharply and Lara lost her grip and
stumbled against a bedside chair. In the same
drunken lurch, the door crashed in against the wall.
Hunter swept through, bringing remnants of wind
and water with him. Without sparing a glance for
her, he shoved the door closed and dragged the sod-
den cloak from his shoulders.

Lara dug her nails into the arm of the chair to keep
from being pitched to the floor and watched him
manage the storm with little effort. His steps were
certain as he lit a lantern, then made his way to the
brazier and crouched down to stoke the coals. Damp
from head to toe, his clothing clung to him like a
second skin and outlined the contours of a body well
honed and lithe, muscular but without excess.

Lara felt an unfamiliar reaction in her chest, something as undefinable and elemental as the storm. Fear
perhaps of his strength and virility, or merely a
weighty dose of ordinary dread. Though she had
solicited his help in a desperate time, it was still difficult to be near him, to see how he had changed and
grown, to try to gauge his thoughts or temperament.
A part of her felt she knew him well enough to predict
his next word or gesture, but another part of her

found him to be a complete and utterly unpredictable stranger.

In spite of her animosity toward him, she was intrigued and studied him while his back was turned. The glow from the brazier illuminated the area in which he crouched in a halo of warmth. Masculine and beautiful, the converse terms fit him perfectly. Just as he had a decade ago, he alternately fascinated and terrified her. She realized now what she had not known then, that rapier wit and demon charm coupled with the beauty of physical presence were daunting combinations for a girl of seventeen to stand against.

A woman of twenty-seven as well. Her gaze wandered swiftly over him, trying not to linger, but it was hard to ignore the way his shirt clung to the musculature of his back and his wet pants hugged his derriere.

She'd heard whispers of a widow's discontent but had never thought the term would apply to her. George's lingering illness had not only deprived her of a husband but of the close comfort of one. The fact that no man had managed to stir her feminine appreciation of the opposite gender the way Hunter did didn't help her lonely situation either.

She found herself resenting the way God had shaped him in a manner so appealing she had to take care not to admire him openly when he grabbed the tails of his damp shirt and drew it over his head, revealing a broad back that was deeply tanned.

Lara pulled her gaze away from his blatant immodesty and became absorbed in the rich colors and patterns of the carpet beneath her feet. The sight of his naked back raised too many memories, and it was painful to recall what they had been together, what they had done. It was unlikely that he remembered it with any special fondness either, but she couldn't help but wonder if he ever thought of the weeks they had spent aboard his ship or the days on the small island where they had taken refuge, wondered if that time had been memorable or just one segment among many for him.

He'd been so wild then, his hair long and black as sin, like his soul, beautiful but tainted. His smile had been just as wicked, a compelling flash of white against bronze. She remembered how tempting she'd found that smile, and the rest of him as well. Bold and confident in every movement, his amethyst eyes glittering with secrets, he had beckoned her away from her instinctive caution and tapped the fertile and susceptible ground of her curiosity.

He had done it with the hands of an artist and the body of a pugilist, skillful and deft in every movement. She remembered the day with crystal clarity, for it had marked the beginning of the demise of her youth. On the balls of his feet, he'd walked backward across the sand toward the waves, holding out his hand and calling to her.

Come, Lara . . .

Shirtless and smiling, his canvas pants riding low on his hips, his entire being had been an invitation as the waves began to cover his ankles.

Come, petite ange. *Come touch the water.*

He'd meant touch him.

A shiver coursed through her even now as she remembered his voice, dark and thick with the accent of his Cajun heritage. She remembered moving toward him, the feel of his long fingers wrapping around her wrists, his hands pressing her own to the sun-heated flesh of his chest. It was her first feel of a man, of the ridges of tightly woven muscle beneath skin. He had moved like the wind, strong and carefree, as he swept her up in his arms.

But his eyes had mirrored the world.

She had not known to look deeper than the beguiling amethyst surface to the jaded core beneath. Her seduction, begun that afternoon and ending later in his cabin, had been so easy, her innocence forfeited so carelessly. She wondered if he still smirked at how effortless a target she had made, just as he had laughed that night when she innocently poured her heart out only to have it shattered.

She tried to force the past aside and watched him stir the coals to life, but she felt the tightening in her chest again, the old hatred. *Petite ange*. Little angel, he'd called her. Indeed, when he'd had only a devil's intention in mind. The bitter animosity and lingering attraction all mixed to form an ugly knot in her stomach. In her naïveté she had thought he would marry her, thought he *had* to after what they had done. She remembered even now the sound of his startled laughter when she mentioned it, the amazement in his eyes when he'd rejected her.

She understood now how silly and lamblike she must have looked to him, but she had died inside that night, and she never wanted to feel such crushing betrayal again. Though he hadn't taunted her after the initial shock, she had hated him so badly in the succeeding months it had consumed her.

The emotion had been too complicated and demanding to carry after John Byron's birth, and pointless as well. With the love of a son to fill her, there was no place for hatred to linger. She had managed over the years to let go of the draining burden of viewing Hunter as an enemy, but she could never see herself placing him in the role of friend.

There was nothing in her that trusted him enough for that. He was suited to the task of reclaiming her son, and she was grateful for the superb strength of his body and the quick aptitude of his mind, but it was hard to feel any other worthy expression toward him when fear and mistrust were the basis of their association.

The coals stirred to life, and he sat back on his heels and raked the worst of the water from his hair. Droplets clung to the ends, sleek and shiny against absolute black. A bit like the man himself, she thought. Brilliantly magnificent on the outside, a colorless soul beneath.

That dearth of conscience had Lara's fingers tightening on the arm of the chair. It frightened her that he knew of John Byron, that he now had a claim on her son. There was no doubt in her mind that he had no use for a baseborn child, but he made his own rules, chose his own morals, and he stood by them at all cost. He would rescue John Byron because he had agreed to do so—a man of ethics in his own uncivilized way.

But what price would he demand for it?

He rose and chafed his hands over the flames, easily adapting to the pitch and sway of the ship, shifting the weight of his body when necessary to maintain equilibrium. By the glow of the low fire he turned to meet Lara's stare for the first time since entering the cabin.

"Like what you see?" he asked.

Lara suffered another drop in her stomach as the ship plunged, and she stumbled a step, then reached for the bedpost and clung. "You have aged very little, just matured."

An indolent grin tipped the corner of his mouth. "Shall I say the same about you?"

Lara shook her head and grudgingly yielded a small smile. "No. It would hardly be the truth."

"Ah, truth. A rather undependable word, I've found."

Her smile faded and she instantly lamented the fact that she let the barb strike home. She nodded toward the portal. "How long will the storm last?"

"The worst is over."

Hunter turned back to study the red-hot glow from the brazier, letting the visual image of heat help warm him. It was a trick he had learned in his teens. Damp and shivering aboard a bootleg vessel, he would raise his face to the sun and be absorbed into its light and heat for as long as he could get away with it—until someone older and stronger snatched him by the hair and shoved him back to work or dragged him belowdecks to be their cruel amusement.

He spared Lara an expressionless glance. "It's too cold to be anywhere away from the fire if there is a choice."

She noted the irritation in his voice. "I should think you would be used to it by now."

Hunter merely gave her an innocuous look. Farming arpents of cotton and sugarcane in a blazing southern sun bore little resemblance to his old life at sea, but he was no stranger to it either. He still had the shipping business when wanderlust and salt water beckoned like a lusty mistress who wouldn't be denied her slice of him.

He stepped to the side and motioned. "Warm yourself before you catch your death. You're shivering from head to toe."

Lara looked down as if to verify his statement, then back up to verify his intent. His expression had not changed, but there was a slightly mocking glint in his eyes at her caution. Aggravated that he could so easily read her, she let go of the bedpost and tested her footing. The ship was rolling more manageably now, with less abrupt drops. She made her way over to the brazier, but found nothing there with which to brace herself. Hunter took her arm and smiled at the annoyance in her expression.

"You despise needing me."

"I despise needing anyone," she said honestly.

The fire was soothing, stealing some of the dampness from the air and Hunter's skin. He smelled of rain and cold, refreshing despite the memories that seemed determined to crowd Lara every time he was near. His grip on her arm was firm but painless, his presence both menacing and reassuring.

Suddenly, desperately, she wished it were George beside her, wished she could curl up in his arms and let his fortitude and comfort chase the fears away. But she would never again be allowed that indulgence, and it was best to put that part of her past life aside.

Hunter watched the pensive look shadow her face. "You have changed," he said. "Grown up, I think."

"Have I?" She glanced over at him. She didn't feel grown. She felt as scared and helpless as a child left alone in a dark room. She forced herself not to move away when his thumb began stroking the fabric of her sleeve, an idle gesture apparently without intent, though with Hunter one could never be certain.

An accompanying tremor crept down her arm, and she drew a quick silent breath and tried to ignore the unwanted apprehension. So many years had passed. She should not be able to recall the scent and texture and unholy magnetism of him as if it were only yesterday. His touch was complicated, familiar yet foreign, undeniable and frightening. It held the same determined heat that she remembered, an odd and unsettling mixture of warmth and dominance.

She tried to lose herself in the flames, but it was a useless effort. She was too aware of his presence, too aware of everything. She had never forgotten him— this intimate stranger who had forever changed her life—and she had never forgiven him. Because she had never thought to see him again, she had certainly never imagined that the carefully erected barriers raised to shield her from the memories would crumble away with nothing more than a touch.

Her eyes burned from staring into the fire and she closed them, shutting out the world, unable to block out the man. His presence was everywhere. Not only beside her but filling every corner of her memory as well. Unlike a decade ago, his cabin was no longer filled with a menagerie of clothing and junk pieces collected like driftwood and flung haphazardly about. Forest green and rich burgundy were now the dominant colors in furnishings carefully chosen for their quality and comfort.

But she saw only the old things when she closed her eyes: a battered brass spyglass, a dented lantern, a scattered pile of clothing in desperate need of mending. A rumpled bed with the scent of passion and lost innocence still clinging to its sheets. Her eyes flew open and she focused on the things at hand.

Wealth and good taste permeated the room.

"Are you still afraid of storms?"

Pulled from her reverie, Lara shook her head. A mild blush threatened, but she wouldn't allow it to surface and give him the satisfaction of knowing she remembered the night her terror of a storm had overridden her fear of him and thrown her into the shelter of his arms. It had not been a safe place to dwell.

"No. I've learned there are too many real things to be more concerned about than a little wind and rain."

"Sweet Lara, you've grown cynical. A pity. You were so ready at one time to take the world by the tail and shake it."

She gave a lost, bitter laugh. "The world shook back." She glanced away and added quietly, "Wasn't it unforgivably simpleminded of me not to know that it would?"

"Naive perhaps." A hint of amused scorn tinted his words but they were not cruel. "You were just so *impossibly* naive."

Because she could not deny it, she inclined her head. "More than that, foolish."

"And spoiled. And proud."

"You needn't remind me. I paid for it with my life."

Not one single word was said with malice or remorse, and admiration for her filtered through all the other emotions buffeting Hunter. "And you don't regret it."

"No." She twined her fingers together, unknowingly digging her nails into her palms. "I regret that George's greedy brothers are still alive while he lies in a cold grave. I regret that the land they already hold isn't enough for them. I regret that they can't let John Byron and me live in peace. I—"

She cursed the tears burning the back of her throat and took a deep breath to contain them. The very idea of breaking down in front of Hunter was unthinkable. "I regret that John Byron is not George's rightful heir."

He watched it all, the color draining from her face, the ramrod stiffness of her back, the lace at her throat rising and falling in cadence to her deep quick breaths. Her eyes were dry but her mouth pinched, her grief and guilt so tangible, he could feel them. "You will get the child back, Lara."

Her eyes blazed into his. "Will I? Tell me again so that I may believe you. Swear it to me!"

She was unaware that she had grabbed his arm until his hand covered the back of hers and began caressing the fine bones of each finger. There was nothing solicitous or comforting in the gesture. Every stroke was a seduction. She bit back a scathing retort and eyed him calmly, as if nothing he did or said could disconcert her.

He smiled. "I merely offer a diversion."

She snatched her hand from beneath his. "Entertain yourself at someone else's expense."

"But who else is there?" He took her hand again before she could step away and brought it to his lips. "Amazing, Lara. Even after all this time, you still inspire in me the most magnificent lust." Her hand spasmed in his but her expression remained cool and fixed. He released her and stepped back. "*Adieu, 'tite ange—*"

"Don't!" she cried without thinking. "Don't call me that."

He smiled. "Why? It still fits." He went to a sea chest and grabbed a fresh shirt. "Try to rest. It will be daylight before we reach our destination."

Her stomach contracted but she said nothing. She wouldn't ask what he had planned, for any method he chose to rescue her son had her full support. She made her way across the room and curled up in the bedside chair, tucking her feet neatly beneath her. At his sardonic look she glanced at the bed, then met his indigo eyes with severe quiet. "I would never be able to sleep."

"So politely done," he drawled. He collected his cloak and swept it over his shoulders as he moved toward the door. "Use the bed. If I'm back before dawn, I won't wake you." He turned to leave and was almost through the doorway when he paused. "Put your fearful imagination to rest, Lara. I would never touch you . . . not without your consent."

Lara only stared back at him in silence. She had no authority here and knew it, not this night or those a decade ago, despite what he said. But none of that mattered. Getting John Byron back was the only thing she cared about.

She waited until he left, then rested her cheek on the arm of the chair and let the exhaustion of too many sleepless nights carry her toward oblivion. She need do nothing now but gather her strength. Hunter would take care of things. As much as she had once hated him, as unsure as she was about how she felt now, she knew one thing: She had complete confidence in his ability to accomplish anything he set out to do.

Lara fussed unconsciously at the jostling, then sighed in contentment as her head sank comfortably into the soft pillow. She noted vaguely her slippers being removed and told herself to awaken and help Tess with the rest of her garments. Freezing cold hands slid her gown from her shoulders and over her hips, drawing a disgruntled murmur of protest from her. A shoulder nudged her, and she scooted over to allow room for . . .

Her eyes flew open. She fought a moment of panic

when she couldn't recall her whereabouts, but the day's events slowly came into focus and she realized she was aboard Hunter's ship. He must have moved her from the chair to the bed and climbed in beside her.

His body was chilled. She could feel the cold permeating her chemise everywhere their bodies touched. Trepidation fluttered in her stomach at the realization that he had removed her outer clothing. She tried to ignore the warning tremor that crept through her. He had done nothing further to incite her ire. Still, she lay very still, not wanting him to know she was awake.

His arm stole over her waist, and her breath caught and held.

"A person will die without air" was all he said before his own breathing fell into the deep and regular pattern of sleep.

It was the lack of warmth that woke her. Disoriented, Lara sat up and pushed the hair from her eyes, then hugged her arms against a chill. Hunter stood at a basin, rinsing lather from his face. He sent her an unreadable look. "Go back to sleep, Lara."

Confused, she glanced around, noting the absence of natural light. The sun had not yet risen and he had been shaving by lantern light. "Have we arrived? Do you go now?"

"At dawn," he said, then added in a more brusque tone, "Do you wish to delay me?"

"No, of course not . . ." she began, bewildered, then realized his gaze had strayed. She snatched the covers up from her lap and clutched them to her chest. Hope filled her with a burgeoning sense of joy mingled with fearful anticipation. After months of agony, she was near her son, yet the outcome was still far too uncertain. "I want to come with you. Please, I will be very careful, follow every instruction."

"No. You would be too . . . distracting."

Hostility flashed in her eyes. To be this close yet do nothing to help was nearly impossible. "You do this to punish me."

"Don't be absurd," Hunter said gently. He pulled on soft, unpolished black boots that blended with the dusty black of his pants. He would fade into the night and move unnoticed with the dawn. "Connie remains aboard to see to your comfort and safety. Do not, however, test his patience by trying to leave the ship. His graciousness to you will extend only the length of my orders."

It was a warning that Lara did not need made clear to know its importance. She would never defy him when her son's life hung in the balance. "You still don't trust me," she accused softly. "You think this is some trap, but I would never use John Byron to—"

"I make certain you do not," he interrupted. "Sheathe your claws, *'tite chatte.*" He smiled. "You'll need your energy later."

Lara knew nothing of the layout of the castle, so Hunter made his way cautiously up the steep rocky incline by his instincts, followed by his cohorts. Gal stayed closest, strong and agile as a young soldier, as gutter-wise and suspicious as her upbringing. She stayed alert for every sound, every movement in the surrounding land. Weasel followed, his darting scurry irritating yet advantageous. He created havoc and confusion everywhere he went, and there were those who swore he could pop up in two places at once and be seen at another in a thrice.

The path cut in dirt and stone was centuries old and eroded, nothing more than a hazard winding upward toward an old fortress overlooking the bluff. Unaware of the lay of the land, Hunter had had to wait for first light to tackle it with any hope of safety, but the gloomy overcast sky made dawn a farce. Shadow blended with shadow and their footing was precarious, their passage slow.

His muscles burned when he reached the top of the rise, but he remained in a crouched position and scanned the grounds for any sign of life. All was still. The only sound to penetrate the heavy mist was that of nature awakening to a damp and sluggish morning.

The old Scottish stronghold loomed ahead, a monstrosity of ivy-covered stone. The arrangement was ill designed, without a hint of elegance or beauty to soften the look of the main hall. To a man used to Doric columns, sweeping green lawns, and gracefully handcrafted ironwork, the malformation before him was an architectural disgrace.

Silent as a cat, he signaled for his followers to spread out, then made his own way forward across the stubby yard. Skirting the front and sides, he reached one of several back entrances and concealed himself in the shadows to wait. The kitchens were off to the right, a collection of stone outbuildings comprising a bakehouse, smokehouse, and buttery. The voices within carried the muted hush of early-morning laborers not yet fully awake.

A maid emerged from the bakehouse, carrying a covered tray, and walked briskly along the cobbled path toward the doorway nearest Hunter. He kept well back until she passed, then entered behind her and began following at a discreet distance.

The main building was a labyrinth. Through narrow halls and dank empty rooms, he followed, staying as close behind the maid as possible. At times, the sound of her footsteps was the only thing keeping him on target when she would turn another corner into obscurity. A catacomb of arched hallways and corridors presented itself around every turn, a maze no doubt designed to snare the unwary invader and keep an enemy going in circles.

Gal's sense of direction was phenomenal. She would have no problem navigating the keep if she chose to enter after inspecting the surrounding area, but Weasel was likely to scuttle himself right into oblivion.

The maid apparently knew *her* way, for her steps never faltered. With brisk efficiency, she moved through the ground floor without pause to finally reach a dark stairway. She didn't even bother with a candle, but mounted the steps with confidence.

Hunter dared not follow too closely, though it was imperative to keep her within a reasonable distance. The hallway was pitch black, every footfall of the maid's a soft tap echoing like muted drumbeats. He

kept to the balls of his own feet and moved sound-
lessly, hoping he wouldn't reach a dead end and become trapped with a hysterically screaming woman
once she became aware of his presence. There was
no alcove or crevice in which to hide should she turn
around and retrace her steps, nothing but damp, cold
walls that were hardly wider than his shoulders.

After a minute, the stairs turned sharply to the
right, and Hunter hung back. He heard the clink of
dishes as the maid shifted the tray, then the creak of
rusty hinges. Soft yellow light flooded the upper turn
in the stairway. He crept up enough to see around the
bend and found a small landing at the top where a
door stood ajar. To the left was a tall window covered
by heavy velvet draperies. Voices carried within the
room but the words spoken were unclear. Hunter
crept up the last few steps and slipped behind the
moldy drapes into a window embrasure to listen.

Lara paced along the rail of the ship, anxiety growing with each step. Hour upon hour, she had been
waiting to catch sight of Hunter returning with John
Byron, and the gnawing anticipation in the pit of her
stomach had long since turned to cold dread. Gal and
Weasel had returned long ago, but they only eyed her
with veiled disdain and kept whatever knowledge
they possessed to themselves. The sun was slipping
closer toward the horizon and only a matter of minutes remained until twilight.

"Lady Chalmers."

Lara whirled to find Connie behind her with a tray

of tea and biscuits. "What's keeping them?" she asked for the hundredth time since noon.

He shrugged as he had at every inquiry and gave the same answer. "He's a careful man, doesn't take any undo chances. I'm certain he's just making sure everything is safe."

She turned back to face the imposing coastline and gripped the rail until her knuckles whitened. "Nothing is safe."

"No, but he'll make it so for the boy, you'll see."

To release the tension increasing inside her with each minute that passed without word of her son, she wanted to rant and argue that Hunter should be back by now, but she knew it would accomplish little beyond making her look demented. Her head ached from worry and her eyes burned from staring too hard at nothing but towering cliffs, crumbling rock, and incessant waves.

"Lady Chalmers, you've not eaten all day."

She shook her head. "I can't just yet."

"A little tea perhaps?"

She didn't want tea or talk or reassurance. She wanted John Byron back. Everything else in the universe was insignificant beyond that one single fact. "What is keeping them?"

The question was spoken softly, but Connie heard the rising desperation beneath her tone. "Drink the tea," he said firmly, and was surprised when she turned and took the cup. He decided to press his luck and handed her a biscuit. "Eat this. It'll help."

She did little more than nibble absently at the edges as she turned back to the cliffs, but Connie was satisfied that she wasn't going to perish from starvation while in his care. He decided to press further and took her arm lightly. "Come, let's get you down to the cabin. I'll have the men prepare a nice warm bath—"

She rounded on him like a gale and snatched her arm away. "I'm not leaving here until they are safely aboard!"

He smiled slightly and took a step back from her wrath. "Just a suggestion, mind you." He had just turned away when he heard the sharp intake of her breath and the unmistakable moan of anguish. He turned slowly and saw what had caused it—Hunter descending the steep, rocky path at a quick pace.

Very much alone.

Lara's hand went to her mouth to hold back the sob rising in her throat. It seemed an eternity that she stood frozen by the rail, dead inside to everything but the grinding pain of disappointment and confusion. She watched the dinghy row toward the ship, a horror inside her that went soul deep. Before Hunter stepped onto the deck, she was running toward him.

He watched her approach, panic in each step that brought her closer, a desperate and frenzied look in her eyes. He caught her before she could plow him down and held her at arms' length.

"He's not there, Lara. We searched everywhere."

"No!" she denied fiercely. "He must be. There is nowhere else! Their note demanded I bring my solicitor here." She pulled out of his grip and stared wildly at the rail as if she would throw herself over and swim to shore. She wavered only a second before realizing her insanity. Her eyes cleared and she stood braced instead, fists tightly clenched. "He has to be there!"

Hunter cut a glance at Connie who merely shook his head. "Gal and Weasel found nothing."

"Could they have moved him?"

Lara looked back and forth at the two men and felt the pain of fear and hopelessness trying to crush the breath from her. She shook her head, denying both of them their silent, vile opinions. "No, he has to be there!" she cried again as if the sheer force of her convictions would make it truth.

Hunter gave Connie a hooded look. "Send Gal to me." He took Lara's arm again. "Let's go down to the cabin and sort this out."

Chapter Six

Lara's steps were quick as she allowed Hunter to escort her to the cabin. A hundred denials spun through her mind, but she maintained perfect control —the upper-crust English arrogance of rising above one's situation so as not to be immersed in the muck that lay beneath. But as soon as the cabin door closed behind them, the facade fell.

"He *is* there." The hint of accusation in her tone was overshadowed only by a stronger fear that she might be wrong and they had wasted precious time in coming all this way.

Hunter moved to his desk and withdrew a sheet of paper, then made a rough sketch of the castle's main hall. "He's not in any of these rooms, on any floor. The damnable place is a maze but I covered every inch. There's not one piece of evidence that a child has even been there."

Lara studied the drawing through vision blurred by the residue of helplessness and frustration. When the first tear splashed on the page, running the images together, she quickly turned her back. "He has to be there!"

Hunter rounded the desk and gripped her upper arms. "Where, Lara?"

She tried to pull away but his hold was tense and unbreakable. "I don't know, but he has to be! Don't you understand? There is nowhere else . . . they own no other property . . ." She turned her face aside and struggled to keep her voice steady. "I will go myself."

"Not tonight. The path is too treacherous, impossible in the dark."

She rounded on him then, her fingers gripping his shirt front, her eyes bright with panic and unshed tears. "What have they done with him?"

Hunter felt the roiling despair inside her manifest itself in the gouge of her nails in his chest, the tremors wracking her body, and the unstable light of terror in her eyes. He pried her fingers from his shirt and said levelly, "I will go back at first light—"

She jerked out of his hold with a wounded cry. "I can't wait that long!"

Her fear was painful to watch, even more devastating to feel. How dare she make him consider this unknown child, product of an ill-fated alliance? He had been denied John Byron all these years; he shouldn't feel the slightest concern, the razor-sharp pricks to conscience that made his voice abrupt.

"You don't have any choice, Lara. The mission would be foolish in the dark." Interrupted by a scratching at the door, he called over his shoulder, "Come in."

Gal entered, eyes solemn. Dressed in dull colors that somehow suited her topaz eyes, she spared Lara only the briefest, resentful glance, then went straight to Hunter and took his hand in both of hers and laid her head on his arm. He stroked her golden hair gently but his voice was cool. "Have you displeased me?"

She nodded into his sleeve.

He closed his eyes briefly. "What have you done?" He continued to stroke her hair as she groped inside her mannish jacket and produced a dagger with a jeweled hilt. Hunter swore softly, viciously, and pushed her at arms' length. "Who?"

Though her fingers still clung to him as if he were an adored demigod, her eyes grew frigid and unrepentant. "A guard. He tried to touch me."

"Did you kill him?"

"Guard?" Lara rushed forward and touched Gal's sleeve. The younger woman recoiled as if she'd been struck and slid around to the other side of Hunter. Daunted, Lara looked to him for help. "Please, it may mean something."

Hunter looked at Gal. "Where?"

"The building in back, by the south door—"

"No." It began as a statement of fact, icy and undeniable, then a terrible demand. "No!" Lara's shrill cry sent Gal burrowing deeper into Hunter. "It's the tower. My God, they've got him jailed in the tower."

Her composure shattered completely, and she rushed past them toward the cabin door. It didn't matter how steep the incline, how sheer the cliffs, how impossible the footing in the dark. It only mattered that Robert and Claude's hatred of John Byron was deeper than anything she had imagined if they could lock up a child in the tower. She wrenched the cabin door open, but Hunter was close behind and grabbed her around the waist.

"You can't do this, Lara." His words were harsh as he struggled to keep her from rushing pell-mell into foolishness.

"I will go to him!" she cried. "I must!" She twisted like a cat and hurled herself beneath his arm. Pain sliced through her hip when she hit the corner of the doorway, but she continued to press forward, mindful of the necessity to escape. Her heel caught in her hem and she heard the fabric rip as she fought to get free.

Hunter caught her again before she could gain her footing and clamped his arms around her waist. "It's impossible tonight," he said calmly, dragging her back inside the cabin. "You can't go without a light, and a lantern or torch would alert them immediately. You'll only make things worse." He ignored her laborious breathing and the suppressed sobs that punctuated each intake of air. Kicking the door shut, he turned to Gal. "What did you do with the guard?"

She cast her eyes to her toes. "Knocked him cold and dragged him into the shrubs."

Hunter's accusation came at her like a whip. "And stripped him clean, which will not only raise the alarm in the castle but into the village as well."

Gal's eyes flared with fierce, wounded pride. "Did not, you stinkin' whoremonger—"

"Gal!" His voice was a whisper-soft warning.

Her face blanched white but she wouldn't back down completely. "Did not!" she repeated childishly, then fled from the room.

Lara struggled to follow, but Hunter's hold around her waist was as unbreakable as the despair gripping her heart. She fought anew, murderously desperate in each twist and turn. "I won't leave him there another night!"

"You have no choice," he returned. "You don't even know for certain that he *is* there."

"I won't leave him another night." She repeated the words over and over like a litany, until each writhe and countertwist grew slower and weaker. In her mind she still fought frantically, but after a time her body just wouldn't respond. Her hands gripped Hunter and her eyes cried out terrible heartache. "He's just a small boy, don't you understand?"

His eyes were cold, his expression removed. He understood only too well men's avarice and dementia. In truth, he doubted the child was still alive. "He's their bargaining tool. They won't risk harming him yet."

It could have been hours or mere minutes before the impossible truth finally seeped into Lara's consciousness. Hunter would do nothing this night and she was helpless to do anything as well except wait until dawn while her son spent another night in a dank cold cell. The horror of what John Byron must be going through, the misery of too many months of watching and waiting and wondering drained her with debilitating force, and she went limp in Hunter's arms.

There were no tears, nothing inside her but a vast, numb emptiness. A flower too fragile to fight the storm, she folded into herself.

"At first light, Lara," Hunter said as he led her to the bed.

She did nothing, just sat on the edge in a semi-rebellious stupor, her sightless gaze fixed on the floor. Hunter waited for a time but still she did not respond, and he began loosening the ties and hooks that bound her clothing. She didn't help nor did she fight, and that more than anything convinced him of the tenuous hold she had on her composure. He stripped her down to her chemise and removed her shoes and stockings, then stepped back to remove his own clothes.

Her gaze lifted and she watched him, coldly lethargic. The pins that held her hair had come loose in their struggles and the heavy sable mass spilled in disarray over her shoulders and breasts, making her look a little wild, a little demented. Her eyes never left his as he undressed. Though he had never been modest around women, the dead look in her expression was disconcerting. In nothing but his breeches, he took her hand and pulled her to her feet, then reached around her to fold back the counterpane.

"Do you have a nightdress?"

She looked confused a second then nodded.

"Shall I fetch it for you?"

She shook her head and glanced over at her portmanteau. The steps she would have to take to retrieve it were too much. Everything was too much. With a small, hopeless cry she dropped back down to the bed and curled into a ball, hugging her knees tight to her chest.

Hunter stepped forward, then stilled. Lantern light played in ghostly shadows along her small, crumpled form, outlining her shape beneath the sheer chemise from her updrawn knees to her slender hips. Her bare arms looked frail hugging her legs but she had no lack of strength. He'd felt every ounce of it when struggling with her earlier. Her hair flowed over her shoulders and the bed linens like dark watered silk, so sleek a man could drown in it. His jaw tensed and he turned away. With a mild curse, he grabbed his cloak and headed for the upper deck.

Lara lay on her side, trying to insulate herself. The struggle to breathe between dry, silent sobs was a monumental feat. She pressed her face to her knees, but nothing could stop the hollow, soul-searing loneliness. If she didn't get John Byron back, she would die like this, suffocated beneath the crushing pain.

If she didn't get John Byron back, she didn't care.

Hunter watched the clouds drift across a black sky to obscure the moon. It was a perfect smuggler's night—a night for stealth and sly deeds and illicit opportunities. It no longer made his blood run hot or his heart thud with the anticipation of the chase. Though he would never rid himself internally of the stigma of his past, he had managed to temper its impact on his present. He took no pride in the ill-gotten pleasure and wealth he had gained at the expense of others, but neither did his past have the power to destroy him with guilt. He neither regretted the memories nor enjoyed them. That part of his life was dead, gone, a facet of him lost to political machinations and maturity.

But Lara was back, silken and beautiful, a part of that past he had endeavored so hard to forget . . . and had so successfully failed. Due to the efficiency of his spies, he had known her movements over the past ten years—her hasty marriage, the birth of their son, her civic and charitable works in the community surrounding Folkstone. He knew her minor failure to secure, through her husband's influence, a position at the university for the mathematician who had tutored John Byron, and her greater accomplishment of sponsoring a budding young scientist whose papers were beginning to receive notice within the academic community. He knew who designed her clothing, which shops she frequented most when in London, and the names of her closest friends.

He did not, however, know anything about her thoughts or feelings or contentment. Had George Chalmers inspired her admiration? Had he managed to take the traumatized young woman who had left Hunter's ship and make her happy? Had he cared for her illegitimate son as the child's true father had not been allowed to?

There was bittersweet revenge in the knowledge that Lara had been forced to come to Hunter to rescue the very child she'd kept from him. Not that he would have made an admirable father. He had been a rogue seaman with few scruples and even fewer morals, who had taken her out of revenge against her father. Not exactly a sterling recommendation for parenthood.

No, he could hardly fault Lara her decision—his life had had little room for a family and his chances for survival had been sketchy at best—though in some twisted sort of reasoning he did condemn her for it, for not giving him the chance to prove her right or wrong.

Methodically, he studied the cloud cover overhead and ticked off the minutes until sunrise. Meticulously he planned his approach and search maneuvers for the following day. But he could not, no matter what diversive tactics he used, forget the painful sight of Lara curled in upon herself in his bed.

Through a haze of restless exhaustion, she felt his presence at her back and buttocks and thighs. The rhythm of his breathing beat softly against the nape of her neck, a pulse that sent odd tendrils of warmth fluttering all through her. Caught in that first instant between sleep and wakefulness, she imagined it was George coming to her bed in one of his rare displays of affection. Her heart plummeted when she realized it wasn't George and never would be again. She was not safely tucked away at Folkstone with John Byron only steps away in the nursery. She turned her face into the pillow and began to sob.

Hands stroked her. Gentle, callused, unwelcome. No matter how comforting their intent, they were still *his* hands and she despised the conflicting feelings they stirred within her—warm comfort, chilling fear. He was a man capable of loving her and betraying her without ever once losing his brilliant smile.

After a time, he turned her toward him. Bleak moonlight shone outside the portal but darkness cloaked the cabin, and she couldn't see much more than the silhouette of his face. His hand went to her cheek and brushed back her tears and the wisps of hair clinging to the moisture at her temples. His palm glided slowly down her neck to her shoulder, then seemed to pause, uncertain. He curled his fingers into her flesh only briefly, then placed his hand at her back and pulled until she was tucked under his chin.

His warmth surrounded her, but there was no succor in it beyond the false and temporary feeling of security. His body, his scent, was foreign to her, no more than a memory. The way they fit together felt alien despite the undeniable familiarity.

His words whispered over her forehead, stirring the curls like a soft breeze. "A tray of food was sent down just after eight o'clock," he said. "If the boy is there, he's being fed."

A cry leapt into her throat and rattled her entire being. She pressed her face into his chest, breathing raggedly and rocking against him to the beat of a painful inner keening. If she let the cry escape, all her sanity would pour out with it. "You . . . were there . . . and you didn't get him?"

Hunter felt the movement of her mouth on his flesh. The heated accusation seared his skin. "I couldn't get close enough."

"Oh, oh . . ." The words were breathless, skipping over one another as she struggled to contain a wail of anguish and fury. "I want him back!"

He cinched his arms tighter around her, not for the more noble reason of comfort but to stop her pain from invading him, from making him feel things he had no desire to feel. If he could hush her, he could remain detached and offer her a harbor of stability until she pulled herself together. He needed for her to pull herself together.

He drew her deeper into him. From shoulders to knees they collided, and a decade of changes slammed into Hunter with the force of a blow. The fullness of her breasts was against his chest, the wider span of her hips nestled into his groin. Her scent wafted over him like a caress. His reasons for holding her—whether noble or indifferent—faded to nothing, leaving only the core of lust that seemed his constant nemesis when around her.

His head dipped and his arms constricted tighter. He'd always had control but he'd never had any willpower around Lara. His mouth found hers, crushing, absorbing her shocked outcry. Her tears wet his cheeks and made their mouths slippery, but he ravaged her without regard for her state of bereaved confusion or his own sudden derangement.

Within his arms, Lara's body trembled and convulsed, then arched away in horrified reaction to the real longing inside her to bury herself farther into the solidity of his strong body. Her hands rose and grabbed him fiercely by the hair, but his mouth left hers only a second before crashing back down. She tugged again, and he winced at the pain but only slashed his mouth across hers more hungrily, a ravenous beast too long denied a morsel.

She felt the movement of his body begin a deep, sensuous rocking before his hips ground into hers with the heavy force of his arousal as he rolled her beneath him. His shoulders reared back and the look on his face was as fierce as it was passionate. "Damn you, Lara," he whispered. His fingers winnowed through the hair at her temples to keep her head impaled to his pillow. "Damn you."

The tortured sound of his voice calmed her as nothing else could have. A coolness settled in her breast. Her fingers relaxed their punishing hold on his hair and caressed instead. Her back arched slightly as his mouth left hers to travel over her neck and shoulder, and her body became malleable beneath him. When his hand slid down her side and grasped the hem of her chemise, she remained quiet. When he shifted his weight and pulled the shift above her hips, she only closed her eyes.

Her breath caught at the feel of his naked body, lean and hot against hers, but she didn't move, didn't fight him. Not yet. She waited while his body covered hers, strength against softness, a position that put them both on the teetering edge of compromise. Her fingers slid from his hair and she cupped his face.

"I want him back," she whispered savagely.

He stopped her words and the underlying manipulation with his mouth. She turned her face aside but the feel of him was almost her undoing. Euphorically beautiful and wildly terrifying, a decade of circumspect living vanished beneath the touch of his hands and mouth. Her breath caught and she jerked her head to the side, fighting to resurface and reclaim her reasoning.

"I want him back!" she repeated, more breathless but no less fierce. She winced when his fingers dug into her scalp and turned her face back, but she did not retreat. She spoke against his lips, her voice cold as ice, her determination unflinching. "I will give myself to you, and in return you will leave immediately to rescue John Byron. Immediately!"

His eyes were fierce as they bore into hers, his smile cruel. But she could feel the heat and evidence of his passion and knew she still had some power to bargain. His hand slid up the sleek skin of her thigh then gripped the soft flesh of her buttocks and pressed her to him in counterattack. "Will you whore for me, Lara?"

The word came flat and emotionless and easy. "Yes."

"Damn you then." His voice was as harsh as the hands that gripped her thighs suddenly and parted them. He settled himself in the cradle of her body, then took the hem of her chemise and pulled it over her arms and head. She shivered when the night air hit her naked flesh and gripped the corners of her pillow to keep from covering herself. Her teeth bit the inside of her jaw to keep from crying out.

She remembered all that he was capable of and tried to prepare herself for anything—savage violence, exquisite tenderness, a heat that could burn them both to cinders. But nothing prepared her for the brutal shift of his body as he rolled away.

Crushed beneath his weight one moment, free the next, Lara's body contracted and she grappled for the sheet to cover herself.

Hunter sat on the edge of the bed, his head in his hands, contemptuous laughter shaking his shoulders. "I should do it anyway. I should lay you down and quench this insane desire you ignite in me."

Lara blushed at the rough passion of his words and felt the beginning of helpless panic clutch again at her heart. "I want my son back."

"Offering yourself like some noble sacrifice won't get him tonight." He gripped the edge of the mattress. "The risk is too great before daylight. We gamble everything by going in foolishly."

She didn't want to understand. She remembered Hunter as a man of wild daring and thoughtless defiance, not a cautious and calculating strategist. She turned her face away and huddled under the sheet, bereft of all feelings save resentment and the constant fear for her son.

Hunter rose and stalked to the window. Her warmth called to him like a siren's treacherous melody. If he stayed beside her he would either make her earlier charge of rape accurate or use her like a whore. He gripped the edge of the portal and cursed himself for having found some sort of contemptible conscience over the past decade.

Weak, gray light heralded dawn as Hunter and Connie made their way up the steep path. Once at the top of the incline, they waited. Weasel darted into view not ten seconds later and handed Hunter a spy-glass.

"He's mean-eyed this morn. Gal must have conked him a good one."

Hunter studied the area near the south entrance where Gal had encountered the guard. The lecherous turnkey sat against the outer wall, filling his belly. Another guard stood near, talking in between bites of his own breakfast. He held up his empty plate, then headed back toward the kitchen buildings. No one else was in sight. Crouching down among the shrubs growing wild along the castle wall, Hunter signaled Weasel to the left and Connie to the right, then made his own way forward a foot at a time, pausing to look and listen for any disturbance.

A circling falcon cried shrilly, but little else broke the early-morning hush. Within three feet of the tower, he stood abruptly. "Good morning," he called civilly.

Startled, the guard choked and scrambled to his feet. "Now see 'ear—" he began before Weasel slammed a cudgel against the back of his skull. The guard dropped like a felled tree, and Connie dragged him out of sight before binding his hands and feet. Hunter slipped through the tower door and paused while his eyes adjusted to the dim light.

The room appeared to have once been a storeroom. Musty sacks lay in piles along the wall near stacks of woven baskets. A clump of rusty tools was heaped in one corner next to a hill of spoiled straw. The smell of damp mold and mildew permeated the air along with the ranker stench of dried urine. Hunter stared into the dark corridor ahead and listened intently, but he could hear nothing beyond the scurry of rats and his own heartbeat.

He took a rushlight from the wall and lit it, then moved forward cautiously. The fire illuminated the hall in an eerie glow that made shadows waver like specters in the drafty air. He passed stall after empty stall, hellish little cubicles cut into stone with iron bars for doors and the smell of death still permeating the rotted straw. His stomach recoiled at the ghosts of atrocities suffered in this place, and he fixed his mind on finding a child he had never seen or strangling Lara if she had played him false.

It was only a faint murmur at first, an echo at the end of the hall. He paused, listening intently to dissect the sounds, then pushed forward at a quicker pace. The tones of muffled crying grew more distinct the deeper he went into the darkness. When he reached the last cell, he raised the torch high and almost recoiled at the sight before him.

A small child with jet-black hair huddled in a corner, his mouth pressed to his sleeve to muzzle his crying. Spilled food littered the dirt floor and two rats snarled at each other for the spoils. They blinked their beady eyes at the sudden light, then scurried off into a dark crack in the wall. The child kept his face averted and cowered deeper into the corner, his sobs breaking off into monosyllabic gusts of fear.

Hunter only stared, mute, feeling the stillness and absolute quiet of complete rage immobilize him. It suspended time and energy and momentum, so that he couldn't move or speak or react. Like an implosion, the anger over such vile and meaningless hatred coalesced inward. He knew such atrocities existed, of course, but it had been years since he'd seen such a manifestation of malice firsthand. It took deranged, conscienceless men to carry it out—or greedy ones.

He commanded motion from his limbs and gripped one of the iron bars of the cell. "John Byron."

The voice was deep but soothing. The child heard no taunt or accusation in the tone and lifted his head only enough to peek over the top of his filthy sleeve. He found a stranger dressed in black, holding a torch high enough to illuminate the room without blinding him.

"I've spilled my breakfast," he said in a pitifully thin voice.

Curly black hair. Strong yet delicate bone structure. Deep amethyst eyes. There was nothing so simple as family resemblance carved into the child's features, but a definitive self-portrait staring back at Hunter, a mirror held up with two decades stripped away.

It stunned him, though it shouldn't have. The insidious streak of engendering resemblance had woven its common thread throughout the generations since their lineage had begun to be counted. His sister Acadiana could have been his twin though many years separated them. Her children, notwithstanding the occasional reference to their father's eyes or nose or chin, could have been his own.

As far back as recorded, the distinctive mark of

kinship had flooded the line, too often exposing indiscreet liaisons through their unfortunate offspring. There were Nanette and Nicolette . . . but he could not think of Nan now, not while he stared into the young, sunken eyes of John Byron.

The rushlight wavered over the child's small ravaged face, and he understood better why Lara had chosen to live a country life with her son. He placed the torch in a wall sconce and knelt on one knee to face the consequence of his revenge.

"I've come to take you home," he said in a low tone. "We must be very quiet, and we must hurry." The child dropped his face back into his sleeve and began to sob anew. Hunter jerked on the cell door and found it locked, as he had suspected. He slipped a wire and pick from his pocket and began working on the mechanism with deft speed. As soon as the lock clicked, he opened the door. "I've come to take you to your mother."

The boy's head lifted and his eyes blazed with wounded resentment. "I was naughty, and she doesn't care for me anymore."

Hunter's breath hissed out between his teeth at the lie. "No, she has come for you," he said levelly. "She couldn't get to you for the longest time, but now she has and she's waiting."

Fearful hope flickered in the child's eyes. "Uncle Robert said she sent me away."

"No, she would never do that. You know this, no matter what you've been told." Hunter reached out a hand. They didn't need to linger. He would take the child by force if necessary, but he hoped it wouldn't come to that. "We must leave now."

John Byron backed away instinctively. Urgency sang through Hunter's blood, but he wouldn't make it far with a hysterical child. "Do you want your uncle or the guard to return before I can get you out of here?"

The child's eyes widened, but not from Hunter's words. They were focused on something behind him.

Hunter dropped his forehead to the bars, sickened by his neglect. He had allowed the child's likeness to disarm him and now he would pay for the lapse. Wondering where the hell his people were, he rose slowly to his feet and turned.

A short, balding man stood behind him dressed in tailored English clothing. His features were round and friendly, but his hands were perfectly steady on the gun pointed straight at Hunter's chest. Perplexity narrowed the man's eyes for only a moment, then understanding seemed to dawn. His mouth turned up at the corners and he began to chuckle triumphantly.

"So," he said with smug glee, "the little bastard has a father after all."

Chapter Seven

The gun never wavered, nor did the man take his eyes off Hunter when he spoke. "Come along, boy."

John Byron, his face devoid of everything save exhaustion, looked back and forth between the two men then dutifully walked out of the cell. Rage washed through Hunter. He knew in that moment that his suspicions had been correct. The child, the cell, the filth—it had all been a magnificent ruse. Lara had betrayed him.

He wanted to laugh and weep and howl like a banshee at his own gullibility. He would crush Lara if he ever got his hands on her again, snap her beautiful neck like a twig. None of his murderous thoughts showed on his face, however. The pistol pointed at his heart didn't allow for overt expression. He watched the boy—Lara's treasonous son with his own hair and face and eyes—edge past him and move forward with absolute trust to the older man's side.

Robert smiled and motioned Hunter into the cell with the pistol. "Donald, come entertain our friend."

A burly man emerged from the darkness, his beefy arms and thighs straining against the thin weave of his worn homespun clothing. His pace was lumberous, his dim eyes a glaring reflection of his mental competence. He stepped into the cell, smiled a semitoothless smile, then sent a meaty fist into Hunter's abdomen.

The force slammed Hunter back against the wall. Unprepared for the big ox's speed, he suffered the first blow with a kind of demented appreciation but made certain he dodged the second. His reactions were sluggish in the cramped space and his breath wheezed inefficiently in and out of his lungs. He managed to duck a third blow and found himself highly resentful of being thrown back into a way of life he had left behind. He was too old for a common brawl, his tavern-room tactics rusty.

Outnumbered by persons and weapons, he bided his time by swerving and sidestepping subsequent swings and wondering where the hell Weasel was. A nasty right clipped him on the edge of the jaw and made sparkles dance before his eyes. He crouched and evaded instinctively, knowing the next blow would put him out.

The swing went wide and he lunged forward, ramming his head and shoulder into the giant's gut. A grunt and small stagger were the only indications he'd struck the lummox at all. Another blow caught him under the ribs and doubled him over. Warning bells screamed in his brain. He scrambled back against the wall, needing time to gain enough breath to reinforce his waning strength.

The ox wasted no time coming after him. Hunter waited for his chance, knowing he would get only one. When the idiot got close enough, he lunged up with locked fists and caught him in the crotch. A gurgle rose in the man's throat and he stood immobile, holding himself and shaking his head from side to side. Hunter put all his strength into an uppercut that caught the man on the chin and toppled him onto his back.

"Enough! Enough!" Robert Chalmers called like a petulant child. He took dead aim with the pistol, and Hunter realized his little struggle had only been for sport. "I'm very disappointed in you, Donald. Shackle him." The giant rolled awkwardly to his feet and trudged forward, too few wits to show anger as he chained Hunter's wrists to the wall. Saliva mixed with blood drooled down one corner of his lopsided grin, and Hunter found himself wishing someone would take the overgrown bully home and clean him up.

He sent Robert a disgusted look. "What do you hope to gain by all this?"

"Where is Lara?" Robert asked.

"Don't you know?"

Robert gave an almost imperceptible nod to the ox, and Hunter tightened his muscles a split second before the blow caught him in the solar plexus.

"Again, where is Lara?"

Through gritted teeth, Hunter smiled charmingly at Robert, marking time, plotting revenge. His lungs

were howling for air but his chest felt as if it would
cave in if he indulged in even a single deep breath.
The concern here, the ultimate goal, was to live long
enough to implement his own brand of torment.
"She's about. Shall I get her for you?"

Another nod and the blow slammed into Hunter's
kidney. He jerked against the manacles, scraping
more flesh from his wrists. Blood began to make a
slippery mess of his forearms. His mind tried to slip
into the protective gray mist of unconsciousness, but
his will could not allow defeat without a fight. Grinding his teeth against the pain, he brought both feet up
and rammed his heels into the ox's gut.

The move sent Donald reeling back against the
bars. Hunter's only defense was time and weakening
the brute's strength so that the punishing blows directed at him were tempered by the lackwit's own
pain.

"Uncle Robert!" John Byron's childish cry came
from the depths of the shadows. He crept forward
into the light and looked up solemnly, his eyes too
grave for a nine-year-old. "You've been very naughty
to lie to me." With one broad sweep, he swung his
foot and kicked his uncle soundly in the shin at the
same time he shoved both fists into the man's gut.

Astonished, appalled, Hunter dropped his head
back against the wall. Robert would kill the child
now and there was nothing he could do to stop it.
"I've got Lara!" he shouted to draw Robert's attention. He need not have bothered. Robert's attention
was fully engaged by the child, who had recovered

the dropped pistol and had it aimed right at his uncle's belly.

The young face was studiously defiant despite its unhealthy pallor, but the small hands shook like dry leaves in a gale. Hunter moaned on a shallow breath at the absolute fruitlessness of this frail nine-year-old trying to stand against a grown man, but he took what small advantage he had at the moment and said calmly to the ox, "Unlock me, Donald, before John Byron blows your master's innards all over this room."

Confusion clouded the dimwit's eyes as he looked back and forth between the two men and the boy. No one moved or breathed. No one dared. The very air filled with the tension of waiting and wondering until it felt ready to explode.

Hunter said quietly, severely, "Keep the gun pointed at your uncle, John Byron. If he so much as moves, even one small inch, shoot him and run out of here as fast as you can. I have people waiting outside who will help you." He turned his head slowly toward Robert. "Order your lackey to release me. Neither one of us is in a position to make demands, so we had better come to some mutually beneficial agreement. Allies or enemies, Robert, we are much the same. We can settle this like gentlemen or . . . not." He smiled. "Your choice."

Rage and frustration lay banked in Robert's eyes. He had been called both charming and cunning by acquaintances. But he had never been called a fool. He could overpower the child with only the smallest risk to himself, but he didn't know where Hunter's people were or if the gun would discharge in a scuffle.

Damn the little bastard for having more courage and stamina than he'd given him credit for. He watched the pistol waver and knew the child's strength was waning fast. He could hold out.

Hunter's silken voice flowed out sweetly, sharply. "If you can't hold up anymore, John Byron, go ahead and shoot. If you don't, your uncle will lock you back up and you will never see your mother again."

Thwarted rage choked Robert's throat and the veins in his neck and forehead swelled and stuck out. "Release him!" he snarled peevishly at Donald.

Donald's bewildered features relaxed and he plodded over to Hunter and unlocked the manacles.

Hunter slumped back against the wall, rubbing circulation back into his wrists with careful nonchalance. If he was not grossly mistaken, some of his ribs were broken and he couldn't afford any sudden moves. It would be all he could manage just to stand upright. He pushed himself off the wall and approached the cell door with studied care, thankful for the dim lighting.

"Donald," he said soothingly, "unlock this door or the boy will blow your employer's gut apart." The warning was for Robert alone. Hunter knew the ox wouldn't obey him.

Donald looked to Robert for permission. When the reluctant nod came, he shuffled forward and did as bidden. Hunter slipped through the door with graceful precision, the advantage his but just barely. As long as he could keep his injuries hidden, he had a better chance of maintaining the upper hand. He eased over to John Byron, fighting the blackness that threatened to overtake him.

"I'll take the gun if you like," he said in a neutral tone, his eyes trained on Robert. John Byron nodded gratefully, but the exchange was tricky. One second's hesitation or fumbling and Robert would be on them. Hunter reached over and aligned his hands with John Byron's. "One sound, one move . . ." he hissed at Robert, his finger on the trigger.

Sweat beaded Robert's brow. "A gentleman's agreement," he temporized. "I'm certain we can come up with something beneficial to us both."

Hunter motioned the older man into the cell. "You agree to lie down away from the door, and I agree not to kill you. I find that beneficial."

Robert saw the deadly warning in Hunter's eyes. He entered the cell and shut the door himself. "Don't be a fool," Robert spat. The power was slipping right through his fingers, and he was incapable of watching his plans go awry graciously. "You'll get nothing from this. Lara won't share so much as a shilling of the child's inheritance with you. Join with me and I will reward you handsomely."

Hunter glanced over at John Byron. The child had crumpled against the stone wall, his face turned to the side and resting on his knees. His filthy clothes were loose on his thin frame, his cheeks sunken. Hunter noted the drooped shoulders, the trembling legs, and the obvious signs of starvation. He turned back to Robert and smiled so nicely only his intimates would recognize the fact that Robert Chalmers had already sealed his fate.

"I'm certain we will come to an arrangement at another time. But alas, for now I must be off. I suggest you count to a thousand several times before you start screaming," he warned lightly. "If I have to kill your people, there won't be anyone to let you out."

John Byron didn't hesitate to rise, but his movements were slow and uncertain as he faced Hunter. "Will you take me to my mother now?"

If both of us can stay alert long enough, Hunter thought grimly, but only nodded and motioned the child to proceed him down the dark corridor. "We still must be very careful," he warned. "There may be others."

The child nodded tiredly, too wasted to show fear. Hunter noted the bleak look in his eyes, the sickly cast to his skin, and knew it would take a miracle for the child to make it under his own power. Hunter also knew he would be of little help. If they didn't get away before Robert's men found them, they wouldn't get away at all. His only hope was that his own people were waiting outside to help.

He held his ribs tightly with one arm and leaned down. "Can you make it to the entrance?"

John Byron nodded but his intentions far outweighed his ability. He crossed six brave yards before he slumped against the wall. "Sir . . ." he whispered.

"Never mind." Hunter sighed, gritted his teeth, and quickly scooped the child up onto his shoulder before he lost his nerve. Pain tore through his body, blinding him. Incapacitated, he leaned against the damp wall, panting dryly as he fought nausea. "We're a pair, aren't we?" he murmured softly, and waited for the worst to subside.

He tried to be grateful for the child's unnatural listlessness when he began to trek toward the entrance. Any sharp movement would send him right over the edge in a black faint. But mild alarm began building inside him at the small arms and legs that hung lax, the skin that was too dry and hot, the rattle in the thin chest every time John Byron took a breath.

Hunter continued along the corridor as quickly as he dared, trying to outrun the suspicions and his own pain before it stopped him. The hurt had gone beyond a throbbing in his side to a screaming agony that demanded he stop and rest. He would ignore it as long as his physical limitations held out, but he knew when pushed too far, his body would simply refuse to cooperate, and he would collapse.

He reached the tower entrance and paused to catch his breath. The stone wall was rough against his back. The smell of moldy straw and the chill of centuries seeped into his shirt, making his aches keener, sharper. He shivered, though sweat trickled down his brow. Lethargy began winding its way insidiously through the pain and he knew he must move.

He crept forward, keeping to the shadows as he peered out. The surrounding grounds were quiet. Whoever or whatever had alerted Robert was not evident at first glance.

Weasel popped up from the nearest shrub and

hissed, "You're safe, good! Saves me from havin' to go in after you. Connie got himself conked on the head but he's comin' around. I had me some trouble and couldn't get to you when I saw the gent go in. Hurry, we don't know who else is waitin' to nab us."

Hunter smiled grimly. "Yes, I can see that." He nodded at something just beyond Weasel's shoulder. "Turn around and say hello to . . . Claude, I presume?"

Weasel spun around to find a gent with a gun. "Well, of all the dirty tricks!" he spat as if insulted. "I'm glad we've our own to take care of sneaky blokes like you."

The click of a cocking hammer froze the victorious smile on Claude's face. "If you even breathe, I'll blow your friggin' skull apart" came a softly feminine threat.

Weasel darted forward and stripped Claude of his gun. "Oooh, very good, Gal. I knew you'd come through." His elfin features beamed up at her like a doting papa. "I'll take care of this pretty fellow. You go along and help Hunter. He's in a bit of a fix, if I'm not mistaken."

Hunter gave Gal a wry grimace. "You were supposed to stay on the ship."

She rolled her eyes. "Catch me if you can."

Hunter nodded, conceding the win graciously. "Guard my back."

Weasel and Gal took their positions. Hunter braced John Byron against his ribs and crossed the lawn as quickly as his body allowed, then took the rocky path down at an even slower pace. The descent was tricky enough without the use of both arms, near impossible with the child's added weight. John Byron was silent and limp, his body folded over Hunter's upper torso like a ragdoll's. His eyes were open but vacant, his face unnaturally wan.

Adrenaline seared Hunter's injured body and his pace hastened. He took the old stone steps at a dangerous, jarring stride. His own stamina would not last much longer and he must reach the bottom while aware. "John Byron, can you walk at all?"

The child gave no response, and Hunter's nerves twisted at the bluish tint around the child's lips. He could feel some of Lara's earlier panic flood his limbs. Cold rage infused him, giving him a spurt of energy that lessened the pain and quickened his pace to a dangerous, uneven gait.

His own breathing was little more than quick shallow gasps as crumbling stone fell away beneath his boots. He took the last several yards down on his hip, using his feet and one arm for leverage.

He didn't feel the skin tear away from his palm or the thorny shrubs and rocks making a mess of his upper thigh and hip. The only thing he felt was the grinding catch in his chest; the only thing he heard was the wheeze in John Byron's as the child struggled for air. He finally gained his footing near the bottom and took the last three feet at a lumbering stretch, feeling like the brainless idiot who'd done this to him.

The dinghy loomed ahead, rocking gently in the shallow waves. Sunlight glistened off the water, crystal drops with jewel colors. It beckoned him like a woman's satin arms, sleek and cool and soothing. Two steps more would get him there. Just two . . . just one. The wood was suddenly solid beneath his palm, welcoming as he tumbled over the edge. He lay in the bottom and stared up at the sky, panting shallowly, John Byron sprawled across his aching ribs.

Weasel and Gal exchanged glances as they followed him into the boat, then pushed off and rowed back to the ship.

Hunter talked to John Byron as the water slipped by, inane bits of conversation that said nothing, meant nothing, beyond trying to keep himself and the child awake. The child's color had worsened and his breathing had grown increasingly harsh. His nostrils thinned and flared, his chest caved in and out as he tried to draw breath. It appeared he had hung on as long as he could. His fortitude and stamina were gone, leaving only an undernourished boy too weak to fight more battles. By the time they reached the barque, he was either sleeping or unconscious.

Lara's cry rang out, heralding joy and relief as Weasel hoisted John Byron over the side of the ship into her arms. She scooped her son into her chest and pressed her cheek to his.

"You're back . . . I have you back." It seemed all she was capable of saying, the verbal reassurance meant to convince no one but herself. She repeated the words over and over as she rocked him against her breast, taking profound comfort in his nearness. She turned to thank Hunter but found Weasel and Gal helping him over the side. He looked at her with dull eyes and limped slowly forward. "Lara—"

The fact that John Byron was unresponsive, his skin much too hot and his breathing irregular, was already seeping into her consciousness. Frightened, she looked around her. "He's ill."

"Get him to the cabin," Hunter said.

Lara took off at a run, clutching her son to her in disbelief. She'd finally gotten him back, but for what? The door was half open when she reached Hunter's room. Gal was already there, turning down the bedding. She took one look at the child in Lara's arms and her expression went blank.

Lara laid John Byron on the bed and began stripping off his filthy clothing. Her eyes lifted to Gal's. "Would you get me water, please? He's ill . . ."

Gal shook her head, staring at John Byron with obsessive fascination. "He's small."

"I need water!" Lara pleaded.

"Smaller even than Ollie."

"Gal!" Lara pleaded frantically.

"Water's coming," Weasel said. "Never you fear, Connie's gittin' it." He bore Hunter's weight on one shoulder and helped him into the room. "Come along, Gal, I need you over here."

Lara noticed for the first time the ashen look on Hunter's face, the lines of pain around his mouth and eyes. "What happened up there?" She turned back to her son and stroked his feverish brow, listened to the windy sounds of his breathing. "What did they do to you?" she whispered over the tears clogging her throat.

Gal drifted to Hunter's side, but her eyes stayed fixed on the child. "No denying he's your get."

Hunter ignored the statement. "You should have helped Lara."

Gal shrugged, unconcerned. "Won't do any good." She peered at the child. "He's got your hair and bones. If he lives what will you do with him?"

The question startled Lara. Her head whipped around and she shot Gal a scathing look. "Of course he will live."

Gal's eyes were vacant as she stared back at Lara. "How do you know? Most die when they sound like that." There was nothing in Gal's voice to purposely inflict hurt, no mean intent at all. She was merely stating the facts as she perceived them.

Lara's heart constricted. "He won't die because we will save him."

Gal's empty look vanished and smug cynicism entered her eyes. "You don't know that." She backed away to lean against the wall, seemingly negligent and unconcerned. She cocked her head toward Hunter. "What about him? He needs help too."

Guilt flooded Lara. She looked more closely and noticed the blood saturating his wrists and hands. "You're hurt." She took a step toward him, then glanced back at John Byron, torn.

"Tend the boy," Hunter said in disgust. "I'll wait."

"At least come sit down," she begged.

Hunter shook his head slowly. If he moved he would pass out—instant calamity. He closed his eyes and tried to distance himself from the pain while searching for a place of strength to remain standing.

Connie brought water and Lara began bathing the grime from her son. His arms were spindly, as were his legs. The outline of each rib was clearly defined. Her heart broke a little more with each wipe of the cloth, but her tears remained checked. She mustn't fall apart, mustn't give in to the crushing fear. Guilt moved through her like poison as she stroked back the damp curls from his precious face. She had not been able to protect him. She didn't know how to now.

When he began coughing, she looked over at Hunter. "I think it may be croup."

The word splintered through him like a bullet, shattering bone and sinew. He stared back at her, blank. He had stitched wounds and set broken limbs. Once he'd even cut a hole in a man's throat to insert a hollow reed so the sailor could breathe until they got him to shore. But he had seen croup at its worst and he didn't know how to help this frail boy, this small replica of himself, when he could barely stand upright.

His hand slid along the wall and gripped the door frame, then he turned his back and limped from the cabin, simply walked away from the destroying pain of his inadequacies. He could not watch this again, would not.

"Hunter!"

Her plea shivered through him. Paralysis stiffened his limbs after only the first step, and he was unable to move, to escape. He turned back and railed silently at Lara, *Damn you for bringing him into my life, making me see him, feel him—lose him.* The muscles in his throat constricted. "What do you want from me?"

Lara cringed at the resentment on his face but her

voice was clear and even. "We need a doctor, for both of you."

It was impossible. They were strangers, immediately suspect if they ventured into the village, whereas Robert and Claude would be well connected there. "It would be suicide."

Cold fury flared in Lara's eyes. "Did you rescue him to watch him die?"

Gal pushed off the wall and sauntered toward the door to take her place beside Hunter. She pointed an accusing finger at John Byron. "Some old leech can't do nothing for that. You'd best make a croup tent."

Desperate hope entered Lara's eyes. "Yes, I've seen it done in the village at Folkstone, but—" Her gaze flashed to Gal. "We need something to make a tent, and we need herbs . . ." Her hands fisted at her sides. "I don't know which herbs."

Gal sent her a look of complacent superiority and slid past Hunter. "I'll find some. Won't do no good though."

Fits of coughing wracked John Byron's thin body over the next few hours. Although the sound tore at Lara's heart, it meant he was getting rid of the phlegm in his lungs that could drown him. Feverish and exhausted, he lay limp in her arms, but his breathing was easier now, his color not so frightening.

Her chin rested on the top of his head as she floated in and out of sleep. Only now did she feel the cramps of stiff muscles in her body, the bone-weary tremors of exhaustion and residual fear. With supreme effort she lifted her head and dropped it back against the chair, only to rear back up in alarm when she felt John Byron slipping from her arms.

Hunter loomed over her, his own face pale, his eyes dark. Gal stood beside him with John Byron in her arms. "She's only putting him to bed," he said.

Lara hadn't realized her look was accusing. She glanced over at the bed with longing, then back at Hunter. She noted that he was shirtless and someone had bandaged his ribs and wrists. Though darkly tanned, his chest showed the effects of the brutality he had suffered in unpleasantly colorful ways. Tears of overwhelming gratitude rushed to her eyes but her voice was steady. "Are you badly hurt?"

"I've had worse."

Gal placed John Byron upon the mattress and just stared at him. "Stronger than he looks," she murmured tightly. "Ollie and Nan . . . they just weren't that strong."

Hunter didn't comment, nor did his gaze linger on John Byron. The years stolen could never be reclaimed, and he pulled back to protect himself from the anger and relief and myriad other feelings assailing him. Staring at the child was like facing himself, a mirror reflecting back at him all the sin and corruption of his youth, his total disregard for others. He turned back to Lara. "You need rest too."

She was almost giddy with exhaustion. She felt oddly euphoric, as if she had run a great race over perilous terrain and won. She tried to move, but her limbs were suddenly lifeless. She gave a strained, perplexed laugh and glanced up at Hunter with eyes much too bright. "Will you have Gal tuck me in as well? It seems I haven't the energy to rise from the chair on my own."

The tears started then, quicker than a water spout. They rolled down her cheeks in huge droplets, alarming because she hadn't felt them coming. "Oh." She gasped, stupefied by the utter loss of control over her body. Trembling all over, she wrapped her arms tight about herself and tried to stop the shivers or at least contain them. Sobs grated in her throat, and she fought to hold them back.

Gal snorted something sarcastic beneath her breath, then glanced at Hunter. "Want me to slap her?"

He shook his head, fighting an inappropriate smile. "Go to her," he said softly.

Gal crossed to Lara at his command and pulled her from the chair. "There, there," she crooned in a matronly voice as she helped Lara to the bed. Sitting her down, Gal pulled a blanket around Lara's shoulders. "I've seen it happen to the brawniest man after a bad winter storm. It's the tension, you see. It's got to be let out."

The cosseting was humiliating for Lara. She turned away and buried her face into the pillow, muffling her sobs.

Hunter nodded permission for Gal to seek her own bed, then eased down beside Lara. He stroked her back, feeling her tremors in the stinging abrasions of his palms. His inclination was to quiet her, but he refrained and let her rid herself of all the pent up anguish.

"I . . . I'm s-sorry," she attempted, but her chest convulsed so that she couldn't get the words out.

"No, hush." He plucked the pins from her hair and smoothed the long mass of sable curls down her back, his sweeps rhythmic and lulling. Grimacing at the painful effort, he eased down on the bed until he lay full length beside her. She tried to turn but he gripped her shoulder. "Lie still," he said between his teeth. He pulled her back to his chest, tighter when she wept, gentler as she calmed. She kept turning her face into the pillow so as not to wake John Byron, but her child slept on in docile depletion.

"I'm s-so . . . ashamed."

"As well you should be." Hunter felt the last of her tremors fade and stroked her hair again, the tresses sleek as sherry-colored satin in the lantern glow. He swirled his fingers in the rich texture, ignoring the low, stirring heat of temptation besetting him.

His hand slid down her back, massaging, comforting, feeling the warmth of her flesh beneath fabric. A light floral scent rose from her hair, fresh and teasing, a reminder. He lowered his head to hers and inhaled the fragrance. Her noisy crying had quieted into the aftermath of shuddering skips of breath and an occasional exhausted sigh. Her chin was tucked against her chest, her spine rounded, knees drawn up in a protective curve. Her hand had crept along the sheets and found her son, her palm on his chest to absorb the reassuring rise and fall of his regular breathing.

"Thank you," she said into the quiet. "Thank you for bringing him back to me."

Hunter watched a mother's delicate hand touch her child. He could not reconcile the Lara he had known, the flighty seventeen-year-old with the world at her feet, with this woman of stalwart strength and valiant determination. He mourned the loss of the funny and frivolous creature who had made him laugh at the same time she sparked desire in him— the Lara he might have easily disregarded.

In her place stood a woman he didn't know, a woman perhaps worth knowing, one who churned him up then turned his lust into something cheap and tawdry.

He watched her face relax, transform, as her breathing took on the regular pattern of exhausted slumber. The innocence of young Lara was still inside her; it whispered out at him from every line of her delicate bone structure, from the way she curled up into her son like a child herself. She might have grown strong and mature and intelligent, but she was still completely vulnerable to malignant forces like Robert and Claude.

There was nothing meager about her fortune, a healthy estate and thriving village, but wealth alone couldn't stop men of Robert and Claude's nature. She had everything to lose; they had everything to gain. She was a woman alone with a child of questionable birthright against two men of unquestionable claim. Did she realize how vile and ugly it could all get before it was over?

Hunter watched them sleep and knew, as much as he might regret it, as much as she would abhor it, that there was no question of returning them to Folkstone.

Chapter Eight

Lara tilted her face to catch the warmth of the morning sun. John Byron rested in the chair beside her, blankets piled to his throat. Though the morning air was crisp, Lara wanted no such encumbrances herself. She felt free, as if a ballast had been lifted from her shoulders. She caught a glimpse of Hunter at the forecastle rail. His commanding height and the way his presence seemed to dominate his surroundings left curiously unsettling impressions on her senses— a hint of brilliance with shadows of the macabre.

Dressed in a full-sleeved white shirt and snug black pants, he looked every bit the pirate he had once been —still was in many ways, she suspected, beneath the handsome veneer of sophistication and polish. It was more like a protracted or peripheral opinion. Something one knew without being able to prove.

He stood in utter stillness, absently holding his ribs and searching the horizon. She wondered if he looked for ships that might be following. His face was wan and lines of strain etched his mouth and forehead. She knew he should be in bed, had told him so at dawn when he prepared to leave the cabin, but he had only made an intimate remark in a caustic tone, then gone on about his business as he saw fit.

The wind flattened his shirt to his chest, a gauzy fabric that showed right through to the bandages beneath. His ink-black hair was tied back with a tattered piece of apricot silk that fluttered in the breeze like a pennant and gave Lara a start. It seemed oddly familiar, like an old melody one could hum but not recall the words. She strained to catch a closer look but it was nothing more than a faint, peachy blur from time to time when the wind tossed it over his shoulder.

She reached down and instinctively stroked John Byron's dark curls, an old habit he had begun to disdain before the kidnapping. Instead of pulling away, he turned his face into her palm, breaking her heart into small sharp fragments. She had hated his march toward adolescence, his self-conscious squirming when forced to hold her hand in a crowded place, the kisses to her cheek that had become perfunctory obligations. She wished all that back now, the normal progress of childhood rather than his clinging to her in fear.

His cheeks were cool against her palm, so she tugged the blanket up closer about his shoulders. He had spent a restful, if exhausted, night, and she felt confident enough to bring him on deck to sit and enjoy the morning sun.

In spite of herself, the ribbon in Hunter's hair continued to rouse her imagination, drawing her attention back repeatedly until she gave up and studied it openly.

She jerked suddenly as hot color bathed her cheeks. The torn strip of cloth, unmistakable even from this distance, was a sash from a dress.

A dress she had worn the day John Byron was conceived.

The wind picked up the trailing ends again and fluttered it against Hunter's cheek, teasing as a caress. He reached up as if to push it back but let his hand linger, rolling the silk between his fingers, studying its texture as intensely as he studied the vast expanse of sky and sea. Lara felt the touch in every cell of her body.

She wrapped her arms around herself, then turned her thoughts to a safe and bolstering pique. She couldn't believe his audacity in wearing the ribbon, flaunting it like some prize. It was juvenile and insulting and . . . she couldn't think of just what it was or represented. What diabolical reason did he have for taunting her, reminding her? She refused to be baited, and turned away to converse with her son.

Beneath hooded lashes, Hunter watched Lara bend to speak with John Byron. Her smile was warm, relieved, overshadowing the still strained look in her eyes. Her face and mannerisms held charming animation when she talked, an escape from her usual soberness. The funny girl had been set aside by the mature woman, but with the child he could still see echoes of young Lara behind the curtain of reserve.

The breeze tugged at the proper chignon at her

nape and tossed several locks free to play around her temples. She pushed them back with an impatient hand, as if unused to the disorder, but Hunter remembered a time when it hung free down her back, windswept into stunning chaos that swirled around her cheeks and into her eyes and mouth . . . and his hands. Her dress was finely cut and perfectly fitted. Modest and stylish, it gave off the same air of reticence as the rest of her.

He wanted to take it off, to peel back the layers of refinement she so properly hid behind. He reached up and fingered the strip of silk again, running it through his fingers over and over, just as he had that day on an island paradise, when a girl of intrepid fancy had danced out ankle deep into the surf with her skirts tucked up to her knees. The sky had been an impossible blue, enhancing the color of her eyes. Her cheeks had been flushed with heat, and she'd put flowers in her hair.

Sly as a little bird, she stole from the ramshackle fisherman's hut where they'd taken refuge from the storm and sneaked down toward the beach when she thought no one was watching. Intrigued, he followed and lurked beside a tall palm tree, wondering what misconduct she was up to. She had that look in her eye: guilt pushed aside in favor of mischief.

She'd been aboard his ship for two months now and he had studied her intently, sorting out her weaknesses from her strengths, teaching her to trust him. She was a product of her upbringing, uncomplicated and unremarkable for the most part, yet there was a beguiling spark of audacity hidden beneath all the layers of propriety and etiquette cultivated from the cradle. It shone as hauteur when she remembered to be offended or entitled arrogance when she became afraid, but there was about her a quality that did not lend itself to snobbery.

Deep down she was an explorer, thrilled by the act of discovery. Innately warm and affectionate, she loved sunshine and nature and the enchantment of small creatures. A ladybug on a leaf, a spider spinning a web, a tiny hermit crab scrambling for its hole. And she loved risks. The sense of adventure was almost too much for her to contain. Mostly, he supposed, because she'd never been allowed to indulge it.

He watched her tiptoe closer to the edge of the jungle, his own heart thudding now with the sensation of adventure he could feel radiating from her. She stayed sheltered within the cool green shadows and waited, looking in every direction, poised just at the edge of daring. He knew the exact moment she decided to defy the standards with which she'd been raised and race for opportunity. Her eyes flared and her chin lifted the smallest notch. She made one last sweeping glance down the stretch of white sand then ran for the water.

The wind whipped her unbound hair in a thousand directions, strand after shining strand flying into her eyes, her mouth, around her throat. She tried pushing it back but the breeze played like a flirty boy with each sleek lock. Finally she gave up, stripped the apricot sash from her gown, and tied the heavy mass back. The gesture stilled something within her, sparked something else. Her hands paused, elbows uplifted, stretching the fabric of her bodice tightly across her breasts. Her eyes narrowed.

Hunter could see her mind churning as clearly as if there existed a window to her thoughts. His own began a reckless stirring that twisted him in opposing directions.

She looked slowly down the beach again, searching and studying both the shoreline and the fringes of the jungle. She put a hand to her mouth, obviously aghast at her own thoughts, but the smile beneath that dainty palm was purely an imp's smile. Confident of her privacy, she unbuttoned her bodice and stood for a moment, waiting. When the sky did not fall in upon her for such a brazen act, she tugged at the shoulders and let it fall to her waist. Bold, silly, she turned in a circle, holding her arms out and flinging her head back to let the sun kiss the creamy flesh of her throat and bosom above her linen chemise.

Hunter smiled at her melodrama, certain she had never revealed so much of herself beyond the safety of a dressing screen. Had he been a gentleman or even a speck more noble, he would have called out a mocking retort that would have sent her scrambling back into her clothes. But he was twenty-three, lawless, and nothing of nobility lay within his jaded soul for the daughter of the man who had stolen a year of his life. He wanted Lara at this moment more than he had ever wanted anything in his life, including revenge. Like a voyeur he watched and waited for what she would dare next. After a thrilling moment of hesitation, she again abandoned caution and peeled off her gown completely.

In nothing but a flimsy scrap cloth with peach ribbons at her breast, she tiptoed down the beach and tested the water. In the next instant she gave a girlish cry of delight and splashed in ankle deep, then skipped like a child in the waves. But her body, outlined perfectly beneath the soaked fabric, was that of a woman.

Small, high breasts strained against the sheer linen above a narrow belly. Her hips were nothing more than a faint flaring out from her waist, her legs slender and long. Succulent and coltish had been the only way to describe her—that and stunning.

Hunter leaned against the palm for a moment longer, absorbing the sight of her in gay abandon, tensing in every muscle and tendon of his body. Every ounce of her unbridled joy seeped into his bloodstream, warming his extremities to feverish hunger. He straightened and walked toward her with only one thought in mind.

"Petite ange, how daring you've become."

She gasped when she saw him and instinctively crossed her arms over her breasts. "A gentleman would not look!" she accused. The heated pink on her cheeks made her look all the more innocent, but the wet chemise clinging to her skin called an ancient allure.

"Am I a gentleman, chère?"

"You are wicked!"

Gulls circled overhead, their sea-cry shrill in the

poignancy of the moment. She tried to say something more, a rebuke, but her reckless behavior was unforgivable, and she couldn't seem to formulate the words or hauteur to hide her embarrassment.

He stole softly, calculatingly, into her thoughts. "There is no one here to chastise you. No one will blame you." He pulled his own shirt off over his head and flung it away, then started toward her slowly, careful not to cause her to flee. "No one will even know."

Silence fell around them, tight and distended as an indrawn breath. The crash of waves against the shore seemed muted now, a backdrop rather than accompaniment to the sharp bird calls.

Staring at his approach with shy fascination, she pushed a lock of damp hair from her eyes with the back of a trembling hand, but the rest of her was motionless, precariously balanced on the thin line between staying transfixed and dashing for cover. The sight was so different, more splendid than anything she had allowed herself to imagine—and she had imagined plenty over the past two months. Or so she had thought.

His skin was darker than her daydreams, more sun-bronzed, and sleekly stretched over taut muscle. His hair shone like jet in the sun, a wild mass black as sin that hung down his back and curled at the ends in the way women fought to achieve with hot irons and curling rags. Yet there was nothing at all feminine about him. His breeches rode low on his hips, a loose-weave homespun the dull color of sand, but his eyes sparkled like jeweled amethysts with dangerous secrets. It made her heartbeat throb unsteadily to look upon him, and she found her breathing catchy and fast.

Hunter moved toward her with fluid grace, a smile on his face, but his pulse hammering out darkly a warning to leave her alone. He had been everywhere, done everything. This girl had nothing he hadn't seen or touched or tasted in a dozen different ports with twice as many women of greater beauty and experience. But the desire to have her had overrun him days ago, and he was weary of trying to outdistance it.

He had become a thing to be despised, he supposed, a hypocrite of sorts. The spoiled hedonist who had to have something merely because it was there for the taking. He felt his muscles contract, an attempt to reverse the dissection of self. He could turn back and leave Lara with her virtue. By stealing her innocence, he still would not own it, would not be able to recapture whatever small glimmer of integrity he himself had once possessed. But she was a keening in his blood now, a challenge too tempting to ignore.

He took another step closer. He had stolen Henry Winthrop's only child and insured his revenge by keeping her long enough for her reputation to be thoroughly ruined. Having studied Winthrop down to the most minute aspect of his personality, Hunter knew his moves, his motives, his life goals. His only child represented chattel, a bid for even higher respectability among the ton. *Whatever Henry could not accomplish with his own illustrious career, his daughter Lara would through marriage.*

But it was Lara herself who drew Hunter this day, not vengeance against Henry. He smiled and took a step closer, compelled and so amused by the artless fascination of her disposition. She had known it was brazen to strip and wade in the surf, but she hadn't cared until she got caught.

He understood her so well. Consequences were not a thing she liked to consider. He would wager his last gold doubloon that she had lived her sweetly pampered life up to this point believing it much better to beg mercy later than to ask permission first.

He noted the mild panic in her eyes and smiled in reassurance. "A nice day, chère. A beautiful day for a swim." He drew near, near enough for the scent of the flowers in her hair to tease his nostrils, then strolled blithely past, staying well away until he could gain her confidence.

"I . . . I cannot swim," she said, breathless, waiting, wanting so badly to stay while knowing she should flee.

"Ah, but I can teach you." He could see her mind churning over the possibilities and reprisals. "It's easy. I'll help you."

The consternation on her face mirrored the tug-of-war in her mind, but Hunter knew already who would win. She wanted this chance, this impudent defiance, wanted to be able to return home and whisper to her covent-schooled peers what shocking things she had done. A stab of guilt tried to find a foothold in Hunter's scarred soul as he circled her like a shark closing in for the kill. She did not yet understand the ramifications of being with him this long. She had done nothing; therefore she was blameless. She did not understand that her world would not care.

He could warn her; he should. Give her some sort of fighting chance. But that was not how the game was played. He spun and moved backward into the surf on the balls of his feet, holding out his palm. "Come, Lara," he said. "Petite ange, come touch the water."

"Come, John Byron."

Hunter brought his surroundings back into focus and suppressed the shudder of raw desire resurrected by the memories. And the mild twinge of guilt. He had been in his own youthful arrogance as foolish as she, thinking revenge would even the score and his sins would have no bearing on his future. Revenge had done nothing. It had not redeemed his time spent on the hell ship; it had not ruined Henry Winthrop. The only one it had hurt was Lara.

He looked away, knowing he still would not have traded that one day, wishing he were admirable enough to at least want it recalled. His ribs ached abominably with every breath, every movement, and he attempted to focus on that pain in order to deflect his thoughts from the past. But one could not outrun a memory and if he had learned anything from his misspent youth, it was that there were always consequences to pay. He turned back to the chore of navigation, but his energy had waned, and he was little good for the running of the ship.

He gave Connie orders and made slow and painful progress down to the galley. Weasel was there, stirring an atrocious stew. Hunter took one bite, then headed for his cabin. He needed rest to heal and time to put things into perspective. As much as he might wish otherwise, rescuing John Byron was not the end of things but only the beginning. Other plans were needed to insure the child's continued safety.

Instead of an empty room, Hunter found John Byron tucked into bed while Lara sat nearby reading aloud. He came up behind her and plucked the book from her hand.

"Oh!" She jerked and craned her head around sharply. Her hand flew to her heart and she gave a small, breathless laugh. "You startled me."

Hunter quirked an eyebrow. "Did I?" He studied the slight smile on her face, the dewdrops of color in her cheeks, and thought of the truly startling things he could manage if given a few hours alone with her.

"Yes, I'm still a bit jumpy." She smiled as if to mock her silliness, but there remained a hint of tragedy in the depths of her eyes.

He handed the book back with a polite nod but his thoughts were far from charitable. They cluttered his room, this picture-perfect mother and son, a Gainsborough-quality domesticity that didn't fit aboard a ship whose very sails were once hoisted for the purpose of plunder and spoil.

In some warped manner, he found it blasphemous that they invaded his bachelor's domain with such homey endeavors. He had come seeking solitude but could not in good conscience send them away. Vexed, he eased down into the overstuffed chair and stretched his legs out toward the brazier, then dropped his head back and closed his eyes.

"Can I get you something?"

It was Lara's voice, solicitous, concerned. Hunter could picture the worry line between her brows. "A hot bath of fresh water in a deep tub, a bottle of French brandy." *Lisette's bread pudding and remarkable hands.*

"Ah." He could hear the smile in her voice. "I'm sorry. Tea instead?"

"Brandy. It's behind the doors there. The small table."

He listened to her rummage around a bit before the tinkling of glass let him know she'd achieved her goal.

"Do you want it warmed?"

A suggestive remark flashed instantly to mind, and he wondered at the detestable turn his life had taken since she'd walked back into it.

"It doesn't matter," he replied, and held out a hand. He tossed the brandy down immediately and didn't even open his eyes, just let the motion of the ship and alcohol lull him.

"Sir?" It was the boy's voice, shy and tentative, remarkably guilt-inflicting. "Thank you for saving me. I'm sorry you got hurt."

Buzzards plucking at his entrails would have been more welcome than the clear cool tones of this child's gratitude. "You saved my life as well," Hunter said. "Were quite brave actually. Let's call it even."

"Yes, sir."

Blessed silence. Hunter hadn't known how important it was to him.

"Sir?"

Damn. "Yes?"

"I've nearly all my strength back."

Was he supposed to care about this? Of course, he just couldn't conjure the proper response or enthusiasm. He had fulfilled his part of the bargain, gotten banged up in the process, and was now ready to put his life back on its usual course. But that wasn't going to happen. He knew it, sensed it. It only lacked confirmation of one sort or the other to which he was certain he would soon by privy.

"So he says," Lara responded, "but I think a bit more rest would not be amiss."

Hunter thought a bit more silence a rewarding thing. He opened one eye and gave John Byron a look of patent male commiseration and took inadvertent pleasure from the child's secret smile.

Lara splashed more brandy into his glass, and he inhaled the bouquet before sipping this one more slowly, feeling the first euphoric buzz in his head, anticipating the further dulling of his pain with relish.

"Sir?"

Bloody hell.

"I've a model ship back home just like this one."

Hunter opened one eye and shot Lara an inquisitive look. "Just like this one?"

She looked away, wondering why everything she had done in the past, no matter how small and harmless, seemed so determined to twist back upon her. "If you have rested enough, John Byron, we'll take another short stroll then ask Mr. O'Connor to place a chair for you near his own upon the deck."

As was his nature, Weasel popped up out of nowhere, startling mother and son. Only Hunter, accustomed to such, didn't flinch or fluster at Weasel's propensity to show up right in the middle of a room without anyone seeing him enter. Hunter had long since ceased trying to figure out how the clever little man did it.

"I've come to fetch the boy," Weasel exclaimed. "Connie and Gal want to see him."

Hunter watched the brief moment of panic in Lara's eyes when John Byron asked to go, then resolution as she came to grips with whatever worried her. Weasel plucked John Byron from the covers and hauled him, blanket and all, out of the cabin. The entire commotion left an unsettling silence behind. Hunter watched a pensive smile touch Lara's lips as her son disappeared, and in her eyes was hard-won contentment.

"How resilient children are," she murmured. She glanced at Hunter then away. "I still feel supremely fragile, as if I could fly apart at the slightest thing, while he's ready to tackle the world again." Guilt suddenly flooded her expression and she turned back. "And you? How are you really faring?"

He grinned wryly. "Not as bravely as he. I'd like

nothing better than to curl up in bed and have my dinner served on a tray."

It was impossible, with their past standing between them like a thorny hedge, for Lara to express the profound gratitude she felt toward him for rescuing her son. It almost shamed her to see his discomfort and to remember that he'd had no one to tend him last night when all had scrambled feverishly to make the croup tent to save John Byron's life.

"Come along," she said with a slight smile, and held out her hand.

Suspicion narrowed his eyes. "What evil are you planning, Lara? I'm an injured man, quite incapable of defending myself."

She laughed lightly, as she had not in too long. "You're being a coward."

He went along peaceably because he'd never seen this side of her and it intrigued him.

She only led him to the bed and ordered him to lie down, which he did with a rakish glimmer in his eye but no comment. "Stay here," she commanded, then left.

He eased up against a pile of pillows, wishing she had lascivious motives, though he knew he couldn't do a thing about it if she decided to strip naked and crawl in with him. She returned in less than a quarter hour with a tray. He winced when she bumped the bed. "If you are planning to debauch me," he said, "I'll need laudanum."

She ignored the remark and sat on the edge beside him with the tray in her lap. "I'm going to pamper you."

Hunter grimaced at the tea and biscuits when she lifted the napkin. "I'd rather be debauched."

"It's medicinal and will restore you faster than anything but rest, which you shall have also." She broke a biscuit and buttered it.

"How properly you have raised him."

The words came out of nowhere, stilling the motion of her hands. "Yes, I was too afraid he would turn out like his father if left to his own childish whimsy."

He gave her a devilish smile. "Or his mother."

Her expression sobered. "Yes. It terrifies me that he could turn out like either of us, without a thought for his future or how his actions might hurt others."

"Don't suffocate him," Hunter warned. "It's not worth the rebellion. If you lose him, you've gained nothing by trying to mold him to your own standards."

She knew he spoke from experience. It resounded in the inflection of each word. "I do not intend to."

She held the biscuit out to him, but he took her wrist instead and fed himself from her hand, his lips brushing her thumb, his teeth grazing her forefinger. He watched her eyes for a hint of her emotions, but she guarded them well. A small shiver was the only indication that she was not as composed as she appeared.

She pulled her hand away and clenched her fist in her lap. "All I've ever wanted for him was a normal life, one without the fear and shame of discovery hanging over his head."

Hunter dropped his head back on the pillows and

stared out the porthole. "For every action there are consequences to pay."

"What have you paid?"

She sounded almost bitter. Hunter thought of the hundreds of arpents of sugarcane grown on his plantation. Making a living off the land had been his father's dream and his sister, Acadiana's. They had always felt a oneness with the rich earth and found fulfillment in the labor of their hands. He had built that dream, the one his father had not lived long enough to, but instead of it being his catharsis or redemption, it had done nothing but leave him cold and hollow inside.

He glanced toward the porthole and watched the clouds gather on the horizon, felt the familiar rush of energy in his blood. Tempest-tossed waves were the nourishment upon which he fed, life to his tarnished soul. He thrived on the danger and challenge of a winter gale, revitalized in the calm warm waters of a tropical island.

He rolled his head back toward Lara and knew why he'd been possessed with having her. She had been an enigma, a creature of privilege and polish who had wanted more than the restricted indulgences afforded a protected young lady of the *ton*. He had understood her need for adventure, her desire for risk.

But Lara hadn't known, and he had refused to reveal, that there would be a price to pay for exercising a moment of thoughtless abandon. She knew now and moved with caution and care, every action or plan thought out ahead of time for its inherent danger. Hunter pitied the slaughter of her natural enthusiasm, but his guilt lasted little beyond a small twinge of regret. The desire he had felt for the girl a decade ago had not diminished a whit, but was decidedly enhanced by the woman she had become.

She was a much greater challenge now, for she knew what he was about. And he wanted to get past her guard, *needed* on some level he did not choose to explore to break through her shell of cool sophistication and tap the heat of passion again, to see the startled wonder on her face when he touched her, hear the small gasps of hunger ring from the depths of her need.

"What is it?" Lara asked.

He closed his eyes, hiding the unruly fire, and turned his attention elsewhere. "Decisions must be made."

"Decisions . . ." She felt queasy in her stomach and limbs. She turned away from him, uncomfortable, and gazed out at the endless blue sky, as if there might be answers there. Her hand rose then dropped back uselessly. "I don't know what to do."

"You cannot go back to Folkstone or the country home in York or the London residence."

She didn't bother to ask how he knew so much about George's holdings. "What else am I to do? Go into hiding, suffocate my son?" She whirled to face him. "I am not without resources. I will hire protection—"

"And George's brothers will bribe them. There is no end to the cycle, Lara."

She stared at the trailing ends of the ribbon in his

hair. It lay across the pillow, obscene in its tattered state, prurient in what it represented. Resentment flared, but she managed to keep her voice low. "I suppose you have a plan?" The words were cold and resentful, because she had none of her own and she didn't know how to stop the nasty tide that was forming, rising higher and moving in closer to swallow her up.

Not by so much as the flicker of an eyelash did Hunter expose any hint of emotion. "You know, Lara. I don't need to spell it out."

"Yes, you do," she said, the first tremors of alarm threatening her composure.

"Fine. You'll stay with me."

The distress on her face slowly faded to self-protective bewilderment, as if she didn't really believe what she was hearing. "I cannot possibly do that."

"Why?" His intense gaze grew piercing and it took everything in her not to run from that look, from the knowledge in his eyes.

"I simply cannot. You must understand—"

He smiled, that odd twist of lips that held no warmth or humor or encouragement. "I understand perfectly, but I can't let you take him from me."

Lara set the tray carefully aside and rose from the bed. "You cannot stop me." Though baiting him was foolish in the extreme, she couldn't back down. "People will know," she said tensely. "It only takes seeing the two of you together . . ."

"Horrifying, isn't it?" he said lightly before his voice turned cruel. "Everyone will finally know for certain what they only suspected all along. That someone else touched every inch of your virtuous body months before the Earl of Folkstone even glimpsed your face."

Her hand swung out and would have slapped his cheek had his reflexes not been quicker than her intent. He grabbed her wrist in a hurtful vise, but the effort cost him. A growl of pain tore from his throat at the sudden movement.

Her startled gaze seared him. "Stop it, Hunter, before you harm yourself worse!"

"Oh, that's rich, Lara. I'm supposed to allow you to slap me senseless but must beware of my aching ribs?"

She jerked on her hand. He grimaced but didn't let go.

"You can't have John Byron," she said with cold assurance.

The look in his eyes was terrifying. "Try to stop me."

She fought to keep the panic from her voice and failed. "Think of what this will do to him. You cannot force me—"

"It will keep him alive," he interrupted in a soft and vicious voice. "And you're right. I won't force you to do anything. *You* may go anywhere you please, but John Byron stays with me."

The cry of outrage came from deep within her, a conflagration of wild hopelessness and terrible foreboding. Not once, in all her planning, had she considered the possibility that Hunter wouldn't allow her simply to walk away with her son after the rescue was over.

"You cannot do this," she hissed between her teeth, but she didn't know how to stop him. Exposing John Byron's parentage even to speculation would harm him most cruelly in the years to come. Gossip was constant. It would ever be rampant at Court and in the country, but without a husband to shelter them, the slander would be more than just ugly whispers behind elegantly gloved palms. Lara would not subject John Byron to open ridicule. "You can't take my son!"

"My son as well," he shot back.

She wrenched her wrist out of his hold and held herself erect. "No," she whispered cruelly. "Your seed perhaps, but not your son. You gave up that right when you refused to marry me."

The ungracious statement hit home with acute accuracy. Hunter closed his eyes briefly to absorb the impact, then said softly, "Be that as it may, you have no choice but to leave him with me or accompany us. I won't cast you aside, Lara, but I will gladly leave you behind."

She began backing away, though where she was headed escaped her. "You cannot have him," she said with cool finality. "Do you hear me?"

"The entire ship can hear you," he answered.

Every reason and argument she might give him swam through her mind like flotsam as she headed for the door. Her heart hurt with indecision, and she could not collect her thoughts enough to make a rational rebuttal. At all costs, she must keep John Byron safe, but they could not spend the rest of their lives in hiding, sailing from one port to another. There were so many things to consider, so many decisions to make—so alarmingly few options. One angry tear slid down her cheek unnoticed as she fled the room.

She tripped on a coil of rope when she reached the open deck and almost fell. Bracing herself, she stood against the mast and breathed deeply to calm herself. She had not yet reached the end of her resources, and until she did she would neither give up nor give in. From birth her life had not been her own but dictated by parents, nannies, teachers—society, propriety, morality. She'd never been allowed the freedom or luxury of making her own decisions. Even her hobbies had been chosen for her.

Marriage had been immensely better. She'd been free to choose her own friends and interests. Though invisible walls remained, the perimeters were much broader and she had never risked taking advantage of them by pressing beyond their bounds. Her life had been peaceful if unexciting, safe and comfortable. Though she would never again chance the winds of excitement, neither would she go back to having every move she made dictated and manipulated.

Her lips bloodless, she strode toward the deck with staunch determination stiffening her backbone. The only time in her life she'd openly rebelled against the convictions of her upbringing, she had paid dearly. It had begun on a sandy beach and ended on a stormy summer night aboard a pirate ship. Casting upbringing and social conventions to the salt-laden winds, she had flouted them all. For one small moment in time, she had taken hold of the world and held it in the palms of her hands. And she had been free.

The sharp intake of her breath came fast and overloud. Lara paused midstep and pressed her fingers to her lips. Shocked realization flooded her, as taunting as the ribbon Hunter had worn to remind her. She remembered the night he had stripped it from her own hair and let the damp locks fall over his hands and arms and chest. *Not rape. The seduction of innocence, perhaps. But not rape.*

She pressed the heels of her palms to her eyes, wondering how she could have forgotten, how she could have so altered and manipulated the memories through the years to fit her comfortable mold of the wounded innocent.

Come, Lara, he had said in a voice she would never forget. Her knees had trembled violently when she took that first step toward him, but each step after had been faster and easier. Wickedness was like that. The instant of indecision was the hardest, that place where guilt could be acknowledged or ignored, where one could turn back. But once the first step was taken, the chains of conscience fell away. Mesmerized by the mixture of thrill and panic, she had walked toward his outstretched hand, noting the way the sun glinted off his hair, how bronzed his exposed skin was in the open neck of his shirt.

When she had drawn close enough, he had reached out and touched her shoulder where the skin was turning pink from too much sun. He had then leaned over and pressed his lips to that same spot, just where her neck and shoulder joined, and she had shivered all over as if from a chill. Though not one single inch of her had been cold.

"Come, Lara."

Her hands flew from her eyes, pushing back a decade of empty longing and regret and flinging her into the present. He was standing on deck, his hand extended, confusing her, mixing past with present. Her breath snared in her throat, and she felt a tremble in her knees. She need only take that one step, one small motion that would thrust herself back into his reckless care.

"Come, let's discuss this rationally in the cabin."

The cabin. Her mind cleared and with it came shame. She could not be rational now. For whatever reason he had come after her, she couldn't be near him. It was just too difficult.

With an inarticulate cry, she moved past him, not caring if he thought her absurd. She would put an ocean between them if she could. Barring that, she'd steal one piece of time for herself, one moment in which she could gather her thoughts and try to come up with a solution.

Long fingers closed around her arm and she was brought up short. Anger turned her blood to ice. "Let go of me."

Locks of her hair slid loose and swirled about her face. She grabbed for the slipping ivory comb, a gift from George, and cried out when it tumbled to the deck at her feet. She bent down and snatched it up, holding it to her breast as if it might disappear.

Hunter let go and stepped back, his voice calm

but laced with cynicism. "Do forgive me." His eyes roamed her, lazy and insulting. "You were pressed against me from breast to thigh last night. I didn't know touching your wrist this morning was forbidden."

Her face flamed and she tried to summon up an unruffled countenance, but everything about him confused and alarmed her. Like standing on unstable ground, she was never quite sure of her footing.

"No, forgive me," she bit out between clenched teeth. She swallowed. "I *know* a decision must be made. I just do not feel certain enough to make one right this instant."

She tried to tuck her hair back up, a motion she had done a thousand times, but her hands trembled too badly to accomplish it. She flung her arms back down and crushed the comb in her palm, ignoring its small teeth biting into her flesh. Almost as if from a distance, she felt him take her wrist and turn it, then unfold her fingers. He slipped the comb from her palm.

"Small things seem huge," she whispered. "Big things are impossible."

He understood only too well.

She stood in silence while he gently lifted her hair from her nape and swirled it back atop her head, too aware of his presence beside her, surrounding her. She knew now what had so captivated her ten years earlier: the lure of the forbidden, the knowledge that she was stepping beyond every allowed boundary. As much as she despised herself for it, she could feel the temptation still.

The breeze, heavy with the smell of the sea, whisked tendrils of hair about her face like delicate flags snapping in the wind. He fitted the comb in place as his eyes devoured her with an intensity that made her blood rush hotly to the surface of her skin. She had seen lust so openly displayed only once before. Ten years ago she hadn't even known what it was. Sheltered, she'd never been exposed to the naked hunger of a man for a woman. What she had seen in Hunter's eyes that day had both alarmed and excited her.

She looked away. She had not then, nor did she now, want to see herself as a creature of desire, one capable of such carnal thoughts and feelings that they corrupted the very foundation of her upbringing. She wanted, *needed*, to see herself as the martyr and victim of a scoundrel's base nature, not a foolishly headstrong young woman who had incited his passion and joined him in her own downfall.

"Lara."

She tried to ignore the husky timbre of his voice, or rather its effect upon her heightened senses, but she had come to know herself fairly well in the past few moments and acknowledged that there were parts of her she would rather not recognize. She tilted her head to face him. "I would never leave my son, not with you or anyone else."

"It's settled then?"

"Not in the manner you would like."

He leaned back against the ship's stairway, holding his ribs tighter, a whiteness around his mouth. "Don't make me take him by force to protect him, Lara. He's been through enough."

Chapter Nine

Distressed, Lara followed Hunter back to the cabin to finish their discussion. It would not do to have things unsettled when they reached port. She stepped inside to find Gal sitting in the bedside chair, her head bent over a book. Sunlight streamed in through the portal and shimmered off her hair, turning it almost silver. Curled up in the chair, her face intense, she looked young and vulnerable. Not at all the mysterious street hoyden, as Lara had begun to think of her.

Gal looked up when they entered. She dismissed Lara with a glance but followed Hunter's every movement in a manner that could only be termed as worshipful. Before John Byron's rescue, Lara had had no time to ponder the girl's relationship with Hunter but she wondered at it now. She saw an enigma: a young woman with the face of an angel who wore boy's apparel with ease and held herself as aloof as royalty.

"Jane Austen giving you trouble?" Hunter asked.

Gal shrugged and closed the book. "Ironic comedy. Seems conflicted to me."

"Because you've never lived a country life."

Gal's eyes seemed to dim, and she abruptly changed the subject. "Where's your boy?"

Lara suppressed the urge to utter something uncharitable and remained silent to study the young woman who both repelled and fascinated her with her streetwise bluntness and blank eyes. Independent and remote, Gal seemed to need no one, and Lara was intensely envious of that sense of self. Yet, contrarily, Gal appeared obsessively devoted to Hunter. Lara wondered if it was by choice or some sort of moral weakness. The promise of beauty so evident in the young woman's bone structure and natural bearing made it hard for Lara to see the boyish clothes and abominable manners without trying to change her.

"Lady Chalmers."

Lara was startled to find Gal speaking directly to her.

"I thought I could teach your boy to play." Gal dug in her pocket and brought out a deck of cards.

Lara didn't know whether to be pleased or leery. She paused too long in her reply, making the silence awkward. Gal's lashes lowered in haughty reticence.

Hunter stepped in smoothly, filling the rude gap so easily Lara wondered if she was making too much of Gal's overture of friendship. "John Byron will be along shortly," he replied. "You may ask him if he's interested."

Gal stuffed the cards back in her pocket and stared

at the closed book on her lap. She traced its binding idly, then finally lifted her head. "What will you do with him?"

"I haven't decided yet," he said. "Do you have a suggestion?"

It was the first hint of overt compassion Lara had witnessed in Hunter. His expression, his voice, everything about him bespoke calm reassurance.

Gal gripped the edges of *Sense and Sensibility* for a brief moment, then seemed to recall herself and opened her fingers with an air of disinterest. "Keep him if you like," she remarked. She nodded in Lara's direction. *"She's* not been able to."

Lara's spine stiffened. Flayed enough by her own guilt, she certainly didn't need more perpetrated by this outlandish waif.

Hunter smiled. "Go along, Gal. Weasel's got sweets in the galley."

The young woman unfolded from the chair and stretched like a cat, seemingly unaware of the sensuous picture she made of lean, feline grace and girlish innocence.

Lara waited until Gal disappeared through the door, then rounded on Hunter in mild pique. "Why is she with you?"

One eyebrow rose in inquiry. "Does it matter?"

"It's not acceptable, a young woman traveling alone with a man—"

"It's a little late," he interrupted with amused sarcasm, "for either of us to pretend outrage at such unacceptable behavior."

Lara looked away, chagrined but unable to let the

matter rest. "She is obviously enamored of you, though you award her little more than your passing attention. Is she your . . . friend, ward—"

"Mistress, lover?" His voice changed abruptly. "No, Lara. Even *I* am not so debauched as to enjoy the favors of an adolescent. Gal is barely thirteen."

Lara's eyes widened in shock. "Thirteen! Has she no parents, no guardian?"

"No." His voice was unnaturally soft and darkly forbidding. "She has no one. Let it drop. We are not here to talk about Gal."

"But . . ." It was too distressing to Lara's maternal sensibilities to let it drop. "What are *you* doing with her?"

Hunter turned and gave her the full force of his icy stare. "I bought her."

He watched the shock hit her in several forms—the flaring of her nostrils, the color draining from her fair cheeks, the expression of stark bewilderment.

He finished tonelessly, "I told you to let it drop."

"Bought her?" It was weaker than a whisper, a raspy breath of abject disbelief. "You do not just *buy* people, especially young girls!"

Hunter pitied the muddled outrage on Lara's face. It was cruel to shock someone so, to savage the very conscience that kept them civil. "Do not be naive, Lara; men have done it for eons. Reprehensible though it may be, the purchase of one human by another existed long before you or I were born and will continue long after we are gone."

"Slavery?" she said in a horrified whisper. "You purchased a child from a slave trader?"

Hunter smiled grimly. "No, my ingenuous Lara, I purchased her from a brothel."

Lara's eyes narrowed in contempt. Her sensibilities were so violated she could hardly breathe. She didn't how her heart could hurt so agonizingly when it suddenly felt emptied. "You disgust me," she rasped, then turned and fled the room.

There was nowhere to go.

It took Lara precious few seconds to realize she had no place in which to flee. She gripped the rail and stared out at the sea, but saw nothing beyond the tears of loathing in her eyes. Her heart hurt still, made worse by her mad dash to nowhere. It was an actual pain in her chest, crushing and bitter. She knew what Hunter was, but she'd never imagined him capable of anything quite so despicable.

She pressed her fingers to her mouth. Had she truly entrusted the rescue and care of her son to a man who purchased young girls? The question raced frantically through her mind but could find no fixed answer, nothing sane with which to reason it out.

Because nothing about it made sense.

Her reason began to clear and shuddering relief poured through her. No matter what she thought of him, Hunter wasn't capable of something that horrid.

. . . *even I am not that debauched.*

She remembered his words, clung to them, and felt the tightness ease up in her chest. Hunter was many things—she knew firsthand the seductive power of his charm—but he would never stoop to buying human flesh for carnal pleasure. He would never have to.

She breathed deeply to collect her composure and began the journey back to the cabin. The breeze scattered loose curls about her cheeks and into her eyes. She pushed them back impatiently and almost ran headfirst into Connie.

"Here now," he said, grabbing her forearms to keep her from falling. "What has you so tied in knots that you're frowning worse than a thief before a judge?"

"Hunter did not purchase Gal from a brothel, or not for the reason he implied."

Connie glanced over his shoulder briefly. "Did he imply a reason?"

Lara colored. "No. I did. Tell me why he did it."

"What does it matter?" Connie said. "Is there any reason good enough?" The fierce expression on Lara's face said she would not back down. He threw his hands up, then pointed to a thick coil of rope. "Very well, if you want the sordid details, sit down. I will entertain you."

Lara remained standing, uncertain now of the wisdom in pushing him. She thought of dissembling, but he had already begun the tale and there was nothing left but for her to listen.

"We walked into a New Orleans bordello one night just after docking. The air was festive, charged with an unusual intensity. The clientele were gathered in a cluster, cheering, and we assumed one of the girls must be putting on a show."

Lara shied away from the suspicion building in the

pit of her stomach, but she couldn't get the words out to stop him.

"We pushed through the crowd to get a look. Standing in the middle of the room with her hands tied behind her back was a seven-year-old girl in a sheer nightdress." His eyes narrowed dangerously but his voice was devoid of all emotion. "She—the madame—had put a wreath of tiny flowers woven with ribbons in the little girl's hair. I don't know why that seemed to be the worst part, but to this day, I can still see those white satin streamers shimmering in the candlelight. Madame was auctioning her off for the night—the original vestal virgin."

Connie could hear her feigned accent even now, raised to cover the din of mesmerized clients. *'Ow much*, chère? *What will you give to sample this tender babe? You must be gentle with her*, oui? *She is such a tiny thing.*

"You should have seen Madame's eyes glimmer with greed as she milked the lecherous fools for every ounce of their week's wages."

"Don't!" Lara begged. She couldn't hear more of anything so hideous.

"Squeamish, Lara? You should have seen those who bid. Madame had them in such a frenzy, they were practically salivating. I could tell by the gleam in her eyes that already she was anticipating how best to sell and resell the child before her marketable youth wore out."

Shaken, Lara gripped his sleeve. "Stop. I will not listen to more—"

"He could tell too. I've never seen that look in

Hunter's eyes, and hope never to again. I don't know what I thought. That he would do something to Madame or start a brawl, but he merely started bidding. He bought Gal for two hundred gold pieces and took her upstairs. I found out later that he thought he could talk the child into escaping, but he realized that Madame had Gal so drugged she could barely walk. He ended up stealing her away and putting her aboard ship."

Lara didn't stay for more. She grabbed up her skirts, turned on her heel, and rushed back to the cabin. Her expression was fierce when she entered. "You didn't buy her," she accused. "You rescued her."

"Dear Connie. What sweetened pap has he been feeding you?"

"Why did you let me think otherwise?"

He stood at the porthole, staring out at the sea. "Look around you. What a pleasant way for a child to grow up."

There was such self-derision in the words, Lara didn't know what to say. No words would make it prettier or cleaner or right. "It is better than what she had," she murmured.

"Is it?" He turned to her and shook his head. "She will never be like other girls. She has an uncanny intellect and can be as bookish as a scholar, but she would never survive an academy education or even a finishing school. She is a social cripple. Cast into society, she would quickly become a pariah."

"Yes," Lara agreed. "But what were her alternatives? The life of a slattern?" When he did not an-

164

swer, Lara flung her hands up. "I cannot believe I am defending you!"

Hunter smiled grimly and glanced back out at dusk blending into the horizon. "I could have taken her to someone to raise—I intended to—but we got caught up in the Battle of New Orleans, with *your* country, and the time was never right. Later she wouldn't go."

"And you would not make her."

"No."

The slow simmer of injustice began to burn in Lara's heart. "Why?"

"I think her parents abandoned her and her little brother. Gal isn't certain. She can't remember much beyond hiding the boy while she scavenged for food behind the bordello. Both were picked up by Madame. Gal had been through so much already, I couldn't bring myself to force her to do another thing."

"You coward," Lara said in quiet anger. "It was wrong to keep her, Hunter. Any number of families would have taken her in had you just tried to find one." She pressed her lips together to stop the flood of indignation but couldn't dam the flow. "You are hardly even kind to her. You punish her for clinging to you but won't send her away."

Banked fury simmered in his eyes when he looked back at her. "Do you really think me that callous?" he asked. "She had seen and done too much. She *knew* too much. No decent family would keep her more than a few days." He turned away, his shoulders tense and unyielding. "I tried three. Every time she clung to me and they had to take her by force. For nights I would hear her screams in my sleep. And every time they brought her back. I suspected Gal made certain of it, but I couldn't subject her to another *well-intentioned* family.''

"I didn't realize," Lara whispered. It was all so vile, it was still beyond her comprehension to imagine such meanness existed, even though she had just experienced it herself with John Byron. She softened her tone, a penance. "Why did you let me believe that you were responsible, that you were so despicable?"

"Am I not?" He turned back suddenly, his smile blinding, and his eyes caressed her too boldly to be excused as anything but sexual. "Don't bet on it, Lara."

The ship rose and fell comfortably as they traveled south toward the English Channel. Lara longed for Folkstone and the comfort of things familiar, but they would not be putting in at Hythe or Dover. Instead, they would dock at some port unknown to her.

Lara had talked, argued, with Hunter until she thought she would tear her hair out, all to no avail. He would have his way by any means, and those means had been to inflict guilt and blame and responsibility upon her until her head ached from trying to fight back the fear that everything he had said was true.

She could not prove that she could keep John Byron safe. Hunter, at least, had proved capable of trying.

She wandered the cabin, feeling confined and restless. It was terrifying not to have even an inkling about what the future held. John Byron played cards on the floor with Gal, fussing good-naturedly when he lost, squealing in triumph when he won. The only time over the past few days that Lara hadn't see Gal trailing Hunter like a shadow was when she was with John Byron. It was easier to see, now that Lara knew, how young a child Gal really was. Her skin, too tan by society standards, was still fresh and youthful, her small frame not yet fully developed. It had been the gutter wisdom in her eyes that had confused Lara, the look that said Gal had seen and done it all, and none of it had been pretty.

"You can't remember any of your given name?" Lara asked on impulse.

Gal's eyes stayed fixed on her cards, but her shoulders stiffened. She said nothing for the longest time, then whispered, "Anne."

Lara felt as if she'd just opened a box of explosives. What lay within could be fantastical or deadly. "Does anyone know?"

"Ollie, my little brother that died, he knew, but he called me Gal like everyone else." She never looked up but her breathing grew faster. "Will you tell *him?*"

Shocked to her toes that Gal had divulged information that even Hunter didn't know, Lara said calmly, "No, there is no reason for me to if you haven't." Her voice remained carefully neutral. "Anne is part of my name as well. It has a nice sound, though I've always found it rather boring."

Gal's brow knitted for a brief moment, then seemed to relax. Her mouth almost curved in a smile. "Not so boring as Gal."

Lara's heart softened. For all the girl's tough exterior, she was still a child inside who wanted to be recognized for herself. Undeniably, they had just bridged part of a huge gap, but Lara also sensed the silent barriers, too long erected to erase in one conversation. She wanted to reach out farther but didn't dare risk ruining in one thoughtless moment what had begun so tentatively.

Gal propped her chin on her fist and studied her cards. Her hair fell forward, cornsilk against sun-browned skin. Her features were flawless, her bone structure delicately carved. Lara wondered how anyone could have taken in this exquisite child years ago, then sent her back like discarded rubbish.

Lara's heartbeat stumbled and she squeezed her fingers into a fist. Cravenly she turned away. Her life with her own child was in such turmoil now, she didn't have the stamina to embroil herself in another's. The sound of the children's play swirled behind her, like eddies on a calm sea, but she refused to listen, hurting inside because their lives would not stay intertwined and there wasn't enough of her left right now to give two youngsters everything they needed when she could barely protect the one.

She turned back abruptly. "I'm going on deck for a stroll. Would either of you like to come?"

Gal and John Byron exchanged glances, then shook their heads and went back to their game.

Lara sighed and headed for the door. On deck she leaned her head back and let the cool air freshen her troubled spirits. The stars were brilliant overheard, the sounds of the sea below soothing. She closed her eyes and listened to the splash of waves against the hull and inhaled the salty scent deep into her lungs. There was peace here; though temporal, she would grab every second.

"This was your favorite spot."

She nodded but didn't turn. She had heard Hunter's approach but hoped he would leave her to her musings.

"The sight of you in moonlight has stayed with me all these years."

Her heartbeat quickened. "Why?"

"The way you turned your face up to drink in the breeze with your dark hair flowing down your back, you always seemed to meld with the night, as if you could become part of it. I envied that."

"You were no different," she said. "You would stand on the deck for hours doing the same."

"No. I always chased the night, tried to conquer it. There were dangers to be avoided, ships to outrun, hiding places to seek. I never could find contentment in it the way you did." His shoulder brushed hers as he moved to her side, purposefully crowding. She could move away or accept the slight intimacy. "It will all be for the best, Lara, you'll see."

The switch in topics jarred her for a moment until she realized he meant their destination. "How can I see anything when you've told me nothing?"

"Just trust me."

She gave a short laugh. "I heard those same words ten years ago."

"And you should have heeded them," he returned with a hint of ire. He cupped her chin in his palm and turned her to him. His touched burned, and she was so cold inside, but he offered nothing she could accept. "Why did you leave me?"

She snatched her face out of his hold and gripped the rail. "What else was I to do? Follow you about from port to port like Gal does, begging for crumbs of favor with a bastard child in tow?" Her breath hissed between her teeth as the pentup anger of ten years came pouring out. "You were a renegade privateer out to destroy my father. When you couldn't get him, you got me. How do you think it made me feel to find out all your sweet words had been false, meant to lure me into the trap you'd set? You used me! How long before you would have abandoned me?"

His voice was constrained, hollow. "How did you find out?"

"I overheard. . . ."

The years came pouring back, and with them all the feelings of hurt and betrayal she felt as she stepped on deck that day to see Hunter's tall lean presence overshadowing Connie's shorter stance, and Connie's accusing words as he lashed out at Hunter, "It's gone too far! You've gotten revenge on the girl's father by ruining her reputation, now let her go back to her family."

Tears had tightened her throat and her voice had been husky and unsteady when she rushed across the deck. "No, Connie!" She remembered looking back and forth between them, so frightened, so determined. "He's going to marry me; he has to."

How lamblike she must have looked to them both, how inexcusably innocent. Even now the memory of

Hunter's startled laughter and Connie's embarrassed cough left a bitter taste in her mouth.

She gripped the rail tighter, fighting hard not to feel the hatred and humiliation clawing at her, failing miserably. "Damn you, Hunter," she whispered. "You left me no pride."

He had no defense against her words. They were all true, but there was a bigger truth as well. "You left me nothing at all," he said. "You took my son and let another man claim him."

"As if you mourned him!" she scorned. "You laughed in my face. I have never been so deeply ashamed."

Hunter closed his eyes. "I was shocked by the depth of your naïveté, Lara, that you actually supposed just because you had shared a man's bed . . . had shared *mine*, a notorious privateer, that I would have to marry you." He ran his fingers through his hair without thinking, then winced at the pull in his side. "We could have settled things better, if you had not run off."

"Oh, of course," she spat in resentment. "What would you have had me do? Remain your mistress until you tired of me or until you discovered I was with child? Then what? Hide me away until John Byron was born, then turn him over to a foundling home?" Her voice trembled with fury. "Or perhaps I should have flaunted him before the world as a pirate's bastard."

Ten years sped away, swept by her fury, and she was left feeling old and tired and cold. She took two steps away from him, her voice as calm and merciless as her emotions. "How dare you judge me? You offered me nothing. I was alone; I was scared. In one blind moment of passion, I had forsaken my virtue. My own father could hardly look me in the face when I returned; all my mother could do was cry. How dare you blame me for doing whatever necessary to protect myself and my son from public disgrace?"

Her chest burned with the pain of holding back angry tears. She took a deep breath, feeling as if she would collapse from the outpouring, as if the force of her righteous anger had been the only thing supporting her all this time. But she was not that seventeen-year-old who had lost her innocence. She drew herself up straight, as regal as a queen, and said icily, "George was a good father and provider. Don't ever malign his memory or my decision again."

With that she turned and walked away. Hunter watched her go. For ten years his feelings for her had been put aside, but they rose now, ugly and undeniable. He hated her, he adored her, he lusted for her. But he had no right to go after her.

John Byron was unnaturally quiet when Lara reached the cabin. He was still sitting in the middle of the floor, thumbing through the cards, but he was alone. She bent and stroked the hair back from his face. When he looked up she saw confusion in his eyes.

"Is Gal coming back?" she asked. He shrugged and looked back down. "What is it, John Byron?" When he didn't answer, she sat in the bedside chair, then held out her arms.

He rose from the floor immediately and climbed

onto her lap. He leaned his head against her shoulder and just rested there, as if overtired. Finally he spoke. "Where's Father?"

Lara's heart twisted. He'd had so little time to adjust to George's death before Robert and Claude took him. "He's in Heaven, probably smiling down at us to see if we're having a grand adventure aboard a ship."

John Byron plucked at the ribbons on her dress, twirling the threads round and round his finger. "Mama," he whispered.

Her heart began hammering. She could feel his next statement rushing at her and didn't know how to stop it. "John—"

"Mama," he said again, "Gal says Hunter is my father. She's a silly chit, and I told her so!" He paused as if expecting a reprimand for his harsh tone, then added in a confused voice, "She said she wasn't teasing."

Fear tightened Lara's throat and made her breathing uneven. "John Byron, I—"

"I look like him, Mama. How can that be?"

Lara took a deep, furious breath, but it couldn't stabilize her thoughts into any orderly fashion.

"Because you're such a clever boy." Hunter's voice almost jolted Lara from her seat. He stepped into the room and sketched a dramatic bow. "Or perhaps you are a changeling," he added in a conspirator's tone. "Do you remember what form you took this time last year?"

John Byron smiled, bemused. "I was a boy, that's all."

But the idea had taken root, and it was easy for Hunter to tap the nine-year-old's imagination. "Are you certain? I had an albatross follow me about for a whole week at sea. The fellow sort of looked like you, now that I think of it." He tapped his temple in great thought but his eyes were devious. "And, of course, there was that shark that kept circling—"

John Byron giggled, all other concerns forgotten. "I was only me, a boy. I wasn't a shark."

"Ha! As if one could ever believe a changeling's word. They are so often in league with pixies, brownies, and fairies. They make a most unpredictable lot."

"No, I haven't been with any of those." John Byron laughed. "I can't make myself into an animal or fish."

"I see . . ." Hunter added with quiet relish. "It was the mermaid then."

"No." John Byron's eyes went round as saucers. "You saw a mermaid?"

"She had dark curly hair and—" Hunter's smile grew stiff, fixed by sheer effort. He couldn't say amethyst eyes. The likeness between father and son was already so blatant, he wouldn't long be able to brush the matter aside with teasing games, even with an innocent nine-year-old. He'd never try with an adult. "—she swam after my boat night and day, calling to me." His eyes drifted briefly to Lara. "I could never get her out of my mind."

He held out a hand, and John Byron scrambled down from his mother's lap and took it. "Let's get you tucked in, Master Changeling, before you turn into a bat and fly off through the night to escape bedtime."

The boyish laughter that followed made Lara's heart contract. How long could they carry this charade? How long before the safety Hunter provided at this moment turned into disgrace? She disregarded the tears burning behind her eyelids. The sting had become constant. She rose from the chair with a false smile and rifled through a portmanteau for her son's nightclothes.

"Perhaps a hawk," she could hear Hunter saying in the background, followed by more of her son's laugher. "Or a falcon. . . ."

She had known he would follow her on deck. Perhaps she had wanted him to. The stars mocked her overhead, twinkling their brightness as if the sleeping world were a safe and cheerful place. She sensed his presence close behind her, though she'd not heard a sound.

"Tell me what we are going to do," she said.

"I don't know exactly."

Lara sucked in a harsh breath. It was the first time she'd heard even a hint of indecisiveness in his tone. "I *can* protect him, given the chance. I wasn't prepared before."

But he could hear the underlying panic in her voice, echoes of uncertainty. "I'm not sure either of us can. Oh, I can protect him physically. Emotionally, socially . . . I don't know anymore, Lara."

She wrapped her arms about herself, needing to be held so badly, to feel safe. She could feel the heat of

175

Hunter's nearness beside her, but she wouldn't turn to him. She was halfway terrified that he would scorn her, even more afraid he would take her overtures as an amorous invitation.

On the verge of constant panic these days, she felt as if every direction she turned faced a cliff that dropped off to certain death. Buffeted by strong winds, tired of trying to keep her footing, there were times when she wanted to let go and allow herself to be hurled over the edge. But for every crisis since John Byron's birth, there had been her child to anchor her and the father who had raised him.

George had kept all hint of scandal at bay those many years ago, everything that would have hurt her or eventually hurt John Byron. Hunter, even if willing, could not protect her in that way. His very presence was a declaration of John Byron's parentage.

She would have to tell her son the truth someday before someone else did, before he realized it himself. But she could wait until later, when she was stronger, when she could find the words, when . . .

She closed her mind against the thought, but she could not shut out the fact that Hunter had moved closer. And that she craved his closeness for all the wrong reasons. Even now she could feel him reaching for her, and she could not seem to force herself to pull away. He laid his hands on her shoulders, a heavy, warm weight that pinned her in place with its promise of strength. She swayed into him, feeling weak for allowing it while knowing there was nothing of weakness that drew her. It was an all-compelling force that had been with her at seventeen.

Instead of diminishing with age, it had only matured as she had, stronger, more solid, infinitely more dangerous.

His chest was firm, his heartbeat a reassuring thump against her cheek. "Why are you doing this?" she whispered.

A shiver moved through him as the heat of her breath invaded his shirt, became a part of his skin. "Because you were about to collapse."

"No." But it was true. Her legs were unsteady still.

His hands began to move over her back, massaging, stroking, supporting, making her legs feel worse. She wanted to melt into him. She had been strong for so long, she wanted to rest, to allow his strength to uphold her. Her breasts sank into his chest, and she heard his quick breath, felt the tightening of his hands.

She sensed the motion of his lowering head before she actually felt his lips touch her brow. Then his mouth moved lower, finding hers, taking without permission what she gave too easily anyway.

"Oh . . ." It was a moan, a plea.

He absorbed the sound into his mouth and touched her gasp with his tongue. The pressure of his lips increased, marauding, too hungry suddenly. His intensity frightened her, but she so needed the human contact she didn't care. She kissed him back in desperation, striving upward to increase the contact, urgency in her motion. She hated herself for the neediness and loneliness, but if she couldn't get inside him and hide for even a small moment, she would go insane.

His fingers splayed across her lower back, pulling her in tighter as his lips slashed across hers. His breathing grew ragged, unstable, and his body had begun an undeniable rocking against hers, a timeless rhythm that mirrored only one ending.

His hand slid over her buttocks then back up, and she made a mew of protest in her throat that sounded so much like passion. His hand slid down again, bunching the fabric of her gown, slipping beneath. She cried out when he touched her bare thigh, but the objection died beneath the daring foray of his lips.

His tongue touched hers, then darted away to stroke the edges of her teeth, and she felt deprived until it returned again to dance with hers in a dueling cadence whose intent was hard to distinguish for its gentle ferocity. His fingers stroked her thigh, moving higher, sending her heart rate spiraling out of control.

"No." She gasped. She knew she mustn't allow it; it was utterly crazed, but she had no strength to push him away when she was clinging to him for support.

"Lara," he whispered darkly, and curled his hand upon her.

Her knees trembled violently, as did the arms circling his neck. Her own kisses became reckless and greedy, taking everything from him, her nails clawing like sharp talons into his shoulders.

"Not here," he whispered roughly, and swept her up and away from the open deck and bright moonlight. He didn't go far. His ribs exploded in pain, arresting every movement. An oath hissed between his teeth and he leaned back against the door jamb of a small storage closet.

Mortification flooded Lara as her sanity returned. She tried to pull away, but his hand was tangled in her skirts and he refused to let go.

"Stop," he growled, willing the pain to subside. He dropped his face into her neck, inhaling the fragrance of her hair, the sultry heat of her skin. "You make me insane," he whispered roughly with resentment. "You always have."

He kissed her again, with a fierceness that bordered on the careless. She knew he was in agony and didn't fight him when his mouth took hers or when his tongue caressed the seam of her lips time and time again. But when his palm rose to cup her breast and he began to free the buttons of her bodice, she made a cry of protest and twisted against him. His mouth dropped to her throat on a groan, and she felt the echo of his pain as a hot breath in the hollow of her shoulder and neck. Without warning, both hands lifted and shoved the edges of her bodice apart.

She made a sound, indistinguishable, as he shaped her, and another as he took her into his mouth and suckled as if starved. She could not speak further, or move. Her words were tangled in her throat in a hot, thick knot of desire that seem to trickle down to her extremities, making her weak. This was madness, sweetly honeyed and irresistible but madness. She knew well the price for abandon. His fingers slipped beneath her skirts again and found her, and she gasped out an objection. They were on deck where anyone could happen upon them, and her sense of shame was greater than her desire—but just barely. Given another moment, she would have no shame at all.

"Hunter, don't!" She gripped his sleeves and pushed back.

He countered by stroking her, making her legs tremble and her fingers bite into his arms for support. He reached behind him and opened the door to the storage closet, then stumbled inside in a turning motion that ended with Lara against the wall. His clever hands found her thighs again and she felt herself rushing headlong toward the edge of reason. The little panting sounds in her throat were muted against his lips and echoed back in deep hungry murmurs from his own throat.

Lara groaned on a hot surge of panic when she felt him release himself from his pants. "Hunter, wait—" Her words ended in a cry of despair when he pressed against her, because she wanted him so badly and hated herself for it. He moved against her, stealing her breath and the denial that tried to surface in the last seconds before everything but the feel of him was obliterated. There was no honor in the way her body moved and shifted to accept him, and no honesty in her protest as she fought for one last ounce of control.

His body rocked into hers without gentleness, frustration in each impact that bumped her into the wall as his hands bore her hips down upon his. The growling sounds in his throat vibrated to the tips of her breasts where he laved her with his tongue, and she strained up and into him, wanting more, accepting nothing.

"Lara," he grated out, "why do you fight this?"

He drew her legs up higher around his waist and would have given her all of himself in the small cramped space, would have taken anything she offered in return, but the pain of his injuries along with her objections were more relentless than his passion, making him crazed. He slashed his lips across hers, then dropped his head into the crook of her neck.

No words were spoken. There was nothing between them but a terrible hunger that had built for a decade. Neither would have chosen the small dingy closet for a tryst. It was too sordid for her, too inelegant for him. But both had been beyond their ability to stop it. Only the pain of his injuries had been strong enough to bring a measure of sense to an insane situation.

He arched his head back and laughed coldly, leaving her suspended against the wall in an agony of unfulfilled need and newly blossoming disgrace.

Chapter Ten

A frantic feeling, when we know
That what we love shall ne'er be so.

—Lord Byron

Lara felt her body being lowered to the floor, felt the bunched fabric at her waist drag down to her ankles. Hunter's body rested heavily against hers, his breathing harsh and irregular. She could still taste him on her lips, feel the sticky humidity of passion on every inch of her skin where her clothing clung. One hand was tangled in her hair at the nape, his other braced against the wall to support a portion of his weight.

The terrible moan that followed his self-derisive laughter had nothing to do with passion.

Neither of them could see in the dark, but every breath, every sound was magnified a thousand times. Lara wanted to scream at him to go away but didn't trust her voice. She hadn't even the energy to blush, so deep was her humiliation. She twisted slightly and he limped back, but she found her legs too shaky to hold her. Sliding down the wall, she sank to the floor and buried her face in her knees.

"Lara."

She heard disfavor in his voice and a faint rustling as he straightened his clothing. In the enclosed space, with the scent of their passion lingering on the air, it was all so obscene. Her clothes were askew. She could feel the night air on her breasts, cool in the spots still damp from his mouth. She folded in tighter over her knees, wanting to weep so badly she thought she would strangle on it. She knew now what she had been trying to forget for ten years, what she had been trying to ignore since he had sneaked into her bedroom a few nights ago. She was so needy around him, so susceptible to him, because she was still in love with him.

She turned her head away sharply at the hiss and flare of a striking match. Hunter lit a lantern and hung it on an overhead hook. It seemed cruel to Lara, his illuminating the small area in a dull glow that revealed everything.

At great physical expense, he crouched down and pushed her shoulders upright. He caught one look, one small destroying glance before she turned her cheek into her sleeve. Her eyes were desolate and wounded, her face etched with fear and pain. He tried to push her upright again but she had folded over her knees. He wanted her anger, deserved it, and he didn't know what to make of the frail, almost

184

frightened look he had just seen. His own defenses rose, making his voice sharp and accusing.

"Dammit, Lara, you're not a girl anymore to play the debauched innocent."

He touched her shoulder again and she shrugged him off with a violent twist of her upper torso. He hissed an oath at the streak of white-hot agony up his side. The sound registered somewhere deep inside Lara, arousing both compassion and revenge. On one level, she hoped he hurt abominably; on another, she felt pity for his suffering. He had sustained his injuries rescuing a son he'd never met, and the impact flooded her with more guilt. She quit struggling and sat back against the wall, clutching her bodice together.

"Go," she said tiredly. "Whatever you wanted to prove, you've done so. Now go."

Hunter's gritty tone bordered on sarcasm. "A bit melodramatic, aren't you?"

The words lanced through her, and she rose swiftly to her feet to face him. "God forbid that I should show even a hint of emotion after almost fornicating in a storage closet with a man I haven't seen in ten years only months after my husband's death." Her eyes burned into his, hot as her anger. "Damn you to hell."

He smiled tightly and ran one finger over the hill of her exposed breast. "I've been there, Lara. I much prefer this heaven."

Jerking back from his touch and the dulcet seduction of his words, she tried to move away, but the closet was small and cramped. She turned her back on him and fumbled with her buttons, each movement jerky and fast. "Go away," she pleaded fiercely, "or I'll show you more screaming melodrama than you've witnessed in your lifetime."

Hunter grabbed her shoulders and pinned her back against his chest, then slapped a hand over her mouth and whispered softly against her ear, "Scream and you'll bring everyone on the ship running." His fingers slid from her mouth to cup her chin, and he tilted her face up and back just enough to bring her mouth to his. "They will see your flushed cheeks and disheveled hair and wrinkled skirts. The guilt in your eyes will tell them more than the heated stain of unfulfilled desire that still covers your breasts. And everything they will think . . . I will only be able to wish it had happened."

Lara shuddered violently. The lantern swung lazily with the rolling of the ship, casting eerie shadows across his features. He looked sinister and calculating in the ghostly light, too much the pirate. She cringed when his fingers left her face to drift down her bodice, but he did nothing but finish fastening her buttons with insulting ease. He then released her and leaned back against the wall, his arms folded protectively over his chest.

His stance was casual, but Lara saw the vigilance in his eyes, brighter than the shadows of pain. And she knew what that look meant, had remembered it for a decade—the hunter after his prey.

With a cry she swung past him toward the door, but his hand slammed out to brace it shut.

"Scream, Lara," he whispered. "I'd rather have

you screaming with passion or outrage than turning into the cold shrew again." He turned quickly and pressed full length against her, trapping her against the door. "Scream until your voice is raw, but don't turn into the frigid sophisticate again. She's a liar, Lara. She has no place here."

She felt him everywhere, crushing the breath from her, making her traitorous body tremble with something more than loathing. The wooden slats of the door scraped her shoulder blades, small abrasions magnified a hundredfold. She wanted both to fling him away and curl up in his arms. As always, she was out of her element with him, and she twisted violently, seeking escape.

He ground his teeth against the impact and dropped his head into the curve of her neck and shoulder. His teeth scraped along the slender column of her throat. "She was a stranger, untouchable and unreachable. This is the Lara I remember."

She sobered immediately and went limp against the door. Her breathing was staggered and angry, but her eyes were tragically wounded. "You knew nothing about her," she whispered. "She was just a young girl, with too high an opinion of herself. She only played at being a woman."

He pulled back and brushed the hair from her forehead, then gently laid his palm along her cheek. "She was brave and rebellious and passionate."

Lara turned her face away. "She was innocent."

"Yes," he whispered, "but you are not."

His thumb stroked the high slope of her cheekbone, but she felt him everywhere else—in the thunder of her heartbeat, the jangled nerve endings along her sensitive skin, the tender awareness of her body.

"Don't make this out to be something worse than it is, Lara."

She gave a short, painful laugh. "I am neither your wife nor fiancée nor even your mistress. I bore you a bastard son and pawned him off as another's. How could I do worse than to repeat my mistakes?"

She dropped her head back against the door, hating him, hating herself. There was such a clamoring inside her, a sense of things unfinished, and everywhere the shame of her wanting burned. His arms fell away, but perversely she felt almost abandoned when he stepped back. With shaking hands, she smoothed her dress and hair, then turned and opened the door.

She walked out, but after only two steps, she paused and turned back. "What do you want from me?" she demanded desperately.

His expression was fathomless in the moonlight. "Everything."

She washed and changed her gown, trying to rid herself of the telling man-scent that clung to her. Crawling into bed beside John Byron, she cradled him close, angry and apprehensive. She didn't know how long she could be around Hunter without going mad. Like a pawn in a game of refined wickedness, she neither understood the rules nor the goals. She was caught between two complex factions where John Byron was the prize and she was little more than a necessary complication to both sides.

One thing became clear in the predawn hours. She would have to come to some suitable agreement with George's brothers and make certain they never had a reason to come after her child again. Her life, at least her sanity, depended on it.

John Byron sighed in his sleep and she brushed the curls back from his face and pressed her cheek to his. The warmth of his skin was familiar, his fresh-scrubbed scent so dear after the long absence. She wanted for him the things all mothers wished for their children—comfort and security, education and social standing—but it would be enough now to lead a simple, uncomplicated life as long as she could keep him safe.

The ship docked well after dawn. Lara watched the bustle of activity from the cabin window. The thought of going on deck and facing Hunter was intolerable.

It was full daylight, a beautiful and unusually clear morning. Sunlight glinted off the water in silvery ripples, so bright it hurt her eyes. She put a hand to her brow to shield her from the glare and searched the docks for a clue to where they had put in.

"You can't hide here all day."

She didn't turn from the window. "Where are we?"

"Winchelsea."

She made a small ironic face. "A smuggler's port. How appropriate."

"Would you have preferred London?"

Her cheeks reddened but her voice was controlled.

"I would have preferred Hythe. This is much too far from Folkstone."

"I know."

Confused, she looked back at him for explanation, but he was already departing the room. "Have you rescued John Byron only to put him back in peril? You cannot dismiss this—"

"I already have," he warned in a frosty voice that stopped her cold. "Prepare to disembark, Lara. Connie has John Byron now and will bring him to you. If you care for the child's safety, don't allow him to leave your side for any reason once we're on shore. Is that clear?"

"Yes," she whispered. His tone was so forbidding, his face tense and unreadable. She realized that his casualness was an outward appearance only. Inside, he was alert and aware, and it frightened her that he might be worried when he was always so confident and self-assured. She grabbed up her skirt and raced after him. "What has happened?"

He paused on his way through the door and looked back over his shoulder. "Nothing yet. I want to make certain things stay that way." He departed the room, leaving Lara with a terrible sense of foreboding that he knew something she didn't.

John Byron rushed in with Gal in tow. Connie poked his head around the door frame and grinned. "I'll be back for the urchins in a moment, if you can survive them that long."

Lara smiled and nodded, then turned to find John Byron flopped belly down on the floor. He pulled a deck of cards from his pocket. "Look, Mama, Gal can do tricks. Do the one about the kings."

Gal dutifully knelt beside him and began shuffling. John Byron watched, fascinated, as her nimble fingers sorted and rearranged the cards faster than his eyes could follow. "The ship is docking. Where are we?" he murmured, but was so preoccupied with Gal's adroitness he didn't wait for an answer. "Do that one again."

Gal glanced up at Lara, an odd expression on her face. She looked back at John Byron and shook her head. "I gotta go get my things ready." She handed him the cards, then stood. "Wait till you meet Nicolette. She's so beautiful it'll make your eyes smart." She dashed off before either could ask questions.

Lara took the cards and packed them away, then sat down and pulled John Byron onto her lap. His legs were getting too long to curl up against her, so she let them dangle over the arm of the chair. He didn't fit as well as he had only a year earlier. In another twelve months he might not fit comfortably on her lap at all.

Time passed so fast. She'd lost three whole months with him to those monsters, and she didn't know how long before their life would return to any sort of normalcy. She feathered her fingers through his hair and spoke as soothingly as she dared and still make him understand.

"I don't know exactly where Hunter is taking us," she began, "but it will be some place where I can keep you safe until we get back to Folkstone. I'll never let your uncles near you again, or anyone else who could take you from me."

He nodded and cinched his arms tighter around her neck. "Will Gal come, and Weasel and Connie?"

"Yes, I think so."

"I'm glad, but I want to go home too and see Barrows and the hounds and my toys. But I don't want my uncles to find me."

Lara's heart contracted, and she pulled him in tighter. "We will return to Folkstone soon, I promise, but for now we must be very cautious. Your uncles are madmen, but Hunter and I will see to it that they never come near you again."

"I'm not afraid, Mama. Hunter said he would feed them to the vultures if they even try to speak to me."

Lara shivered at the bloodthirsty fierceness in her son's tone, but she wanted him to feel the confidence and assurance she couldn't find yet. "Did he? Well, your nasty uncles had better beware then."

"And Gal has a dagger with beautiful stones in the hilt. She said she would split their gullets and throw their entrails to the sharks."

Lara stifled the urge to reprimand his distasteful language. "Good for Gal," she said instead, "but I don't think the sharks would have them."

John Byron giggled, which lightened Lara's mood immensely. She would see him playing freely again, but where and how soon?

She stroked his dark hair back off his forehead and tipped his face up. "Wherever we are going," she said softly but firmly, "I want you to remember to stay near me at all times. Until we arrive at our destination, do not let go of my hand, even if it embarrasses you."

"I know," he said tiredly. "Hunter already told me." He gazed up into her eyes, as if seeking reassurance, then suddenly tightened his hold. "I *am* brave, Mama, but I don't want to leave the ship."

She hugged him close, her heart near to shattering. "I know it feels safe here, but wherever Hunter takes us will feel safe too." She believed her own words, at least where John Byron was concerned. For herself she wasn't certain what the future held. Constant close proximity to Hunter was inconceivable.

"Mama? Why *do* I look like him?"

The question threw her. Lara forced herself not to tense up and spoke lightly. "So many people in the world look alike, John Byron. It's in our heritage, our ancestry. We are all descended from Adam and Eve, are we not? So it stands to reason that many times over we will find people in life whom we resemble."

He nodded, satisfied. "Gal says we must be nice to Nicolette."

Lara's fingers stilled in his curls. "Oh?"

John Byron shrugged. "Gal says I will like her."

Lara's heart did something horrid and unforgivable. It thumped twice with jealousy. "Well," she attempted brightly, "perhaps she is a valued servant."

His brow knitted. "No. Gal says Hunter always brings her gifts. We don't give our servants gifts when we travel."

Lara lay her head on the crown of her son's. She could hardly get the words past her throat. "Perhaps she is Hunter's wife."

"Perhaps," he agreed. He tilted his face up and gave her a sad look. "I miss Papa."

"Me too," she whispered, kissing his forehead, drowning in blame. She felt nauseous at the thought that Hunter might be married. It compounded her own guilt over what they had almost done the night before. The pirate she had known was capable of anything, but what of the man he had become? She didn't know if he was a man who would honor or forsake marriage vows, but she knew herself, and she had no right to cast stones. The intimacy she had allowed with him touched not only her self-worth and knowledge of right and wrong but also George's memory. Her husband had barely been gone three months and already she'd behaved so disreputably. Weak and foolish and outrageous, as if her anchor of stability had been removed.

Nine years of caution and care, nine years of maintaining the strictest control over her life had yielded this? A few tawdry minutes in a storage closet as if she were nothing better than the slatterns who plied their wares on London's meanest streets? Her throat tightened, but she would not cry, not over this. She would not give Hunter that much place in her life.

Gowned in dove-gray taffeta with a fall of lace at her elbows, Lara donned a matching wide-brimmed bonnet to conceal her features when they were called to the deck. There was little she could do to hide her son's looks, but a beribboned straw hat covered most of his curls and shadowed his face. He looked like any well-dressed child of his age in a bobtailed coat and knee breeches. Only someone expressly looking for the fifth Earl of Folkstone would be able to single him out.

Lara grasped his hand tightly as they crossed the deck and neared the gangplank. Connie led the way in front while Weasel took up the rear. Gal was nowhere in sight, but Lara sensed her presence as surely as if Gal trailed alongside them. An uneasiness hovered about her, ever-increasing the closer they drew to land. Lara wished suddenly that Hunter had taken them to America where she could hide John Byron indefinitely, at least until the trauma of the past few months had waned and she could think more clearly, plan more decisively. But running away would solve nothing in the long run.

John Byron tugged on his hand and she realized she was squeezing too tight. She murmured an apology and relaxed her grip enough for comfort, but just barely. The docks ahead were crowded, teeming with workers. Everywhere brawny men hefted crates to their shoulders, the muscles in their arms and thighs bulging with the strain. Younger, lankier youths rolled rope and ran errands, their language already showy and ribald in an effort to emulate or outdo the seasoned workers. Peasants pushed overfull carts along the waterfront, hawking their wares in voices pitched high to carry over the din.

The crush of humanity was intimidating—too many strange faces, too many chances for error. John Byron felt it too and pressed against Lara's legs while tightening his hold on her hand. Surrounded, Lara felt both smothered and secure. She strained to catch a glimpse of anyone familiar, but the faces of laborers and pedestrians milling about were unknown to her.

"Ready?" It was Connie offering his arm as escort.

Lara nodded and accepted. "Where are we going?" she asked.

"Now, Lady Chalmers." He clicked his tongue, as fussily as a maiden aunt.

Lara managed a smile. "Faithful to the last," she murmured. "Have you ever done anything that was against his will or want?"

"I am my own man," Connie answered, "be assured of that. But I owe my life to him on more than one occasion, and you'll never see me turn my back on him or betray him like so many have."

Lara wondered if he implicated her in that list. As they neared the end of the plank, her nervousness rose with each step that brought her closer to the teeming crowd. Connie continued forward without regard for the fact that Hunter was nowhere in sight. Lara followed in great trepidation, not knowing what else to do. She glanced frantically behind her to make certain Weasel was still in place, only to find him darting off into the crowd. She turned back to alert Connie only to find him gone as well. Her pulse beat quickened and she clutched John Byron's hand so tight he protested.

People jostled her from all sides, and the smell of unclean bodies and decaying fish was oppressive in the damp heat. She remembered George's funeral, the sweltering heat of a midday sun beating down upon her veiled head, the cloying smell of wilting flowers, John Byron's hand slipping from her numb one as Claude called to him.

She searched around frantically for recognizable faces, expecting her son to be snatched away at any moment. She pulled him into her skirts and prepared to retrace her steps back up the gangplank when the sounds and movements in a small sphere around her seemed to still. An elegantly garbed figure passed through the crowd. Lara blinked as Hunter stepped up and made a slight bow before mother and son, but he no longer resembled a pirate or seaman.

Dressed in fashionable trousers and dress coat, his bearing was regal, exuding wealth and good taste. Just like the night he stole into Folkstone, he could have walked into any English parlor or gentlemen's club and not have his right to be there questioned. Even his manner was properly dignified when he offered his arm for escort, but when Lara turned her stunned gaze to meet his eyes she found just the barest hint of ridicule in the amethyst depths.

She gave a false, engaging smile for any who might be watching as she took his arm. "Do you mock me?" she said under her breath.

"No, my dear. I mock us all." His gaze strayed to the generous expanse of bosom revealed above her gown. "You look quite lovely this morning. Ravishing."

A perfected British accent rolled from his tongue with ease, startling her further. "As do you," she returned in her most cheerfully counterfeit tone. Her eyes flashed with good humor for the populous and underlying malice for him. "Now, if we may dispense with the civilities," she said, "where are we going?"

"In due time, Lara." He escorted her through the crowd until he reached a black lacquered carriage whose door already stood open. He nodded at the coachman standing beside it. "Home, Stevens."

Chapter Eleven

The vehicle was a luxurious combination of velvet-lined walls, leather upholstery, and brass fittings. But by the time Lara had been traveling in it for twelve hours with only brief stops for the necessities, she was tired, sore to the bone, and at her wit's end.

She glared at Hunter. "I simply cannot understand why you won't tell me where we are going."

He sat across from her, head back and eyes closed, arms crossed over his chest. "You might flee at the next stop if you knew." His legs were sprawled at awkward angles to accommodate their long length, and he shifted to ease his cramped muscles. "Patience, Lara."

"Oh, that's well and good for you to say." She sighed in frustration. *"You* know where we are going." She crossed her own arms over her chest and wilted back against the seat. She had found it more than difficult spending the day cooped up inside the rocking carriage with nothing to stare at but

Hunter's too-beautiful face and physique and her son's obvious enthrallment with him.

Fatherhood was not a word she could associate with Hunter in any corporeal or cerebral manner, but John Byron had tailed him like a shadow on their infrequent stops and Hunter had managed to carry out particular duties over the long day, no matter how distasteful, with a certain grace if not good humor. John Byron was now curled up on the plush seat, his head in Hunter's lap.

Lara glanced away from her son's sleeping form. With George gone, John Byron had no manly influence to emulate, no one to lead him toward adulthood. It frightened her that he trusted Hunter so completely, for the time would come when she would take John Byron back home.

Anxiety curled through her. She wasn't at all certain to what she would return. A home with guards instead of gardeners, a prison instead of a haven. These newfound friendships her son had forged just after the loss of his father would be severed, hurting and disappointing him further.

She pushed the curtain aside and stared out at the countryside. "Birmingham?" she queried.

Though he never opened his eyes or regarded her in any way, the corner of Hunter's mouth turned up slightly.

"Ah! It is Birmingham." She sat back, pleased and satisfied with herself until he rolled his head back and forth. "Kent?" she added in mild pique.

John Byron stirred restlessly and she reached over to stroke his cheek in a gesture that had soothed him since infancy. Hunter reached down at the same time and their hands collided in a gentle tangle of flesh and misguided intentions. Lara pulled back first, startled by the charge that passed between them in so simple a gesture. She clutched her hands together and sat back. Hunter seemed so unaffected, she wondered if it were only her. Was she so beset with loneliness that she conjured these impulses? She had never approved or understood the more brazen widows with their titillating innuendos and indelicate talk, but she wondered now if she were becoming like them, flustered as a schoolgirl over nothing but a touch.

She turned her thoughts to her son, but his father captured her attention away from even that attempt at diversion. *Father.* The word echoed in her mind, taunting. Lara tried to dismiss it. George had been the only real father John Byron had ever known. Hunter may have provided the biology to give John Byron life, but he would soon return to his own country, his own life, just as she and John Byron would return to theirs. There was no question of her son ever learning the truth, at least not in childhood. It would only hurt and confuse him, and it certainly had the potential to ruin his chances for a decent future.

Lara sighed inwardly. If she could just come to some agreement with George's brothers and get back to Folkstone, everything would be all right. The future would settle itself. Perhaps not as comfortably as she had hoped, but it would be acceptable. It had to be. She studied John Byron's young face, so innocent in repose. Neither she nor George had ever meant to hurt him with their lies, only protect him. *Protect themselves*. Her mouth pressed into a grim line. Yes, protect their reputations as well, but not at the expense of John Byron.

She leaned her head back, lulled by the rocking sway of the carriage. Nothing would hurt her son again; she would see to it. Whatever she had to do, whatever bargain she had to make with Robert and Claude, she would allow no harm nor hint of scandal to befall John Byron again. Her gaze drifted to Hunter's strong features, and she knew for her son's sake, she must get John Byron away from him as soon as possible.

"What are you plotting, Lara?"

She jumped in guilty reflex and looked away. "How best to go about thwarting you."

He chuckled lightly. "You do that by your mere existence." The carriage slowed, then rocked to a full stop. "We're here, I believe."

Lara threw back the small curtain and peered out into the early-evening gloom. A two-story public dwelling sat back from the road, a welcome lantern hanging from its porch. "A roadside inn?" she asked, aghast. "We've traveled all this way to stay at a roadside inn?"

"Don't be snobbish," Hunter replied.

Concern stiffened her features. "You know that's not what I meant. This is a public place; people will see us—" Tears seriously threatened the composure she was trying to maintain, so she kept her peace when the coachman stepped up to open the door. She stretched gingerly, wincing at the cramped muscles in her back and legs. She leaned over and shook her son lightly. "John Byron."

A moment of confusion and fear crossed his young face upon waking. He blinked and sat up quickly, searching the interior of the carriage frantically to establish his safety. It took only seconds for him to note his surroundings and scramble with relief into his mother's arms, but Lara never wanted to see that look of terror again.

She smiled in reassurance and straightened his rumpled clothes. "Come along, we've stopped for the night."

The inn was cozy and decent. They were greeted with warm enthusiasm by the innkeeper's wife, who bustled about like a plump hen situating everyone to her own inner sense of comfort without so much as consulting the guests themselves. With her rosy-cheeked smile and good-hearted intentions, it was impossible to take offense at being herded around like wayward chicks.

They were ushered over to a long table near the hearth where a low fire burned the chill and dampness from their corner of the room. Lara had only a moment's pause when the jolly woman referred to Hunter as her husband, but the pressure of his hand on her shoulder warned her to keep peace over the mistake.

"Sit," the innkeeper's wife ordered. "Platters will be out shortly and yer rooms will be ready when yer done." With that the woman flounced off to cheerfully boss her next group of customers.

A steaming assortment of breads, mutton, and vegetables were set before them along with pitchers of ale. A cup of milk was brought out for John Byron, and Hunter ordered another for Gal, which she accepted only under protest. It was common fare and bland to the taste, but it provided everything the weary travelers needed after the long, tedious journey.

John Byron nodded off even before he was finished. Gal stood up, yawning gracelessly herself, and mumbled, "I'll take him up."

Connie followed. "I'm done in too. G'night, all."

Weasel, who had long since finished eating, stared moodily into the fire. Lara had never seen him so still. He was an odd little man, nearly irritating at times, but she would forever be indebted to him for her son's life. The quietude was so unlike him, she reached out and touched his arm. He turned his head and gave her a wide grin.

"Pretty lady," he slurred.

Lara realized he was quite into his cups and not suffering melancholia at all. She smiled in spite of herself at the foolish look on his face and stood. "I believe I shall retire also."

Hunter rose and offered his arm. "Shall I escort you up?"

Lara found only polite regard in his expression. If irony was there, it was well concealed.

Her room was small and simple but clean. The only accommodations were a bed covered with a lovely homespun counterpane, a wardrobe on the opposite wall, and a washstand in a corner near the window.

Neither a chair nor footstool had been added. It was a room meant only for passing the night, not housing boarders. At a sound, Lara stilled her examination of the room and turned slowly to find that Hunter had shut and locked the door.

He leaned back negligently against the frame, absently massaging his ribs. "We've been put together. An honest mistake."

Lara kept her voice level. "Where is John Byron?"

"With Gal. Connie and Weasel are on one side, we are on the other."

Her entire body flushed. "You are impertinent to make such arrangements."

"I didn't make them, Lara, though I don't mind taking advantage of them."

"I want John Byron in my room."

Hunter nodded and pushed off the door. "I'll get him." But he didn't leave the room. Instead, he approached her, closing the distance between them with unhurried grace, sleekly powerful even in travel-weary attire.

Lara backed up until her thighs bumped the edge of the bed. "I . . . what are you doing?"

Hunter smiled softly, sweetly, but there was something dark and intense beneath the superficial perfection of that smile. "Nothing you have to be concerned about," he said, "not a seduction. I'm in no shape to try that again." When he was no more than a breath away, he reached up and stroked her hair, purposefully scattering pins until it fell in shiny waves to her waist. He smoothed his hand down the heavy curls with light, soothing sweeps of his palm.

Lara ducked her head to the side but he only cupped her chin firmly and tilted her face up. "Don't," she commanded, and tried to shrug him off.

"What are you afraid of, Lara?"

"You . . . this. You said you would get John Byron," she evaded, before his fingers slid around to her back and began slipping the hooks of her gown free. "What are you doing?" There was no composure in her voice now, but censure mingled with outrage as she tried to twist out of his reach.

"Wait." He stilled her with nothing but a grip on her upper arms. "You've nothing to fear from me. I swear it." He would prove he was no longer the pirate, if not to her then to himself. He pulled her to him and held her there with one hand, while the other resumed work on her buttons.

She twisted and pushed against him, which only brought a sound of deep satisfaction from his throat and that unholy smile to his lips. She could feel her gown going slack on her shoulders. "Stop it," she warned. "I'll . . ."

"Yes?" he whispered, bringing his lips so close that her next protest was against his mouth. "What will you do, Lara? Scream? Call for help?" His teeth captured her bottom lip. "How will you explain?"

Frustration sharpened her tone. "What do you intend?"

He backed up slightly. "I told you. Nothing you have to fear." He trailed one finger over the exposed flesh of her shoulder, then looked back into her eyes. "*I'm* not the one you have to be afraid of, Lara. I never have been."

Hot color scored her cheeks at the implication. She pushed away from him only to have her gown droop to her waist. She grappled with the falling fabric and bunched it at her middle. "Get out."

He smiled irreverently. "No. You'll have to abide my company a while longer. I want to show you something." He pointed at her gown. "Take that off . . . don't look so offended, I've seen you in less. And the petticoats too."

She actually gaped. "Are you mad?"

He shrugged. "More than likely. Come, we haven't got all night. I'm tired unto death, Lara. If you want to enjoy this, you'd better hurry." The look on her face was so outraged and comical, he could hardly contain his own expressionless demeanor. He crossed to her while she stood in shocked stupor and tugged the gown down to her ankles. "Now, the petticoats if you please; you may leave the chemise on. Less than that and we won't have to worry about *your* lack of control, I might not be able to maintain my own."

She stepped over the puddle of her clothing and snatched the gown back up for modesty. "You *are* mad," she accused, feeling exposed and foolish in nothing but her dainty shoes and undergarments. She tried to put as much distance between them as possible but found she had precious little space in which to maneuver.

Hunter waited until she inadvertently trapped herself between him and the bed. She was a stunning sight, all flustered and wary and more beautiful than any woman he had ever known. He had second thoughts about what he was doing, then dismissed the insecurity and caught her up in one quick lunge, cursing vilely at the pain that tore through his side. He placed her on the bed, holding her with one arm and his own ribs with the other. He made no other advance, just sat beside her and waited for the pain to subside.

More curious than frightened now, Lara eyed him suspiciously, but there was simply nothing in his expression to cause alarm, no anger or unchecked passion or anything else recognizable. "What do you want?"

His expression changed, a subtle shift full of shadowy secrets. The pain faded gradually, leaving an intense honesty she'd never seen before. "I want one night with you, Lara," he said softly. "No past, no future. One night clean, free from fear and blame and repercussions. Free even from sin." His eyes darkened. "Tomorrow . . . everything will change tomorrow."

The words were final and underscored with resignation and the faintest hint of despair. Coming from Hunter, the effect was devastating. "You . . . you are frightening me."

He smiled suddenly, brilliantly. "One night then to not be afraid." He took her hand and pulled her forward, onto her knees. "Hush," he warned when she would have protested. He turned her until her back faced him and put his hands onto her shoulders. "Relax."

His thumbs began slow, methodical circles on her back, digging into her flesh with the most wonderful pressure. Her head tilted back slightly. "I don't understand."

"Just feel." His thumbs continued their lulling rhythm, circling round and round, up her neck to the base of her scalp and slowly down the sides of each vertebra of her spine. Tension drained from her with each continuous rotation until her entire body felt limp.

"Here, lie down."

She was insane to stretch out on a bed in little clothing with Hunter in the room. But she did it and gladly as his fingers began working over her shoulders and back, massaging each muscle thoroughly, kneading with the most exquisite gentleness.

"Why are you doing this?"

His hands were so clever as they massaged each silken inch, worked slowly down to the small of her back. She wanted to protest when the tips of his fingers dug into her hips, but she was too afraid he would stop. She bit her tongue and chanced what he would do next.

"Don't tense up," he said, and continued the wondrous motion over her buttocks to her legs.

She blushed three shades of pink as his fingers plied her thigh with the same soothing motion, working each muscle as if it were the most important. Over knee and calf, ankle and foot, no inch went untouched by his skillful fingers.

When he reached her back again, he said softly, "Turn over."

"Oh." It was a moan of despair. She knew it would be completely asinine to roll over and expose herself to his eyes and hands. Her body was completely placid, wallowing happily in the luxury of his massage. She'd never felt anything like this in her life and she was likely never to again. "Hunter . . ."

"Chance it, Lara."

She rolled over quickly before good sense intruded. He smiled. "How daring."

She made a face. "Where did you learn to do this?"

"You don't want to know."

But she did, in a way. In another she wanted nothing but the touch of his hands as they went to her shoulders and began kneading the muscles there, his thumbs caressing the creamy skin over her collarbone. "Have you done this before?"

"What would you have me answer?" His hands worked down her arms to her fingers, where he stroked each one individually.

"The truth."

"Yes."

Lara's eyes drifted open, aggravated.

"Ah. Not really the truth. A lie that sounded like the truth would have been better." He cupped her cheeks, that intense expression on his face, and Lara thought if he kissed her now, everything would be ruined. Laughter lurked in his eyes and she realized he knew what she was thinking.

His fingers began massaging her facial muscles just as they had the rest of her, until her eyes fluttered closed again in sublime rapture. Across the bridge of her nose, the slope of her cheeks, her temples—his fingers had the power to erase months of anxiety and strain.

Lara moaned as his hands moved across her scalp the tiniest inch at a time, making certain no space was left untouched. She began drifting and fought to stay awake. It would be unforgivable to miss one second of such pleasure.

"Why are you doing this?" she whispered.

"Why not?"

"It is decadent."

"Is it?"

She mulled it over dreamily as his fingers massaged her temples. "Yes, I think it is."

"Do you want me to stop?"

A puff of cynical laughter answered him. "I need to tell John Byron good night," she murmured.

"But you don't want me to stop." His dexterous hands drifted back down to her neck and shoulders, stroking the firm skin perfectly, luxuriously, then down further to her bodice. Lara sucked in a strained breath when his palms covered her breasts and he continued the rotation of unceasing motion.

"Don't . . ." How witless she sounded, especially with her back arching up into him like an alley cat's. She grabbed his wrist but he was already moving lower in a gentle gliding motion to her midriff. One rib at a time, he worked his way to her stomach where his hand flattened over her belly, fingers splayed. Then lower still.

Lara reared up, all the lovely feelings shattered.

Hunter lifted both hands and stepped back. "I'm done."

"Oh." Lara kept the vast disappointment out of her voice and rolled onto her side, away from him. The

heat in her body was tangible evidence of her susceptibility. "Why did you do all that?"

Hunter stared at the sweet curve of her back, the
slight dip in her waist, the rounded hill of her hip.
"To prove that every touch between us doesn't have
to be lascivious."

But in the end, he would have taken her if she
hadn't risen up so offended, if his ribs weren't aching
so badly, if it wouldn't have made a complete liar out
of him.

In the end, he had proven nothing and they both
knew it. He was still the pirate, heart and soul and
desire.

"I'll go get John Byron."

"No." Lara rolled over quickly, desperate to understand. "Why is it this way between us? Why must we
either be at each other's throats or . . . worse?" She
could not say the darker words aloud. Even with
George, the husband she had loved and respected,
there had never been this insatiable clamoring inside
her. "Why can we never be merely civil?"

"I don't know," Hunter answer honestly. He
turned and walked to the door.

"Wait," she demanded.

He paused and looked back, something akin to regret in his eyes. "If I stay, I'll have you again, Lara.
You should know that."

Silent and wanting, they regarded each other
across the room. She dared not say a word to stay
him.

* * *

STOLEN DREAMS

Lara watched the countryside roll by and felt a vague familiarity begin to seep into her consciousness. Though she did not recall ever traveling this particular road, she felt a sense of acquaintance with the surrounding area and knew she must be going toward somewhere she'd been before, perhaps from a different direction. The horses rounded a sharp curve and she knew her intuition had been right.

High, walled gates made of stone and iron appeared. As they had for centuries, guards stood their posts on either side of the scrolled ironwork entrance and swung the gates wide when the carriage drew near. A castle loomed in the distance, its crenelated turrets magnificent against the azure sky. The horses clattered over a wooden bridge and passed into the inner countryside of Ravenwood.

The manicured grounds were stunning and seemed to stretch forever before the road finally wound itself to the front entrance. The standard of the lion and raven flew high atop the west turret, signifying the duke was in residence. Lara gripped John Byron's hand and cut Hunter a condemning stare mingled with guilt.

"You've made a grave mistake coming here," she said. "I've not had time to arrange things."

A footman dressed in crimson and silver livery opened the carriage door.

Hunter's expression was bland, his voice coolly politic. "Alight, Lara. We will discuss everything at a more opportune time." He turned to John Byron. "Come, let us see what mischief we can be about."

John Byron smiled and scrambled out. Lara

paused only a second then followed, but her world
felt frighteningly out of kilter, as if she'd allowed everything to run amiss and didn't quite know how to
gather it all back into place. She allowed the groom
to hand her down and watched Hunter and her son
cross the bricked courtyard, one tall, dark, and forbidding, the other small, dark, and trusting.

She wondered what her penalty would be for the
small deception. If Hunter thought he had come to
claim the reward for knowledge of the locket, he
would be sorely disappointed. She hadn't even been
certain she would locate him after all these years,
much less petitioned the estate managers yet about
offering monetary recompense for return of the jewelry.

"Hunter," she pleaded softly as they approached
the entrance. "We must talk."

"At my leisure," he returned, then mounted the
steps to the huge carved doors.

They opened almost immediately. A steward stood
in the entrance, imposingly tall and reed thin with a
shock of white hair that seemed want to grow in spi-
rals. He offered a deep, respectful bow and said in a
well modulated voice, "Welcome home, Your Grace."

Lara's eyes flared at Hunter, but he was already
entering the castle with John Byron in tow. She
rushed up behind him in time to hear him order
smoothly, "Assemble the staff, Jacobs. I wish to present my son."

The earth tilted. Lara felt it fall away swiftly, as if
she were suddenly caught up in a fast-spinning

dream. Hazy white nothingness clouded her eyes, then there was nothing at all.

Lara's collapse flung everyone into motion. John Byron cried out and rushed to her, stumbling over his own feet in his haste. He skinned both knees and palms on the polished stone entry but paid the sting little mind as he knelt at his mother's side.

"It's just the heat and travel," Hunter said calmly, as he examined Lara for injury. Her face was deathly pale and a small bump was already forming on her left temple where she must have struck her head. He slipped an arm beneath her neck and knees and lifted.

"Shall I get the physician, Your Grace?" Jacobs asked.

Hunter shook his head. "I think she's just fainted from exhaustion. Have Mary bring ice and bandaging to the Rose Room." He glanced down at John Byron's terrified face. "Come, help me get her settled."

He crossed the great hall with as much haste as he dared. The injury at Lara's temple was turning a nasty shade of blue-purple but didn't seem to be swelling overmuch. It had been cruel to shock her so, but his staff had not been chosen for stupidity, and any one of them with mediocre eyesight would know at once that John Byron was his offspring. He had wanted to still all tongue wagging before it had the chance to spread beyond Ravenwood. The truth, liberally altered, would have served to temper the tale-telling to a manageable level.

He took the stairs, then veered left at the top down

a short corridor and almost collided with the upstairs maid.

She gasped and bobbed a quick curtsey. "Beg pardon, Your Grace. May I be of assistance?"

"Turn back the bedding in the Rose Room," he requested, "then see if Cook will send up refreshments for our young charge here."

She bobbed again and hurried off to do his bidding. If she thought it odd that the Duke of Ravenwood carried an unconscious lady toward his bedroom with a child of striking resemblance on his heels, it was no concern of hers. Let it never be said that Lydia Crumb was a gossipmonger. She flung open the door to the master suite, crossed the room in a thrice, pushed back the bed draperies, and pulled the covers aside. Beaming with the pride of her profession, she nodded and stepped back. "All's ready, Your Grace."

"The *Rose* Room," Hunter repeated.

Lydia turned three shades of red. "Of course! I don't know what I were thinking!" She dashed into the adjoining antechamber and repeated the entire process with much less flourish. The smaller connecting room was intended to house a valet—which the present Duke of Ravenwood never kept in residence —and served as guest quarters instead, which were seldom used. With four elaborate suites and many smaller bedchambers, there was little need for the room at all. But Lydia Crumb wasn't about to comment upon it.

Neither was it her place to speculate on the lovely young woman being lain gently upon the linen sheets, but Lydia did have a tendency toward curiosity that her mama always swore would get her in trouble. She watched with avid fascination as the duke placed the lady on the high bed, then scooped the child up and sat him at the foot.

"Keep watch," Hunter said as he settled John Byron. He smoothed back Lara's hair from her face, then glanced over his shoulder to find Mary entering with the tray. He took it and placed it on the bedside table. "I'll see to this," he said. "Gal and Connie will be along shortly. Have their rooms prepared and ask Cook to serve an early dinner." He dipped a cloth in icy water and laid it on Lara's forehead, then glanced back at Mary. "Tell Jacobs we won't be assembling the staff this evening after all."

"Yes, Your Grace," Mary said quietly. She paused, not wanting to overstep her boundaries. "Your Grace?" Hunter made an impatient sound and she finished discreetly, "Miss Nicolette saw the carriage. She'll be asking . . ."

His expression softened in pained exasperation. "She wasn't due to arrive for another month." Mary gave him a helpless look, and he almost smiled. "Send her up." He freshened the cloth and placed it back on Lara's forehead. "Oh, and . . . ?" He looked around to see who was still present.

"Lydia," the upstairs maid supplied.

"Yes, Lydia." He emphasized her name as if committing it to memory. "Have a cot brought in for young John here."

"Yes, Your Grace." She nodded politely at the child, pitying the bright relief on the youngster's face.

In her own small cottage in the village, there was no question of a child being shipped off to the nursery or separate quarters. Parents stayed with their young, often in the same cramped rooms. But that wasn't the way of things in large estates. Nannies, governesses, and tutors did the raising, while parents did the doting.

Though Lydia coveted the luxury and grandness of Ravenwood like any girl of her station would, she knew a high personal price also went with such. The lifestyle of the gentry was cold and superficial and, all too often, desperately lonely. She could count on one hand the times over the past five years since His Grace had returned to take control of Ravenwood when she'd actually seen him entertain personal guests.

There were balls and soirees and hunting parties, but he had a secretary who handled all the arrangements. No one doubted that he must have a beautiful mistress tucked away somewhere—he had Nicolette, after all—but he never brought one to Ravenwood. In fact, he was so seldom in residence, Lydia wondered why he bothered to entertain at all.

It wouldn't do to overtax her mind with his odd ways when she had so much else to do. She gave John Byron a warm smile. "I'll have you a nice bed brought up right away. Is there anything else you'd like?"

He shook his head and gave his attention back over to his mother's pale face. "Mama?" he whispered.

"She'll be all right," Hunter replied. "She's stirring now, see?" He moved back a space so John Byron could get an unobstructed view. "She'll have a headache though, so let's keep our voices low." He dipped the cloth in cool water again and placed it back on Lara's brow. "Try not to move," he warned when she began turning fretfully.

She moaned at the pain stabbing her skull and reached up to find the source.

Hunter grabbed her fingers. "Lara, you've had a fall and hurt your head. Be still."

She blinked to focus but the world remained murky. Shadow images swam before her eyes and her head pounded like a thousand hammers. She recognized Hunter's voice but didn't recall her whereabouts. "Did I faint?"

"Yes. And hit your head. Are you in pain anywhere else?"

She didn't think so, but her headache overshadowed everything else at the moment except concern for her son. "Where is John Byron?"

"I'm here, Mama."

She heard the fear in his voice and felt the bed dip as he moved closer. She held out her hand. "You mustn't be concerned," she soothed. "I took a spill, but I'm fine." His small hand crept into hers, and their fingers locked.

Hunter watched the two comfort one another in a manner so natural, they did it without thought or spoken word. The tangible concern on John Byron's face brought to mind his last visit with his sister Acadiana. She had looked at him with that same fierce, bewildered expression she so often wore when he was around.

"Mon Dieu, *Matthew, when will you settle down? You must marry someday,* oui? *Don't you know that your children are a continuation of yourself?"*

He looked at John Byron, so undeniably his, and thought what cruel tricks Providence played on the innocent. He had never wanted a continuation of himself. His parents had been dead since he was fifteen, partially his fault, and he had pushed aside all memories of them in favor of sheer survival. When he let himself think or feel anything from his childhood, he remembered only his sister and everything his rebellion had deprived her of when she had needed him most. The world did not need a continuation of himself.

As if by design, he heard the patter of small feet and turned quickly to brace himself against the small firebrand of energy certain to follow. Like a whirlwind, a petite child of four blew through the door and launched herself into Hunter's waiting arms with a squeal of mixed French and English.

He winced at the blow to his ribs and smiled tightly. "Minx, slow down before you kill me."

Lara stirred at the commotion and attempted to bring everything into focus, but the effort made her head pound all the worse. She could hear a child's excited voice and Hunter's deeper tones, but the language was too difficult to understand. She concentrated, instead, on what she could recall. She remembered the ship, then a carriage ride and their arrival . . . where had they arrived? She blinked to clear her vision, but her senses were slow to respond. Images ran together, like colors on an artist's palette, then finally seemed to conform into individual shapes.

Hunter stood over her, a fresh cloth in one hand, a child in the other. The little girl's mouth formed an oval as she stared down at Lara with compassion.

"It hurts badly, *oui?*" she whispered in heavily accented English.

Lara's frantic gaze flew to Hunter. His features were a masculine contrast and aged by thirty years but, just as with John Byron, he and the small girl were exact replicas. Lara made a strangled sound in her throat and turned her head away to find the soft, concerned eyes of her son upon her. "John Byron," she whispered, and reached to touch his face.

He cuddled close to her side. "Mama," he whispered back, "you gave me such a fright. Are you all right?"

"Yes, of course," she soothed, but she could not recall where she was and wondered, horribly, if Hunter's wife would walk in any minute to fetch their daughter. She glanced back at Hunter and the child he held, and saw at once two things she'd never seen in his eyes—intense guilt and undiluted love.

He said grimly but without apology, "My daughter, Nicolette." He eyed the child narrowly. "Who wasn't due to arrive for at least another month."

"But I am early. Uncle Edward brought me," Nicolette said prettily, then glanced over at Lara. Her lovely eyes narrowed in concern. "Your head, madame, does it hurt badly?"

"Not too badly," Lara reassured automatically, but her confusion was getting the best of her in painful ways. She felt as if she had been hurled into a state of surreal fantasy, a stage play in which all the players knew their lines but her. Hunter had a daughter—a beautiful, precocious child the mirror image of John Byron at age four. It hurt in ways Lara could not begin to comprehend.

She wanted—needed—answers. But her heart hurt and her head ached to the extreme that she could not think of the questions. She glanced around carefully and found herself in a small but lavish room. It was richly appointed with rose damask draperies in a floral design at the arched windows and cherubs frolicking overhead on the plastered ceiling. Soft sky colors provided the backdrop for their play among billowy white clouds tinted at the edges and beyond with the very palest colors of sunset. The effect was soothing, a dreamy place to rest and contemplate before sleep.

She turned her head slowly back to Hunter. "Where are we?"

"Ravenwood."

She jerked at the recollection. Her startled gaze burned into his piercing one. "Imposter," she whispered.

"Now is not the time," he warned.

She heeded his words due to the increased pounding in her skull and the fact that there were children present. Rolling her head to the side, she found John Byron. "Has Gal arrived yet or Connie?"

He shook his head, and she closed her eyes in regret. She desperately needed to talk to Hunter in private but wouldn't send her son off in a strange place or entrust his safety to servants she didn't know. "Well, they'll be along soon, I'm certain—"

As if her will had conjured them, Connie poked his head around the door. "Here's the little scoundrel!" he blustered cheerfully. "Beat us by twenty minutes." His eyes widened in amazement. "And Miss Nicci, too! Where did you come from, darling? I wasn't to fetch you for another month."

Nicolette launched herself from Hunter's arms into Connie's. "Uncle Edward is trading cotton in London and I came with him."

"Well, and glad I am about it! Come along, you too, John Byron, we'll have a pony ride if you hurry."

"Go. I'll be fine," Lara said before John Byron could protest. It was difficult to speak further. Everyone around her knew of Nicolette and Ravenwood except her. What other secrets and conspiracies did Hunter hide?

Hunter swung John Byron off the bed. "Dinner is at six," he said. "Tell Gal she still has to dress."

For the first time since his mother's fall, John Byron smiled. He headed toward the groan echoing in the hallway. "I don't like it either," he said on his way through the door, "but it's better than eating in the nursery. . . ."

The rest of his conversation was muted by muttered commiseration and distance. Lara waited until she could no longer hear the children's voices and turned pleading eyes to Connie. "Do you go with them?"

"Aye," he said, "but Gal will watch him with her life."

"She doesn't care much for me."

"Who's to know with Gal? It takes awhile." He smiled and gave a Gallic shrug. "It is enough right now that she's devoted to Hunter. She would never do anything to hurt or betray his son."

Lara flushed and looked away. She would never get used to such free speaking. She'd carried the secret for so long that the lie seemed much more real than the truth. In every sense of the word, she had given George the son he wanted. George, in turn, had given her child a name and an inheritance. If they had perpetrated a lie on the rest of the world, she no longer cared. Her only other alternatives had been to end her life or live it in shame. She had chosen neither.

From the moment she became aware of conception, there had been no choice but to protect John Byron the best way possible. Now all her carefully laid plans were falling apart and she didn't know how to keep it all together.

She closed her eyes and waited until Connie left the room with Nicolette before facing Hunter, a touch of bitterness in her voice. "However did you pull this charade off, *Your Grace?*"

Chapter Twelve

Just seconds ago . . . looking at her son, her eyes had been softer, though still worried. Turned upon him now, a storm raged in their depths. And deeper, the hurt of another betrayal by him.

"Why didn't you tell me you had duped the whole of England into believing you are the Duke of Ravenwood?" she demanded.

"What? And have your blackmail or bribery scheme fall apart before you'd had a chance to propose it?" He gave a sharp laugh. "I enjoyed too much seeing how far you would go."

Lara's fingers curled into fists. Stultifying fury washed through her. "How it must have amused you," she said scornfully, *just as I provided amusement ten years ago.*

"No." He took the cloth from her forehead and freshened it.

"Why did you do it then," she persisted, "if not for the reward money?"

His eyes flared. "He is my son."

"That has always been true, yet you did not come for him before now."

"He did not need me before now."

She lifted her hand then let it fall back limply to the mattress. "And you have a daughter as well. How inconvenient for you this all must be."

He smiled then and she knew to regret her words. It was the smile of the predator closing in for the kill. "Not too inconvenient," he drawled silkily. "I shall forever after this have a sort of thwarted fondness for storage closets."

She closed her eyes, knowing better than to engage him in verbal warfare when her wits were sluggish. "Are you paid back then for the rescue of my son?"

He laughed outright, but the sound held a dangerously cutting edge to it. "One hasty bit of play for risking my life? You hold your charms too highly, Lara." He picked up her hand and stroked each finger, then brought her wrist to his lips. His warm breath brushed her skin before his teeth lightly closed on her flesh. "He's my son too," he said softly. "Never *ever* forget that."

She snatched her hand back, angry and terrified suddenly by the intense tone of his voice. "You don't love him," she charged. "You don't even know him; you said so yourself—"

"You never gave me the chance to know him," he interrupted coldly.

"You never *deserved* the chance!" she retaliated.

The words were intended to inflict pain and guilt. They both knew it, but the knowledge didn't lessen the blow. Hunter took the hit with stiff grace. Nodding formally, he stepped back from the bed.

"Dinner is at six, if you are feeling well enough to join us. If not, ring for Mary."

"Will your wife be attending?" Lara burst out.

"Nicolette's mother died of a fever when she was two." He turned on his heel and departed, an elegant stranger in the trappings of a duke with the heart of pirate.

Lara turned her face into the downy pillow, feeling coarse and shallow for the relief that flooded her. How ironic that her past had caught up with her at the point in her life when she had finally stopped worrying about it. She had expected it in the early years and lived constantly on the edge of guilt, which had kept her feeling bruised and wrung out. Over time, George's generosity and care of John Byron had made the pain and worry fade until her past was not hers at all but some frivolous young girl's who had allowed herself to be seduced. The grown woman Lara had become would never have been so susceptible to the charms and deceptions of a roguish privateer.

Or so she had thought.

One touch had sent her back over the edge, one helpless moment in a storage closet. It wasn't guilt she felt so much this time as anger—anger at herself for being so needy and anger at Hunter for taking advantage of it. Her pride had been ravaged this time in place of innocence.

She closed her eyes against the piercing headache and conjured George's memory to salve her wounded self-esteem. *You make too much of nothing*, he had often said when she fretted. For all that he was a man who kept to himself and enjoyed scholarly pursuits, more times than not he had scolded her for being the same.

"George," she whispered in her most imperious voice, "how very inconsiderate of you to die and leave John Byron and me in such an impossible state." The words would have touched the contrary side of his sober personality and caused him to turn a rare and dignified smile on her, so she repeated them with even more hauteur. "He has a daughter who looks like John Byron," she whispered, then burst into tears.

The throbbing in her head was no longer constant but a dull reminder that threatened to resurface if she moved too quickly. She rolled slowly and sat on the edge of the bed, waiting to see if her head would spin and debating whether to ring for Mary. She needed to find John Byron, but her dress was a fright and completely unsuitable for anything but a trip to the laundress. She tried to smooth out the wrinkles but gave up and reached for the pull.

As if hovering outside the door, Lydia knocked and bustled in almost immediately, a gown draped over her arm. "M'lady." She smiled and laid the garment at the foot of the bed. "His Grace says you may wear this if you're feeling up to dinner."

Appalled and amazed, Lara stared at the gown of peach taffeta with small crystal beads that made it sparkle in the candlelight. She grasped the hem and jerked it over, searching the once-raveled edge where salt water had damaged it. It had been neatly repaired by adding a strip of delicate lace to the hem . . . and one to the waist in place of the missing sash.

She glanced at the maid then looked away. "Tell *His Grace* that this is a child's gown. I'll wait for the one I am wearing to be laundered."

Lydia nodded nervously. "Begging your pardon, m'lady, but I don't think they can get it done by dinner."

"No, of course not." Lara noted for the first time how young the servant girl was and gave her a reassuring smile. "I don't feel quite up to dinner tonight and thought I would dine here."

Relieved, Lydia beamed. "Yes, m'lady. I'll have a tray sent up."

"Would you also locate my son?"

Lydia's chin dropped slightly but she recalled herself immediately. "You be meaning the young lad? John Byron?"

"Yes. Send him to me please."

The servant nodded and dashed from the room. It might never be said that Lydia Crumb was a gossipmonger, but truth was not at all the same as gossip and she wanted to be the first one out with the news.

"His Grace is *what?*" Cook looked up from the dough she was kneading and sent Lydia a vexed look.

"Married! I tell you he's married to the woman what fainted this morning. She ain't a governess like we thought."

"Like *you* thought. Don't include me in your brainless shenanigans." Cook slapped a fistful of dough down. The comforting smell of baking bread and spices surrounded her, diminishing the offensiveness of Lydia's gossip. "You've lost your wits, girl. Don't you think we'd be informed if His Grace took a wife?"

"Not *took*," Lydia said. "Already has."

Cook rolled her eyes at the gullibility of young maids. "You've got your head in the clouds, lass, if you're thinking to make something romantic out of His Grace bringing a beautiful woman here with her child. Such has been done since time began and it don't mean marriage."

Lydia pursed her lips. "The child is his, just like Miss Nicolette is."

Cook stopped kneading and leveled the servant with a stern look. "Perhaps, but you can't be knowing that for certain, now can you? You're a hard worker, Lydia, but I'll have you dismissed if I hear you spewing rumor again."

Hurt by Cook's disapproval, Lydia snatched a fresh apron from the wall peg and headed for the door. "I heard it from the duke's own lips," she said petulantly. "And the lady abovestairs said the child is hers too." With that, she swung about and headed for the door.

"Get back here!" Cook called. "Lydia!" She rounded the wooden table and headed after the maid only to be brought up short in the doorway when Gal appeared, reeking of manure, stable dust, and horseflesh.

"Miss Gal," she scolded, almost by rote. "You smell

like a team of oxen! Get yourself out of my kitchen and off to a tub of hot water!"

Gal ignored Cook's outrage and shouldered her way in toward the tall arched fireplace. "But I've someone I want you to meet." A huge cauldron bubbled, sending heat scented with venison into the air. Rows of furbished copper pots hung from a wooden shelf, reflecting back at Gal her own untidy, distorted image. On wet days this was her favorite place to spend an afternoon, nibbling on almond cakes while helping Cook stir compounds of raisins, eggs, ginger, nutmeg, currants, and mace to glaze a roasted duck. "Come on," she called to the empty threshold.

Cook watched, astounded, as the Duke of Ravenwood—in a much smaller package—walked into the room. He peered in all directions, lost as how to proceed in the great vaulted kitchen. She tried to smile at the boy, but shock had made her facial muscles unresponsive.

"John Byron," Gal said, "meet Cook. She makes the best sweetmeats in all of London, maybe even the world."

Manners inbred into every bone in his body, John Byron nodded formally. "I'm very pleased to meet you."

Flustered, Cook glanced at Gal for further explanation, but the young miss had already moved away to rummage the cupboards. "Well, and I'm very pleased to meet you too, uh . . ." She wasn't certain how to address the youngster and covered with a cough that fooled no one but John Byron.

"Just call him Lord Ravenwood," Gal said over her shoulder. "Everyone will have to sooner or later."

Confusion clouded the boy's eyes before he set his chin indignantly and said with learned hauteur, "Gal can be such a nuisance. Upon my father's recent passing, I am the fifth Earl of *Folkstone*. You may address me as such, or 'my lord' will do if you prefer."

Cook had earned her position as head of the kitchens by knowing when to argue and when to keep her own council. She nodded gravely at the small replica of her master, no matter who he claimed as father, and said with deference, "M'lord Folkstone, would you care for a cup of tea?"

The child visibly relaxed and even graced her with an angelic smile that so mirrored Miss Nicolette's it made Cook's bones tingle. "That would be very nice, thank you."

Cook caught Gal's smirk out of the corner of her eye and was thankful the girl didn't feel compelled to make more mischief. "And have you seen where Miss Nicci got off to?"

"I got off to here, Mademoiselle Cook!" she chimed in as she swept into the room. Her hair was mussed, her dress a shambles, but her smile would have warmed the heart of the coldest nursemaid.

"So you have," Cook said fondly. "Well, take a seat and I'll have you a spot of tea in a thrice."

She often served a cluster of village children around this table on earthenware plates and had poured many a cup of Rhenish wine for merchants from Dover to Kent, but seldom did she get to bring out the "children's china," as she called a delicate, handpainted set from France that had been purchased a hundred years earlier for the castle children at teatime.

She stared at the three chattering happily around the scarred wooden table, her chest tight with memories. Three years ago they'd lost Gal's younger brother Ollie to the croup, then a year later Nicolette's tiny twin sister Nan. Her eyes welled up like the bubbling stew pot and she grabbed the tail of her apron to dab at the corners. Oh, but little Nan had been a hard one on the duke, him watching the wee one struggle those last hours, then having to tell Miss Nicci when it was over. All his money and connections had been good for nothing against such evil. Something vital seemed to have been stolen from him the day they put Miss Nan in the ground, something Cook wasn't certain he'd ever gotten back.

There were only Gal and Nicolette left now when the duke was in residence, and then only rarely. The table needed children around it, just like the castle did. It had been devoid of the sights and smells and laughter of young ones too long.

Cook didn't claim to be one much for sentiment, but she got misty-eyed all the same. She knew what she knew, and Ravenwood had been lacking too long. Like the duke himself, it had grown cold and impersonal, if such a thing were possible. But she had seen the paintings, those that still hung in the gallery and even the ones that had been stored away. For centuries there had been children at Ravenwood, and she was convinced that there needed to be again.

233

She paused before placing tea and biscuits on the table just to enjoy the special patter of young voices. It was right, natural. The room seemed to fill with it, as if coming alive, but she feared it would not last. The duke never visited more than a month or two several times a year, just enough to tend to business and keep things in order.

Of course, he'd never brought home a son before.

She felt the winds of change and wondered if they would be sweet or rank. Setting down the tray of refreshments, she smiled at the handsome young boy waiting patiently to be served.

Call yourself what you like, lad. But Gal's right. Lord Ravenwood is what you are.

Chapter Thirteen

Lara slid her legs over the side of the bed and stood up carefully to keep her head from spinning. She felt drained but alert and walked to the window embrasure to push back the drapes. The sun was setting, bathing the land in soothing pinks and golds, a benign contrast to the ugly ache in her head. The courtyard below was busy with activity, but voices were kept low as if in deference to the beauty and hour of the day.

Villagers waved good evening, a peddler packed up his wares, the stable master collected ponies tethered on the front lawn. It was all so customary, so expected. Lara felt as if she viewed the happenings at day's end from within a magician's crystal, isolated and cut off from reality. Didn't they know that the lord who inhabited the manner was not the English duke they revered but an American patriot and former pirate?

She leaned her forehead against the cool pane. It

had all gotten so tangled now, she feared nothing could unravel it. She had to get her son away soon. If Hunter didn't tell him the truth, John Byron would hear rumors from the villagers or castle staff. And she had to get herself away, to protect herself from the vulnerability of her feelings.

A draft stirred the hem of her chemise and she sighed inwardly. Lara knew only one person would dare enter without knocking. "I'm not presentable," she said without turning.

"Are you not?"

His steps were muted on the rich carpet, but Lara sensed his approach in the way the flesh on her arms prickled. She pulled a panel of the drape around her for modesty and turned. "I haven't even a robe. If you have any decency, you'll leave."

"Decency?" He chuckled softly. "How addled of you to suggest it. I'm a pirate, Lara. I rape, pillage, and plunder for sport and profit."

Looking at him, no one would ever have believed it. He was dressed for dinner, stunning in a black coat and trousers with a crisp white shirt and neck cloth. In two decades John Byron would look like this —handsome and distinguished, with a hint of rakish humor in his amethyst eyes. The thought brought Lara a moment of pride before panic at the uncertainty of her child's future crept in to destroy it. She gripped the edge of the drape tighter, as if she could hold the impending events at bay by physical force.

Hunter approached with an unhurried elegance that successfully cloaked the panther on the prowl, but Lara felt the power of his advance in each step, the tempered restraint he chose to exercise. She wondered when he would drop the urbane facade and unleash it. He stopped less than a foot away and ran one finger down the edge of the drape, then slipped it inside to touch her flesh. The barest hint of a cavalier smile crossed his face. "You shiver."

Lara's eyes flashed with resentment. "Why did you bring us here? To shame me and John Byron? Did you save him only to disgrace him?"

"I brought you here for protection and to acknowledge John Byron as the rightful heir of Ravenwood."

Lara felt the dizzy sensation of spinning again. Her life, her choices were flying crazily out of her grasp, but she refused to let the overwhelming feelings take hold of her. "Do you hate me so much that you would get revenge by ruining an innocent child?"

"Hate you?" His hand swept out in a wide arc. "Look around you, Lara. I am the Duke of Ravenwood, Viscount of Heathridge, and Earl of Choucester. I own a shipping business, a sugar plantation, and numerous other properties in America. I also hold titles and land in France. All of this I offer to John Byron for the simple price of acknowledgment. Just which part do you protest?"

She looked at him as if he were insane. "The farce of it all. How dare you call yourself Duke of Ravenwood? You are a schemer and a liar, and I don't want my son to have any part of your deception."

His face went cold, his voice colder still. "Your son is my blood, not George Chalmers's. He does not belong at Folkstone. That is the lie, Lara, and you perpetuated it, not me."

A fine trembling seized her, and she gripped the drapes until her knuckles whitened. "Do you care nothing for his reputation? You ruin him by exposing him."

"You risk his life otherwise."

She pressed her fingers to her throbbing head and said with icy reserve, "What do you want? Tell me. Whatever it takes to preserve his integrity, his future, I'll do it."

"Lara, my love." He reached out and cupped her face tenderly, but his eyes were remote. "Haven't you realized yet? You have nothing I need, except my heir. My wealth outweighs your own by more than my accountants can ledger. My titles make your deceased husband look like a pauper."

"But it's all a farce!" she cried. "I don't know how you've done it, but your empire will collapse when someone discovers the lie. I will not have John Byron subjected to that chance."

"How hypocritical of you. His whole life has been a lie." He sighed, then stepped back. "Forgive me, Lara, but the choice is no longer yours."

Her eyes flared in hostility when he rudely turned his back and strode toward the door. She flung the drapes aside and followed after him. "Do you keep us here as prisoners?"

He turned, then stopped, arrested by the sight of her in so little. She stood only in a chemise of fine linen, sheer as a wisp of fog, the heat of anger pink across her cheeks and chest. "The thought has merit."

She fought the urge to cross her arms in modesty,

but she wouldn't retreat from the confrontation at hand. Her mouth was grim but she managed to keep the rancor from her voice. "And what of Nicolette?"

The faintest trace of pain flickered in his eyes only to be replaced swiftly by his cunning smile. "A darling child, a bit spoiled but . . ."

"Stop it, Hunter."

His expression darkened to utmost seriousness. "John Byron is my firstborn."

"Mine as well and my only child. We leave tomorrow," she said evenly. "If you have a care for him, you will provide us with transportation and an armed escort. Once I reach Folkstone, I will set into motion my own protection and send your men back."

There was a look in his eyes, something she could not decipher—a look as deep and unfathomable as the seas he once sailed for amusement and booty. Finally he nodded. "As you wish, Lara."

She recognized immediately that he had given in too easily.

"I don't see why we must leave so soon."

John Byron stood, his small case in his hand, looking as forlorn as Lara had ever seen him.

She took his hands in hers, knowing it was her own cowardice that drove her away faster than any other reason. "Don't you miss Barrows and Mistress Farnsmill?" At his nod she continued, "And your hounds?"

"Milton and Chaucer have surely missed me very much," he said.

It was, perhaps, the hardest thing she had ever

done, to play upon her child's fondness for his animals in order to manipulate him into making this easier for them both. "They have missed you ever so much," she affirmed.

There still lurked a vestige of fear in his eyes. Lara didn't know whether returning to Folkstone would erase or compound it. Her heart, already burdened, felt like an anvil in her chest. "The carriage waits," she said softly.

"But I must say good-bye."

"Yes." She took his hand and walked with him room to room in order for him to make his farewells. At only a little past dawn, Nicolette was still asleep, Gal nowhere to be found. A sleepy-eyed Cook wrapped up almond cakes for the journey and bid them return quickly.

At the look in her son's eyes, Lara almost postponed the trip, but the longer they stayed the harder it would be on both of them.

A carriage awaited departure at the castle entrance. At least four men stood guard; Lara didn't know how many more had been sent on ahead. The morning air was crisp but dry, a prelude to fall. She took John Byron's hand and led him toward the small group assembled near the carriage. She smiled at those she had grown to care for, thankful they had risen so early, though it made things infinitely more difficult. Weasel nodded at her then scurried around checking harness and horses. Connie gave orders to the outriders in a low voice. Gal, looking rumpled and sullen, was leaning against the carriage door.

She crammed her hat farther down on her head and gave Lara an accusing look.

Lara could not say, could not be, what the young woman needed, so she said nothing at all, but her heart constricted painfully and she could not shake the feeling that she was somehow abandoning Gal. She should offer to take her to Folkstone, but Gal would never leave Hunter, so what would that serve? Despite the chilly reception, Lara walked to Gal and kissed her cheek. Gal turned her head away sharply and stuffed her hands in her pockets.

"Thank you for helping me get my son back," Lara said softly. "I will forever be grateful."

Gal shook her head. "I did it for Hunter. Now you're taking John Byron away. I wish we'd left him to rot."

"No you don't," Lara said quietly. She turned away before her heart burst and found her son standing beside Hunter. He stepped forward and opened the door.

Lara didn't trust for one moment his ease about her leaving, but she needed to get away first before trying to unravel his motives. Trepidation weighted each step she took toward him. Studying his extraordinarily handsome face, she wondered if this would be the last time she saw him, the last time she felt the powerful mixture of awe and apprehension in his presence. The thought suddenly frightened her more than anything. More than leaving against his wishes, more than trying to protect John Byron—more than being alone.

She smoothed her dress with anxious palms, then

met his eyes. "Thank you," she said softly, "for everything." The breeze caught her bonnet and she grasped the ribbons at her throat to keep it from sailing off. "I will forever be indebted to you."

He only looked at her with depthless amethyst eyes and said gruffly, "Reconsider, Lara."

"No." She looked down, wavering terribly beneath his piercing gaze. "I cannot." Her feelings for him were a sharp-edged dagger piercing her heart. She ushered John Byron inside the carriage, then followed quickly and pressed her shoulders back against the plush upholstery where she could not see Hunter's face. Her eyes stung frightfully but she would not give in to the need to cry in front of her son.

Hunter pulled the door open wider and stuck his head inside. "Coward," he whispered roughly. "Stay."

Her eyes flickered with anger but she held herself erect, everything within her tightly contained and protected. Her voice was excruciatingly civil. "Fare-thee-well, Your Grace."

"Lady Chalmers, John Byron," he returned in an equally formal tone, then shut the carriage door. "Godspeed."

Lara took several deep breaths, then forced all thoughts aside but the immediate. There was no past, no future, only this exact moment that she must get through. Busying herself with helping John Byron get settled, she also tried to ignore his forlorn expression. Just as she would protect him against anything else harmful, she must get him away from Ravenwood and protect him from discovery.

She pulled a box of entertainments from her traveling case and placed it on his lap. Inside were cards and small toys and even a book. It would be a long and tedious journey, and she did not envy herself or John Byron the restless hours ahead.

The carriage tilted slightly as the driver climbed aboard, but a sudden, high-pitched squeal halted any forward motion. Lara pushed back the curtain as John Byron rose to his knees on the seat.

He smiled from ear to ear. "She woke up."

Nicolette ran toward the carriage, the folds of her nightrail flying about her like full sails. *"M'sieu* Coachman," she said, waving her tiny hand imperially, *"un moment, s'il vous plait."* Her bare feet pattered across the bricked drive while her uncombed hair bounced to her waist in beautiful, messy ringlets. She carried something tightly clasped against her chest. "For you, John Byron," Nicolette said, jumping up and down repeatedly to see in the window. "Come see!"

Hunter scooped her up in one arm as he opened the carriage door, then placed her inside. Nicolette scrambled up on the seat between Lara and John Byron, her cheeks flushed. "Naughty, naughty of you to leave without saying *adieu.*"

"You were asleep," John Byron said.

"Non, I am not!"

John Byron only smirked, and Lara was surprised that her son understood the fruitlessness of arguing with a groggy four-year-old. "We are glad you came to see us off, Nicolette," she said softly.

"Oh, Madame!" the child burst out dramatically and flung herself into Lara's arms. "Must you go? Must you really?"

Lara hugged Nicolette close, assailed by the sleepy-child fragrances of warm skin beneath sun-dried cotton. Sturdy arms clung to her neck and Lara's heart squeezed with a rush of memories: holding a young one tightly to her breast and feeling the robust energy of a healthy child in every sharp angle and soft curve. Blood drained from her face, and she forced herself to put Nicolette aside.

"We must go, Nicci, but perhaps . . ." Lara's words faded off to nothing. Perhaps what? She could not say they would return to Ravenwood, nor could she invite Nicolette to Folkstone where her very likeness would announce her connection to John Byron. She would not make promises to this precious four-year-old child that she would never keep. "We must go."

Nicolette pressed her face into Lara's neck. *"Non, non, non!* I will not let you go!"

Lara squeezed her eyes closed to hold back a tide of tears and pulled Nicolette firmly from her. She glanced helplessly at Hunter but he only gave her a scathing look. Her throat too restricted to speak, she smoothed Nicolette's tousled curls and touched the rumpled package in her tiny fist.

Remembering her mission, Nicolette swung quickly to John Byron and put the gift in his hands. "For you, *mon ami.*"

He folded back the edges of a linen cloth to find a smudged picture on wrinkled paper.

"It is me and you riding the ponies."

Lara could see John Byron was having trouble making out the scribble but he hid his consternation admirably.

"Thank you," he mumbled. "I shall treasure it always."

"Come, Nicolette," Hunter called from the carriage door. He overrode her forming protest by plucking her from the seat before she could utter more than a cry of dismay. He took one last look at Lara, his eyes as accusing as Gal's had been, then shut the door and rapped on the roof for the coachman to be off.

Lara sat back, despondent, foolishly feeling like she had just made the biggest mistake of her life, while John Byron waved and waved and waved, until Ravenwood could no longer be seen.

Chapter Fourteen

Percy paced the little room George Chalmers had always referred to as his accounts' chamber. His hidey-hole, Percy realized now. He felt ill in his stomach and soul with the news he must impart to Lara.

He had rifled through George's private boxes and found hidden accounts of which Lara must have no knowledge. Certainly George's wretched brothers must not or they would never have pressed so hard to have Folkstone turned over to them.

So much of the properties were mortgaged, the money spent on God only knew what. Percy certainly couldn't find much of an accounting of the funds, just vague references to things that made no sense scratched out in a feeble hand. It seemed that George, in his weakening months, had gone a little eccentric and decided to splurge on oddities.

"Lyell: changes slow or violent," one account said. "Joule: energy" and "Faraday: current," others read. There were more listed, with money paid out scribbled by each name. The exorbitant amounts caused Percy's eyes to widen, but "Analise" noted in another column gave him the most pause. Percy dreaded to think what money spent on someone named Analise might suggest, and how was he to go about explaining it to Lara? As George's solicitor he should have been privy to the expenses, but he hadn't even known what George was about.

He closed the ledger on a sigh, then picked up the document that had arrived hours ago by messenger. He would have to tell Lara the gravest of news, and George's excessive spending was not the worst of it.

Lara stared out over the cliffs of Dover, outwardly composed, as cool and flawlessly imperturbable as the marbles that had been on display at Ravenwood. Her gown, of purest white, flowed about her like a silken banner in the breeze and contrasted sharply with the dark sheen of her unbound hair. She had cast off widow's wear to stroll privately. No one would know; no one would care. Least of all George Chalmers.

It was one of the few areas where Lara's husband had not been a traditionalist. "A person of any worth mourns in their heart," he had said once with such acrid passion it had startled Lara. "One need not prove their grief to the world with drab attire that, by its very nature, calls attention to itself!" He had known he was ill, Lara realized later, and already railing against the unfairness and inevitability of it.

She surveyed the grounds in the distance and saw George's influence everywhere, in the neat lawn, in the mathematically constructed gardens, in the precise architecture of the castle itself. He had been an intelligent but unexciting man, and she felt petty and shallow for the resentment that still managed to wind its way into her heart at times, giving rise to an unreasonable animosity toward both Hunter and George over the things she might have missed from marrying so young.

But she had come to recognize the difference between the glimmer of diamond and glass over the years. So many of her early girlhood dreams of courtship and marriage were worth no more than paste. The true worth of a man was not measured in the cut of his coat or the way he sat a horse or the figures tallied on his accounting ledgers.

Lara pushed a wind-blown curl behind her ear and listened to the endless motion of the sea. She had always considered George a man of worth, measuring him by the attributes of steadfastness, commitment, and integrity. Her view had not changed.

But a newer, more uncomfortable realization had begun to seep into her consciousness over the past weeks.

A hot rush of color stung her cheeks, and she pressed her palms to her skin, unable to put aside what she had tried to ignore for so very long. She had fallen for Hunter a decade ago, measuring him by nothing more than the excited way he made her heart race and the handsomeness of his physical appearance. She had loved him with a girl's innocence, then had rushed to marry the staid and dignified George Chalmers who more closely epitomized the type of man her father would have chosen for her rather than the dashing rogue who had completely and irrevocably stolen her foolish heart.

She had loved George; no one could take that from her, but, in reality, the love she had held for him had been more that of a friend and confidant and provider. He had been an excellent husband and father to her son as well, but she had not loved him with the same driving, frightening, painful, fiery emotions she held for Hunter.

Hunter, who did not love her in return.

A quiet, bitter laugh tumbled from her lips and was caught away on the wind—malice revealing itself from the depths of her soul. He desired her, yes, but what was carnal craving compared to the lasting commitment of real love?

For the past month, Hunter had plagued her dreams at night and her thoughts during the daylight. Since her return to Folkstone, she had not known a moment of peace free from his face, his words, the look in his eyes when she left Ravenwood. For the first time since John Byron's birth, her son's features were not merely a vague reminder but a glaring proclamation of the strength and intelligence that was his inheritance.

Lara felt a flutter of alarm in her breast. Her feelings for Hunter were not a juvenile infatuation or mild flirtation that she could ignore. The emotions were as strong and unyielding as the man himself, and they made her completely vulnerable to him. She crossed her arms over the middle and shivered in the cool air. She would not let her guard down and put herself at risk as she had ten years ago. No matter what happened to her and John Byron from now on, she could never go through the pain of betrayal again.

She pulled her gaze from Folkstone and faced the sea again. The cliffs dropped off in chalky splendor to the crashing waves below, an inspiring sight that never failed to both soothe and revive her. But this day she saw only the destruction, the erosive force of water wearing away at stone. She had found to her own consternation this morning that all things could be worn down with time and constancy. Herself included. Which was only one more reason to erect impenetrable barriers to protect herself.

Hunter had known. Somehow he had known when he so blithely allowed her to return home that she would not be able to deal sufficiently with Robert and Claude, that she had not seen the end of their scheming. She heard labored huffing as Smythe ascended the steep path behind her and felt a terrible flicker of guilt. It was inordinately cruel to make him search her out to officially deliver news of which she was already aware. But a terrible lethargy had taken hold of her after the messenger arrived, and she hadn't even had the kindness or inclination to leave a note for him with Barrows.

She glanced over at John Byron playing chase with one of the hounds and feigned a smile, an easy enough task given the deeper, more abiding emotions in her heart. Smythe made the rise, and she turned to him, all warmth vanished from her face.

He stared down at his feet in painful regret. "You already know."

"You are not to blame that they have filed suit against me," she said sternly. "I am convinced that if you could have stopped it, you would have."

He could not bear her exoneration. "But it is everything you feared and worse, everything you hoped to avoid."

"So it is." Her voice was not as strong as she wished, not commanding enough to fool her gentle solicitor into believing she could weather this. "The truth, Percy," she whispered. "Have they a case?"

He closed his eyes briefly. "The answer may be moot."

"Ah, I see. John Byron and I will be ruined either way."

"They will try."

She meant to smile but could not. A horrible despair filled her, but her strength was not yet gone, nor her wits. "Will they settle? I am at least entitled to a dowager's share. I would take less—" Her voice broke slightly. "God, Percy, this cannot go to trial."

"There is more," he said with regret.

"More? How can there be more?" Tempered panic trembled in her voice. "You have not even gone to London yet to answer the charges. What else can there be?"

Percy held out the order, a temporary verdict in essence, that spoke loudly of where she stood with the lower court.

Lara took the note and read, then reread over and over, as if the words might change if she were just tenacious enough to wait for it to happen. Finally she looked up at her solicitor. "I am appalled," she said bleakly. "How can they do this?"

"You are aware of the reputation of the lower court judges. It is obvious Robert and Claude offered bribe money."

"And is it obvious that I will lose as well?"

Percy paused, loath to hurt her, then spoke the inevitable frankly. "In the lower courts, yes." It was hard to look at her, to see the slow destruction of such a beautiful woman of courage and fortitude.

"I have been put out of my home," she whispered. "I cannot fathom it." She turned away and watched the waves crash below, their rhythm and power a strengthening sight that she desperately needed. "How could they . . . does George's reputation as an upright, honorable man mean naught now that he is dead?"

"Lady Chalmers . . ."

She spun to face him, fury in her eyes. "No, I mean it, Percy! Is there no justice? How can the lower court judge think to abolish George's wishes for me and my son with one stroke of a pen? Tell me!"

Percy knew she would not relent until he spoke words aloud that she already sensed in her heart. "The judge has been *convinced* that he is preserving Folkstone for its rightful heirs rather than a . . . pretender."

Lara looked away, suspecting in her heart all along that it would come to this. The truth, spoken by someone she trusted implicitly, hurt terribly, but it was exactly what she had feared and been preparing for secretly over the past month.

"I have done something, Percy. Something not quite . . . honorable." She glanced over her shoulder at him, but only briefly. "After what Robert and Claude did to John Byron, I cannot say I was unprepared for something this extreme. I had merely hoped otherwise."

She began to pace. "I took the family jewels earlier in the week to someone I trust and had the settings copied. I've hidden the originals and have a box full of paste and marcasites in their place. George's blooded mare, his favorite, is on her way to Wakefield, along with more of his better stock.

"I don't know how closed-mouth the servants will be when put to the test, but certainly Barrows is trustworthy and Mr. Hardcastle, who took the mare." She laced her fingers tightly together. "I have money set aside that the brothers will never touch, but it isn't a great sum, only as much as I could secure without raising suspicion. As for everything else at Folkstone, I can only hope it will be returned to me." She spun away from the cliffs to face her solicitor fully. "I tell you one thing, Percy. I will face them all head-on. If Robert and Claude will not settle, then let them go to court. If they win, I will appeal to a higher justice and also have the brothers charged with kidnapping. All who will sit in judgment of me and my son in the House of Lords were friends or acquaintances of George. Surely they will stand by me."

Percy only stared at her. There was nothing certain in life, nothing definitive or absolute.

Foreboding snaked through Lara. "Very well," she whispered fatally. "If I am to be destroyed, every single one of them will see my face and know what he has done."

Percy swallowed hard. Most women in her predicament would be having the vapors. He looked away, abashed that he had thought Lara might succumb, also, when he should have known better. "You will need a barrister. I would find you someone older, more well versed. One of the king's council, perhaps, or . . ."

"Don't be absurd," she interrupted. "I value trust and loyalty far more than experience at a time like this. Until I must, I will not hear of it."

"If it goes to appeal—"

"Yes," she interrupted, "I know I must retain someone then. Let's not speak of it now."

Percy nodded and looked down. "I offer my services freely, then . . . until such time—"

She rounded on him, a fierce and frightening look in her eyes. "Not one half-penny of your time will I take. Every shilling must be accounted for. Do you understand?"

He understood pride perfectly, but she hadn't an extra penny that wasn't tied up since Robert and Claude had filed suit. Bribing lower court judges was a common enough practice, but the order still stood. Not even a stipend for simple care had the court awarded Lara. A paternity suit was such an ugly and unlikely case to bring to trial, no one suspected she would do anything but try to have it kept quiet.

Percy had spoken to her household. The older retainers would stay on. They had money set aside from George's bequest. Those who had nowhere else to go had also agreed to stay until some decision was made or another position offered. Some, with families to feed and enough tenure to make them marketable, were already packing their belongings with the recommendations Smythe had written.

No provision had been made for Lara and her son, and Percy had not even told Lara yet of the full extent of her problems. If Folkstone was handed back to her this day, she would still be in dreadful financial difficulty. But that news could wait until he was more certain of the full extent of George Chalmers's peculiarities.

"Lady Chalmers," he said, "I should present your options."

"No, hush," she admonished gently. "I know what I must do. We will speak of nothing else just now. As you say, it is moot until we find out if Robert and Claude will drop this case and settle out of court."

"But you must be prepared." He had not wanted his own alarm to show in his voice, but the flaring of her eyes told him it did. "It's just that these things cannot be done overnight," he apologized. "You must obtain council now. I would prefer you choose a peer, and you'll need a sponsor—"

Lara whirled on him. "You are certain already that it will go before the House of Lords?" She held a hand up to stop him from answering the obvious.

"Find someone. I can sell the jewels and the mare, if needs be." With obvious finality, she turned away from Percy, composed her expression, and called to John Byron. As soon as he reached her side, she smiled. "We are going on another journey."

His eyes dimmed and he shifted uneasily beside her. "Will Barrows come with us? And Mistress Farnsmill? She bakes the best sugar cookies." He reached down and grabbed one of his hounds around the neck and held on, as if he would not let go. His gaze whipped to Smythe, his eyes desolate and afraid. "It's my uncles, isn't it? They know I've come home."

Not for the first time Lara questioned her decision in returning to Folkstone. For all the strangeness of Ravenwood, John Byron had felt safe there, removed from anyone who would hurt him. Lara herself had been torn between her feelings of physical security and emotional instability. She had come back home to protect herself from her tangled feelings for Hunter and to keep John Byron shielded from prying eyes and wagging tongues. Now it had all come full circle, and she hadn't been able to protect either of them at all.

Such helplessness was untenable for Lara, and she would not give in to it. Whatever had to be done, whatever steps she had to take, she would do it to secure John Byron's future. She stroked his hair, savoring the feel and textures uniquely him, then bent to face him eye to eye. "Your uncles are making trouble, yes, but they will be locked in Newgate if they set foot on Folkstone lands."

A man kept watch less than twenty feet away, another nearer the house. Men she wouldn't be able to afford in another week when her household money ran out. Already she slept with her son in her room and a pistol by her bed. What more must she do? Her senses spun as she thought of the prison their lives had become, the uncertainty of their future. She had met George's brothers only once. Just after her marriage was announced, Robert and Claude paid a visit to George's country estate at Wakefield. Lara had had an uncanny mistrust of them then but never any proof that they were anything but the boorish and sullen brothers they seemed. She knew now why George had remained estranged from them and why she must stay ever on guard.

"The courts will decide if you and I are to hold your father's lands or if they will be turned over to Robert and Claude. For now, they are forbidding all of us the use of Folkstone or any of your father's holdings. I cannot tell you what the final decision will be, but you must not worry. Everything will work out for the best."

Though he didn't understand it, John Byron believed every word.

Lara wished she did.

"Where will we go?" he asked.

She scrambled for an answer that would not come. Her plans had not proceeded that far. "Somewhere peaceful," she said, needing that more than anything.

He looked at her, his great amethyst eyes so like his father's. "Ravenwood?" he asked hopefully.

A cold chill ran down her spine, followed by a flush of heat. "We wouldn't want to wear out our welcome," she answered evasively. She reached out and took his hand, then picked up the hamper they had brought along for lunch and handed it to Smythe. "In any case," she said with forced brightness, "I supposed we should make preparations for travel."

The trunks lay open upon the floor, five in number, along with numerous hat boxes, jewelry cases, and a smaller portmanteau. Lara had no idea how long she would be gone or, in truth, if she would ever be returning. But it was too painful to think of that now. She concentrated only on what she must do for this day, this hour.

Several options had presented themselves, though none were acceptable. Barrows had a sister who would hide them away for a time, but when Lara's money ran out, she could not impose upon the gentlewoman's good graces and meager income.

She folded a blouse and placed it upon the layer of clothing already in the trunk. The idea of returning to Ravenwood had kept rambling through her mind, though she dismissed it every cycle. It would be her last resort and a bitter draft to swallow, but her pride didn't extend over into foolishness. She and John Byron would be safe and cared for there, with none of the endless questions and curiosities that would come if she went begging to a friend.

Every bit of property George had left to her was now tied up, not so much as a gatehouse remained at her disposal. It was unforgivable that men in power thought nothing of her plight, that they could so thoughtlessly dismiss her needs until the matter was settled. They assumed, and rightly so, that no one of common charity would turn Lara and her son away, but they gave no thought whatsoever to shattering her pride in the process. She knew now what a poor relation must feel when knocking upon a benevolent cousin's door or the pitiable spinster aunt turned nanny to earn her keep. How unfortunate that women were expected to be beholden to others rather than self-sufficient.

How much worse John Byron must feel, homeless and uprooted again, forced from everything familiar and precious to him. Anger burned through Lara, tormenting in its intensity, purging everything but determination from her mind. Though Robert and Claude were not allowed use of her holdings either until the case was decided, they didn't need them. They had their own properties and rents in Scotland to maintain them. They had nothing to lose, everything to gain, and, deep down inside, Lara greatly feared that they had right on their side, though their evilness toward John Byron had negated any compassion or guilt she might have felt toward them.

The choice Lara had settled upon was a cottage in the country. Percy had located a small, private house far from Folkstone that would be appropriate for her needs. Lara could not afford to underestimate Robert and Claude. Just because they had filed suit against her did not mean they would leave John Byron alone. She had no doubt that where they had failed the first time, they would not fail again. She had chosen the cottage for its privacy and distance from everyone familiar to her.

She packed several more articles into the trunk, then slammed the lid and lay her head on the top. "Damn," she whispered. "Damn them all."

Chapter Fifteen

Lara was not allowed the luxury of making the journey in one of George's well-sprung carriages. Nothing but her most personal belongings could be taken from Folkstone, and she and John Byron were forced to travel in a hired coach from the Dover station, an indignity she would never have expected to bother her. It wasn't the discomfort itself or the commonalty of traveling in a public conveyance, but the fact that Folkstone had a carriage house full of vehicles needlessly collecting mildew. Or they would be once they were returned. She'd sent several out in different directions earlier to confound anyone who might be keeping watch.

Lara glanced over at her child's forlorn expression. Even John Byron's beloved hounds had to stay behind, cared for by a stranger assigned by the court. The injustice of having an outsider living in her home when she and her son were cast out was almost more than she could bear. A deep resentment blossomed inside her for the men in authority who had so little regard for her and her son that they would allow this to happen.

After a full day's travel, the coach rumbled to a jarring halt at the village posting house of Fairfield Cross, a rustic settlement lying deeper into the countryside even than the village of Fairfield off the Portsmouth Road for which it had been named. The fact that it lay more than halfway between Folkstone and Ravenwood had not escaped Lara. Of the three places Percy had discreetly inquired about, this offered the most sanctuary and safety. It was deepest into the countryside, was a private home not in use and close to Ravenwood. If need be, she was only a half day's ride from shelter and provision for John Byron.

Trying not to think of Hunter over the long month at Folkstone had been futile, though the memories had brought her pain and longing and restlessness. His face as she had seen him that last morning at Ravenwood was ever before her, the disquieting fierceness on his countenance and the underlying plea in his tone when she left. It was a look she did not understand and words she would never forget. *Reconsider, Lara. . . . Reconsider, reconsider, reconsider.*

She fought the recollection. There was nothing to reconsider, and she was foolish to pine over him like a moonstruck adolescent. The carriage door opened and she searched her reticule for funds to hire a man to cart their belongings to the private house where Percy had made arrangements.

The question had been raised by Mrs. Middleton, the housekeeper, about accommodations for Lara's female companion, but no argument had been made when told there would not be one. Mrs. Middleton's only comment had been that she kept a decent place, and Mr. Smythe was to remember that.

The house was clean and neat, a two-story dwelling on the outskirts of the village, perhaps a quarter hour's walk from the green. Lara stepped from the carriage and motioned John Byron to her side. Percy escorted them to the statuesque housekeeper waiting on the front porch.

Tall and stockily built, Mrs. Middleton could have been an imposing woman but her friendly manner put one at ease immediately. "Welcome, Mr. Smythe. You made decent time, I see."

Percy nodded, then introduced Lara and John Byron.

"I'm pleased to meet you," Mrs. Middleton said. Her words, though pleasant-sounding, were garbled, as if she spoke with a marble in each cheek. "I don't know if we've much to entertain a young boy, but we'll try." She sent Lara a resigned look. "We are considered a dull place here in Fairfield Cross, too far from everything to be of any use to anybody, but the town's good doctor came from the noise-ridden streets in the crowded East End of London and says he would choose to rusticate here any day over what he left behind."

It was exactly what Lara had been looking for. She glanced aside at Percy and nodded once, then turned back to the housekeeper. "We will do fine here, I'm certain."

Mrs. Middleton smiled in agreement. "I know you are a widow only recently, if you need a shoulder to cry on, mine are plenty large. If you need anything else, I go to the village once a day."

Lara smiled her thanks but doubted she would ever confide in the housekeeper. Her decision was confirmed over the next twenty minutes as Mrs. Middleton continued to ramble on. The housekeeper was a cheerful inquisitor with a sly way of getting people to talk. She would have Lara's entire life story within days if she and John Byron weren't careful with their answers.

"Well, come on in. I've two very nice-size bedrooms with a small connecting parlor between them on the second floor," Mrs. Middleton explained, finally leading them inside. She stopped in the foyer and turned to Percy. "But for you, young man, I've only a boxy little space on the first floor near my kitchen."

Percy nodded agreeably, as if innocent of the housekeeper's cloaked insinuation. Lara started to speak out then let it pass as well. Bringing attention to a hint of impropriety would only plant the seed deeper into the woman's thoughts. In any case, she wasn't worried about what Mrs. Middleton thought nearly as much as her more pressing concerns of keeping her son safe.

"Come along, John Byron," she said. "Let us unpack and rest before dinner."

The mention of dinner sent Mrs. Middleton rushing

into action. "Here's the key to your room. First one on the left at the top of the stairs. Dinner's at eight." She hurried off to the kitchen to prove her worth as both housekeeper and cook.

Lara handed the key to John Byron and sent him up to do the honors.

Percy raised an eyebrow. "Will you survive her?"

"Of course. She is the least of my worries. In fact, she will keep me well occupied when I don't want to remember sad things. And I will take myself off when I must think and plan." She looked around the charming house with its simple sitting room, cozy fireplace, and hand-braided rugs. The entire dwelling could fit into a portion of Folkstone's west wing. "I can be content here, never fear, for however long it takes." She took a deep, fortifying breath. "Thank you, Percival."

He brushed her gratitude aside with a shake of his head. "Thank me when I have untangled this mess for you."

Her gaze shot back and he could see the fear in her eyes, subdued but not hidden. "Can you do it?" she asked. "Can you untangle this devil's snare before it chokes us all?"

"I will do everything in my power," he promised.

"And you are hopeful?" she pressed. She threw up a hand at his pause. "No, do not answer. Do not lie to pacify me."

"I will do everything I can," he repeated.

"See that you do," she admonished, and looked away, afraid to see more in his eyes than she could manage. "I believe I will go unpack, then meet you for dinner."

The cottage at Fairfield Cross proved to be a peaceful place for Lara to hide away after the trauma of the past months. The mornings were filled with helping John Byron with his lessons to the accompaniment of birdsong and a refreshing breeze outside their window, an ideal scene had it not been for the darker currents swirling beneath their life. Early afternoons were not so fortuitous. Lara found herself with too much time to do nothing but ponder the tragedy her life had become and think of Hunter.

She forced herself to concentrate on other avenues instead, praying for the best but planning for the worst. She felt powerless with the court decision hanging over her head like an executioner's ax and knew she must prepare for whatever decision would be rendered. The outlook was not hopeful, Percy had warned her on his last visit. Lara already knew.

She placed her pen down and waited for the ink on the letter she had just written to dry. She had requested a visit from Harry Wakefield, Lord Southerland, George's oldest friend and confidant. If the brothers refused to bargain and she lost in the lower courts, she needed to know what chance she stood if she appealed to the House of Lords. Harry could tell her—as soon as she got up the courage to post the letter. Ignoring the feeling of dread in the pit of her stomach, she folded the sheet and sealed it. Tomorrow she would have Mrs. Middleton take it into town.

The grounds outside the quaint house were stunning. Lara strolled them at length every afternoon, enjoying the great expanse of rolling green lawn as it spread out to finally merge in a thick forest in the distance. She and John Byron would walk daily with a snack of fruit and honeycake tied up in a square of coarse linen.

They were strange days for Lara, filled with hard decisions and idle hours of which she never grew fond. For the past decade, she had given herself over to charities and visitations, attending lectures with George, mothering John Byron, and wishing secretly for more children to help fill the many empty rooms of Folkstone. Days of idleness were foreign to her, and she missed the familiarity of home and the comfort of her own servants.

But she did find something to treasure at the cottage outside Fairfield Cross. Freedom. For this small moment in time, she answered to neither father nor husband, court nor council. Only her conscience dictated her behavior, and she found an amazing sense of well-being deep within the turmoil of her life. If there were few chances to exercise her bit of liberty, it was of no account. For this short stretch of time, her life was her own and she cherished the small independence. Too soon she would be at the mercy of others again.

Percy had gone to London to meet with the barrister retained by Robert and Claude. Compromise was necessary to Lara, but of little consequence to the brothers. She had sent Percy with an offer that was almost unbearable for her. It gave them everything but one house, a small stipend for Lara with which to raise her son, and a decent inheritance for John Byron when he reached his majority. Too soon she would hear their decision . . . or too late. She wasn't quite certain just what her perspective should be.

Mrs. Middleton proved to be a charming companion and not as meddlesome as Lara had predicted. The housekeeper had plenty of work to keep her occupied and visited only at mealtime, teatime, and a half-hour after dinner. She, too, seemed to need time to herself. Though she slept in the house, she left every afternoon after tea to visit with her grown daughter in the village, then returned in time to prepare the evening meal.

The worst blot on the even-tempered days was the fact that John Byron missed both Folkstone and Ravenwood, and there was little Lara could do. He needed playmates, but there were no children near and it was unlikely that Lara would get chummy with anyone in town. She couldn't afford for her whereabouts to be known.

She tried to stay outside in the sunshine and fresh air as much as possible for her son's sake. Tiring him out was the best way to keep loneliness from ruling his life as it did her own. Though she told herself she was content to spend the rest of her days with her son safely by her side, she too missed the companionship of her peers and the adult pursuits that had been commonplace before George's death.

And she missed other adult things as well, things she would not admit even to herself in the darkest, most secret part of the night when she lay awake and restless in her lonely bed.

"What do you think?" She shaded her eyes from the midday sun and searched the grounds for the best spot.

"Over here!" John Byron ran toward the chosen area with his arms full of mallets and wickets. "When I get the right of this, I'm going to teach it to Nicolette and Gal."

Lara refrained from answering. He mentioned them often, and she hadn't the heart to discourage him. Instead she threw her energies into the game and diverted his attention away from his loneliness into trying to best her. A carriage arrived just as she and John Byron were returning from their recreation. Shiny and well kept, the door emblazoned with the owner's crests, it was obviously neither a peddler's vehicle nor a public coach. Lara grabbed John Byron's hand and hurried around the back of the house, out of sight.

Mrs. Middleton was hanging out wash when she caught sight of the carriage. She dropped a wet sheet and rushed into the house like a woman gone mad. In seconds, she was out the front and talking to the gentleman through the carriage door. Lara couldn't hear the exchange of words, but Mrs. Middleton's tone was hushed and agitated, uncommonly gruff for a servant addressing a caller. Lara tried to catch sight of the visitor without being seen herself, which was next to impossible.

Her biggest fear, that Robert and Claude had discovered John Byron's whereabouts, rushed cold chills down her spine. She pulled her son tightly to her side, pressed back against the house, and waited for whatever would happen next. After a time the carriage left and Mrs. Middleton returned to her wash.

Lara waited until early evening then approached the housekeeper calmly; it wouldn't do to appear too intrigued and arouse her suspicion, but Lara needed to know if someone had been asking about her.

"Did we have a visitor earlier?" she asked.

Mrs. Middleton looked up from the flour she was kneading. "A lost bloke is all. Took the wrong road out of town."

Lara sensed the housekeeper's deception in the way the woman kept her eyes averted and her voice noncommittal. Mrs. Middleton might have elaborated on the man's looks, demeanor, even his carriage, but never would she have said nothing. Lara had no reason to doubt Mrs. Middleton's sincerity, but she knew that a lie had just been told to her. Frowning, she turned away. She no longer felt safe at Fairfield Cross, and she didn't even know why.

The morning was gloomy and overcast. John Byron sat next to the window, chin in his palm, staring moodily at the approaching storm. "I want to go outside."

Lara looked up from her sewing. "It looks foul."

The smell of ginger cookies wafted up from below and John Byron's eyes widened in delight. "I need to visit Mrs. Middleton!"

Lara laughed as he spun away from the window and headed for the door. "Don't be a pest."

"I shan't," he promised. Tearing out of their small suite, he raced down the stairs as fast as he could, putting both life and limb in sufficient peril to fill his bored blood with enough adrenaline to last a good many hours. When he reached the bottom, he rounded the corner and collided with a gentleman just leaving the dining room.

"Here now." The gentleman grabbed the child by the upper arms to steady them both.

Chagrined at being caught racing down the stairs like a street urchin, John Byron looked up sheepishly and found a tall, regal-looking man with hair the color of butter and eyes that looked both stern and friendly. "I beg your pardon, sir," he said earnestly. He would be upbraided by this man, no doubt, then receive a scolding from his mother too if she found out. All in the same morning, for the same crime. The day was not turning out nearly so well as he had hoped.

Instead, the man just stared at him with sharp eyes and an inquisitive smile on his face. "And who might you be, young upstart?"

"John Byron."

"Ah, a poetic name to be certain."

Heartened, John Byron nodded. "Exactly, sir. I was named for John Milton and Lord Byron. My father, Lord Folkstone, said that with an intelligent and dignified name I should become an intelligent and dignified man."

"I see." Understanding and confusion both shone

in the friendly smile. "You are George's son?" At the boy's nod, he continued. "My condolences to your family. I was rather fond of your father."

Relieved he wasn't to receive a dressing down for his behavior, John Byron smiled up at the dashing man. He looked to be in his twenties and was casually dressed in buff-colored riding breeches with a dark-green coat slung over one shoulder. Though relaxed, he carried himself with an air that gave one no doubt he was a nobleman. "And you are, sir?"

"Adam Devereaux, with various and sundry titles attached."

John Byron's small jaw dropped in shock. "You're the Duke of Warrington!"

"Well, it isn't a crime, you know."

"Oh, no, sir." He reddened with embarrassment. "It's just that my father spoke of you often."

"I imagine he did," Adam agreed. "We sat on opposing sides of many scientific arguments"—he gave John Byron an odd half smile—"but agreed on many as well."

"Your Grace, I am most sorry for plowing into you."

Adam waved an elegant hand. "No bother. I was a child once, only last year if the dower duchess were to give her august opinion. *I* would have ridden the banister down, if I'd had the chance." The child stifled a burst of amazed giggles, and Adam sent him a pained look. "I wouldn't have told you who I am if I had known you were going to get all flustered and stiff."

"No, sir. I won't." John Byron decided he liked this

man immensely. "I know another duke," he said on impulse.

"Do you?" Adam queried. "I know several. A stuffy lot, all of them. Except me, of course."

"No, my duke isn't stuffy at all."

Adam's brow arched. "Oh? And who might your duke be?"

"The Duke of Ravenwood."

Trained from the cradle to show only the mildest interest to even the most extraordinary news, Adam merely nodded when the jolt of astonishment shot through him. *Hunter, you sly puss. I thought I recognized your demon eyes in this cherub's face.* Adam smiled sweetly. "I imagine you do know Ravenwood." *And your mother too, though it all seems too fantastical.* It simply wasn't Hunter's style to cuckold another man's wife. "And have you seen His Grace lately?"

John Byron shook his head, rather forlornly Adam thought. "It's been ever so long."

"Well, who knows?" Adam returned flippantly. "Ravenwood might show up at this very place for a day of hunting. Stranger things have been known to happen."

The child's wide, expectant smile made Adam feel like a cad. He hadn't the slightest idea what Hunter was about these days, but he was certainly going to do his best to find out. "Well, I've a hundred things to do, young Lord Folkstone, but I have just one question for you before I'm off."

John Byron smiled up at the handsome man expectantly.

"What are you doing at Fairen Woods?"

"Sir?"

"This hunting cottage, Fairen Woods. It belongs to me."

"John Byron!"

Lara stood at the top of the stairs, her face pale but composed. She smiled gently at her son and held out her hand. John Byron raced only halfway up before remembering his manners.

"Mother, please meet His Grace, the Duke of Warrington."

Lara forced a smile for her son's sake and descended the stairs. "We've met. So good to see you again, Your Grace. It's been too long."

"Lady Chalmers," he acknowledged. "My condolences on your husband's passing. George was a remarkable man."

"He will be missed by many," Lara agreed. Though Adam's words had been more than merely perfunctory, Lara sensed something assessing and unsettling in his sharp gaze. "Did I understand correctly? You own this home?"

Adam nodded. "Yes, though not as part of my family's holdings. The hunting in yon woods is superb, so I purchased Fairen Woods years back in order to have a place to stay rather than the public inn in Fairfield Cross." He smiled. "Have you found it hospitable?"

"Quite," Lara answered, the truth of her situation beginning to settle sickly in the pit of her stomach. "Why did you rent it to me?"

"Oh, your man was very discreet," Adam said, as if

to reassure her. He finally shrugged and held up his hands, too innocent. "Alas, I am a snoop of the first water. When Hunter asked if Fairen Woods was available, I had to find out why he was interested." He glanced pointedly at John Byron, then back at Lara. "Now I know."

Chapter Sixteen

The heat of indignation rose in Lara's cheeks, but she continued to regard Adam Devereaux with a chilly frankness. He had a roguish, polished look that Lara generally found distasteful in the younger set, but she also noted keen-eyed intelligence in the eyes staring back at her.

"Hunter doesn't know I'm here."

He smiled, the cavalier from head to toe. "Doesn't he?"

Further argument was unnecessary. She knew by the look on Warrington's face that Hunter had set this whole thing up, using Percy as a convenient pawn. She wasn't certain how Hunter had managed it or even if she was angry at his manipulation, but she was vastly, albeit reluctantly, relieved to realize that he was still making sure John Byron was protected.

She noted the acceptance on Warrington's face of what he perceived was her clandestine lifestyle. She turned to John Byron and smiled softly. "Go see if Mrs. Middleton will prepare tea for all of us." As soon as he departed, she turned back to Adam.

"Your son is a handsome boy," he said.

"Yes, the very likeness of his father," she returned coldly. She couldn't remain at Fairen Woods now, beneath a cloud of suspicion and innuendo. Despair made a mess of her stamina. Her knees and stomach felt weak, her chest hollow. "I will have our things packed by evening," she stated, and turned to climb the stairs, her only thought to get away as quickly as possible.

Adam touched her shoulder. "Wait, I didn't mean to chase you off."

Lara braced her hand against the polished wooden rail. "I'm not running, merely leaving."

"Your son is a remarkable boy," Adam said. "Will he be dragged into court along with you?"

Lara's face paled. She turned slowly and regarded Adam Devereaux with stony purpose. "Don't," she commanded softly. "Don't make me flee even farther into the countryside to hide him."

An odd mixture of admiration and contempt shone in Adam's eyes. "Let your husband's brothers have Folkstone before they ruin both you and your child by dragging you into public scrutiny."

"Are you telling me not to appeal?"

"I have seen your son."

An anguished cry echoed through Lara's mind but her voice remained level. There would be no need to summon Harry; she could find out just exactly what her chances would be now. "You sit in the House of

Lords. You and George were well acquainted. If this goes to appeal—"

"I have seen your son," Adam repeated.

The finality of his statement, the sentiment, struck Lara like a slap. "Good day, Your Grace," she said quietly, and ascended the stairs.

Her days at Fairen Woods had been well ordered and placid, if a bit boring. She had been her own person, and for the first time since George's death, she had not been afraid. She wondered how long it would take her to forgive the Duke of Warrington for ruining it all so easily.

Lara stepped down from the public coach and searched for Percy. She had sent word for him to meet her at Ravenwood village, but travel was unreliable and she couldn't be certain he'd even gotten her message. An elderly man sat on an overturned bucket outside the village posting house, chewing on a stem of grass.

"Excuse me," Lara said, making her way toward him.

"Givens is me name," the man said, and rose to his feet.

"Good day, Mr. Givens. Do you know if Mr. Percy Smythe has arrived today from London?"

The man wore tattered clothing and a friendly smile. His thin hair stood on end, as if he'd been running his hand through it repeatedly. "Small man? Young and proper-looking?"

"Yes," Lara breathed. "Where is he?"

"Waiting inside."

Having heard the coach, Percy strolled out at that moment, an abashed look on his face. He took Lara's hands, then realized how familiar he must appear and released them. "What has happened? I received only a message saying to meet you here."

"All is well," Lara said calmly. "We'll talk later." She turned back to Mr. Givens. "Have you a buggy for hire? We need to get to Ravenwood Castle." She would not go trudging in on foot, dragging her portmanteau behind her like a displaced housemaid looking for work. She already expected to find Hunter's urbane countenance knowingly awaiting them, and she didn't need any further indignity to amuse him.

The man motioned Lara around to the side of his shop where an ancient nag stood munching hay from a wooden trough. "Ain't a buggy."

Lara stared at the wagon that had seen more prosperous days but wouldn't quibble about the only means of transportation in sight. "It will do just fine," she said.

He peered at her curiously, then nodded and went about his business. "It'll only take a moment."

Lara picked her way back through patches of prickly briars and weeds to the corner of the building where she motioned the coachman to unload their belongings. John Byron stepped down from the coach and raced around the side of the building to stand beside Lara.

"How much for three of us?" she asked Mr. Givens.

The man scratched his head as if he'd never had to multiply a fare, then looked up and paused. His gaze fixed on John Byron, then dropped quickly back to his task. "No charge," he murmured.

Lara cut him a cool glance and ushered her son into the wagon before further comments could be made. A small knot of anxiety tightened in her stomach when they got under way, but she ignored it and tried to enjoy the beauty of the countryside and coolness of the early autumn breeze.

She was going to see Hunter again. Trepidation curled through her, and desire, and a hundred other emotions not so easily defined. She had known it was not over. Somewhere in the hidden recesses of her soul she had known she would see him again, though she had tried to prepare herself for the opposite. Her gloved hands tightened on her reticule as the wagon bounced along. Beautiful rolling farmland stretched far in one direction, while thick forest edged the dusty road on the other side. Low boggy areas interspersed the woodlands and sturdy wildflowers clung to the marshes in odd patches, too stubborn to leave summer behind.

The untended landscape was both haunting and stunning, a moody but vibrant wildness in the midst of beauty. Hunter's image came to mind. This was a place, a disposition, he would understand perfectly.

The woodland began to thin and marshes gave way to sloping green meadows dotted with trees. Livestock grazed in the distance, their slow quiet movements lending peace to the picturesque countryside. The groomed lands of Ravenwood began with a low stone wall and arched entrance gate officially separating the castle grounds.

The wagon lumbered along, miserably uncomfort-able when judged against the luxury of a well-sprung carriage, though not one of its inhabitants minded. The driver was accustomed to the bumps and jolts, the others were too worried about what greeted them at Ravenwood, except John Byron, who felt happy anticipation building in his chest until he thought he would explode with it.

When they reached the bricked courtyard leading to the front entrance, they were greeted by Jacobs who, after a stunned glance, recovered himself enough to send Lara a disapproving frown. "Milady should have sent someone from the village for the carriage."

"We are fine," she assured him. She smoothed the wrinkles from her dress nervously. "Is His Grace at home?"

"He is away at the moment, but come inside. He left instructions for your comfort."

Lara exhaled a sigh of melancholic relief. It was no good lamenting the fact that Hunter had known she would return. With a forced smile, she accepted Ja-cobs's help and climbed from the wagon. With John Byron and Percy following, she led the way to the entrance.

Fresh flowers sat atop a marble side table in the foyer, lending color and aroma from a priceless vase that added just the right proof of affluence. It was all so impersonal, one of a hundred entry halls in as many English manor homes, but Lara felt Hunter's presence everywhere—in the conventional way his servants behaved within the unconventional structure of his life, in the subdued masculine hues chosen to decorate the hall while allowing splashes of bold color from every kind of flower at his housekeeper's whim.

There was a presence about Ravenwood that transcended time and decorum, something both eerie and inviting. Exquisitely and tastefully done, no concession was made either for or against modern times. Pieces were chosen, colors used, artifacts retained in a conglomeration that melded ancient with contemporary in perfect harmony. Lara had not felt these things as a child when she visited here, and she knew it was not merely her maturity that had changed her perception. It was Hunter's presence that had imbued life into the estate once again.

Within seconds, a loud squeal pierced the serenity of the hall. "Madame Lara! John Byron!" Nicolette cried in delight as she hurtled down the steps at an alarming rate. "You have returned!" Unabashed, she flung herself at John Byron, catching him midway between waist and chest, and toppling them both to the floor.

"Silly moppet," he scolded, but his laughter mixed with hers, childish and unaffected. With a huff of male impatience, he pushed yards of fluff and frill aside to find Nicolette's innocent smile fixed on the housekeeper who was scowling down at both of them. His expression sobered appropriately. "Good afternoon, Mistress Mary."

"Lord Folkstone," Mary acknowledged, then turned her frown on the culprit. "Miss Nicolette, where are your manners? You've tumbled milord to the floor like some street hoyden. I've a mind to send you to the nursery."

"Oh, please don't," John Byron pleaded. "I'm so glad to be back. I don't mind at all being tackled."

"Lucky for Miss Nicolette," Mary said with a twinkle. "Come now, let's get you back on your feet." She helped both children up and tidied their clothes with brisk efficiency. "There. Now, can you extend a proper welcome, Miss Nicci?"

Nicolette curtsied prettily, if perfunctorily. "Welcome, John Byron, Madame Lara and . . ." Her eyes fastened on Percival. ". . . and *M'sieu* whoever-you-are."

Mary gasped at her impertinence, but Percy only bowed formally. "Percival Smythe," he managed.

"*M'sieu* Smythe," Nicolette repeated dutifully, then spun to John Byron. "Come see. Gal is sulking. Papa wouldn't let her go with him, so she is pouting in her room and won't let me in to play."

John Byron nodded sagely. "Come along, then. We'll go stand outside her door and make pests of ourselves until she relents." He took Nicolette's hand and they raced up the stairs without a thought for the adults left behind.

Mary turned quickly to Lara. "Lady Chalmers, forgive Nicolette's manners and my own, you must be parched from the journey. I'll send refreshments to the morning room immediately."

Lara only nodded absently as Mary hurried off, her eyes transfixed on the stairs, rapt and appalled by the scene that had just unfolded before her. She had witnessed nothing less than a brother accepting the role of the elder, taking a little sister's hand to offer support. John Byron was only nine, still so in need of care himself, but in an instant he had changed and grown to meet the needs of one much younger. Lara's discomfited gaze flew to Smythe.

"God save us," Percy whispered. "She could be his twin."

Lara only nodded. It was neither prudent nor fruitful to indulge the overwhelming sense of betrayal she felt when looking at Nicolette. "Her mother is dead," she said to forestall further questions.

He took the news with grace, as Lara suspected he would, as if it meant nothing, when it meant so much more than she was willing to admit.

"Do you wonder, Percy, how many more bastard children he has ready to pop up and identify him by nothing but their likeness?"

"No," Smythe murmured truthfully. "I was thinking how astonishingly beautiful his children are."

Lara laughed softly at the insanity of such a comment from the all-too-proper Smythe. "So they are," she agreed, and smiled because crying was useless. "Here is Jacobs," she added. "I will let him see you to your room while I find out if Hunter has returned and secure our welcome."

"Is there a problem?"

"He will not turn us out, no," she said, then smiled wryly, "but we mustn't confuse that with being welcome, either." She sighed. "Forgive my cynicism, Percy, I'm tired. There is a magnificent garden behind the castle, beyond the lawn. I shall retire there for a while. If you need me . . ."

The unfinished statement hung between them, rife with too much expectancy. There wasn't much he could do yet; there wasn't much she expected him to.

The late summer sun slipped behind the low clouds in a dazzling display of color, stretching bands of gold and orange, violet, and rose to warm the afternoon sky beyond what it deserved with its gloomy gathering of storm clouds. Lara felt the humid chill of pending rain and stayed by a patch of late summer blossoms. Their scent and color soothed her, a spot of beauty in the midst of approaching disaster. The garden was an unaccountably peaceful place. One felt both consoled and renewed upon entering the simple wicket gate set into the hedge. Lara had no explanation for the feelings, but she basked in the peace that enveloped this spot. Neither the cliffs of Dover nor the pastures of Fairfield Cross had brought her the contentment of Ravenwood's garden.

The sound of children at play drifted on the wind, a nice accompaniment to the babble of water from the nearby fountain. Herbs and spices grew in neat rows far off in one section, medicinal plants on the other, but in the middle lay acres of paradise, fruit and nut trees, flowers and shrubs. Walking paths had been worn into some of the grassy areas, and marble benches were scattered throughout to best catch the morning sun or midday shade or evening twilight.

Lara leaned her head back against the trunk of a hawthorn, inhaled the scented air, and tried to forget that she stood to lose everything she owned.

If her life of lies collapsed in upon her, she had no

one to blame but herself, but she could not abide with what would happen to her son. Whether because of simple vanity or the surety that his brothers were not fit to run his estates, George had set his own course to secure the comfortable financial empire he had established, and Lara had gone along readily with the deception for her child's sake. If the Scotland residence was any indication, Robert and Claude would run Folkstone into the ground in less than a decade if awarded ownership. She felt certain now that George must have known that. It wasn't just masculine pride that had moved him to claim another man's child but also the need to preserve what his own father and grandfather had built.

She closed her eyes and tried to pray, to beg, but even that consolation was beyond her. Her sins had brought her to this place in life, and she was destined now to reap what she had so blithely sown a decade earlier. She wanted forgiveness and deliverance, but there was nothing in her that regretted John Byron or what she had done to protect him all these years. Her heart clamored for peace but a part of her suspected she might never see it again.

The breeze whispered a new song as it soughed through the trees and tugged the curls at Lara's temples free. She brushed them away with the back of her hand, then paused, the moment captured by a sudden sense of awareness. She recognized a presence long before someone emerged from the thicket, the density of strength and purpose preceding him like aromas from a cookhouse.

He stood off in the shadows, misty gray in twilight,

ground fog cloaking him like a veil so that it was hard to distinguish his features. "Hunter?" she called, but he did not answer.

Lara didn't realize until that very moment that day had waned and twilight was upon her. The moon had risen, casting silvery ribbons through his dark hair. There was a look about him she could not discern, something ancient yet ageless. And there was such compassion in his eyes, she thought it must be a trick of the light.

She rose from her seat, discomfited by his stillness and the oddly powerful kindness in his gaze. She wanted to run into his arms, to hide in the comfort of his embrace, but knew she was being foolish. "I have brought Smythe," she said to break the silence, though she felt certain he already knew. "He is not encouraged, I fear, though he tries to hide it." She looked down at her hands and fought the urge to lash out at him for knowing she would return. "I had nowhere else to go . . . nowhere else I *chose* to go." She had needed desperately to feel safe again. "Thank you for receiving us."

"You belong here" was all he said.

"No . . ." But Lara's heart leapt in her breast at his words. She had thought she might never see him again, and she could not regret this one last chance, just the circumstances that had brought her here. "Still, I thank you—" She blinked and peered into the gloom to find that he was gone, vanished like a puff of chimney smoke. Disconcerted, she searched harder for the path he'd taken. The foliage was thick in places, sparse in others, carefully manicured to offer openness or intimacy. She saw no sign of his passage and wondered at his reticence. She had thought he would taunt her to some small degree. Instead, he had not only let the chance go by but had also welcomed her with words that made no sense and a look in his eyes she'd never seen before.

A breeze blew across the back of her neck, more biting than the balmy afternoon winds had been, almost as if his departure had left a chill in its wake. She shivered and rushed back to the main hall before the storm moved in and caught her unsheltered. She reached the gallery at the back entrance and was greeted by the yeasty smells of fresh bread drifting from the bakehouse, more inviting than the heavy scent of rain rushing in with the dark clouds. She took one last look at the grounds in the fading light, then left the peace behind to face whatever lay ahead.

Passing through the formal dining room, she saw that the table had already been set. Crystal winked beneath chandeliers lit by dozens of scented candles, and gleaming china emblazoned with the Ravenwood crest sat in front of five chairs. Her heart sank at the number. Though she did not particularly relish the thought of an intimate meal with Hunter, she could not find it within her at all to share repast with a group of strangers. She would plead a headache, which would not be far from the truth, and take her dinner in her room.

Children's voices rang in excited echoes, distant at first, then more distinct as they drew closer to the dining room. Nicolette burst through the door first, followed by John Byron and Gal. Their cheeks were rosy from outdoor exercise, their hair too hastily combed, but at least their faces and hands were clean.

"My pony," John Byron exclaimed to the others, "went fast as the wind."

"*Oui,*" Nicolette jumped in, not to be outshone. "My pony is fast, too. Very fast. Her name is Posey and she is my very own."

Gal and John Byron exchanged superior glances but allowed Nicolette her posturing. "I'm so hungry," Gal said, "I could eat a pony named Posey."

Squeals and giggles erupted as Nicolette took off after Gal in righteous affront. Lara wished she could watch them for hours, simply bask in the beauty of their innocent play, but they tempted calamity running around the dinner table like hoodlums. "Girls," she said sharply.

Gal stopped suddenly and all animation left her face. She stared at Lara for a moment, then walked purposefully forward. Her path was direct, her look subtly defiant, but her voice barely rose above a whisper. "You have come back," she said.

"Yes. Am I welcome?"

Stiffly Gal nodded.

"Thank you, Anne," Lara said very quietly. "I am so glad to see you."

Gal's eyes closed briefly, then she spun around and picked Nicolette up and tossed her upside down over her shoulder, which set the youngster to squealing again.

"Come, Mama," John Byron said, obviously excited as he took Lara's hand. "We are to eat with the adults tonight."

"Are you?" Lara glanced at the table and counted off the places again, wondering who had been intentionally left out. She would not condone Percy being treated as a hired servant rather than her friend. "How nice of His Grace to suggest it. I would like to thank him before dinner."

"He's not here," John Byron interrupted. "It was Cook's idea."

"He hasn't been for two days," Gal added, "but he'll be back tomorrow or the next day perhaps."

"But I just saw him," Lara said, "in the garden."

Gal placed a wiggling Nicolette into her chair. "It wasn't Hunter."

"But I saw him," Lara repeated. "He spoke to me."

Gal looked up, mild exasperation on her face. "He's not here. If you saw something in the garden, it was the Guardian." She added matter-of-factly, "He's a ghost or something."

"An angel," Nicolette corrected.

Gal gave her a sour look and continued. "The legend says the Guardian has been here since the beginning, when a woman named LeClaire claimed her rightful place as lady of Ravenwood. Everyone who belongs here sees him."

"Do not!" Nicolette chimed in. "I haven't seen him and I better not! It would scare me silly."

"You're already silly," Gal teased, which sent Nicolette into a serious pout.

Lara threw a hand up to stop their bickering. "I do

not believe in ghosts, and I know what I saw. Hunter was in the garden.''

Gal took her seat in a huff. "Fine."

Which Lara knew didn't mean fine at all, but Percy walked in at that moment and she had no desire to pursue the subject at the dinner table.

"Good evening all," he called. With no servant present, he held a chair for Lara, then looked at the remaining seat. When no one spoke, he looked around self-consciously. "Will His Grace be joining us?"

Cook bustled in, followed by two servants, their arms laden with trays. "Good evening, milady, Mr. Smythe," she said cheerily. "His Grace is away, but you are to make yourself comfortable until his return."

Gal threw Lara a self-satisfied look.

Lara ignored her and spoke calmly to Cook. "I am quite certain I saw His Grace in the garden earlier."

Cook paused, startled, then made the sign of the cross. "Yes, milady," she murmured and hurried from the room.

Lara had been at Ravenwood for two weeks, going slowly mad, when Hunter decided to make an appearance. He took her completely by surprise, strolling into the breakfast room one morning as if he had never been away. She almost choked on the biscuit in her mouth.

"Good morning," he greeted, then served himself from the buffet.

Lara's stomach suffered a weightless lift but her

voice was, thankfully, composed. "Where have you been?" she asked as if she had the right, which she knew perfectly well she did not.

"Settling affairs," he said ambiguously. "How is John Byron?"

"Well enough." She looked down at her plate. "Better now that he is here again. Thank you for having us."

He poured rich dark coffee from a silver service. "You should say it with less resentment."

She smiled. "You ask the impossible."

"Then say nothing at all. I don't want your gratitude, Lara."

"But I am grateful." She looked up at him, stunned as always by the masculine strength and perfection of his features, his beautiful likeness to his son. Her heart beat treacherously fast in her breast. "You know what has happened."

"Yes."

"And will you allow us to stay here until the courts are done with us?"

"You will not be able to avoid a scandal."

She sighed. "I know." Hated tears blurred her vision and she looked away. "I cannot touch my money and I can think of no other way to provide for John Byron properly." She crushed the napkin in her lap. "I will not starve my child to save my reputation, and I could not bear to go begging to friends."

"And I am not a friend?"

Lara smiled self-consciously. "I'm not certain yet. Can you think of another alternative?"

"You could go back to Fairfield Cross."

Anger and disgust flashed in her eyes. "How good of you and Warrington to set that up."

"I was not out to trick you but to protect my son," he said. "I should have known Adam would go sneaking around out there. Now that he has seen John Byron, he thinks you are being unreasonable to appeal."

"Rubbish!" She rose from her seat, her appetite gone. "Women are chattel. Even if he had not seen my son, he and the others would side with the male relatives. What other choice do I have but to appeal?"

Hunter said nothing and his very silence made Lara blush hotly.

"I see," she said scornfully. "I should become your mistress in order to survive and salvage what's left of my reputation. How sickeningly hypocritical!" She flung her napkin onto the table. "Do you know I won't even be allowed to speak on my own behalf. I must have a lord sponsor me and a barrister represent me. Two or more men to do what I could do very well on my own, if given the chance."

There was no use arguing with her. Every word she said, however unfair, was true. "Prepare yourself, Lara," Hunter said. "It could get very ugly before it's over."

His voice was woefully dark, and Lara felt her heart give. She looked out at the vast lawn, so lovely with its clean lines, elegant arbors, and cooling pools. "Forgive me for thinking only of myself. Will it ruin you too?"

He chuckled self-derisively. "Nothing can ruin me. What can they say that I will not willingly admit?"

Her hand tightened into a fist. "I don't care any more," she said fiercely. "Truly, if it were not for John Byron I wouldn't care a whit."

"They will try to crucify you," he warned.

"Fine. Let them. Half of those who would condemn me have mistresses tucked away and wives with peccadilloes of their own. If their younger children bear resemblance to another they overlook that as nothing, but John Byron will pay with his life!"

"As will you," he said quietly.

"I'm so afraid," she whispered, and walked from the room.

Hunter watched her go, her head held erect, her shoulders dignified. He waited for something, a sense of victory, a feeling of triumph.

He waited in vain.

Chapter Seventeen

It was the worst thing Lara could imagine at this point in her life.

"Are you certain, Lydia?" she asked.

"He says it's all arranged and scheduled for two weeks from tonight."

"Then he's gone mad," Lara whispered.

"Beg pardon, milady?"

Lara rose from the desk where she had been trying to pen several innocuous letters to friends explaining her absence. "Lydia, see if His Grace has time this morning to meet with me."

"Yes, milady." Lydia left the breakfast tray on the table near the window and hurried off.

Lara approached it with trepidation. Not because of the cook's excellent food but because of the newspaper lying beside her plate. The first reference to her association with Hunter had begun a week ago, cloaked in fiction. Lara had no doubt that others would be forthcoming soon.

She unfolded the paper and scanned the pages until she found what she had dreaded: the backhanded innuendo that kept gossip flowing like spoiled wine.

The Duke of Dovetree is said to be keeping company with a young and lovely widow from Dover, who has been his house guest for several weeks. How long have the two known each other, and has our elusive and very eligible duke finally found a mate?

Lara slapped the paper down. The garbage came as no surprise and could not be avoided, but she loathed it nonetheless. And what could Hunter be thinking to suggest a ball at Ravenwood and expect her to play hostess to a guest list of England's most prestigious and powerful lords? It wasn't even public knowledge that she had appealed to a higher court, and already she was being ridiculed. It would get much worse when the *ton* found out about the charges brought against her.

She didn't wait to hear from Lydia but abandoned her tray and went in search of Hunter herself. The breakfast room was empty, as was the library. John Byron was at his lessons with Nicolette and her tutor, Mr. Mabry, in the nursery, and neither had seen Hunter since dinner the night before. Lara finally found Gal, a stubborn look on her face, coming up the stairs.

"Have you seen Hunter?" she asked.

"The devil take him" was the only response she got as Gal pushed past her.

"I'll pass your message along, if you tell me where he is," Lara offered.

"The stables," Gal snapped, then disappeared through the nursery door.

Lara left the main hall through the back entrance and headed in the general direction of several out-buildings she assumed were the stables. The smell of manure wafted strong on the wind as she neared, overriding the nicer odors of fresh air and horseflesh. A man sang as he pitched hay from a wagon into an outside trough, and a boy with a strong Cockney accent talked in soothing tones to a young, spirited horse he worked on a lead rope around a pen.

Lara approached. "Excuse me. Have you seen His Grace this morning?"

The old man turned slowly. He was permanently bent at the waist, but his arms still bulged with strength. He pointed at the long building with his pitchfork. "Inside."

Lara thanked him, then picked her way cautiously between the areas that had not yet been raked by the stable hands. Stepping into the cool interior of the long barn, she paused to let her eyes adjust to the dim light, then walked toward the voices coming from the back. Weasel was making admiring sounds as a stable boy threw a saddle over a magnificent black gelding tied to one of the stalls.

"He's a fine one. Lord Warrington will be green with envy."

Hunter stood at the horse's head, stroking its nose with long patient sweeps. "Adam has ten just like this one. He'll not even notice."

"Nay, he takes more stock in horseflesh than you do. He'll be making a bid for this one within a quarter hour of his arrival, you wait and see."

Hunter smiled. "Then I'll have to keep him, won't I?"

"Your Grace."

Hunter turned to see Lara standing in diffuse sunlight, tiny motes dancing in the rays like pixies scattering dust over her hair and shoulders. Dressed in a high-waisted gown of white with pink and green trimming, she looked fresh and inviting in the dusty interior of the stable. He had the sudden urge to pull her into the shelter of his arms, to hold her close against the unsteady heartbeat her presence caused. "Lady Chalmers."

"May I speak with you, please?"

She could do anything she wanted with him, not that he could tell her that. He wanted to be alone with her, away from the rest of the turbulent, intrusive world. Just a few secluded hours where no one existed but the two of them. A thought struck him suddenly, an unconscionable plan in reality, but then he had never pretended to be reputable in either thought or deed. "I am off for a ride, Lara. Would you care to join me?"

"Thank you, but no. I'm not much of a horsewoman and it's been years since I enjoyed a ride. I do need to speak with you, though."

Tiny lines of strain creased her brow. He wanted to run his thumb over her flesh, to smooth away the signs of anxiety. "Allow me to have Briggs saddle a gentle mare for you. You shouldn't have any problems." He turned to his stable boy. "Ready Mercy for Lady Chalmers."

"No, please," Lara said.

Hunter put his finger to her lips. "Say yes."

His voice was sultry and convincing; his eyes glimmered with teasing humor. Lara knew better than to permit herself one second of his byplay, but she felt her guard slipping at the gentle coaxing. Oh, to be able to indulge in a harmless flirtation with him. It held untold fascination for Lara, though she knew it was impossible. She was past the respectable time in her life when such was allowed with impunity. At her age and widowhood, there were no harmless flirtations, only coy invitations.

The stable boy hurried off to do his lord's bidding, and Weasel darted around the edge of the stall with a wide grin. "Give her a try, milady. You'll like Mercy, she's gentle as a lamb. Best take a cloak though. Storm's moving in and the wind's whipping up something fierce out there."

Hunter cut Weasel a sideways glance. "We won't be gone that long."

"But I'm not dressed for riding," Lara said, noting that Hunter was superbly turned out in a dark-blue velvet hunting jacket and tightly fitted breeches that buckled just above his tall boots.

"Your manner of dress makes no difference here, Lara," he said, and led the horse out into the hay-littered aisle.

She stepped out of the way of the gelding's frisky shifting and hoped Weasel was right about Mercy. Briggs returned with a small chestnut mare, and

Libby Sydes

Hunter took Lara by the waist and hoisted her onto
the saddle before she changed her mind. She jerked
her skirts back over her ankles with one hand and
held the reins tightly with the other.

Hunter led both horses outside before mounting,
then gave Weasel a solemn look. "We'll ride to the
east near Wolfsglen Forest. We should be back by
noon."

Weasel opened his mouth, then snapped it closed.
"Aye, whatever you say."

Lara gave her mare a cautious kick and was
pleased with the horse's sweet disposition and comfortable gait. She enjoyed riding immensely, but it
had been years since she had done so. After George's
health failed, she had been content to stay by his side
when she wasn't seeing to his affairs and running
Folkstone. The breeze was cool on her cheeks, the
sun fickle as it slipped in and out between drifting
clouds. A darker sky loomed in the distance, spreading across the horizon in shades of gray and black.

"Are you certain the weather will hold?"

Hunter kept his horse to a sedate pace beside
Lara's mare. "It will hold as long as we need it to,"
he answered. "What did you want to speak with me
about?"

"Lydia came in this morning with some nonsense
about a ball. She says that I am to play hostess in two
weeks to some of England's most influential families."

"Nonsense, yes," he answered, "but true nonetheless. And not just a ball but an entire weekend party.
Whole families will be invited. I have arranged a

304

chaperon for you, someone I can trust to say she's been here the entire time, which will alleviate rumors of any impropriety."

Lara gritted her teeth against the news and clutched Mercy's reins so hard the little mare began to sidestep nervously. She relaxed her grip immediately, but her voice remained tight. "What, may I ask, is the insane purpose behind such?"

Hunter shrugged. "Win them to your side first, and they'll think twice about deserting you later."

"Ah." Cynicism laced her tone. "Your reasoning sounds so logical, but what makes you think it will work?"

"Absolutely nothing," he admitted. "It's just better to face the *ton* standing. When the accusations come, they will expect you to cower."

"They will expect it, but they won't respect it."

"Exactly."

"So," she said with sugary sarcasm, "I win them to my side, then show no wavering later when George's brothers try to ruin me by proving nothing less than the very truth. This, in turn, will preserve my integrity, and John Byron will never have reason to be ashamed."

Hunter cut her a sideways glance. "You sound a bit leery."

Lara laughed softly in frustration. "Do I? I can't imagine why." She glanced over at him briefly. "It's better than screaming and tearing at my hair."

The look in his amethyst eyes said he understood perfectly.

Something inside Lara shifted suddenly with the

understanding and compassion she saw there from such a cold and guarded man. Warmth trickled in through the icy barrier she had erected, softening her countenance and her reserve. He understood her dilemma and was trying to help in the most expedient way. He did not patronize her nor feed her lies and false hope, he merely did what he thought best. None of it would avail him anything. In truth, it could potentially damage his own reputation and standing among the *ton*. Although Lara knew he wouldn't care, she did for his sake.

"You don't have to do this," she pleaded. "It will profit you nothing and may not be worth the risk."

He smiled, clearly the pirate. "I thrive on risk, Lara."

No inch of her was immune to the power of that smile; no inch of her ever had been. Less confident of her seat than the need to put some distance between them, she kicked the mare into a faster pace to escape everything but the wind in her face and the rolling gait of the mare's strong stride beneath her. As the ground sped away, she let her thoughts go, if only for the briefest span of time, and allowed herself the freedom to feel only the moment: her hair being torn from its combs to whip wildly behind her, the cold air rushing over her clothing and exposed skin, the thunder of the mare's small hooves taking her away from her troubles.

She flung her head back and shook the few remaining pins lose, needing to be free of all encumbrances. Lightning cracked in the distance, charging the air with an intensity that matched Lara's need for escape. Thunder followed, rolling across the fields as if it chased the descending darkness. She barely noticed the approaching storm, just continued letting her body flow with the steady rhythm of the mare's gallop, as if she could outrun the trauma her life had become. And the riotous feelings Hunter inspired in her.

He followed at a short distance, knowing what she ran from, wondering what she ran to. He glimpsed a younger Lara in the wild flight, in need of excitement and adventure, and his pulse picked up the strong, rhythmic urgency of her desire to go forth recklessly and leave everything behind. The sloping meadow gave way to sparse thickets of shrubs and trees with the denser forest ahead. Lara continued on without a thought for the terrain, the distance, or the time of day. Hunter wondered if she was even aware of how far they had traveled from Ravenwood. He nudged his horse to catch up, careful to watch her, alert for any misstep or stumble.

Suddenly the rain came down in hard, gray sheets, pelting them both with enough force to sting, and the skies darkened with no trace of sun or cloud. Within seconds, they were soaked from head to toe.

Hunter pulled alongside Lara and reached over to take the mare's bridle, holding tight until both horses slowed to a manageable pace. "Through here," he shouted over the storm, and turned onto a path leading into the forest.

Lara wiped the rain from her eyes and felt her heart rate slow. Her exhilarating ride was over and she was exhausted from the energy expended in the reckless pace. A chill began seeping through her dripping clothes and into her bones, and she shivered. Little sunlight filtered past the storm clouds through the forest walls, and the darkness was almost complete beneath the canopy of trees. Noise was magnified, rain splattering on leaves, the wind howling through the trees. Lara shivered again and rubbed her arms briskly to bring up some warmth. Her fingers were growing numb and slippery on the mare's reins and her muscles had begun stiffening from the cold.

Through chattering teeth, she called to Hunter, "How long will this last?"

"Duck," he called back, and led them into a thicker copse of trees.

Lara leaned low over the mare's mane until the forest thinned again. Sitting back up, she saw a house just ahead, unoccupied by the look of it, yet well maintained. Hunter walked the horses to a lean-to around back, then helped Lara dismount. She turned her face aside to keep the rain out of her eyes, but her hair and clothing were drenched, hanging on her like seaweed. She pushed the hair back from her face. "Where are we?"

"Ravenwood's hunting lodge. We'll be able to dry off inside. Go ahead while I put the horses away."

Thankful, Lara hurried around the lodge to the front door. Its hinges were rusty and she couldn't get it to budge, so she huddled under the eaves until Hunter returned. The storm seemed to be worsening with each passing second.

He worked on the stubborn door for several minutes until it finally gave and swung open. The interior of the lodge was dark and smelled of wet and dust and old wood smoke. Sheets covered the furniture, making huge lumpy shadows throughout the room. Lara walked to the hearth and began stacking logs. Her hands were trembling but no worse than the rest of her frozen body.

Hunter crouched down beside her and took the firewood. "Get out of your wet clothes before you catch your death. I'll get a fire going."

Lara gave him a sharp look, then glanced down at herself and blushed. The drenched white lawn dress clung to her, sheer and revealing. She hesitated less than three seconds before rising and stalking away. There wasn't enough modesty in the world for her to dissemble. She snatched a sheet of coarse linen from a large chair and retreated to a dark corner. Behind the cover of draped furniture, she removed every item of wet clothing and dried herself as best she could, then wrapped her still-shaking body in the sheet. By the time she was done, a fire was blazing in the hearth and she rushed forward to huddle in front of it.

Hunter backed away and removed his own soaked clothing and returned minutes later, also draped in a swath of linen. He carried their wet garments over both arms. Lara took the pile of dripping fabric and began spreading each piece over chairs he had pulled to both sides of the fire. Once done, she went back to the center of the hearth and sat on her knees on a fur rug in front of the blaze. She closed her eyes and concentrated on the heat radiating outward from the crackling logs. She was cold and tired, but a part of her reveled in the remnant of excitement left over from the exhilarating ride.

Rain pounded on the roof overhead and lashed at the windows. The fire hissed and popped in countertempo to the tempest outside. Steam rose from their clothing, sending familiar scents into the musty air. Hunter crouched down beside Lara, but neither said a word as they focused on getting warm and dry. As the chill finally began to leave Lara's limbs, the awkwardness of her situation seeped into her conscience and with it a sudden, startling realization.

She tilted her head to the side to look at Hunter, anger flushing her cheeks, accusation in her tone. "You knew we would be caught in the storm."

His hand went to his bare chest in a show of maligned innocence. "I can't predict the weather."

"You knew!"

"I guessed."

Lara's heartbeat jerked with an adolescent rush that both thrilled and appalled her. With an indignant breath and half-hidden smile, she turned back to the fire. Hunter lifted a thick lock of hair from her shoulder and squeezed until drops of rainwater formed a tiny puddle on the floor beside the rug.

"You've been kidnapped, Lara."

His voice was low and warm and sultry. She almost laughed in girlish response, which appalled her even more. "Why?"

"I wanted no interruptions to my devious plans."

Feeling giddy and fearful and ridiculous, Lara's

words came out horrifyingly breathless. "You didn't kidnap me, I came along willingly."

He released her hair, then leaned over and pulled a sheet from the nearest chair and began drying the long tresses. "I tricked you. Now you're trapped in a deserted hunting lodge, unclothed, and at my mercy."

It was difficult to think, much less answer back, with Hunter's ministrations. His chest was broad and dark above the sheet that rode low on his hips, and Lara knew that beneath he was as bare as he was above, beautifully so, and it both thrilled and embarrassed her like nothing else had in a decade. She would have liked to lay the flat of her palm on his chest, to feel the heat and solidity of him. Surrounded by the smell of dust and dampness, his skin was a fragrant contrast that teased her senses deliciously. His hands were gentle and sure as he briskly rubbed the dampness from each curl, and gooseflesh pebbled every inch of Lara's exposed skin. Once done, he threaded his fingers through her hair and spread it about her shoulders and back, as if it pleased him to do so.

The simple gesture was compelling and suggestive, a seductive whisper into her willful reserve. Lara trembled in response and Hunter's voice came dark and soft near her ear.

"Still cold?"

She was far from cold. Heat spread throughout her body at an alarming rate, flushing her cheeks and breasts with a telling tide of pink. She reached up

311

when his hands fell to her shoulders and grabbed them tightly.

"Hunter . . ."

His fingers flexed then spread, creeping forward over her collarbone to the hills of her breasts. "At my mercy," he whispered into the shell of her ear. She felt his chest at her back, warm and solid, with nothing separating them but the thin sheet. She leaned forward to escape his questing hands, but he only leaned into her, a wonderful, heavy warmth against her spine, and slid his fingers beneath the cloth until it loosened and fell to her waist.

"Don't!" Anger underscored the word but it was directed at herself, at the desire that was so weighty inside her she could feel it pulsing in her veins. She scrambled to her feet and whirled to face him, clutching the linen to her breasts. "Stop this now, or I'll . . ."

"What?" he asked, rising also.

Lara backed up. "I don't know, but something."

He stalked her, step for step across the lodge floor, until her heart beat crazily in her throat and her cheeks grew hotter.

"Stop," she warned again, one hand held out as if that silly gesture would stay him.

He took her fingers and pulled quickly, bringing them to his mouth. Lara dug in her heels and tugged against him, but his eyes sparkled with unholy mirth and she knew he was not yet ready to give up the game. Worse, she found herself sinking unforgivably fast beneath the titillation and excitement of his roguish behavior.

She braced her palm against his chest to hold him at bay and gained her earlier wish. He was as warm and firm as she had imagined, sleek taut strength beneath her fingers.

He noted the flush in her cheeks, the too-bright eyes, and the weak protest in her voice. "Lara," he crooned silkily. "I think you enjoy this."

"Don't be absurd—"

He pulled suddenly and she was in his arms, surrounded by his heat and magnetism. His lips covered hers but there was no force behind the kiss, only an incredible gentleness more devastating than anything she could imagine. Her body melted into his with shameful quickness and her hands struggled to hold her sheet in place while she twisted in a half circle, one last effort to keep herself from being consumed by him.

He enfolded her in a tight grip, his chest pressed to her back, his forearms covering her breasts. "How long has it been, Lara?" he asked. "How long since you were stirred like this?" His mouth moved down the nape of her neck. "You shiver, you burn, and still you deny us both." His palms flattened on her breasts, callused and strong, each vein on the back of his hands visible beneath his bronze skin.

Lara gasped and covered his hands with her own, protesting vehemently with a writhe that only abraded her sensitive flesh and intensified the ache. Everything in her wanted to push him away, but she couldn't summon the words or gestures when everything in her also thrilled to his touch so badly she hurt with it.

She dug her nails into the backs of his hands and heard him hiss by her ear, felt his hot oath shiver down her neck and raise sharp tingles along her sensitized skin. The sharp intake of his breath was the only other sound before his lips claimed the tender flesh on the side of her neck just below her earlobe. The warmth of his mouth caressed her, sending molten heat to her lower abdomen and raising a keening inside that seemed to reverberate in echoes to her extremities. His hands began to move, making slow circles on her breasts, lifting, shaping, making her aroused and anxious. When his palms slid lower, she lurched back into him with a distressed cry.

"Hunter . . ."

He whispered her name, then tilted her face back and up to his. His mouth captured hers, absorbing both protest and passion. "Why do you fight this, Lara?" he sighed against her lips, then touched her deeply with his tongue.

She reached behind and grabbed his hair at the nape and pulled him into her, hungry for fiercer contact. She devoured him as he did her, with flesh and breath and desire, but quickly, before she came to her senses. Too long deprived to be satiated in an instant, too aware of just what such abandon would harvest, she released him and pulled back before she lost herself to his touch and scent and skill. Scrambling out of his hold, she faced him beyond arm's reach, her back to the fire, her hair falling around her wantonly.

Hunter's breath groaned between his teeth. Every ounce of him throbbed with an unfulfilled desire that only this woman could ignite, only this woman could quench. He laughed a bit shakily. "Come back here, Lara."

She held the sheet tightly to her breasts. "No."

"Why?"

"You know why."

She was magnificent with the firelight behind her casting sherry glints through her hair like spilled wine. Her shoulders were pale above the sheet, cool porcelain with the blush of passion still staining her in heat patches. He moved toward her and she scooted away, skittish and beautiful and too aware of her own susceptibility to allow him to get close again.

"You want this, Lara."

"Yes."

"Then don't deny us."

Her mouth was dry, her breath rapid and shallow. "I must."

"Why?"

Ire flashed in her voice. "You have two children at Ravenwood. I don't know how many elsewhere, and you've never been married. Need you ask why?"

"Then marry me."

Her eyes widened and everything in her went still and cold and painfully hollow. Time paused, as if all heat and motion had been suddenly stripped from the universe. Her expression fell and her voice came out as nothing more than a rasp of wounded pride.

"That's cruel and cheap. Even in your youth, you did not play such a mean trick to lure me into your bed."

She turned away, too devastated to look at him, and curled her nails into the palms of her hands. Her body felt ravaged by passion, her emotions shattered. When she was able, she turned back to find the door slightly ajar and Hunter gone. She pressed the heels of her hands to her eyes. She would not cry. She would not!

Crossing to their clothes, she turned them, then tidied the room, then wandered window to window to watch the rain—to watch. Through it all she fought the terrified thought that if Hunter had caught her with her guard just a little more down, she might have leapt into his arms at any casual invitation and made an utter fool of herself.

When he finally returned to the lodge, he was soaked anew from head to toe, including the sheet that still wrapped his lower torso.

He had to be freezing. "You'll catch your death," Lara scolded, then busied herself with turning their clothes again to avoid further contact.

He would not allow her any respite. He stripped his shirt from her hands and draped it over the chair back, then turned Lara to face him. His gaze was sharp and piercing. "You enjoyed the idea of my kidnapping you, Lara. It made your blood run a little hotter, your pulse race a little faster."

"Don't!"

"It did the same for me." His fingers bit into her upper arms, unyielding, just at the edge of hurtful. "In fact, it made me so hot I almost lost control. I wanted to lose control."

Lara struggled against his hold, fighting to get away before he finished with the awful truth.

"Is that what you wanted, Lara? Did you want me

to lose control so you wouldn't be responsible for the outcome?"

"No." She twisted again, tears blurring her vision at the terrible realization. "Yes." She faced him, her eyes desolate, her pride wanting revenge. "I want what I can't accept. But you want me too, Hunter, and you'd like any excuse to take me and salvage your own conscience, to act the pirate without really being that ignoble."

She pulled out of his grasp. "You can't have it both ways. Are you the pirate or the lord, man or beast?"

Something stark and painful flashed in his eyes, then was gone. Calmly he dropped the sheet at his waist, then grabbed Lara and pulled her to him. "The beast," he said with a note of regret, as she collided with his chest. "Forever the beast."

Chapter Eighteen

In the end, Hunter turned out to be neither saint nor sinner. Lightning struck a tree and sent the horses into a screaming frenzy. With an oath, he released Lara and threw his pants on, then rushed out into the storm to quiet the animals before they injured themselves. Lara collapsed into a chair, her mind and body in a turmoil of confusion.

What would Hunter have done—what would she had done—if Nature had not intervened? The thought was both so titillating and frightening that Lara flung her arm over her eyes and slouched down in the chair, as if she could hide from her own libidinous urges.

Over the ensuing minutes, she found to her distress that she could not escape the attraction she felt for Hunter, nor had she the energy to fight it any more. Her emotions were shredded, her resolve gone. She drew her legs to her chest and laid her forehead on her knees, a wanton widow in the throws of a moral

319

dilemma, as tragically wretched as the poor souls in the newspaper serials that circulated weekly.

Huddled within the tight circle of her arms, she ached and burned for a man from her past whom she had summoned into her present. She longed for the magnetism of his touch, the comfort of his embrace, the power of his passion. She longed for him to love her as she did him, with reason and comfort and gentle assurance. Instead, he disturbed her peace and disrupted everything she had thought she knew about herself sexually, turning her normal female yearnings into a grasping, depraved lust. In essence, she typified the foolish proverbial moth, hastening toward the flame.

She pulled her knees tighter to her chest and rocked. She had lain with him only once, a painful and awkward experience that held no great memory that she should want to repeat it. It was what had come before that she craved: the tenderness, the whispered words of adoration and seduction, the banishing of empty, aching loneliness. And what would come after: the quiet, regular breathing of exhausted slumber; the scent and texture of his warm, damp skin pressed to hers, proof of another's presence beside her, proof that she was not alone. A gripping despair filled her. In truth, she wanted more than all that. She wanted what she had never been with him—to be completely at peace, whole and loved.

Rain running off him and his mud-splattered breeches in rivulets, Hunter stormed back into the lodge. "Get dressed."

Lara rolled her forehead back and forth upon her knees. "No."

He ran his fingers through his wet hair and cocked one eyebrow. "No?" He marched to the chair, in no mood to humor her. "Will you not?" he whispered threateningly, and pulled her to her feet.

"No," she repeated in kind, and threw her arms around his neck. She pressed full length against him and tugged until their mouths collided in a tangle of frustrated passion and need.

"You've gone mad," he growled against her lips. He grabbed her arms to set her aside, but she clutched him tighter and hung on as if he were a lifeline. "Lara—"

Yes, she had gone mad, wanting him so, needing him beyond all reason and right. She would have this one moment, this small slice of time to pretend that their lives were in one accord, not tangled threads of past grievance and hopeless future. She would have with him now what she would only dream of later.

Hunter succumbed to her kiss, to her, allowing whatever she wanted to carry him along in its wake. She was small and lithe pressed against him, smelling of rainwater and violet-scented soap. He would neither advance nor retreat, just savor the moment as long as she pursued it. He didn't doubt that she would come to her senses any second and end it all, leaving him more frustrated than when they began, but at this moment he didn't care.

Undone, his hand slid down her back over her buttocks to her thigh, where he pulled her leg up to wrap around his waist. He cradled himself against her, wishing he could dissolve into her heat and passion, needing to merge into her softness and giving. She sighed his name and held him closer, their bodies melding, one a complement of the other. Her mouth returned to his time and again in a devouring dance of desire, clumsy and unchoreographed in her haste to escape the virtuous, circumspect behavior that had forever been her life.

Shocked and aroused to the edge of danger, Hunter ran his palm over her hair and shoulder, then down the narrow ridges of her spine. "Lara," he warned, but she only pressed tighter, searing him with the daring foray of her tongue as she swept his mouth. Frightened now of his ebbing control, he tugged at the sheet concealing her, thinking she would balk and it would be over, finding himself startled and so inaccurate when it came away like a vapor.

Her breath hitched and she pressed harder against him to shield herself from his gaze, and he echoed with a gruff murmur as the sleek, silken flesh of her breasts and midriff pressed against his ribs. Her skin was cool in the damp air, pebbled in places exposed, hot where she meshed with him. He tried to push her at arm's length, but she protested and clung tighter, consuming him with her eyes and mouth and ravenous ardor.

"I want to look at you," he said huskily.

She made a sound in her throat, distress coupled with embarrassment, and ran her hands over his back and shoulders and chest, making him forget he'd asked for more.

STOLEN DREAMS

He held her flush against him and moved to the fur rug in front of the fire, then lay her down in a wild tangle of sable hair and scattered emotions. In ten years he had not touched her the way he wanted, the way he had imagined time and again. Given the liberty now, he tried to keep a small distance to see her, to cherish her, to allow himself to burn even hotter with the voracious fervor he'd not felt in a decade. But she clutched him tighter, not allowing even a modicum of distance. Nothing that would allow her to come to her senses and know the terrible mistake she was making. She focused only on him, felt only what she wanted—the desperation of her passion, her starved need for closeness and fulfillment, the overwhelming desire to be loved.

He tore at his breeches; she helped him between demanding kisses and the devastating urge to keep her flesh next to his, to become a part of him, to merge both body and soul. His knee pressed between her thighs and she opened for him without reserve. He tried to calm her agitation, to quiet the graceless frenzy of her need, but she only arched into him, scattering his good intentions to the winds.

Shocked by the heavy weight of him against her belly and thighs, she bit her lip to keep from crying out, afraid he would stop and she would never know this again, never feel him fill her. Perspiration beaded his forehead and his eyes were dark and intense, almost fierce in his attempt to hold back and control the momentum of their passion.

Lara closed her eyes, then dug her nails into his buttocks.

On a groan, he lurched into her, too fast, too painful, too far gone to stop the rocking rhythm of his desire as it overtook compassion and consideration and caution.

"Lara, damn—" It was a plea that availed nothing. She only gripped him harder and rode the storm as it swelled and built to a fury.

Hunter gritted his teeth, cursing silently, aspirating a cry aloud, but it was too late to collect his will or temper his movements with her small, sharp nails biting into him and her tight body rising against him in complete, unbridled offering. He took her with an unforgivable strength and quickness that sent him spinning off toward a maelstrom of dark, sweet spasms.

Too much, too soon, too intense. He withdrew suddenly and lay panting and shivering in the aftermath, drained and oddly bereft but still hungry.

He slumped upon her, caught in the limbo of heaving breaths and sluggish thoughts, and cursed his lack of prowess. She trembled beneath him, and he heard a muted sob repressed deep in her throat. "Don't!" he demanded in a frightening tone. "Don't you dare cry, Lara. Don't you dare blame me for this."

"I don't! I won't," she managed, then flung her forearm over her eyes.

Her small, slender chest heaved as his did, but not from spent passion. He wanted to bury his face between her breasts, to cup and shape her around him and find succor in the acceptance she kept just beyond his fingertips. He wanted her delirious sigh of fulfillment rather than her slowly awakening guilt. He cupped her face, spoke her name, as if he could ward off the impending regret closing in on her.

Lara could not move at first, could only lay with him sprawled over her, feeling bruised yet wishing for . . . something. The yearning she felt when near him, the love she foolishly held for him was not diminished at all. It clamored inside her still, a craving centered on him that was never complete. "What's wrong with me?" she said flatly. "What moral ineptitude compels me to act so wantonly around you?"

Hunter jerked his head back and stared down at her. Tears dampened her cheeks, but her expression was more studious than ravaged, as if she must try to solve this question. *Moral ineptitude?* Christ, only Lara would come up with that explanation. "It's not that."

"What else could it be?" Her bottom lip trembled but she forged on angrily. "I lose all sense of who I am, what I am supposed to be, when around you. I am like some jungle native with no sense of how to behave in polite society."

He pulled her arm down from her face. "You think this does not happen in polite society?"

"Of course it does," she admitted, jerking her arm back over her eyes, "but not to me."

He shifted his weight to her side and ran one finger beneath the tender underside of her breast. "Then to whom?"

"Other women." She shivered and scooted away from him.

"Lara." He rolled to grab her too late. She had

325

already snatched up the swath of linen. She pulled it around her like a blanket and sat huddled before the fire, isolated and inviolable as she stared into the leaping flames.

"Women of greater passions or supreme loneliness," she continued moodily, as if it were a malady she had spent hours contemplating but still could not figure out. "Women who rebel against their marriage vows or their God or their lives." She glanced over at him briefly. "But not to me!" She returned to the flames dancing and swaying in the hissing wood. They threw shadows along the hearth and walls, insubstantial images that seemed to mock her. She had loved her husband, but she had never had to contend with these overwhelming emotions. "With George, I was satisfied. His weekly visitations to my bed were . . . comforting. I never looked for this or longed for it. I can't say that I truly care for it."

Hunter closed his eyes, accepting the blow to his manhood with chagrined grace. "That's unforgivable."

"What?" She looked back at him, her chin on her bare shoulder, delicate and beautiful in the firelight.

"The fact that you don't care for it much." He reached for his breeches, regrettably, and pulled them on, then sat up next to her. He traced the edge of her shoulder and felt her withdraw, though she didn't move a muscle. "You haven't explored it enough, studied it. Weekly visits be damned, Lara. If you were my wife, the visits would be hourly."

Her eyes widened, horrified . . . intrigued. She studiously avoided looking at him.

"I didn't help any," he continued, "rushing like a schoolboy at his first tumble."

She blushed outrageously. "Hourly." The word was little more than a delicate snort of disbelief. "I don't care to talk about this."

"I don't believe you."

Her brow knit. "It's so . . . unseemly."

"Of course, that's why it's so much fun." He nipped her shoulder with his teeth, then sighed and nuzzled his face into the crook of her neck. "Give me a few minutes and I'll show you how much more unseemly it can be."

Lara quivered and shook her head, fear beginning to trickle into her bloodstream like poison. Somewhere in the back of her mind she had known it would come, had tried to ward it off, but it rushed at her like a wave. "I cannot."

"Coward," he whispered.

She rounded on him. "How dare you? It's not you who would suffer the stigma of being unwed and with child." She stood, cringing at the tenderness of her body, and began snatching her clothing from the chair. Panic hovered near in each jerky movement, ready to pounce when she allowed herself to acknowledge what she had done.

Hunter saw the alarm on her face and rose to his feet. "Lara, don't. It was one time—"

The tears scalding her eyes began to fall. "Oh, please," she begged, "at least leave me some dignity. It was foolish and irresponsible."

How to explain what she obviously didn't realize? "I . . . practice what the French call *la chamale*."

327

She looked distracted, then confused.

"The retreat."

The realization of just what he meant was a slow process that transformed her face from bewilderment to shock to angry scarlet. "You *practice*," she repeated distinctly, as if she must get it perfectly right. "Children practice their letters, musicians practice their repertoire, opera singers practice—" Her scornful gaze seared him, and she began to tremble uncontrollably.

His jaw clenched. "Don't you dare judge me."

Her smile was flippant, bitter. "How often do you practice?"

He wouldn't do this. He wouldn't continue to trade spite with her out of jealousy or whatever else they were feeling. Her remorse was like a knife in his heart. "Do you regret it so much?" he whispered roughly.

She looked away, wounding him in a manner he had never thought possible. "The risk. I cannot believe I was so foolish when I know the consequences."

"The risk is minimal."

A gust of anger sounded in her throat. "To *you* perhaps." Her hand slashed down, fist clenched. "It cannot be minimal enough for me!"

"Then marry me!"

The world fell still. She looked at him in silent horror, her face blanched white. He did not toy with her; she knew it instantly by the fierce, cold expression on his face. "I cannot," she said, devastated that he should, after all these years, finally feel compelled to make a gentleman's offer.

She stumbled back a step, then turned and began collecting her damp clothes. She was going to cry any second, noisily, uncontrollably. The prospect was humiliating. "No one saw us," she said in a reasonable tone to avoid the complete breaking apart of her emotions. "No one knows. We are not compromised," she continued mechanically, "not like before."

They returned to Ravenwood in silence. Neither willing to risk the other's censure or spite or any other painful barb they were both so good at hurling. Percy was waiting for Lara at the stables. She knew by the look on his face that the unthinkable had happened.

"They won."

"In the lower courts, yes."

"Oh." The word was weak, full of anguish. "What is there to do now?"

"I have met with a barrister and had him file an appeal."

"It will go to the House of Lords."

"Yes." Percy swallowed and looked to Hunter. "She will need a sponsor."

Hunter gave the solicitor a clipped nod, then handed his reins over to Robin, the stable boy, and walked toward the main hall.

Lara stood in her chemise and stockings, her emotions mixed about the gown Lydia held up before her in awe and excitement. It had been two weeks since her ill-fated jaunt to the hunting lodge. She had seen Hunter so little, she wondered at times if he still resided at Ravenwood. When they were together, he was so chilly and unresponsive, she had given up trying to be civil.

But she missed him. Even matching wits and words with him would be preferable to the icy silence and long absences. She missed his strength and confidence and assurance. If he told her everything would be all right, she would believe him. She had that much faith in his ability to accomplish anything he set out to do. But he had not told her that. In reality, he had kept his distance even more since a hearing date had been set. In only three days, Hunter would be in London to sponsor Lara in her appeal. This evening's entertainment was designed to precede that event and sway things in her favor.

With a sigh of resignation, she raised her arms for Lydia to slide the gown over her head, then turned to be fastened. She had no choice but to go below and see the farce played out or stay in her room and give those due to arrive any minute even more fuel for speculation.

Lydia sighed dreamily. "It's perfect, milady."

Lara agreed. The gown was exquisite, but not perfect, not when it had been designed and purchased with Hunter's money. He had promised half mourning, something dull and gray. To believe that was naive. Sober gray had turned out to be closer to a silvery blue that enhanced the color of her eyes. The shoulders dropped daringly low, exposing her bosom in a way that defined elegance and maturity, while the mutable color gave the illusion of innocence. The contrast was a manipulative ploy to catch a man's interest while leaving its wearer innocent of any guile. At the rap on the door, she caught the neck of her gown.

"Your Grace." Lydia curtsied when Hunter stepped into the room. "Don't she look lovely?"

"Quite lovely," he agreed, his eyes burning with admiration and something more that Lara could not discern. "Mary needs help below, if you would."

"Of course." Lydia bobbed again and hurried to do his bidding.

Lara gave Hunter an exasperated look. "I could have used her a moment longer."

He walked over and turned her to face the full-length mirror. His dexterous fingers worked the hooks as deftly as Lydia had, but his eyes stared at Lara in a manner far removed from servant to mistress. His hands slid over her shoulders, sun-brown against her fairness.

She shivered at the terrible longing his touch created inside her and looked away. His fingers stirred, and she tried to step aside before disgracing herself with a gasp or a sigh or some other girlish crooning.

His hands tightened and he held her fixed in front of her reflection. "You look both seductive and frail," he said, "impossible for a man to ignore."

He loomed behind her, superbly dressed in black with accents in silver and blue that matched her own gown. Lara felt the warmth of his fingers against her flesh, saw the heat in his gaze, so different from the cold and impersonal stranger he had been all week. "Impossible for you?" she taunted softly.

"Most of all for me."

She shook her head, mocking his words. "I can't see where looking seductive and frail is beneficial," she said. "It seems a comparison unworthy of a man's intelligence."

"Intelligence," he scoffed, "rarely, if ever, over-rides a man's base nature, unless the man knows he's being played for a fool."

"And do you play these well-educated men for fools?"

"I merely play upon their good manners. England's finest will both want to protect you and bed you. They will not, however, want to destroy you."

Lara wished it were true. "I have spent so much time here, I fear I am already doomed."

His lips dropped to her shoulder. "There is nothing they can say, your visit has been above reproach. Especially with my aunt chaperoning us every waking moment."

She shivered beneath the heat of his breath, the feel of his lips on her flesh. "There is no aunt."

"Of course there is. It is unfortunate she has the headache tonight or you could meet her."

Lara smiled wryly. "I wish I had your cunning mind."

"No." He ran his hands lightly over her arms, then laced his fingers through hers in a rare and genuine intimacy that seemed to have no sexual connotation. "I would never want you that jaded, Lara."

She looked down at the striking gown. "I can't see how this will help."

"It would destroy their sense of gallantry to turn someone so tender and beautiful over to the wolves."

"Ah, the wolves," she said, feeling herself slipping beneath the intoxicating spell of his caress. "And your sense of gallantry?"

"I have none. I am the biggest wolf of all."

She laughed lightly at the self-derision in his voice, and for the first time her heart softened. He was a predator, yes. She would never be so foolish as to forget that, but she sensed that he almost regretted it. She turned in the circle of his arms and placed a hand on his chest, wishing she could rest her cheek there, as well. "Not always the wolf," she said earnestly. "You are sometimes the gallant knight come to the rescue."

His heart twisted. A mask fell over his features and a brilliantly cold smile emerged. "Never, *ever* underestimate me, Lara, nor crown me with hidden virtues." In his eyes was a look she had never seen, a mysterious mixture of fierce determination and painful self-loathing. She almost flinched when his hand lifted, but he only cupped her cheek tenderly. "Soon enough," he whispered roughly, "you will come to hate me."

He stepped back and offered his arm, chivalrous again, his every movement a mirror of gentility.

"I could never hate you," she said solemnly, "not after what you have done for John Byron. For me."

One mocking eyebrow rose over his stunning eyes.

"We shall see, my dear Lara. When this is all over, we shall see."

The carriages were arriving when they descended the winding staircase. A low fire burned in the massive stone hearth to dispel the dampness from the air, and every door stood open to allow the breeze to freshen the room. A thousand candles lit the ballroom, and fresh flowers created scent and beauty on every available tabletop. Tapestries of incalculable worth hung on several walls, giving one a sense of reverence at the timelessness of Ravenwood.

Lara stood erect in the receiving line, supremely composed, not one ounce of discomfort showing on her face. Hunter stood by her side, a bored smile on his face, a calculating look in his eyes.

Jacobs announced each guest that entered. "Lord and Lady Haversham . . . Countess Collingswood . . . Lord Darby . . ."

Only when His Grace, the Duke of Warrington, chose to make his entrance some forty minutes past fashionably late did a look of genuine appreciation enter Hunter's eyes. "Adam," he said, "so good of you to trouble yourself."

"The trouble was all mine." Adam turned to Lara, a rakish twinkle in his smile. "Lady Chalmers, it's been some time."

"It's been no time at all, Your Grace," she responded.

Adam's smile widened. "Hasn't it?" He took in her gown, his gaze forward and without apology. "What a lovely color for mourning, not at all dreary."

Lara's expression tightened into a show of heartfelt pain, not all feigned. "George could not abide the custom. It was his last wish that I endeavor to preserve the life and friendships we had sown. It has been difficult to carry on outside of tradition, but I feel I am honor-bound to try to uphold his wishes."

Whispers and titters floated throughout the room at her bald statement, allaying the concerns of many, fueling the gossip for others. Other than calling her an outright liar, they would have to accept the statement as fact and the reason for her breach of etiquette.

"Very good," Adam said quietly.

"Very true," Lara seethed beneath her breath. "I am told," she continued cordially for all to hear, "that the university is always grateful for your support, Your Grace."

Adam dismissed her changing the subject with a flourish of his jeweled hand. "A pittance. I wish I could do more, but there are so many needs, so many causes." He glanced back at Hunter. "Well done, Your Grace. We will talk later, I presume?"

"Of course," Hunter agreed.

By ten o'clock, Lara was desperately tired of smiling at people of whom she had only a passing acquaintance. Those of a scholarly bent she knew from her marriage to George and had to suffer through their confused expressions upon being invited to the Duke of Ravenwood's gathering when they never had been included before.

They simply could not put it into proper perspective. They assumed the invitation came because of

Lara, except that Lord and Lady Chalmers had never held such elaborate soirees. And now, of course, the earl was dead and it was in much too poor of taste to consider that his lady had stepped out of widow's weeds early to sow wild oats with the notorious Duke of Ravenwood and still include them on the invitation list.

Lara genuinely felt for their bemusement. So many were trying, out of their respect for George, not to malign her unfairly, and there was little she could do but continue to play the charade.

Lady Fitzworth tittered like a little bird when she finally reached Lara. "My dear, what a sly goose you are. Why didn't you tell me you knew Ravenwood personally when we were here last?"

Lara only smiled. She had buried George and lost her son only days before that mad dash to Ravenwood with a plan to lure Hunter into helping her. Little had she known then that she not only knew Ravenwood, but knew him intimately. She only waited for one of George's acquaintances to remember John Byron's features and make the connection.

Lady Fitzworth peered up at Hunter. "Marvelous display of Elgin marbles. Do you propose to host anything else in the near future?"

"I only await your suggestion, dear lady," Hunter returned, which caused Marion to titter even more.

"I shall think upon it and let you know," she stated, and moved off into the ballroom to spread the news that, being personally acquainted with the duke, she was being solicited for her sage advice.

Hunter snagged two glasses of champagne from

the passing waiter and handed one to Lara. "You're looking a bit frayed."

"I can't imagine why," she drawled. She sipped the bubbling liquid slowly, wondering if it would quiet her raging headache or make it worse. Her facial muscles felt permanently frozen in a false smile.

"Buck up, my dear. The worst is almost over, at least for tonight."

By the time Lara left the receiving line, she had consumed two more glasses of champagne and was feeling a bit more relaxed but infinitely more despondent. Hunter took her arm to lead her in for the first dance, and she responded with as much enthusiasm as a drugged pup.

Taking her in his arms, he smiled nicely for the benefit of those watching. "Smile, Lara."

"It's all so inappropriate," she lamented. "I should still be mourning George, no matter what we've told them."

"Nevertheless, my dear, play the game as if your life depended upon it."

The waltz began and he swept her into a turn that had her clinging momentarily to him for support. She caught the rhythm of it soon enough and spent the next few minutes swaying and stepping to the lovely strains of a superb orchestra.

"I can't believe I once craved this," she said. "It all seems so frivolous now."

"It can be fun," Hunter countered.

"Can it?"

They made another turn and Hunter's arm brushed

her breast. Her eyes widened; his grew sultry. "It can be as much fun as you let it."

In retaliation and without forethought, she moved quickly and swayed her hip gently into his groin, then took immense satisfaction from watching the startled heat flare in his eyes. "Yes, I suppose it can."

Embarrassed by her own brazenness, she kept to safer topics after that, until the last notes died away and they parted to dance with others. Hunter chose Marion Fitzworth, collecting an ally should he need it later. Adam approached Lara. She tried to turn away but he was quick and sly.

"This dance is mine, I believe," he lied, offering his arm.

She took it, knowing she must, loathing him for the manipulation.

"I only seek to help," he said, as he led her back to the dance floor.

"Why?"

"Gad, Lady Chalmers, must I have a reason? What of chivalry and gallantry and all those other high-flown notions?" At her tight silence, he relented. "Oh, all right. I respected George immensely and wouldn't like to see his widow destitute. I am also very tight with Ravenwood. It's obvious why he's helping you, even to those who have never seen your son."

Lara's eyes widened. "What do you mean?"

"Why, he's mad about you, of course. It's quite sickening, really, when you consider that he has already procured an heir in Nicolette. Unlike some of us, he could live the free, unfettered life of a single nobleman, if it weren't for you."

"Me?"

"All that disgusting pining. Is it obvious to all but you, my dear, that he won't be happy until he has you?"

Lara's heart thudded sadly in her breast. "I don't know what you're talking about, and I daresay neither do you." She looked away from Adam's handsome face and too-charming smile. "You play a nasty game, Your Grace. I pray you aren't thinking of spouting the same balderdash to Hunter."

"I'm certain he already knows it."

The dance ended and Lara took her leave with quick steps through the crowd, her fingers to her temples as if she suffered a headache. Searching for the nearest hiding place, she slipped into the library and collapsed into a plush leather chair beside the cold hearth. Adam's words taunted her, repeating themselves over and over in her mind. She would that it were so, but the very idea of Hunter pining over anything was so ludicrous, she knew Adam was just stirring up trouble. When she could no longer stand the shrill silence of the library, with only her frightful imagination for company, she returned to the ballroom.

Feigning fatigue, she declined the next dance and stood off to the side, watching those who would sit in judgment over her dance quadrilles and waltzes, consume copious amounts of spirits or punch, and flirt outrageously with each other's wives and sweethearts and lovers.

She despaired to think that had it not been for her marriage to George, she would have become like them—shallow and flighty little butterflies flitting from one pursuit to another, one man to another, one charity to another. Their lives had no meaning. Boredom was the bane of their existence. They had too much money, too much fun, too much leisure. They did too much, went too much, were too much. Everything was at their disposal, which made everything less valuable.

By a very young age they had played every game, won every medal. But Lara had learned that life must have meaning, existence purpose. Since theirs had none, they supported churches to make them feel holy, charities to make them feel benevolent, university chairs to make them feel intelligent. And they flirted, both covertly and outrageously, with each other's wives or husbands to make them feel desired.

Watching it all, Lara greatly feared she would have become just like them if she had not paid the consequences of one night's abandon aboard a pirate ship.

She glanced over at Hunter and bit her lip at the wicked smile he bestowed upon the elderly Lady Channing, a smile that never reached his eyes. He indulged them, he imitated them, he stroked their egos until they postured like peacocks basking in the glow of his favor. But he gave nothing of himself in return.

He glanced up and their eyes met and held for one brief moment, then he looked away. No, not all, Lara realized. He played no game with Adam Devereaux, Duke of Warrington. She saw mutual respect and friendship between the two men. Though Adam was every bit as devilish and whimsical as the rest of the shallow crowd, there was an intelligence behind his eyes that said he knew it was all a farce. Life was a game to be played and won until such time as he chose to get serious about it. Lara at least respected his honesty with himself.

And Hunter played no game with her, Lara admitted. When he had looked over at her moments ago, he had been deadly serious.

Tired to the bone, Lara crawled into the high bed and sank down into the feather mattress in glorious relief. Her feet ached, her back ached, even her smile ached. She could not say that she had accomplished one single thing with the farce played out below, but it was over now and she could rest.

Moonlight spilled in her window, illuminating the bedclothes in an ivory glow. She ran her hand over the cool sheets and let her thoughts drift at will. Hunter's face came to mind, dashing and handsome, his smile beautiful but cold. She sighed his name and started when an answer came back.

"A rousing success, my dear."

He stood in the doorway, his cravat hanging loose, his shirt front open to reveal the dark, crisp hair of his chest. Lara sat up in bed and pulled the covers to her neck.

"Was it? I couldn't tell."

She sensed the shift in the atmosphere. He had a look about him that frightened her, determination mixed with contrition, as if he regretted what he was about to do but would do it anyway.

Her hands tightened on the covers. "Why are you here?"

"Don't be afraid."

"I'm not, but why are you here?"

He pushed off the door frame and strolled into the room, lithe and strong and silent. He stripped the cravat from his neck and let it fall from his fingers, forgotten before it drifted to the floor. He reached the bed and leaned over it, his fists planted on the mattress so that Lara tipped toward him. She could smell the brandy on his breath.

"You are intoxicated," she accused.

"Am I?" He smiled. "I suppose I am, at least when near you." He leaned closer and grazed her lips before she could pull away.

"I'm ready for bed"—she saw instantly the ribald response that sprang to his lips and countered before he could speak—"and so should you be. In bed, I mean." Flustered, she gripped the covers tighter, her knuckles growing white upon the satin counterpane.

"I agree, Lara." He stripped the shirt from his pants, then dragged it from his back and slung it to the floor. Before Lara could utter much more than a shocked protest, he had his pants off, as well, and was jerking her covers back to crawl in beside her.

"This is unconscionable!" She nearly screeched.

"Isn't it?" he agreed, and cupped her cheek in his palm. He was fully naked, his flesh hot where it touched hers, radiating heat even where it did not. His mouth stopped her next words by taking her lips in a searing kiss that left little to the imagination of his exact purpose. "Ah, Lara," he breathed, "I have dreamed of this so long."

Her thin cotton nightrail was little protection against the sharp angles and rounded planes of his magnificent physique. Every muscle and tendon fitted itself to her, point and counterpoint, perfect symmetry. His lips took hers, humid and hot, his tongue a gentle penetration that she could neither accept nor reject. He traced her teeth, feeling the uneven edges of each one, listening to her breathing quicken.

She grabbed his face in her palms. "You've had too much to drink," she said, pronouncing each word. "Think what you are doing."

"I've thought of nothing else," he whispered against her lips.

His intent was undeniable as he covered her completely, his weight and warmth a luxurious danger Lara found hard to rail against. His tongue stroked her mouth with the same rhythm that his body rocked against her, and she found it more than difficult not to follow the cadence.

She wanted him so badly she ached with it but knew it was impossible. "Hunter, no," she breathed, the words sounding as weak as he made her feel. She forced his face up, but he only turned his mouth into her palm and stroked each finger as he had her mouth, his breath hot and wet against her flesh. "Don't do this," she pleaded, knowing intrinsically that she could not stop him, that he must be the one to pull away.

His hand slid along her side, down every curve and crest, warm through the fabric of her gown. When

343

his fingers slipped beneath the scalloped edge to touch the moist heat of her, she gasped and pulled away. His gaze flew to hers and held, piercing and knowing, then he withdrew and reached over the side of the bed to fumble with something in his clothing. When he righted himself, he held a small thin packet.

Curious, Lara peered over to see that it read "Lambskin Sheath, for the Prevention of Conception." Aghast, she reared back, her cheeks flaming.

He flinched at his inopportune timing. "You were worried about this before. I only thought to allay your fears."

She could not find command of her voice, so startled and astounded was she. "I . . . I didn't know there were such . . . *things* available." She rolled back toward him and snatched the little packet from his fingers. It was thin, almost weightless. "What does it do?"

"Do?" Hunter opened his mouth, then closed it. He thought he actually blushed. He knew he was aroused by her fierce, innocent curiosity. "It . . . covers."

"Covers?" She looked up, inquisitively rapt, then realized what he meant. Her face flamed and she dropped the salacious little device back into his palm. "However did you get up the nerve to purchase this?"

"I had three children out of wedlock," he said quietly. "It took no nerve at all."

Her heart plunged to her toes. "Three?"

"Nanette. Nicolette's twin. She died of croup two years ago."

A twin, not another pregnancy. It made things better somehow. But there were unspoken echoes in his ravaged voice that would never be made right. "I'm sorry. Truly."

"So am I." He tossed the indecent little package from palm to palm, slanting Lara a brief, testing glance. "French letters, English hats, condoms. So many sly names for one little convenience. What do you think? Without fear of exposure will it erase man's guilt of fornication and adultery?"

He had purposely left the subject of his daughter behind, ignoring it, running from it, throwing illicit jargon at Lara to appall her and divert her attention. "What of Nicolette's mother?" she asked.

He flipped over onto his back beside her and sighed. "It's not going to happen, is it? I wanted it to be tonight." *I leave tomorrow and everything will change, Lara. I need tonight.*

"What was her name?"

He made a sound—distaste, disgust, impatience— Lara could not be certain, just that he didn't want to discuss it.

"Tell me, Hunter."

"Lisette."

It had a lyrical ring the way he said it, as if his tongue unconsciously caressed each syllable. Lara could not quite look at him. "Did you love her?"

He had to mull it over. "I wanted to." Needed to, for the girls' sake. He shot Lara an accusing look.

"She wouldn't marry me. I would never let myself become completely attached."

Lara's emotions teetered. "Why wouldn't she?"

"It was complicated. I don't want to discuss her." He rolled to his side and his hand began a questing journey over her shoulder, then across her breast.

Lara flipped onto her belly to escape. "Complicated how?"

On a muted growl, he flung himself back again, one arm over his eyes, one resting across his lower stomach. "I want to make love to you."

She refused to acknowledge the jolt of awareness that shot through her. "How?"

"More ways than you know. As many as I can count."

She jerked and felt her face grow hot. "No, how was Lisette complicated?"

Without warning, he rolled her swiftly to her back and placed his mouth at the hill of her breast. "So lovely," he murmured. "So very beautiful."

Lara's breath hissed between her teeth but she managed to pull his head up. "How?" He turned his face into her hand and nibbled each finger, ran his tongue over every tiny inch of flesh. "I will not be detoured," Lara warned, though she quivered inside and wondered how long she could hold him at bay. There was no real middle ground. They would either go forward or he would leave and return to his room. Both were unthinkable to Lara, so she held onto him a bit longer, in the most acceptable way she could. "How was it complicated?"

He sighed deeply, obvious surrender. "Lisette

346

found out she was descended from a quadroon mistress. Her grandmother was one-eighth Negro. Lisette was afraid, if she married me, she would be discovered one day. When the twins were born, she knew they could not be raised in both worlds. Once across the barrier, there would be no returning." He ran his hands over his eyes, exhausted. "Lisette had no ambition. She wasn't willing to risk it all coming apart one day, so she left me. She chose to raise the twins as part of the New Orleans demimonde, but she died of a fever when they were two. I don't know where their grandmother was. Their great-grandmother was raising them, as she had been raised, to be quadroon mistresses for some unsatisfied New Orleans aristocrat." He breathed deeply. "I took them from her. She will never forgive me."

Chapter Nineteen

Lara touched Hunter's arm, in comfort and compassion. "You were right to take them away from that life."

"Was I?" he asked. "Nanette might still be alive if I hadn't." He rolled over suddenly, pinning Lara beneath him. "Love me," he whispered roughly, then took her mouth in a flaming kiss.

His words rushed through her, a liquid fire igniting her own emotions to a feverish longing. She wanted to respond in kind, to tell him of the feelings that so frightened her, but she lay still and quiet, allowing his impassioned attempt to escape the past. He touched her hair, her shoulder, then cupped her breast. She stiffened at the caress, murmuring a plaintive sigh of yearning at the feel of his rough palm on her cool flesh. She called his name in a plea for clemency, but he was ruthless in his determination to break free of his past and through her crumbling barriers.

His mouth lowered to the bodice of her nightrail. He wet the lace over her breast with his tongue, tasted the dry starchy flavor of cotton, created havoc inside Lara. Her nipple pebbled against his lips and he pulled the fabric aside, stirring latent fires until she began to simmer beneath the pull of his mouth, the nip of his teeth. She arched into him, against him, murmuring protests that neither of them believed. His hand slid beneath the nightrail and pushed it up, the edge pooling over his dark arms like a sail unfurled.

Tormented, she sighed his name, then his fingers found her and there was nothing left but a gasp and cry and the bowing of her body. She was humid, ready, and he covered her fully and sank the full weight of his desire into the cradle of her body. She received him on a protest, her mind much less reconciled than her body, but she arched into him all the same when his hand slid between them and began to kindle a greater fire within her, one she had never experienced in the limited sensual avenues of her life.

She cried out when he stroked her, a delicate flower unfolding to the hottest sun, and he entered her with the slow, dynamic purpose of a man who knew he had come home. She flung her head back, cognizant of little beyond the wondrous, frightening tension in her body and the rocking compliment of his thrusts. She felt like a bow strung too tight, ready to snap and fly apart in a million pieces. She called his name in a distressed breath, straining into him, growing frantic with each rushing pulse of blood in her veins. Her extremities felt swollen and taut, hungry for respite.

The sheer joy of joining with him overwhelmed her, swept her away into the beauty of their dance. Everything within her was reduced to the small inferno of their passion, and she began to pulse and throb in a rising tempo that took her breath until only an exhaled cry was left.

She called his name and cambered high into him, one with him.

He held her suspended against him, one arm under her hips, the other clutching the carved headboard, as he poured himself into her, mindless and grasping, the embarrassing little packet forgotten on the cold wooden floor.

Lara drifted back to reality by degrees. Her limp arm lay over her eyes, her palm turned up in repletion. Her chest rose and fell with shallow breaths, her legs felt like jelly. She could not move or speak. Her being was trapped in a limbo of sublime wonder and slowly fading euphoria. Her skin felt clammy, and the musty scent of passion filled her nostrils.

Hunter's weight was warm and heavy and not unwelcome. She reached down and clasped his hand tightly in her own. Too soon, she would come to her senses and regret what they had just done with every ounce of her being. She pressed her face into his shoulder and inhaled, took his essence into her as she had his body, a memory to keep locked away when she no longer had the reality.

Hunter watched her sleep. For hours he lay awake with Lara cradled to his heart, trying not to think of the daylight that would come and steal the perfect peace of being replete in her arms.

Lara searched room to room, but could find no trace of Hunter. She had fallen asleep, her head nestled into the crook of his shoulder, pretending things were as they should be. He had loved her once more near morning with a desperation she had not understood but had been powerless to refuse when her own emotions were so tied up with loving and wanting him. She did not expect him to feel the same, she did not demand it, but her heart hurt from wanting it.

No mention of the future had been made. She was no longer naive enough to believe that one night of passion meant anything to him beyond just that. But to her it meant everything. Her heart was sealed now and she would never be able to retrace her running path away from him. In her mind and heart and soul, she loved him. No matter what he was or had become, she would forever belong to him—in her heart if not reality.

Lara pushed the heavy drapery back to stare down into the courtyard. Her heart felt laden. There would not be another night. Never again would she know the strength of his caress, the wonder of his tenderness. For her son's sake, she would not become Hunter's mistress. No matter how fatefully she loved him, she would not compromise herself and John Byron. She would take her one night, and she would not regret it.

Oh, but the joy of his possession, the fulfillment and completion she had found in his arms. How would she ever return to her lonely bed, her lonely life, now that she knew?

How would she tell him?

She found Jacobs in the morning room and discovered that he had carried Hunter's bags down after breakfast, so it could be assumed His Grace would be gone some time. Hurt, Lara searched for Lydia to see if Hunter had left a message with her, but he had said nothing to the young maid. As a last effort, she went to the nursery to see if the children knew anything and found John Byron and Gal hard at their studies, while Nicolette pouted from a small chair by the window.

"Oh, Madame!" she cried, leaping up to rush headlong into Lara's skirts. "You must save me! *M'sieu* Mabry is being horrid!"

Gal rolled her eyes. "You were being a pest, Nicci. Watch you don't get worse for lying."

John Byron glanced up from his mathematics sheet and nodded. "She was, Mama."

Lara looked to the much-maligned Mr. Mabry. "Shall I take her for a while?"

Arthur Mabry inclined his head. "Whatever you think best. I am at my wit's end to determine just what is best anymore where Miss Nicolette is concerned." He also had yet to determine the connection between John Byron, Lady Chalmers, and the duke. A family resemblance was unmistakable, but no one had offered him anything but the briefest introduction. He directed his sternest instructor's stare to the recalcitrant child. "Miss Nicolette is by far one of the brightest students I have ever tutored. When most her age are only capable of playing with dolls and hanging about their nanny's skirts, Miss Nicolette is accomplished at ciphering small numbers, writing the alphabet, and reading many passages from scripture. She wastes my time and her own by causing trouble."

"As you say, Mr. Mabry, she is very young," Lara said. "Most her age don't even have tutors." At the sudden flaring of his nostrils, she hurried to reassure him that his employment was not in jeopardy. "Perhaps the time spent in formal study could be shortened to accommodate her youth?"

"But His Grace is paying me—"

"For Nicolette to learn," she interrupted gently. "If she adequately covers the material, what does it matter if she finishes early?"

"But she could learn so much more!"

"Not if she stays in trouble." Lara watched Mr. Mabry's frustration peak then dissolve in reluctant understanding.

He sent her a pained smile. "Quite right. Dear me, I should have seen that, but I've never had a pupil of Miss Nicolette's age advance so rapidly. Truth to tell, I've never had a pupil of Miss Nicolette's age at all. In fact, I've never been called upon to tutor young girls unless they already have older brothers at home."

Lara could see that Mr. Mabry might be convinced to go on for some time with very little encouragement. She took Nicolette's hand and turned her to face her tutor. "Please apologize, Nicolette, then we'll go find something else to entertain you until Gal and John Byron are finished."

Nicci curtsied dutifully; she knew when she had the advantage. "My apologies, *M'sieu* Mabry. I will try ever so much harder tomorrow."

"See that you do, Miss Nicolette," he said importantly, then nodded at Lara and turned back to his more biddable students.

"Have you seen your father?" Lara asked the child as they descended the carpeted staircase.

"He kissed me and John Byron good-bye when the sun was still asleep," Nicci said with a pout, "and said he was off to London with *M'sieu* Adam. He said he would bring us a treat."

The vision of Hunter kissing his children good-bye in the predawn hours tore at Lara's resolve. What would have been impossible a decade ago, she could easily picture now—his tall frame bending to accommodate a child's small bed, a look of reserved longing on his face. Lara had never thought to see him in that role, but he doted on Nicolette, even spoiled her outrageously, but he could also be stern when her demands gained advantage over the other children's rights. His parenting was decidedly unconventional, at least by English standards, but Lara suspected he might just have the right of it.

She left Nicolette munching an almond cake beside Lydia in the kitchen. She needed answers and knew of nowhere else to find them. Percy had also left that morning for London with the barrister Hunter had retained on her behalf. A delivery had been made days ago, but Hunter had not divulged the contents of the package, much to Lara's annoyance. She knew the delivery concerned her, and she feared that

Hunter's secrecy and early disappearance meant something horrible had occurred, especially since he had rushed off to London a day early without so much as a by-your-leave.

She had a strong sense of things gone awry, beyond her control and knowledge. Frustration sharpened her determination and helped override her more emotional feelings about Hunter's absence. She slipped into his study unnoticed, much as she had that day months ago before she knew Hunter and the Duke of Ravenwood were one and the same. Going through his private papers was sneaky and dishonorable, but Lara didn't care. She had reached the end of wisdom and decorum, and had only her wits to cling to now.

Glancing around surreptitiously, she pulled open the top drawer of Hunter's desk. It contained sheets, quills, nibs and inkpots, but nothing wrapped in brown paper. Sliding it closed, she then tugged on a side drawer. This one was heavier, filled with stacks of documents filed alphabetically by a heading sheet on the top of each pile. Most were correspondence concerning lands and properties he owned. It appeared he took great pains to be kept informed about every aspect of his belongings.

Lara rifled through page after page of boring accounts of beans and barley planting, cattle purchases, household disputes, and small investments. She set that stack aside and picked up the next, then the next until she reached one with the heading "Our Lady of Mercy." It piqued Lara's curiosity and she slipped the first correspondence free.

STOLEN DREAMS

Your Grace:

It is my regret to inform you of little Mary Whiston's passing on Monday last. You will recall how weak she was when we got her. Be comforted that her last hours were peaceful, and she has been laid to rest in the churchyard next to the young lad we called Ted.

There is news of a more encouraging nature. Master Roderick is coming along nicely since Dr. Johnson's last visit, and the Canfield twins are almost back to normal. Sister Agnes says we will be getting two new additions come Tuesday. The first is a female infant from Ramsgate left in a basket on the docks. She appears in good health, our Lord be praised, and will arrive with a nurse by coach. The other is a boy, approximately three years of age, found wandering in the same area. It is supposed he might be the infant's brother but as of yet that has not been verified. Both will be welcomed with all warmth and consideration, as are due all our little angels.

I remain gratefully yours, in the service of our Lord and Savior Jesus Christ, Father Timothy.

Lara stared at the letter, her face hot, her eyes stinging. There were stacks of letters just like this one, detailing the hardships and joys of individual children of Our Lady of Mercy Foundling Home. Each letter was a personal account, with successes and failures along with many requests for additional funds, and always Father Timothy's gratitude for the Duke of Ravenwood's generous support.

357

She could see things now that had not been clear to her months before, blinded as she had been by her attraction and resentment of the man Hunter had been rather than the man he had become. These letters were private and painful, not merely solicitations of charity—the hidden portrait of a man whom others rarely saw.

Her hands trembled slightly as she put the papers back into the drawer. The letters only confirmed what she already knew. He was a man of compassion and generosity, one to be admired and respected. It would be more than difficult to take John Byron away from such a person than the seductive, lawless pirate she had known. She closed the drawer quickly before her intentions crumbled completely and opened the one below it.

Marry me. The words ricocheted through her mind, making her fingers stumble. There had been no profession of love, nothing to make her believe he had done more than salvage a belated sense of duty. And he was cunning enough to preserve his future. If the question ever arose, he would be able to tell John Byron that he had offered for Lara and she had been the one to refuse. She smiled sadly. She knew he desired her, but carnal affection was far removed from the love she wanted from him. She would not, could not, accept anything less.

She slipped another stack of documents free but found nothing that resembled the one delivered over the past week. The Folkstone seal had been stamped upon its face, but it had been addressed to Hunter and Lara had not been allowed to see the contents.

She rifled through another set of papers. She had little hope of fully retaining all of George's holdings, but she had told Percy to have the barrister fight for Folkstone and dowager provision. No one could deny she was George's widow, after all. If she managed to retain Folkstone, she would return there with John Byron and lead a quiet country existence. She did not need social acceptance. She'd had only one year of balls and soirees and rides in Hyde Park, and she did not need them now. The pomp and sparkle of a London season faded to useless frivolity in light of the true seriousness of life. She had learned that lesson early enough to not miss it too dearly, though the vision of a young girl dressed in white staring dreamily over the balcony of her father's ballroom still haunted her at times.

Sixteen and drilled in every aspect of proper deportment, she had waited in flushed excitement for her name to be announced so that she could make her entrance. Her coming out had occurred only months before Hunter, before everything she knew of life had sheared off drastically in another direction.

Since last night, she felt as if it had sheared off again. Her limbs felt heavy with the bliss of utter contentment still flowing through her blood, and her mind was wont to wander into an idle euphoria she had never known. Hunter had given everything of himself with a desperation that had consumed her, and she had given back in return all the love she kept hidden in her heart. She was forever changed and knew it. She just wasn't certain what it meant or how she would deal with it.

"Spying, Lara?"

She spun around. Adam stood not ten feet away. His smile was angelic, his blond hair shining in the sunlight streaming through the tall windows, but his eyes were sharp and intelligent and cold as ice. Lara slammed the drawer shut and schooled her features. "I can't find my solicitor's last letter, though I know it must be here somewhere."

"In Hunter's desk instead of your own? How unusual."

Lara only smiled with the same feigned innocence. "I thought you were off to London."

"I forgot something and had to return." Adam walked to the desk and opened the same drawer Lara had just closed and pulled a packet from the bottom.

Lara fought the urge to reach for it and curled her hand into a fist instead. "Do you return with Hunter?"

"Within a week," he replied, then dropped the veneer of politeness. "He has ruined them, you know. I don't approve but"—he shrugged and handed her the packet—"neither do I blame him."

To Lara's dismay, it was not the package delivered earlier in the week. She took it, bewildered by Adam's words and the reticence in his expression. She slipped the knot of twine free and folded back the outer wrapping. Contained inside were promissory notes, so many of them Lara could hardly comprehend the importance of their numbers.

"Robert and Claude's debts," Adam said. "Hunter bought up their markers, every one, and is calling them due. They are ruined, of course, as he intended."

Lara held her breath. She did not understand the importance of Adam's words or the implications of the notes in her hand. "I . . . don't understand."

"No matter what is decided in the appeal, Robert and Claude lose. This changes nothing in the court proceedings, but it may mean that Folkstone is lost if you do not win."

Anger flashed in Lara's eyes. "And you do not approve?"

"I understand why Hunter did it, but no. It is an ignoble act to call in a man's debts when he has no hope of paying. Hunter does not need the money."

Lara's eyes narrowed. "Let me assure you, they are not men, they are animals. They would have killed my son." She slapped the package back into his palm. "Now, if you will excuse me, I have a letter to locate."

Ignoring Adam, she began going through the desk again until she finally spotted a small, thin bundle near the bottom. It wasn't the package itself, but the wax seal that caught her attention. The Folkstone seal was clearly stamped on its face. After pulling it free, she placed it on the desk, mindful of Adam's sharp gaze as she opened it. Confusion was her first reaction, when she found George's neat, precise handwriting detailing several transactions. Odd sums of money were attached to even odder names: Jack—Bow Street, Richard—Newgate, and several others, with slashes marked through each one, as if George were angry when he wrote it.

A sinking feeling assailed Lara. She knew instinctively that these were not the names of the scientists to whom George had faithfully made endowments over the years, and she knew Hunter would not be in possession of them had Percy not turned them over without her knowledge. Her breathing grew agitated and she turned to Adam. "Who are these men?"

Adam glanced at the sheet briefly. "Bow Street Jack and Newgate Richard are cutthroats. I'm not familiar with the others." He tugged at the lace on his cuff and sniffed delicately. "I think Jack is dead now, an altercation in America. New Orleans, I believe."

Lara's face drained of color. Hunter's words came back, full of venom. *Someone has been sending one henchman after another for ten years.* "No!" she cried in denial, but the terrible truth was seeping past her loyalty to George with devastating effectiveness.

Glancing up, Adam smiled coldly. "No?"

"Whatever you're thinking, I had nothing to do with this. And George . . ." She couldn't finish.

Adam only stared back at her laconically, neither accusing nor exonerating her.

"I must go to London," Lara said.

"I leave in an hour."

"I will be ready."

She slapped the papers down and sped from the room, as if she could outrun the ugly insinuation and confusion besetting her. Picking up her skirts, she raced for the garden and the peace that had eluded her for a decade.

Her thoughts tumbled over one another. Robert and Claude were ruined. No matter how she tried to gloat, she felt nothing but deep sadness over the entire affair. Adam had been right; it solved nothing. The courts could still decide in the brothers' favor.

She stumbled through the gate, catching her hem on a jagged root. God have mercy, George had been the one. Tears blinded Lara as she made her way to the fruit and nut trees, their shade offering respite from the midday heat. Sunlight filtered through the leafy branches and dappled the lane in speckles that shifted and danced with each sway of the tree limbs. Oh, George, why? How could her staid, patient husband have been so corrupt as to hire men to murder Hunter? She felt ashamed and responsible and betrayed. Had everything she loved about George been a farce? Had he too played false her youth and innocence all those years past?

Ten years earlier, Hunter had represented everything young girls were warned against, George had represented everything noble. Yet it was Hunter who had come to her son's rescue and gotten revenge upon his kidnappers; Hunter who collected children like treasures, then seemed to consider himself unworthy of their adoration; Hunter who sent giddy flutters to her heartbeat and made her pulse race as George never had.

Hunter who had dodged her husband's murderous henchmen for years, yet still came when Lara needed him.

She plucked a rose carefully from its thorny stem and pressed her face into its fragrant petals. Her heart was burdened, her thoughts a tangle of regret and admiration. She knew only one thing for certain.

She must get to London immediately. She had to look into his eyes, to confirm her heart, to lay before him all she knew and felt.

The wind heralded her passage, the sweetest tinkling through the trees, soft as the beat of an angel's wings. Soft as the notes of a love song.

The carriage pulled beneath the portico of a whitewashed stuccoed mansion in Berkeley Square. Elegant and impressive, the entire street exuded the old-money prestige of its owners. Though her body was exhausted from having slept little over the day-and-a-half journey, Lara paced restlessly in the exquisite sitting room. She had arrived in London an hour earlier only to discover that Hunter was away.

So she waited, filled with nameless and blindless energies, feelings that demanded to be released. She needed one more look into his eyes, one more chance to lose herself in the intensity of his gaze and return back to him everything she knew and felt when near him. Minutes passed, seconds dragged by, and she paced as if her life depended on the constant motion.

What would she say to him, how much would she allow herself to reveal? In her mind, she rehearsed speech after tender speech in which she laid bare her heart and soul, reserving nothing for her own safe-keeping but offering him all, then discarded them one after the other as nothing but words, too inept to display the true, abiding emotions within her.

Where was he? She glanced at the ormolu clock on the mantel, then resumed her determined pacing. The world had never seemed so clear and so demented at once. In reality, she did not know if she could utter the strangled words from her throat and leave herself once and for all completely vulnerable to Hunter, but she didn't know how she could do less.

In one swift moment, with one thoughtless heartless word, he could destroy her. But she would have to chance it. In her entire life she had thrown caution to the wind only twice. When she conceived John Byron and when she called upon Hunter to rescue him. She would dare everything again.

Adam, who had been patently amused by her relentless and restless pacing, had excused himself minutes ago in search of refreshments. Lara heard the door open and turned to regard him fiercely. "Where is he?"

"Right here," Hunter said. He appeared behind Adam, but his eyes were for Lara only, fathomless and dark.

Strangely, incomprehensibly, the past entered with him, and there were only the two of them, separate and contained within their own sphere of time—an innocent debutante of seventeen and a dynamic, hardened youth of twenty-three. Danger crackled in the air around them, charging it with an electrifying intensity that seemed to burn hotter the longer they stared into each other's eyes. It reached a point of blinding white obliteration, then slowly, gently, began to fade, taking the past with it, cleansing them of bitterness and fear and long erected defenses.

All of Lara's being, her thoughts and senses and corporeal flesh, were focused on Hunter, attuned to every nuance of his expression. All of her practiced speeches and carefully chosen words drifted like ashes from her mind, leaving only one thing. Love. No matter the past or the future or the outcome of this day, love was the one thing that would last. The only thing that was real.

"Hunter," she whispered, needing to tell him, to show him, to make him understand what she had not known herself for so long.

"You need not have come," he said, his words deep, strained. He looked stunning in formal attire, dashing and powerful, but his eyes were tired and his body stiff as if braced.

She wanted to hold him and thank him and ease the concern on his brow. She wanted to tell him what he meant to her and beg his forgiveness for things beyond her control. From the corner of her eye she saw Adam withdraw his pocket watch and desperation hit her. There was so much to say, so much she needed to reveal.

"I had to come," she began. Her hand lifted, but Hunter made a sudden, jerking gesture with his shoulder, as if he would ward her off.

And the time for truth passed.

There was nothing to be said here, with Adam present and her fate swiftly ticking away.

"It is time to go," Hunter said. "We've been sent for a day early."

A moment of panic flashed in Lara's eyes. She felt the velocity of her circumstances gaining momentum, spinning out of her control, stripping her of the time she needed to tell Hunter what she must and thrusting her toward things that demanded her immediate attention.

"Please," she begged, and for one small, infinitesimal instant Hunter's guard dropped and he revealed himself. Lara saw a promise of her own feelings reflected back in his eyes.

His emotions were quickly and brutally covered, layered behind a hard veneer of dark, urbane intelligence, but Lara had seen the truth if only for that one unguarded moment, and her heart took flight, soaring with exquisite lightness and resounding hope.

Adam cleared his throat, a delicate taunt. "The distinguished House of Lords awaits."

Lara seared him with a look, then turned back to Hunter. "Tell me what you will do," she said, her throat arid. "What will you say to them?"

He held still for a moment and searched her eyes, as if he might determine her thoughts. He started to speak, then something akin to pain and a terrible concern flickered through his expression. He shook his head fatally. Turning away, he took his cloak from the butler and walked through the door.

Lara followed, frightened by his expression, his silence. "I want to come with you," she demanded.

Hunter glanced at Adam, then back at Lara and nodded.

As soon as they were settled and the carriage was under way, Lara pulled George's incriminating paper from her reticule. "I had nothing to with this," she said. "Please believe me."

Hunter glanced at the documents only once, then closed his eyes and nodded. Relief spun through him,

cleansing away the sludge of old hostility and bitterness. He reached over and took Lara's hand, holding
it tightly for the rest of the journey.

With her son's entire future to be decided over
the next hour, Lara thought the trip seemed overly
long. Finally the carriage rolled past St. Margaret's
Church, founded in the twelfth century as the parish
church of Westminster and declared for two hundred
years as the national church for the use of the House
of Commons. The peaceful interior adorned with
unobtrusive Elizabethan and Jacobean wall monu-
ments had been a fashionable place for weddings for
two centuries, and its churchyard an equally fashionable spot for burials.

Opposite St. Margaret's stood Westminster Hall
and to the south opened Old Palace Yard outside the
House of Lords. The carriage slowed, then rocked
gently to a stop. Lara took a deep breath, then another, the rise and fall of her chest the only indication
that she was not completely serene.

Hunter felt for the thin bulk of documents in his
breast pocket before rising from his seat. The packet
sat there like a lead weight, damnation or deliverance. He wouldn't know which until later. He
glanced over at Lara and saw the love, the faith, the
trust in her eyes. And felt as if his heart were being
ripped to shreds.

One hour too soon, ten years too late.

She would hate him once this miserable day's work
was done. Though she might also be grateful, he had
no doubt she would despise him for the machinations
and contrivances.

Chapter Twenty

Hunter had been to both the House of Lords and the House of Commons several times and suffered none of the awe or fear most experienced upon making the trip. Unlike Adam, he found politics neither heroic nor inspiring, and certainly unworthy of the environment in the transformed London of the Regent and his architects. The grandiose building schemes of the prince and his town planner, however, did not extend to Old Palace Yard and St. Stephen's. The Commons sat in a congested pit lighted by oil lamps, while the Lords sat in a chamber eighty feet long, forty feet wide, and thirty feet high, which was beautifully tapestried and had three semicircular windows and numerous chandeliers. Both Houses were desperately overcrowded on any occasion of great debate.

It was often said that the treatment for an overserious attitude toward either House was to go look at it. Having obtained an order for admission to the visitors' gallery, one could look down into a dim, lamp-lit den where some three or four hundred ordinary-looking men congregated. It was frightening for some to view the collective wisdom of the nation leaning against pillars with hats cocked at jaunty angles, lolling on benches, stamping their boots, and snorting into neckcloths. The most illustrious assembly of freemen in the world were an assortment of plain persons who whispered, coughed, whinnied, yelled, and, at times, even howled like hounds at feeding time.

It was enough to make a politically conflicted, conservative radical like Hunter stay as far away as possible. Adam, on the other hand, thrived in this setting. His smile, full of both cunning and good cheer, stretched as he handed Lara down from the carriage. Extending his arm for escort, he asked, "Shall we venture into the lion's den?"

Lara, her nerves too mangled to speak, glanced over at Hunter instead and took his arm.

Three abreast, they strolled briskly toward the appropriate entrance of the House of Lords. "Since I have come, will I be interviewed?" Lara asked. Her palms were already growing clammy and she curled her gloved hands into fists.

Adam cut Hunter a glance. "If all goes well, my dear, you'll not be called upon to speak at all."

Lara stopped in midstride. "What do you mean?" Her gaze darted between both men, frantic and hopeful, afraid to be either. "Have you discovered something?"

"Nothing as dramatic as all that," Adam said calmly. He searched her face intently, all the normally roguish animation gone from his own. "The goal, as I understand it, is to preserve the integrity of your son and yourself at all costs. Am I right?"

"Yes."

"Does it matter how it is done?"

Lara squeezed her eyes closed, wondering if it did, wondering how far one could go before selling one's soul. She thought of John Byron, his gaunt face and ravaged eyes when Hunter had rescued him from George's brothers.

"No," she said with conviction, "it doesn't matter."

Hunter squeezed her arm. "Let us get this done."

Once inside, Lara was escorted to a small, richly paneled sitting room and left there. The colors were masculine and somber, the wood dark and gleaming. The fragrance of beeswax and pipe tobacco clung to the drapes and upholstery, neither scent dominant but both befitting the room, giving the occupant a sense of timelessness. If no one entered this room for a century, the scent would remain, as constant as the polished wood.

Lara paced from window to door to window again. The sky had darkened and condensation collected on the glass and rolled down in a constant trickle. Traffic below was frantic. Everyone seemed intent on getting somewhere before the downpour. Men rushed about in the rising wind, hats held in place, while peasant women juggled young children and bulky brown packages with equal finesse. Ladies with parasols walked briskly toward the next shop and the next, not at all mindful of the servants trailing them with arms full of purchases. The inevitable downpour came, clearing the crowded streets in seconds.

Deliberately circumventing the frenetic energies of both the weather and her circumstances, Lara pressed her forehead to the cool windowpane and tried to concentrate only on taking slow deep breaths, rather than on the discussion concerning her son's future going on this very minute.

Meeting across a green-clothed table with the Privy Council had never been a harrowing experience for Hunter as it could be for others. The gentlemen of this stately scene were not proud and heartless noblemen of ancient lineage. In fact, no one in the room save Adam had the blooded connection of centuries that Hunter did.

The prime minister, Lord Liverpool, was only the second of his noble line. Robert Stewart, Viscount Castlereagh, was a courtesy "lord," a man of distinction and eminence in a plum-colored coat with a gold ring on the small finger of his left hand. Even with his fair looks, careful dress, and courteous manners, he was quite unpopular, and the awareness showed behind his tired eyes. Home Secretary Henry Addington, Viscount Sidmouth, was the son of a fashionable medical man known for having dispensed port to the younger Pitt. And the lord chancellor, John Scott, Lord Eldon, was the son of a Newcastle coal merchant who had worked his way to prominence from a grammar school by means of an exhibition to Oxford.

Though their emotions were well-hidden behind intelligent gazes and smiles of exemplary patience, these men were in awe of the Duke of Ravenwood, "the noble noncommoner," he had once been called, who seemed to have the people's attitudes, a king's treasury, and a deference for steering clear of politics. The last attribute suited each of them just fine. They never doubted that the man would be entirely too dangerous if he ever decided to step into the political arena.

Adam Devereaux, Duke of Warrington, however, they knew all too well. An incendiary if there ever was one, Warrington plagued their every decision-making session with whatever ammunition he chose to fire at the time, whether it be verbal warfare in the House of Lords, letters to the dailies, pamphlets he funded and circulated, or spouting his views at the many social gatherings he chose to attend.

The lord chancellor, feeling much maligned by this powerful show of unity, stood and whispered to the servant behind him, then turned back. "Your Graces. If you will, there are others who must be considered in this matter." He waited until Robert and Claude Chalmers were shown in and seated to Adam's left.

Hunter smiled. "How good of you both to come." He glanced at Adam. "Show them the papers you brought, Your Grace."

Rolling his eyes in droll boredom, Adam produced the markers for the brothers' inspection. He might not have approved Hunter's revenge, but he did enjoy the sight of the blood draining from the brothers' faces only to return a mottled purple within seconds.

"Consider each argument you might make carefully," Adam warned them quietly, then turned back to the council.

"Lord Chancellor." Hunter inclined his head, his eyes bright and hard. "As I do not wish to burden the busy Council with either trivialities or formalities, allow me to get straight to business and dispense this matter quickly so that each of you may get on with much more important issues." He pulled out a packet of documents and placed the first one before the Council.

"This, as you can see, is a marriage certificate showing Lara Anne Winthrop legally married to Matthew Huntington Hamilton, Duke of Ravenwood, Viscount Hearthstone, Earl of Chouchester, and other varied and sundry titles, on the fourteenth day of June in the year of our Lord 1811."

Murmurs rose quickly among the distinguished gentlemen, and Hunter allowed them a moment to digest the first document, then placed the second down. "This," he continued, "is a marriage certificate showing Lara Winthrop officially married to George Samuel Chalmers, Earl of Folkstone."

The murmurs rose to a crescendo, then fell off as the lord chancellor pounded the document. "What defense is this? You are saying that Lady Chalmers is a bigamist, Your Grace."

Hunter waited while the brothers' expressions filled with smug hope. "Not entirely," he said, then produced the third document. He looked each man in the eye before he continued. "This is a letter of bereavement, issued by the United States Government, consoling my dear wife on the death of her husband while in service to his country." He scrutinized each man accusingly, imparting individual responsibility. "You remember the war, I assume. Your country, *my* country by birthright, attacked—unprovoked—the United States, where I had been raised and owed my allegiance. I was missing and presumed dead. This letter of condolence was sent to Lara, who could only assume the same."

Lord Sidmouth, a balding man with pleasant features, folded his hands in a show of interest and great humor. "But you were not dead, Your Grace."

Hunter smiled. "No, Henry, I was not. I was wounded and unconscious. I won't go into the details of my long recuperation, but it was almost a year before I was able to return to England in search of Lara. I found to my horror that, grieving and finding herself widowed and with child by a man her country would have considered a traitor, Lara had accepted George Chalmers's offer of marriage. George, as you will recall, was an astute man and excellent judge of moral character."

Hunter slapped the last document down before them. "George Chalmers knew his brothers well. As soon as a male child was born to his wife, he legally adopted John Byron as his son and heir in order to secure his properties from his greedy brothers and to provide for the wife and child he truly had grown to cherish."

Hunter returned to his seat. He had thrown everything at them, but he had no way of knowing how they would react. He could be branded a traitor, his lands confiscated in the name of the Crown, his titles stripped from him. He could be jailed, even hanged, but he had not come forward expecting the worst. He glanced over at Adam. He had powerful friends and knew well the value of connections, even if he disdained the theory behind it.

These men, these nouveau lords, could hardly attack the house of Ravenwood and hope to come through unscathed. The Dukes of Ravenwood had long had the admiration of the common man as well as the gentry, and Hunter didn't think the Privy Council would want to upset the balance of power. Keeping Ravenwood in the background afforded them much greater peace of mind than having him as an enemy. No matter what they could prove with the documents, a court trial could go either way, and, either way, their personal popularity would be adversely affected.

"Well," the lord chancellor said, looking a bit anxious as he glanced at Robert and Claude. "Do either of you have anything to add?"

Adam tapped the gambling debts idly and watched the sweat break out on Robert's brow. "Speak up, man. We haven't got all day."

Robert sent Hunter a murderous look, then gave the Council his attention. "We were unaware of the full developments of this situation." His throat grew tight beneath Hunter's gaze and he choked the last words out. "We rely on the mercy and good intelligence of the court to decide in this matter."

The lord chancellor rose. "We have much to mull over. Allow us a few moments, if you will, and we will come back to you with a decision."

"All that long?" Adam drawled silkily. "I should think you would be ready to decry the outrageous demands of two Scotland-dwelling mongrels this instant."

Lord Sidmouth, known for his affable manner, nodded politely. "Nonetheless, Adam, I will not be pressured into hastiness."

"I do trust you for that, Henry," Adam responded in good humor.

Hunter and Adam both left the Privy Chamber, but only Hunter joined Lara in the small minister's room where she'd been left to wait. Her eyes were frightened when he walked in, and there was nothing he could say to avert her fear.

"They are pondering."

Her breath came out in a huff. "Pondering! As if the fate of a child can be determined by such an ignoble, passive act." Her expression fell in despair and she spun away and pressed her hand to her mouth, fighting hard for control. "I saw them," she whispered. "I saw Robert and Claude go in after you. I wanted to kill them."

Hunter crossed the room and pulled her against him. "Don't do this."

She turned her face into his chest and clutched at his coat, her breathing fast, her hopes caving in too rapidly for her to make much sense of things.

"Tell me what the Council will do!"

"I don't know yet."

"What did you say to them? What possible hope do I have?"

He shut his eyes and stroked her hair, pretending that she had come to him of her own affection, pretending she already knew what he had done.

A rap on the door parted them quickly. A young solicitor stuck his head in. "Your Grace? They are ready."

Lara thought she might collapse when Hunter left the room. She hastened over to the settee to sit and wait for the minutes to tick away like eons stretched toward eternity.

In only moments he was back, his expression tight, his eyes devoid of anything she could name. "What?" she said, frightened.

"It is over, Lara. You have won."

She squeezed her eyes closed, afraid to believe him. "It's not possible. Do you mean I have managed to retain a dowager share?"

"No, you have won. Everything."

She looked up, pale and shaken, afraid he played some horrid trick. "John Byron's inheritance is secure?"

"Yes."

Joy spun through her, bursts of warmth that made her cheeks flush with relief and elation and disbelief. "Oh, thank God," she whispered, afraid to say it too loudly lest the dream be stolen away. Hunter nodded and looked aside. It was then that she remembered his voice, his tone, the look of icy reserve on his face. She pressed her fingers to her lips. "What is wrong?" Her voice began to shake. "Something is wrong."

"Come. We'll discuss it in the carriage." He took

her arm and she moved woodenly beside him, her hopes fading.

When they reached the carriage, she hurried in as if the world would swallow her up if she did not move fast enough. She sat down, shoulders pressed hard against the seat, arms crossed over her middle to protect herself. She only hoped he would tell her quickly because she could not ask. She could barely breathe.

Hunter climbed in beside her and rapped on the roof to signal the driver to commence. As soon as the carriage was under way, he withdrew the packet of papers from his coat. "I want you to understand that this was the only way I could see to handle this situation with any chance at all of victory." Taking a deep breath he began to present the documents to her, one by one, just as he had the Privy Council. "This first is a marriage certificate."

Lara's eyes widened, first at her own name then at the other. "Matthew Huntington Hamilton?" Her head snapped up. "You? Is this you?"

"This second is self-explanatory," he continued as if she had not spoken. "Among other documents, I had Percy procure your certificate of marriage to George from Folkstone. This third is a paper of legal adoption and the fourth a notice of death."

Lara's hands were trembling so, she could not pick the papers up. "Explain them to me," she said, her voice little more than a vapor, "slowly."

He did, just as he had with the Privy Council. When he was done, he gathered the documents back up and started to tie them in brown paper. Lara's hand slammed down on the stack.

"This!" She picked up the marriage certificate validating her marriage to him. "Where did you get this?"

He accepted the ice in her voice, the angry flush in her cheeks, but he had not expected the hurt bewilderment in her eyes. "I obtained it from the records at St. Margaret's. It was registered there ten years ago."

Lara's eyes widened further. "It can't be real. We never . . ."

"It's real enough." He looked out the carriage window, not seeing the splatter of rain and the gray gloom outside. "It would have held up in court if necessary." He glanced over at her, his eyes troubled and tired. "I ran away from home before my fifteenth birthday, abandoning both my parents and my younger sister. Only my sister survived. I knew nothing of my right to Ravenwood until after I met you. If it had not been for Adam standing beside me when I claimed it, I might not have the right to it now."

He ran his thumb idly along the edge of the marriage certificate. "I had nothing to offer you ten years ago, Lara, but I could not abandon you, not like I had the others. My revenge against your father turned on me." He smiled faintly. "Revenge always will. I had this drawn up and registered at St. Margaret's for your protection, but you married George Chalmers and didn't need it to provide John Byron legitimacy."

Lara's trembling fingers rose to her mouth. "You could not have known I was with child."

"No, only that there was a chance. I found out later that I had been correct."

380

"And these?" Lara picked up the adoption paper and the letter of bereavement. "What of these?"

"Complete forgeries, both of them."

"Oh, God." She closed her eyes.

"But George's wishes nonetheless. You, who knew him best, cannot deny that."

"Oh . . ." Tears pooled in her eyes, then began to spill over. "Am I married to you now?"

Hunter's chest tightened. "Yes. It was the only way."

"And if I choose not to be?"

"You will have to legally divorce me. The marriage cannot be annulled because of John Byron."

"And if I do not choose that either?"

His brow creased and he dropped his head back against the seat. "Do what you like. You are the dowager of Folkstone, the Duchess of Ravenwood, along with a half-dozen other titles. John Byron is heir to it all. You are no longer without resources, Lara."

He looked exhausted, sprawled back against the seat, his long legs stretched at odd angles. Powerful and dynamic, he was so handsome it stole Lara's breath. But it was the other expression that touched her heart. He looked defensive, as if waiting for the final blow that would finish him. "What do *you* want me to do?"

He opened one accusing eye to regard her, then shut it again. "What I want is of no concern whatsoever."

"Is it not?"

Suddenly he felt her hand, in a place where the proper Lara Winthrop Chalmers Hamilton had never dared touch him before. His eyes opened wide, but before he could say a word, she threw herself at him.

"Oh, you wretched man!" She climbed fully onto his lap, utterly wanton, her skirts billowing up to her thighs. With half of London just outside the carriage window, she took his face in her hands and pressed her mouth to his. "Say it!"

His hands slid beneath her skirts and he grabbed her hips and held her tightly against him. "What, Lara? What would you have me say?"

"You know! Say it or I'll leave this very day and return John Byron to Folkstone."

"And I'll follow you," he threatened.

"Then say it."

"I want you to stay with me, be married to me. Love me."

Her tears made their lips slippery and uncontrollable. "Why?"

"Why? How can you ask why?" His hands flexed on her flesh, firm and demanding, possessive and protective.

"I need to hear the truth."

"I love you, Lara. I always have."

"No." She shook her head, her voice constricting. "Not always."

"Always. Even when I didn't want to. All those years I tried to put you out of my mind."

She made a sound, a small cry of painful wonder. It was hard to speak the words she had so guarded for a decade, so hard to finally be free to feel their meaning. "And I've loved you, so much, too much. It almost ruined me! We were so foolish to let go of each other."

He clasped her to him, his chest expanding with relief so vast and painful he could not consider it happiness. It was joy, that deep and abiding sense of well-being that comes from believing and experiencing pure, undiluted love. "Lara . . ."

She pressed kisses to every inch of his face, gladness bursting inside her like champagne bubbles. "I can't believe it . . . all these years. I have loved you all these years—"

"And hated me."

"For hurting me so. You left me to face them alone."

"No, you left me."

"Because you didn't want me!" she cried.

He held her tight. "Never that. I could not make the kind of life for you that you deserved. You were everything good that I was not; you were nothing bad that I had become. I could not bear the thought of immersing you in the darkness of my world."

She stroked his hair, his face, reveled in the strength of his heartbeat against her cheek, but her voice was sadly despondent when she spoke. "I feel as if all those years were stolen."

"Lost. But we grew up, Lara, grew better."

"Yes, but we cannot start over."

"No, we'll start now."

"Now and forever," she echoed.

Epilogue

John Byron stood near the banks of Bayou Teche and watched a bass dart through the dark water. His mother stood less than fifty yards away, a soft smile on her face as she held his aunt Acadiana's locket. Hunter stood near, smiling at Nicolette's antics, his head bent to accommodate her tiny height. The fecund smell of rich earth and lush vegetation surrounded the plantation of Bayou Oaks, and John Byron found himself drawn to it, to everything in Louisiana.

Gal would think he was silly, but his heart beat here in a different way than in England. He couldn't explain it but he felt it every morning when he stepped out onto the veranda of the plantation house and watched the breeze stir the palmetto and palm and azalea, smelled the perfumed camellia and magnolia. He knew a secret. He whispered it every evening when the frogs and katydids began their eerie evening symphony along the black shadows of the

Teche. He was going to come back here when he was grown and live in his father's plantation outside New Orleans. He hadn't told anyone yet, but he knew.

Graceful willows draped the sloped bank and dipped to the water's edge. Oak and cypress trees made huge shade canopies to stroll beneath. He couldn't remember all his cousins' names yet, but their faces were his own. And Nicolette's. And his father's.

He had turned it over in his mind many times but had yet to fully understand how his mother had been married to Hunter, then to George Chalmers, then to Hunter again.

But he understood happiness, and his mother's face was aglow with it these days. Mama said it was all right to still miss Papa and love Hunter, which he did, even though it made him feel guilty sometimes at just how much more he seemed to love Hunter. Gal said he couldn't help it, that it was in his blood and his bones and his skin, and he felt better when he remembered that.

A mockingbird called from the high bamboo hedges, and he listened as a whippoorwill answered. He liked very much that he had aunts and uncles and cousins, almost more than he could count, and none of them like Robert and Claude. A shiver ran down his spine and he searched automatically for his mother. She stood in a cluster of adults, smiling at Grandmère and Uncle Jonas and Uncle Edward. Most of all, he liked that he and Gal and Nicolette would have a new baby soon, in the winter, his father had said.

Gal had told him how babies were made but he didn't believe her. He made a face at her across the green lawn, teasing because Mama had made her wear a pretty gown "as befitted a young lady," and Gal ended up liking it so much she wouldn't even chase him around while wearing it.

He smiled. But Nicolette would.